The GREEN RAY OF the SUN

Reinhardt Suarez

THE GREEN RAY OF THE SUN

Book copyright © 2012, 2014, 2020 by Reinhardt Suarez

Music and Song Lyrics Copyright © 2012, 2020 by Wes Alexander

All characters and events in this book are fictitious. Any similarity to actual events, locales, or persons living, dead, mostly dead, exiled to the Bog of Eternal Stench, or trapped in a closet is purely coincidental.

Revised Printing, 2020

Interior design by Reinhardt Suarez

Cover design by Risa Rodil (www.risarodil.com)

ISBN 978-1-7337106-4-0

ISBN 978-1-7337106-5-7 (paperback)

ISBN 978-1-7337106-6-4 (ebook)

ISBN 978-1-7337106-7-1 (audiobook)

www.thereinhardtexperience.com

This book was written for Tenuta San Carlo
and is dedicated to Samantha Lotti.

Part One

Il Raggio Verde del Sole

Tutti mi dicon Maremma, Maremma . . .

Ma a me mi pare una Maremma amara.
L'uccello che ci va perde la penna.
Io c'ho perduto una persona cara.

Sia maledetta Maremma Maremma
Sia maledetta Maremma e chi l'ama.
Sempre mi piange il cor quando ci vai
Perché ho paura non torni mai.

Everyone tells me Maremma, Maremma . . .

But to me it seems a bitter Maremma.
The bird that flies there loses its feather.
I have lost my beloved one there.

Damned be Maremma, Maremma.
Damned be Maremma and those who adore it.
My heart always cries when you go there
Because I fear you shall never return.

— *"Maremma Amara"*
Traditional Tuscan folk song

One

"The present is the only time that truly exists in this universe," insisted Herr Cutter. He glowered over me, seemingly unbothered by the sheets of rain pouring down on his head. Also my head. "It is of the essence—time, I mean."

"I get that," I told him. "But this storm is hella crazy."

He turned away with a grunt and continued down the muddy trail, reminding me how deathly allergic Herr Cutter was to anything fun—and apparently to anything resembling common sense. How the hell did he become a world-renowned botany expert?

My money was on some kind of satanic ritual involving an ox stomach, a bag of moldy turnips, and episodes of *Big Bang Theory* constantly playing in the background.

"This sucks!" I called out.

"How do you propose to use our time?" he yelled back.

"I don't know—paint each other's toenails and sing sad, sad Taylor Swift songs to each other," I said, catching up to him. "Preferably somewhere dry."

He let out a disdainful snort and kept walking. Which meant I kept walking. Making matters worse, we had dragged poor Raffiano, the manager of the farm where we were staying, through this ordeal. He'd tried to warn us against going out when the rain was just a minor drizzle. But *noooooo*. Herr Cutter had his dainty lace *Regenschirm* (German for "umbrella stolen from my neighbor's five-year-old daughter") to keep us dry.

"Uno disastro ecologico," Raffiano moaned as he trudged behind us.

"How far to the ocean?" asked Herr Cutter. Raffiano looked down, puzzled. That's when Herr Cutter turned to me and said, "Miss Taggart, translate my question." And I would have done so. If I had known Italian. Maybe he should have asked before schlepping me halfway around the world to be his research assistant. Oops, too late.

I raised a finger with a thought to explain this to him but thought better of it. More words meant more time in the rain. So I whipped out the waterlogged Italian-English dictionary I bought at the Rome airport and flipped through the pages while fat raindrops punched into them.

"Uh . . . *il mare*?" I said. "¿Donde está *il mare*?" That's right. I was speaking Spanish to Raffiano—a language he didn't understand—completing this delightful circle of non-comprehension. Thankfully, he got the *il mare* part of what I had said, enough to point down the path and say:

"Uno chilometro."

"Eh?" Herr Cutter grunted.

"It's a kilometer farther," I said. "Uh, give or take."

"Not so far, then," he said almost cheerfully. "Onward."

Alright, that was it. I put my foot down, which unfortunately made me sink faster into the mud.

"Herr Cutter, this is not cool. Can we please go back?"

"Miss Taggart." I hate being called that. *Miss Taggart.* Not that my first name—*Ryland*—is much better. "I must have samples of *hypochoeris radicata* and *crepis capillaris.* Our work here is important."

"Yeah, but look!" I pointed to Raffiano, who looked all Jolly-Green-Giant-after-stepping-on-a-puppy. "You see that, Herr Cutter? That is the look of ultimate suffering. My heart made that face when Tasha Yar died on *Star Trek: The Next Generation.* Raffiano looks like that now."

"You are an erratic person," he said. "Nevertheless, we are already behind. We shall proceed undeterred."

I then resorted to the argument style espoused by the greatest masters of debate: "C'mon, man!" I tugged at Herr Cutter's jacket. "You're miserable, I'm miserable, and besides, the samples are under, like, four feet of water."

"Hmm. Your point does have validity. I had not considered it." Leave it to Herr Cutter to forget about water in the middle of a rainstorm. Raffiano, bless his soul, waited while we argued without so much as a peep. I felt so sorry for him, almost as much as I felt sorry for my ass cheeks. Chafing was a merciless mistress.

"Dobbiamo andare avanti?" I had no idea what Raffiano just said. I tried to find a lifeline in the dictionary, but the pages were too stuck together.

"Very well, Taggart," said Herr Cutter. "Tell Mr. Raffiano that we shall try again tomorrow." At that, he started walking back toward the farm's grand villa, leaving me and Raffiano to get drenched. I turned to the big Italian and shrugged. Pretty sure he understood.

"I take it that your efforts today were not very fruitful," said Tania, the farm owner, placing down the bell she had just rung to call for refreshments. Herr Cutter and I were back inside the villa, sitting at a long wooden table with place settings for ten. But it was only us two, along with Tania, who'd be enjoying our post-failure afternoon tea. Herr Cutter warmed himself by cupping his hands around a mug of hot bitters, a personally created blend of teas that smelled like rotten feet. I, not being a connoisseur of zombie-flavored beverages, settled for chamomile. It hadn't been cold outside since it was the height of summer. Just really, really wet—enough to send a chill into our bones despite the heat.

"We were unprepared for rain," said Herr Cutter, wearily.

"As were we," said Tania. "It complicates an already complicated situation." The "situation" Tania referred to was the reason we were there. She had originally contracted Herr Cutter to study why the farm's crop yields had been getting smaller and smaller in the last decade. The previous year had been especially bad. Now, with the abnormal rain on top of the mysterious die-off, the farm could lose the entire year's crop.

"I tried to get him to buy an umbrella," I said.

"Not now, Taggart."

That's how just about all our conversations ended—*Not now, Taggart*—which brought up a valid question: why exactly did he bring *me* halfway around the world? I was scarily ungifted in all things biology-based (we shall not speak of the "Great Sea Monkey Holocaust" of 2007). And I was for sure the worst student in his class last semester. There wasn't any sort of dirty-old-man reason for picking me, either. I'm a baby dyke—*lesbian*, in the parlance of our times—and I concluded from his love of fuchsia-colored ascots and the way he fluttered his hands whenever he went into high-and-mighty mode that Herr Cutter was as queer as I am. And he obviously wasn't too keen on taking practical life advice. Whatever, man. I'm sure there were plenty of other students at UT that deserved this more than me. But was I going to turn down an all-expense-paid week in scenic Tuscany?

Hell no.

Literally on cue, Gina, Tania's live-in cook, brought in a plate of tiny cakes and biscuits. She was an older lady with a butch cut who spent most of her time out on the porch chain-smoking when she wasn't cooking up food from the gods. Not a hoax, not a dream. She birthed pure ambrosia from that stovetop and standing mixer.

"How are your rooms?" asked Tania. "I trust they are comfortable."

"The room is acceptable," said Herr Cutter. "But . . ." He

let the pause run its course, then overrun into awkward silence. Then, after sipping his bitters and poking a raspberry mini-tart: "There is a smell."

"A smell?" said Tania.

"Yes, a smell. It is not unlike the smell of wet cardboard, mixed with brimstone. You don't have a mold infestation here, do you?"

"Absolutely not!"

"That's too bad. I would have liked to study it. Taggart—" He swung his eyes in my direction, which was terrible timing, as I had a mouth full of cookie. "You say your room is fine."

I nodded.

"Then switch with me. It is a curse, this delicate olfactory sense of mine. It has helped me as a professional, but alas, it is also my weakness."

"I will have your bedroom inspected to see what the problem is." She rang the bell again, and a moment later, Gina was right there at Tania's side to receive her marching orders delivered in a pleasant yet distinctly firm tone.

"There," Tania said as Gina excused herself to go up the steps. "It will be taken care of."

"I still must insist on another room," said Herr Cutter.

"It's fine, you guys," I said, feeling both of their stares. "We can switch. Not a big. I used to sleep in a barn."

"That's settled!" exclaimed Herr Cutter, slapping the table. "I will go prepare my things now." He excused himself to pack his things up, leaving a half-eaten piece of shortcake and his half-empty cup of butt-smelling swill to permeate the room.

"That is quite strong, is it not?" said Tania.

"Ugh. A giant Thermos of the stuff every single class," I told her. "You'd think I would have gotten used it, but the smell still makes me want to die."

"You mentioned that you used to sleep in a barn."

"Mmm-hmm. I grew up on a cattle ranch in Wyoming."

She raised her eyebrows. "The professor—" She nodded upstairs just as Herr Cutter's voice pierced the peace—*Miss Gina, you absolutely cannot move my shoes! My shoes! My shoes! Meine Schuhe!* "He is not the kind of person I would have expected. And you are not the kind of person I expected him to have as a—what is it exactly that you do for him?"

Ah, the hard question. If I didn't count the NOT translating Italian and the NOT reinforcing his scientific ego, the answer was painfully obvious: I was a slightly more sociable Renfield to Herr Cutter's Count Dracula. In our not-even-a-day at the farm (we had landed in Rome the previous night), my duties included: unpacking his stuff, laying out his toiletries in the bathroom according to a written list of specified places where his toothbrush, comb, shampoo, and other accoutrements belonged, pre-tying seven bow ties that he had brought with him ("Not too tight! I do not want my nose getting caught!"), and bolstering his self-esteem. *You look like Ricardo Montalban, sir. Circa Wrath of Khan. Yeah, with the chest.*

I couldn't admit that, so I said: "I double check his math."

"I suppose that's important. Would you like some more tea?" I waved her off and downed the rest of my chamomile.

Miss Gina—don't . . . ! Taggart! I require your assistance!

9

"I should go up and help him. I'd hate to see what happens to Gina if she touches Herr Cutter's toe booties."

"Would you mind helping me clear the table?" I helped Tania stack the cups and saucers and silverware into a neat (if precarious) pile and then balanced it all on my arm.

"Impressive," she said. "I've never seen this trick."

"Watch me pull a rabbit out of a hat."

"Come. The kitchen is this way." I followed Tania, passing through the huge main hall. On the walls hung a series of family portraits. The big central frame showed a mother and father flanking their young son and daughter. A small plaque inset into the bottom part of the frame read: *La Famiglia Rossi—Eduardo, Annalise, Tania, Leo.* Poor Tania. If I had a picture of me in a baby blue dress and equally hideous bowtie headband, I just might "accidentally" dunk it into a vat of battery acid.

And then came the kitchen. One word: *whoa*. Back in Austin, my kitchen consisted of a microwave nook next to my bed, a single bowl that I cleaned only when direly necessary, and my prized stash of pink, shrimp-flavored Ramen packs. Tania's kitchen made my setup run home and cry for mommy. There was a huge pork hock hung over the sink on a giant iron hook. Bowls (plural!) of tomatoes, onions, and garlic took up much of the counter-space. And inside the cabinets were obviously the good china with gold inlays, not the mere silver-filigreed guest dishes we had used for lunch. I laid them in the sink and turned to Tania.

"I should go up."

"I have things to attend to as well. Buongiorno, Miss Taggart."

We went our separate ways—me toward where we were, and Tania back toward the back door of the villa. I ventured up the stairs, turned the corner to Herr Cutter's room and saw Gina backing up from his doorway at the end of a broomstick he had managed to yank from her hands.

"Gina?"

"Taggart, what took you so long?" Herr Cutter called from inside the room. "Please explain to Miss Gina that her services are not needed."

"I don't—" I started to say, but what the hell did it matter? "Gina . . ." I began. "It's okay."

I think Gina took the hint, because she continued to backpedal toward the stairs. When she passed me, she placed her hand on my shoulder, lowered her mouth to my ear, and whispered, "Dio mio." Then she went down the stairs, mumbling an unknown number of Italian curses under her breath.

I walked into Herr Cutter's room, where it looked like a suitcase nuke had exploded inside. All his stuff—once neatly arranged—was now strewn about, with him at the epicenter of the destruction. He sat on the bed, rubbing his temples.

"Miss Taggart, I am happy you are here." What's this? A compliment from His Stinginess? Hardly. While Herr Cutter reclined on the bed, it was I who hauled his stuff into my room ("I have problems with my lumbar region."). Then I arranged it all ("The panoply of possible storage choices addles my sensitive mind."). Finally, I lugged all his botany texts and notes down the stairs to the living room table so that we could begin formulating a plan for the rest of our stay at the farm ("The dangers of vertigo have not been as thoroughly investigated as the lay man is wont to believe.").

Me = sucker.

I waited at the base of the stairs for Herr Cutter to join me. And waited. A lot. Where the hell was he? I started to go back up, but then thought better of it. The last thing I wanted was to catch him doing something horrifying like plucking his ear hairs or exfoliating his armpits—the kind of shit you can't unsee. Instead, I sat at the table and cracked open a fresh notepad. I figured that I could pass the time by making to-do lists. That's scientific.

Step 1 – get plant samples

Step 2 – don't kill them

Step 3 – something involving science . . .

So much for that. I got up and started to pace—my customary thing to do in situations like this (AKA shitty ones). A series of photos hung on the walls caught my eye. They were black and white pictures of the farm grounds. The pictures were very old if the hand-written years in the corners were accurate—1913, 1936. The latter one had a whole family standing in front of the villa: a father, mother, and two children—a young boy who looked around ten and a baby held in the mother's arms. Next to these pictures was a framed map with the farm's name etched into a blackened piece of brass nailed to the frame: *Podere Graziela*. It gave me an idea.

I took the map, frame and all, and laid it on the table. It looked like the property was divided into alternating bands of forest and field leading all the way to the Mediterranean, where we had tried to go that afternoon. If I could just find a list of plants Herr Cutter wanted to get, I could group them by habitat and plot out a course around the property so that we wouldn't be needlessly wandering. One had to be in his stuff somewhere. Unfortunately, when I started leafing through his notebooks, endless lines of German stared back at me. Umlauts galore.

"Tania?" I heard a raspy voice call out. Standing at the doorway that led to the kitchen was a gray-haired man holding his hat. He was soaked top to bottom, and left a puddle on the floor where he stood.

"Um. Hi?"

"Eh?" said the man. "Inglese?" My English must have intrigued him enough to come closer. But upon seeing that I had taken the map down from the wall, he snatched it and hung it back up, all the while hurling sharp-tongued Italian that sounded like one long impossibly-syllabled word.

"I'm sorry," I blurted out. "I didn't . . . I . . . ."

"Paolo!" said Tania sternly from the hallway. She closed her umbrella and shook off the water. For a solid five minutes, Tania and the old man lobbed hyper-speed Italian at each other. Their voices got steadily louder as they argued, until one point when Tania screamed and pointed back down the hallway. The man grumbled and stomped his foot, but ultimately relented and disappeared down the hall. Tania turned to me with her steady, unnerving voice: "In the future, ask before you touch anything. Some things are not what they seem. Over here," she said, pointing to a tall set of drawers tucked into the corner. "There used to be a porcelain vase with pieces of jade inset into it. I'd stare at it for hours. One day, I just had to touch it, so I jumped up to try to grab it, but only managed to knock it onto the floor. It shattered. That was my grandmother's vase, one of a kind. Now it is gone forever."

"I'm sorry," I began. "I wanted to . . . I mean, I was using the map to, sorta, plan how we—Herr Cutter and I—would get plant samples. For when the rain stops."

"I appreciate your dedication." Tania walked to the large window at the back of the room. She crossed her arms and stared out at the tall, skyscraper-high trees being battered by the rain in an eerie silent movie. "Sometimes I think we do not belong here," she said, her eyes not wavering from the scene. "We have a song—'Maremma Amara.' It means 'Bitter Maremma,' referring to these lands when they were swamps teeming with malaria. I have always wondered when nature would finally be tired of us and take back what we claimed." She turned away but kept her arms crossed in front of her. "My uncle can be difficult. I will talk to him."

"It's cool," I said.

"No, it is not," she said. "I am his employer, and he will not treat guests in that manner."

"You're his boss?"

"Yes. I must see what he wants. Oh, and you may use the map. I never look at it, anyway." She disappeared down the hall—I assumed to the kitchen to confront her uncle—and only then did Herr Cutter amble down like nothing doing.

"What took you so long?" I said.

He squinted at me. "Your precision leaves much to be desired, Taggart. I had to rearrange my belongings into their proper configurations." What? I followed every part of his 9-page, 8-point-font instruction manual. Whatever, man. Herr Cutter pulled up a seat, and together, he and I studied the maps of Tania's property. The property was clearly delineated into two parts: *terreni agricoli* (farmland) and *foresta nazionale* (national forest). Tania had provided a list of crops that she grows on her farm and crops that her neighbors tended to grow (olives, wheat, pine nuts, and sugar beets), and we made a note to get samples of each. Herr Cutter then listed down native Mediterranean plants he wanted samples of. On several sheets of notebook paper, he sketched out a circular route we were to take around the property, collecting samples as we went. In this realm—botany—Herr Cutter was definitely the one-eyed man in the land of the blind (complete with a prissy eye-patch).

We worked into the evening. I didn't notice it was nighttime until Gina brought out an *assalumi* platter of freshly sliced Tuscan ham and some crumbly sausage that reeked of fennel. Both of these on a piping hot piece of *schiacciata* flatbread . . . pure mouth-gasm.

"I'm never washing my tongue again."

"For my sake, I hope you reconsider," said Herr Cutter. "We are working in close quarters."

"Gina, is Tania eating with us?" I wasn't sure she understood. I repeated myself, and when I said Tania's name for the second time, she shook her head.

"Ah . . . no come. No come."

Herr Cutter and I turned in early to finish off our lingering jet lag. It was cold in my new room—much colder than the rest of the villa. Once I crawled under the doubled-up comforters, it felt like lead fishing weights had hooked onto my eyelids. I plunged into sleep, but not before noticing the gunpowder smell that Herr Cutter talked about earlier. Slowly, it became stronger, more concentrated—enough to feel the grit between my teeth and taste its bite on my tongue.

I awoke—or at least thought I did—expecting to see the bedroom, unlit and silent, the far corners where the walls and floor and ceiling met engulfed in shadow. But that wasn't what I saw. There was only blue overhead—like a pool of sky-colored paint. As I stared at the arc above me, I noticed that my bed was gone, as was all the furniture. I was standing in the middle of a marble colonnade, like an old Roman temple. Around me were figures dressed completely in white—all men, all old and stoic looking. They didn't move, and at first, I thought they might have been statues. But every time I blinked, they seemed to appear closer. Closer. What would happen when they got close enough to touch me? I tried to stop blinking, but that only made it harder to keep my eyes open. What else could I do? Run away? I'd never make it through that obstacle course without being grabbed. Beg for mercy? For what?

And did I deserve it?

The men drew closer. I gave into the blink, crawled into a ball on the ground and shut my eyes tight. *Better to just get it over with*, I thought. In a second, other hands, fingers as hard and cold as the stone floor, took my wrists. They lifted me up, pushed and pulled my shoulders until my back was straight and my head faced forward.

"Bene," I heard in my ear.

My eyes opened, and I found myself in the arms of one of these men. We turned in the center of the floor, stepping only to the sounds of fabric on fabric, the jingling of coins in his pocket, the groan of his old boots. These were the notes of our silent waltz, a tune only my partner could hear, a dance only he knew the steps to. We spun—faster, faster. His grip grew tighter to keep me from falling. My grip grew tighter because it was the only thing I could do. Soon, the whole world blurred into a swirl of ever-changing colors.

"What's going on?" I asked. That's when I noticed his eyes, black and glassy, staring back at me. No—they stared *into* me from two sunken sockets in his leathery face, crisscrossed by wrinkles like deep ravines. His ratty beard halfway hid sunken cheeks, thin as onion skin. He started to talk, his skin stretching, perhaps tearing, underneath his beard. But no words came out. Correction—I heard sounds come from his mouth, but they were only fragments of words. Bits and pieces I could barely hear above the *wooshing* sound created by our spinning, and the other half were unintelligible fragments of Italian. Then, as suddenly as he appeared, he let me go. I fell and kept falling.

I woke up, my sheets drenched in sweat. Tania stood in the open doorway to the bedroom. She held a lit candle by her waist, keeping her face in shadow.

"I heard you thrashing."

"I . . ." I began. "I must have been dreaming."

"Most definitely," she said. "May I come in?"

17

"Okay." It was her house. She didn't need permission.

She sat down on the bed next to me, the candle situated on her lap so that her body became a black silhouette outlined by the orange flame. "This was my room when I was young. Nothing has changed about it. The bed, the dresser—all is the same. The windows are old and let the wind in," she said, noting the candle flame teased by the breeze. "That is also why it is so cold, even in the summer."

"And the smell?"

"It has always been here—for as long as I can remember," she said. "May I ask what you were dreaming about?"

"It's stupid."

"No." She turned to face me. Orange pinpoints danced in her eyes. "Dreams are many things. But they are *never* stupid." She was serious. Like deadly so. "If you do not wish to share, that is your choice. But do not dismiss."

I sat up. Took a breath. "There were these columns. And all the colors were bright, and I was dancing, and this man—we were dancing."

"Did he say anything to you?"

Now this was freaking me out. "How did you . . . ?"

"An innocent question, Miss Taggart. Nothing more."

"Okay," I said, not completely buying her answer. I thought about it, closing my eyes to bring myself back to the dream, to sound of the man's voice, dry as sand on a sidewalk. "No. Nothing that I can remember."

"I see," she said, setting the candle on the nightstand before standing up. "Let this burn as you sleep. It will quiet your mind. I am sure Professor Cutter will need your wits about you tomorrow."

Two

In the morning, I did my best to stumble down the stairs. No small feat, considering that my legs felt like Jell-O and my head felt like it was under a thousand feet of water. I found Tania eating breakfast at the dining room table. Bright and cheery. Ugh.

"Buongiorno," she said, looking away from her newspaper. I couldn't muster anything more than a mumble as I sat down and stared at the cake in the center of the table. "I'm afraid to ask how you feel."

"What's Italian for 'like shit'?"

"Di merda."

"Yeah. That," I said, resting my head on the tabletop. "What time is it?"

"Eleven o'clock. I had Raffiano accompany Professor Cutter to help him. I told him you had a bad night sleeping. When you are ready, I will take you to where they are."

"Wait—outside?" I looked out the huge, panoramic window and saw why the villa's architect had put it there. Outside, the sky was a deep, thick blue. One thing was sure: it wasn't raining.

"Cut yourself a piece of cake if you are hungry," said Tania. At seeing the cloudless sky, I felt totally famished. I guess my body wanted some fuel to get out there and enjoy the Tuscany that you see in the guidebooks. "This cake is called *Ciambellone allo Zafferano*." It tasted heavenly—a mix of cream and orange—but I couldn't eat slowly enough to really enjoy it. I guzzled down tea after every bite, and when I was done, Tania told me to get dressed so we could go find Raffiano and Herr Cutter.

A Ziggy Stardust t-shirt and a pair of culottes later, I met Tania at the front of the villa, where she handed me a pair of heavy rubber boots. I couldn't help but notice Tania's own choice of wardrobe: tight pants ending in knee-high boots, a white shirt, and a small red jacket—a jockey's uniform.

"I'm going riding later today, after I drop you off." She bunched her hair up into a ponytail while I finished putting on the boots. It was only then that I noticed the wrinkles around her eyes and her slightly sunken cheeks. These were hidden behind the dark blonde locks of her hair, but now her face was naked to the light. I hadn't really questioned Tania's age at all. She was definitely older, and when she talked, she made sure you knew it. But just how old was she? If her uncle was in his eighties, which was my wild guess, then Tania might have been as old as . . . No. She didn't look a day over thirty-five.

I admit it. I kinda had the hots for her, not so much for how she looked—although that was very nice—but more for how she spoke: authoritative and yet completely mysterious. As the schmuck who always ends up making the hard (and wrong) decisions, having someone else insist on taking charge felt like a guilty pleasure.

"Something on your mind, Miss Taggart?" Tania said.

"Nope," I said abruptly. "I'm fine. Let's go!"

The farm had awoken from a long, wet sleep. As we walked along the trail that would take us into the forest, we crossed paths with a group of men on million-Euro race horses that were, as Tania put it, "on vacation" and tractors pulling wagons of hay to the pens with the spiral-horned Maremman cows. Once we reached the tree line, Tania stopped walking and looked up. I didn't know what had caught her attention until I saw movement in the canopy.

"What the . . . ?" I strained my neck watching three men climb and swing from three different umbrella pine trees (*pinus pinea*) that were almost forty feet tall.

"They are cutting the excess," said Tania, pointing out that each man had a small chainsaw attached to his belt with a rope. "If the tops are too thick, sunlight does not reach the floor of the pineta. And if the tops are too heavy, the wind is able to blow them down. The roots are very shallow." She pointed farther into the forest. A huge tree, almost fifty feet tall, lay on the ground, its bare roots reaching out like scraggly claws scraping at the air. "Watch this," she said. She pointed to the man in the tree directly above us. It was then that I noticed three things. First, he was smoking a cigarette. Second, he didn't have a harness or rope or any other safety device. And third, he was the same man who laid into me the previous afternoon because I'd dared to touch a map on the wall.

"That's your uncle, right?"

"Yes," she said, like it was normal for Paolo to balance on a branch forty feet up, arching his chainsaw to trim branches inches from his face. When his cigarette had burned to the filter, he let the chainsaw dangle from his belt, calmly dug into his pocket for his pack, grabbed a square with his teeth, and lit the tip with his free hand. Fuck me. "He is teaching the other two. Boys from Capalbio have been coming here for years to learn this." The other two tree-cutters looked younger, less sure. Unlike Paolo, they hugged the trunk close to their bodies for dear life.

When he started his descent, Paolo used the branch stumps like a ladder going down. When he passed a few, he would pause, saw the stumps completely off, and then continue on his way. By the time his feet touched the ground, the tree was properly pruned to have a thick—but not too thick—upper canopy and a clean-looking, bare trunk all the way down.

"Not bad for an eighty year old," I said.

Tania laughed. "Paolo is my father's *older* brother. He was eighty almost twenty years ago."

"So . . . how old are you, if you don't mind me asking?"

"It makes no difference. I am sixty-two," she said. "C'è il sole—finalmente!" she said to Paolo.

"Bah," he answered, "Non c'è fine. La pioggia si ferma solo per uno periodo breve."

"Good morning—I mean *buongiorno*," I said, trying to

once again ingratiate myself. It didn't seem to work. He only looked at me funny before saying, "eh."

"Lo apprendono rapidamente?" said Tania, pointing to the two boys still up in the trees.

Paolo shook his head. "Troppo lento."

"He says that they are too slow in learning."

"How long have they been doing this?" I said.

"This is their first day."

Tania turned to Paolo. "Stiamo cercando a Raffiano. È con il Professore Cutter."

"Il Tedesco. Bah!" At that, he turned back toward the trees and the boys and started barking at all of them. Tania and I continued to walk down the trail.

"Wow," I said. "He really didn't like something."

"My uncle does not like German people."

"Really? Did Germans do something bad to him?"

"A small thing. In America, you call it World War II."

Pwned. I shut up for the rest of the hike.

I had no idea where we were going. Sometimes we went off the trail, and sometimes we stayed on the trail. Tania pointed out that when a trail was very choppy and muddy, a wild boar had made it. Other than that, she didn't give any indication of how she was finding her way. Eventually, we spotted Herr Cutter's frilly parasol poking above the bush. He and Raffiano were safe, sound, and sane. Well, they were safe, anyway. Those other things? Well . . .

"Mister Raffiano, it is essential that you know the scientific names of plants. This is, after all, the land over which you preside! So repeat after me: *thymus vulgaris.*"

"Buongiorno!" said Tania. All at once, the expression on

Raffiano's face switched from despondent to elated. He walked over to meet me and Tania coming up the trail.

"È pazzo," he said to Tania softly. Then he turned to me. "A lei mangerà alla mia casa."

"I . . . I don't understand."

"Raffiano just invited you to dinner with his family," said Tania. "You should say yes."

"Uh, yeah! That sounds cool."

"Heh. Cool." Raffiano said his goodbyes and walked back up the trail. By the time we had reached Herr Cutter, he had somehow tangled his upper body in a bunch of thorny vines. He danced around, attempting to free himself from their grasp.

"Rubus caesius! Rubus caesius!"

The *Rubus caesius*, or European Dewberry, is a hearty plant related to the raspberry and blackberry. Its roots can span more than ten meters from where it comes out of the ground, and it is characterized by its thick, thorny brambles, which Herr Cutter had found out about firsthand. Tania and I pulled the vines off him—carefully and slowly, much to his dismay—until, scratched on his face and breathing heavily, he emerged once more from his eternal nemesis: nature.

"You see, Taggart," he said between great big breaths, "most people do not know the dangers we botanists face on a daily basis. If you were not here to help—"

"I am sure Raffiano would have aided you," said Tania, fighting her smile. "But now that I have reunited you two, I must be off."

"So soon, Miss Tania? I would think that you would want

to tour with us a bit," said Herr Cutter. "I have already found evidence of something . . . some affliction."

"Tell me."

"It is too early to say exactly what it is, but there is *something*. When Miss Taggart and I are done collecting samples today, we will go back and analyze them. Then we can tell you more."

Tania looked satisfied at that. "Good. I have instructed Gina to cook your lunch. It will be ready at one o'clock. Be prompt." After she took her leave, I waited until she was out of sight before asking Herr Cutter what he found.

"As I told Miss Tania, it's still too early to tell," he said, shaking his head. There was a tone in his voice that I had never heard before—uncertainty.

"But what do you think?"

"Miss Taggart, we are scientists. We are not here to measure what we 'think.' Science is about posing a question and finding a definite answer, whether we like it or not." He brushed his jacket off and made sure all the contents of his shoulder bag were present and in order. "We do not know how long this respite will last before the rains come back, so we must get as much done today as possible, yes?" Herr Cutter handed me a written list of plants I was to look for. "When you see one, stop, and we will collect the sample."

So Herr Cutter and I started collecting samples, a process that included trudging through the mud, bending down, looking for just the right leaf, and carefully placing each sample in a labeled bag. After an hour or so, we paused for lunch. He was not his usual annoyingly talkative self at the table, and I, still groggy from lack of sleep, didn't fill the empty space. Besides, the food—a "simple" lunch of caprese salads with bread and thinly-sliced sweet soppressata—was too good not to savor. Herr Cutter's tight lips unnerved me though. The lack of conversation spanned into the late afternoon, and by that time, we had gathered almost every sample that Herr Cutter had wanted.

Then there was one—one last sample to get. Herr Cutter took out the last empty bag he had prepared this morning. The label read: *Atriplex hortensis. Atriplex hortensis*, or garden orache, is one of the oldest plants used by man and is even referenced in the bible as "salt herbs"—plants collected and eaten by outcasts from society. For this sample, we headed straight west to where the map put a little old thing called the Mediterranean Sea. We wound about on a path that grew less muddy and more sandy as we followed it, and kept walking until the trail curved to reveal a wooden sign that read "Il Mare." Soon after, we came upon the beach.

Holy shiz-nit.

I was standing at the edge of the world. Speechless. The massive pieces of driftwood that lined the beach stayed rooted in place like I did, their stories locked up inside. We were brothers and sisters at the end of time, feeling so small, so *blink-and-you're-gone*. All of us little specks of dust programmed and predestined—fated—to disappear in an instant quietly and without much effort.

"Here, Taggart!" Herr Cutter called out. I turned around to see him standing next a pristine specimen of *Atriplex hortensis*. "Now collect the last so we can go back."

"Go back?" I asked. "What's the hurry? I mean look at

that!" I pointed to the water. "Is that not the coolest thing you've ever seen?"

"It is water and salt, Taggart. Nothing special."

"Nothing special? Aren't we water and salt?"

"Mostly. Now be careful. I want a full leaf and stem. Don't cut it too short."

"I know what I'm doing," I said, losing a little bit of my cool. I mean, not that anyone else has to appreciate the shit that I like, but c'mon. You're staring creation directly in the cajones, and you're not awed at all? I snipped the leaf and stem like he specified and sealed it all up in the last bag. I held it out for him to take, but didn't let go when he pulled. "Don't you think that there's anything out there that science can't explain?"

"No." He pulled again, but I held the bag fast.

"Isn't that sad?" Why was I was harping so much? Herr Cutter was a scientist. Flights of fancy and imaginary indulgences were alien to him. So I wasn't surprised at his answer—just a little disappointed.

"It is neither sad nor happy. That is simply the way it is. Now please let go." I released the final specimen, and Herr Cutter packed it away. Then he started back up the path. I watched the sea roll for a few more moments, noting the clouds along the horizon. I certainly hoped that this wouldn't be the only sun I'd see during my week-long stay, but it didn't look good.

I turned away to follow Herr Cutter before he got too far ahead. When I reached him, the sound of the water pushing and pulling itself was no more than a whisper in my ear.

The bottle of grappa on the table taunted me, dared me to try and fit more into my stomach. The meal at Raffiano's had been too awesome to stop eating, even though I'd been defeated for a full twenty minutes (about halfway through my third helping of roast wild boar). I also didn't want to be rude to Raffiano or his wife, Gemma, who must have spent hours in the kitchen cooking up this feast. Romaine and carrot salad, *crostini lardo* (which was basically pork fat spread on toast), spaghetti carbonara, roasted wild boar, a cream desert called *panna cotta* with raspberry syrup, and espresso with chocolate. Finally, there was the digestive: a thick, clear liquid that smelled like turpentine—grappa. Raffiano had matched me bite for bite, though he had the excuse that he was a hardworking farmer with the frame of a grizzly. I, on the other hand, was a lazy American from the land where Texas Hold 'Em and barbecuing brisket are competitive sports. Back home, I could out-eat and out-drink any frat boy that dared to test me. But this guy . . . if I ever get a tapeworm, I'm going to name it after Raffiano.

As per Raffiano's invitation, Herr Cutter and I joined Raffiano and his family for dinner at their house, which was only a little down the road from Tania's villa. The house felt warm and lived in, and the second you stepped inside, the air crackled with energy—due in no small part to Gemma and their four (yes, 1-2-3-4) daughters.

"Salute!" cried Raffiano. He happily downed the grappa

and set the glass on the table. I was too busy holding my head up to take a shot. I did, and instantly, Gemma was there to pour me another—this in her tireless pursuit of hostessing perfection. She had spent a total of fifteen minutes sitting down and the rest of the time shuffling plates, serving food, and asking her daughters about school.

Raffiano's daughters (oldest to youngest: Daniella, Fiorentina, Vittoria, and Ottavia) sat at the other side of the table completely mesmerized by my predicament. They had kept their eyes on me the entire meal, not saying anything. But whenever I'd poke my food or look confused at it, they'd giggle. It was cute. And unnerving.

"Somehow, Taggart, you have eaten more than your body weight," said Herr Cutter, who had cruised through the meal taking nibbles and bites, but mostly leaving his food untouched. He blamed his sensitive stomach. I blamed him for not liking food with real flavor. "I do not know whether to marvel at this breakthrough in four-dimensional physics or to vomit in solidarity."

"Ha ha, sir." Then I tossed back another shot of grappa. God, it felt like liquid fire going down my esophagus, coating everything it touched in red hot lava. I finally understood why it was considered a digestive. Warmth coursed through me, and I knew I was going to have an interesting night.

"Ti piace?" asked Raffiano. I had heard this enough to know that it meant *do you like it?*

"Si. Mi piace."

Raffiano lifted the bottle of grappa and extended it toward my glass. I put my hand in the way.

"No more. I'm done. Thanks, though."

Gemma sat down at the table finally, after taking all the plates and putting them in the sink.

"Thank you . . . I mean, *grazie*," I said to her.

"Prego," she said. Note to self—"you're welcome" is the same word as the off-the-shelf spaghetti sauce. Mnemonic devices like that helped me remember the bits of Italian that I learned.

"Now, if you'll excuse me," said Herr Cutter, getting up from the table, "I must get some work done before going to sleep. Thank you, Mister Raffiano and family for your hospitality." Way to make it sound like a wake, Herr Cutter. He glanced down at me and raised his eyebrow. No. I didn't really feel like getting up or moving at all. That and I was having fun just watching the girls zip around the table, whisper things to each other, and take turns being the apple of Raffiano's eye.

"Will you be alright heading back on your own?" I asked Herr Cutter.

"Of course, Taggart. It is a short distance to the villa." Herr Cutter was exactly right. And in the daytime, I probably wouldn't have even thought about it. But outside, it was pitch black because the cloud cover had returned, and Herr Cutter was directionally brain dead.

"Well, if you get lost, just scream. We'll all hear you."

"Hmph. I will see you in the morning, then."

Herr Cutter made his exit. I watched as he walked out of the range of Raffiano's porch light and into the darkness. I wondered if Gina would be out smoking on the porch. At least then someone would be there to help him out, since

Tania wasn't home. In fact, thinking about it, she hadn't been home in the evenings at all. Late night/early morning, yes, but neither Herr Cutter nor I had eaten a single dinner with her. I wanted to ask if Raffiano knew where Tania was, or what she did in the evenings. I got as far as opening my mouth, but nothing came out. The language barrier was too fierce, too imposing. And that's when it happened.

"Come si chiama?"

"I'm sorry, but I don't—"

"What is your name?"

I did a double take. I looked around the table and saw Daniella with her eyes pointed my way. She spoke. In English. She had been able to the entire time.

"Uh, my name?"

"Yes. My father wants to know. He calls you *la bionda*." I was the blonde girl.

"My name is Ryland. It's weird." She looked puzzled. "I'm pretty sure my dad made it up."

"Papa, si chiama Ryland." Now he looked confused.

"It's okay," I said. "Even English speakers don't get it."

"Mama," Daniella called out. "Lei può aiutarmi con i compiti inglesi?"

"L'hai chiesta?"

"Ah—can you help me with my homework for English?"

"You speak okay," I told Daniella.

"Writing . . . not so easy."

So, after helping the family clear the table and pile all the dishes and silverware into the sink, I played teacher with Daniella at the kitchen table. The rest of the family relaxed in front of the TV in the back room to watch dubbed episodes of *Walker, Texas Ranger*. Ah, Chuck Norris—even in the land of the Romans, you are still a paragon of kick-assitude. As soon as Daniella cracked open her text book, she revealed what she really wanted to learn.

"Tell me about boys."

"Um, is that part of your homework?"

"No."

Shit. Not only was I not a very good expert on the mind of the modern male, I happened to be a foremost authority on how NOT to have relationships with other people. What I knew about the straight dating world was restricted totally to observation, such as: if you have at least three out of four limbs attached to your body and can complete a sentence, chances are that there's a guy out there catching glimpses of you when you're not looking. Witness: I have no ass, I have no boobs, and I don't do dresses. Even so, I've been an unwitting crush for guys. Why? Fuck all if I know. Sometimes the fact that I'm into girls gets them more excited (read: delusional). In full disclosure, I have kissed a guy, but I have never done the sideways polka with one or even entertained the thought. This chica likes boobs and girl-junk and always has.

"What's his name?" I asked.

"Fabrizio."

"What do you like about him?"

She scrunched up her pixie face. "I like . . . pantaloni."

Pantaloni. I thought about it for a second, then: "You like his pants?"

"Si! He has many colors, like red, and blue, and the other color . . . come le viole."

"Purple pants. Really."

"Si. He is so cool."

"Have you talked to Fabrizio?"

She shook her head vigorously. "No."

"But you like him."

She nodded.

"Try this—tell him that you like his pants."

She smiled sheepishly and curled her head into her shoulders.

"No. I can't."

"Yes you can. Just go up to him before class starts and tell him. It'll be over quickly."

Gemma stuck her head into the doorway to see how we were doing on Daniella's homework.

"Bene, mama," Daniella said to her mom. "Lei mi sta aiutando molto."

He took my arm, and when my skin touched his, I shivered. His forearm was ice cold and smooth like tanned hide. Together, my dance partner from the other night and I walked down the same path that Herr Cutter and I had tread upon during the day. It was nighttime, and the moon was full, casting everything in a bright sheen. Even though the wind stroked my cheeks, carrying upon it the faint traces of gunpowder, nothing moved—like the entire world had been shellacked.

"Poco tempo rimane," he said. That, for sure, was not a trick of the wind. Those were his words, and it was his voice rasping through a dry throat. "Dovete fare la vostra scelta." If I didn't think I was crazy before, this was enough to send me over the edge. It sounded like Italian. It felt like Italian. But it couldn't have been. Because I didn't know Italian, and how the hell was I dreaming in a language I couldn't speak?

"Who are you?" I asked. He ignored me and pulled me along. I recognized the sign that we passed—*Il Mare*—and a second later, there was the beach. In the moonlight, the huge pieces of driftwood were crooked fingers emerging from the sand, and the sea was a dark void that absorbed light rather than reflect it. Despite that, the rhythmic rumbling of the waves—push, pull—sounded like they were inside my own ears.

"Presto," he said. At that moment, the tug of the real world tingled the tips of my fingers and toes. I groped for the last Italian I remembered and spat it out.

"Come si chiama?"

He looked as if he was about to answer, but the next thing I knew, I was lying in bed, my eyes flooded by the shade of orange you see when light shines through your eyelids. I sat up, spotting the shadows cast onto the ceiling cast by the candle on the nightstand.

Christ. I was ambivalent on out of body experiences or other new-agey bullshit. And I for sure was not into ghosts. But this was more than an indigestion-fueled hallucination. Though lit, the candle was still tall. Tania must have left it on the nightstand not too long before.

Three

"Professor Cutter is gone," said Tania, pouring me a glass of blood orange juice at breakfast.

"What do you mean by *gone*?"

"Early this morning." She lightly tapped her soft boiled egg-in-holder with a spoon. "He said little before leaving. Only that he needed specific facilities to analyze yesterday's findings. I had Paolo drive him to the train station." Tania wasn't too worked up about this development, but I was thrown. The whole point of me being there was to help Herr Cutter. And now . . . ?

"Do you know what he found?" I asked.

"No," she said. "More tests. That's all he'd say."

"Tests. Where exactly did he go?"

"Munich."

"Munich. As in Germany?"

"Full of questions this morning, aren't you?" She chipped a piece of the egg shell and, like unwrapping a bandage from a wound, she pulled the shell away in one long piece. Then she dug into her prey. "He wanted to wake you, but I told him to let you be."

"You're joking."

"I have a terrible sense of humor, Miss Taggart."

I sipped juice to wet my throat.

"Did he leave a phone number? An address maybe?"

"I have his mobile. You may try and call him later."

"I think I should." *Yeah. I think I should take out a contract on him. Do hitmen take cafeteria meal swipes?*

"Originally, you and the professor were supposed to be here through Saturday morning. That is because on Saturday evening, I am having an event here at the farm. We could use your help setting up, if you are willing. Of course, I could not pay you in traditional ways, since you are technically a tourist, but I can offer you room, meal, and the service charge of changing your plane ticket back home. It would only be one more day."

I wasn't in any hurry to get back home. What did I have to return to, anyway? An empty dorm room? Soulless hours as the resident bitch waitress at Spider House Café? Sidelong glances from sellout hipster townies with their double-wide strollers? If Tania's offer spared me from that—even just for one day—I was gonna take it.

"I'm game."

"Good," she said. "You will help Paolo."

Oh. *Great.*

After finishing breakfast, I took a shower, changed up, and tried phoning Herr Cutter. No answer. I hate leaving messages, so I figured I'd call him a bit later—the better to catch him off guard for the beatdown of the century. I mean, who does that? Sure, I wasn't a minor, but without him, I was an impressionable young gentlelady all alone in big, bad, patriarchal Italy. That was a good enough excuse to be spray-painted on the bridge I was going to drop on his face.

When Paolo came back from dropping Herr Cutter off, he wandered into the villa in his usual grumpy mood. He stood in the doorway to the kitchen while Gina put away dishes, complaining to her about something while she opened and closed cupboards. She'd either become an expert at ignoring him, or had found amusement in his endless criticism. Whatever the case, she finished with her job and took her cigarette break. She spotted me on the way out, giggled, and went on her way.

"Pazzesca," Paolo muttered when he set his eyes on me. Nice to see you, too, partner.

"Paolo," called Tania from the living room. He and I walked over to see Tania standing and watching out the window while sipping a cup of tea. It was no wonder—a second day without rain. The clouds had dissipated, leaving the blue sky and the sun and nothing else. She gave him instructions, which—surprise, surprise—started a fight between them. Barbed Italian flew back and forth like a blizzard of ninja stars. At the end of it all, Tania shouted something at Paolo, causing his eyes to widen. Then he looked at me and stormed out.

Tania sighed. "I apologize," she said. "He does not like being told what to do."

"Or who to do it with."

"Trust me, it is not you. He is just . . . Sometimes he makes things difficult because he thinks they ought to be difficult. In five minutes, go outside. He will be out by the car. Do not say anything. Just get in, fasten your belt, and let him drive."

"What exactly am I supposed to be helping with?"

"Assorted errands," said Tania, who rang her little servant bell. "Paolo will tell you. Now, if you will excuse me."

"But . . ." Never mind. She was already gone.

I took Tania's advice about Paolo and waited in the foyer for a couple of minutes before venturing outside. Sure enough, Paolo was waiting there, seated at the wheel of his car, grinding his teeth. I got in, fastened my seat belt, and prayed to any god that would hear me. The car rolled out, and we were on the road. And you know what—I just couldn't resist. When someone is mad at me or has a beef with something that I did, I can only hold it in so long.

"Do you have a problem with me?" I said. "Look, I'm sorry for taking down the map. I didn't know it wasn't cool."

Paolo's grimace melted into what may have been shame. He turned away from me to look out the side window. I did the same out mine. I couldn't imagine what the journey would have been like in the rains of two days before. Some of the roads were still flooded, but instead of swelling pools of gray, mirrors dotted the ground, reflecting tiny suns shining upward. The hills were as amazing as any I had seen back home in Wyoming. Capalbio, with its castle towers, loomed in the distance.

"Are you okay?" I asked, hoping he could understand the sentiment, if not the actual English.

38

"Bene," he said, keeping his focus on avoiding the large standing pools of water on the road. I sat back in my seat and stayed silent the rest of the way there. Whatever it was could wait until he wasn't behind a steering wheel. Instead of staying down in the modern part of town, we journeyed upward into the old part with its narrow, cobbled streets.

The last time I was in Capalbio, it was drizzling and pitch black. I'd been in no mood to sightsee. So driving in with Paolo was the first real good look I'd gotten of it. The town seemed to wind about itself, its hub being the town's central *piazza* and its bustling marketplace. I pressed my face against the glass to catch every nuance: how the vendors moved their hands to seal an impending sale, how townspeople—and some very touristy looking folks, I might add—either shrewdly inspected everything they laid their eyes on or ambled about looking ripe for a pickpocket.

After parking on a steeply inclined road, we got out and descended back to the piazza, melting into the throngs of marketgoers. The marketplace was all cloth-decked wooden booths bursting with jars of red sauce, garlic on stalks brandished like swords, and vines of tomatoes held aloft like cluster bombs of flavor. No signs in any language marked where vendors ended and customers began. Rather, both sides on this battlefield spilled into each other. Your best chances at survival were a strong pointing finger and a fast tongue to fire off negotiations and counteroffers. The trick I learned from following close on Paolo's heels was *never stop moving*. If you stood still for a single moment, you'd get trampled by a grandma launching a tirade over the unrivaled freshness of her artichokes.

We stopped at a booth at the other end of the piazza. An older, big-shouldered woman presided over a fine collection of hand-carved wooden picture frames. They looked plain from afar, but on closer inspection, you could see that each of them was whittled out of a single piece of wood. These frames weren't assembled—they were sculpted.

"Paolo!" she called out. He batted away her greeting with a limp-wristed swat and a *bah*. They started to converse, obviously about me from how they stared and pointed.

"L'hai presentata a Giuseppe?" the woman asked Paolo.

"No!" He looked back at me and smiled. "È pazza." They went on with their conversation, leaving me to have a looksee around. Each frame had a different picture of a famous actor or politician or landmark stuck inside of it— the Italian version of those place-holding generic pretty couples in Target-brand frames. As I browsed, one frame caught my eye. I picked it up for a closer look. Inside the frame was a black and white photograph of an old man wearing a beaten hat and propped up against a post. The butt of his rifle rested on the ground near his feet, and his right hand was curled around the end of the barrel. He looked bloated and pale, like a corpse a few hours after dying. Wait—that's exactly what I was looking at, like those old west photos of outlaws taken as proof that the deadly deed was done. But the face in the photo—it was the face in my dream. The old man with the beard who spoke to me in my sleep was now there when I was awake.

Holy shit, holy shit, holy shit, holy shit.

"Um . . . cuanto cuesta?" I said to the woman, trying to stay composed. Thankfully, my Spanish translated over to

Italian fine enough. She held up her hand, all five fingers outstretched. Five Euros. I reached into my pocket and pulled out the cloth bottom. I had nothing.

"Cinque, si?" said Paolo, reaching into his own pocket. He took out a blue-colored note and handed it to the lady. "I pay," he told me. "You pay me back, eh?"

So he could speak English. Well, well. This was progress.

I nodded, and he returned to his conversation. I looked back down at the picture—my picture, thanks to Paolo. I thought that I was seeing things, but after a second or two of staring, there was no question. It *was* the man from my dreams—the one who danced with me, who walked with me, who insisted in telling me stuff in a language I couldn't speak. Obviously, he was someone of repute, ill or not. A picture of his corpse would not have been placed in this frame if he was just some dude. I waited patiently while Paolo indulged himself in conversation, which was funny, because his frown showed that the last thing he wanted to do was talk to the frame lady. Afterward, we milled about a little more before walking back through the piazza and up the hill toward the car.

"Hey, thank you—I mean, *grazie*—for the frame."

"Eh."

"Do you know who this is? The man in the picture?"

"Domenico Tiburzi."

"Who is he?"

"Il Re di Lamone! He is hero to Maremma. Domenico Tiburzi took money from the rich and gave to the people."

"Like Robin Hood."

"Bah. Tiburzi kills Robin Hood."

I didn't care who was better than who. I got a name, and that's what counted.

So, it turned out that we weren't going just yet. There was that whole helping Paolo with . . . with . . . oh God. I really hoped I wasn't about to learn the Italian term for "castrating a bull." With mild trepidation, I followed Paolo as he climbed a few staircases and passed under a couple of archways until we came to a door. He got out the keys and unlocked it.

"What's the dilly-o, bossman?" I rethought that question and restated: "What should I do?"

He shook his head. "Lei parla sciocchezze. Pazzesca." That word again—*Pazzesca!* I took a mental note to look it up, then a second later thought better of it. Maybe I didn't want to know. "Benvenuto a casa mia," he sighed.

So this is where you live. The apartment looked like time inside had frozen forty years ago. The walls had been white, but accumulated grime had turned them a sickly looking yellow. The front room itself was bare except for a table with four chairs around it, three of which had caked-on layers of dust. Bookshelves lined the walls on both sides of the room. A painting of Padre Pio, famous Italian saint, leaned against the far wall.

Paolo walked into the back room, leaving me to lounge in the front. With nothing else to do at the moment, I started scanning the big bookshelves at the far end of the room and plucking out books I thought looked interesting. I know—douchebag move, but with any luck there might have been an Italian phrase book (my dictionary was still recovering from its near drowning). As it turned out, many of the books were in English. Most of them were pulpy sci-fi paperbacks from the 1950s. Others were guidebooks to places like Mauritania and Fiji, also from the 1950s and 60s. From the images on the covers (buxom, luxuriantly coiffed ladies swooning in the arms of absurdly buff men—with even nicer hair), I guessed that the Italian language books were romance novels. I didn't peg him for a bleeding heart, but here was the proof.

Scanning the rest of the spines on the shelves, one book in particular caught my eye. The faded brownish cloth cover was basically rotten, the threads that bound the pages frayed and unspun like corn flax. I pulled the book off the shelf. It was an English translation of *Le Rayon Vert*, or *The Green Ray*, by Jules Verne, copyright 1883. On the title page was a handwritten note:

P—

You can borrow my book, but you must return it to my library.

—D

I flipped through the book, careful to keep all the pages together. Stuck into the last few pages was a photo of a woman in a nurse's outfit standing in front of a single house amid the burned-out husks of surrounding buildings. Despite the devastation, the girl smiled wide and pretty. The shutter captured that moment just before she broke out into laughter. My mom always said that that's when things are the funniest—not when you laugh, but right before, that split-second when the laugh is still an electric impulse. It's in that moment that you feel the funny in your face and your chest and your knees and you have to explode.

On the back of the photo was this note: *Munich 1945.*

I heard Paolo's footsteps coming back my way. Since I didn't want to find out how much less he could like me, I put the book, photo and all, back where I found it. Just in time. Paolo came back with both arms draped in wooden folding chairs. Through a combination of pantomime, guttural grunts, and nose pointing, he conveyed the plan: he brings out the chairs from the back, and I take them and load them in the car. Easy peasy. Right.

Fast forward about twenty minutes. The chairs were in the car, and both of us were sitting at Paolo's table, sweating waterfalls. He reclined and enjoyed a snack of bread, cheese, and lemonade, while I held a slab of meat to my forehead. Let's just say this—those stairs were steep, those chairs were heavy, and the word for "pain" sounds the same in Spanish and Italian.

"Why you come here and not speak the language?"

"Well, Herr Cutter—"

"Ah. Il Tedesco. Si. Stupido."

"I've learned a little bit while I've been here."

He leaned forward. "Si? Okay. You tell me."

Shit. Me and my big mouth. "Uh . . ." I held that god-awful note while I desperately tried to remember anything that Tania or Raffiano or Daniella had said to me. And then there, way in the back, I found something. So I grabbed onto it and held it for dear life: "Dovete fare la vostra scelta."

"Eh? You know what that means?"

"No," I said. "Not at all."

44

"*You choose. You must choose.* Where you learn this?"

I shrugged. "I must have heard it somewhere," I said, pretending that I didn't know exactly where I'd heard it and who I'd heard it from. Now that I knew his name, I could even tell Paolo if I wanted sound like a crazy person: *In my dreams, from Dominico Tiburzi.*

Paolo made me a little cheese sandwich and pushed it in front of me. "Mangia," he said. I nibbled it, and then took a long drink. "You like?" he said, pointing to the lemonade.

"It's good. You made it yourself?"

"Si. It was ice—eh, *frozen.* I mix with water."

"Nice," I said. "So, what kind of event is Tania having at the farm this weekend?"

"Fine settimana? La festa?"

"A feast. Like a party? Who's coming?"

"The families of the workers. Every year Tania does this."

"And your family? Are they coming?"

And he laughed. His face looked like it was going to rip at the seams. For a second, I saw a completely different man, someone who maybe wouldn't complain so much about the rain or who wouldn't care so much if some strange girl was looking at a map a little too closely. It was nice. But it passed quickly. "No family. Only me and Tania."

Back at the farm, we left all the chairs in the villa's living room. According to Tania, they'd be set outside on Saturday morning, but in the meantime, they'd stay piled on the floor. Paolo went out to inspect how the novice tree cutters were faring without his instruction ("incompetenti," he muttered as he went out the door), while I sat at the dining room table phoning Herr Cutter. No one picked up. I hit redial. Voice mail again. Third time's the charm? Nothing.

This time, I left a message: "Hi, Herr Cutter. It's Ryland Taggart—y'know, the girl you abandoned in rural Italy? I know you're probably, like, jumping into a vat of weisswurst or something, but maybe if you could call me back and explain, I'd think you were less of an asshole. Pardon my Spanish. Hugs and kisses!"

Tania came in from the kitchen with a cup of tea and slice of cake.

"Did you reach the professor?"

"No. I think he's scared of me."

"I have no doubt of that." She put the tea and cake under my nose and sat across from me.

"So, do you guys eat all the time?" I asked.

Before answering, she put a forkful of the cake in her mouth and chewed slowly. Then she washed it down with tea. Finally, she said, "Yes. All the time."

"I mean, that's cool. I've always wanted to be five billion pounds." I shrugged, took a bite of cake, and my mouth exploded with light, buttery, lemony goodness. "What do you call this?"

"It's a simple cake," she said. "Gina made it this morning, but that's not important now. I wanted to ask if you have had any more dreams."

"Yes," I said. "But you know that. There was a candle in

my room last night." Tania had to know something. Otherwise why even bring it up?

"I heard you talking in your sleep."

"What was I saying?"

"I could not tell. You were mumbling."

"Does the name Domenico Tiburzi ring any bells?"

She paused and weighed what I said. I tried to figure out the change in her expression, but it passed too quickly. "My father told me stories about him when I was young."

"Paolo said something about a Robin Hood guy—stole from the rich to give to the poor."

"He stole from everyone and made sure they knew it," she said. "This man was a murderer and thief. He killed and robbed many people."

"Yeah, well now he's robbing me of a good night's sleep."

"You dreamed of Tiburzi? What did he say?"

"Hell if I know," I told her. "I don't speak Italian. And he doesn't speak any English." *Wow*, I thought. *That sounded* more *insane that I thought it would.*

"Of course not—" She abruptly stopped and took an overly long sip of tea. "Let us talk about something else, yes?" Another sip. "You are in for a treat tonight. Gina is making her lasagna. Dinner is at seven o'clock. In the meantime, you may do as you please."

"Cool. Will you be eating with me?"

"No," she said.

"I don't want to pry . . . well, I guess that's what I'm doing. Are you on a special no-dinner diet or something? Where do you go every night?"

"You want to know?" she said. "Okay. Meet me at the

front door to the villa at six. If you are not there, I will leave without you."

I spent the rest of the afternoon wandering the grounds around the villa, and then looking over all my shit—including the now useless botany guides I brought from Austin. I had no idea what to expect on the other side of six o'clock. I wasn't sure how to dress, if I needed to bring a date—that sort of thing. Turns out I didn't have to worry. I showed up to see Tania in her jeans and boots, a backpack slung over her shoulder.

"We are going out there." She pointed straight ahead at everything that wasn't the villa.

"Where exactly?"

"I do not know exactly," she said. "We will find it when we find it. Gina packed food for you, so we will eat when we get there." And then she started walking. All I could do was follow. We walked for a long time without talking. I was having a hard enough time keeping up with her long strides. She seemed to be following a trail that only she could see through the comfy bed of pine needles carpeting the forest floor. The woods here were darker than the ones close to the villa. The ebbing light from the setting Sun darkened them even more.

From there, she zig-zagged us around trees like a slalom skier—around the left of one, around the right of the next, always making sure to lay her palm on the still-damp bark of each tree. Don't think that I didn't try to leave a mental trail of breadcrumbs behind. Mama didn't raise no dummies, and I liked to be on the side of knowing where we were just in case. The farther we pressed, the more every patch of moss looked like every other patch of moss, until I finally had to admit that all my Girl Scout training had been defeated. Right about that time, as if she could read my mind, Tania announced that we'd arrived and laid her butt on the soggy ground. I sat next to her and took the sandwich she handed to me. I unwrapped it and took a bite.

"Egg salad?" I said. "Not exactly fine Italian cuisine."

She took a bite of her sandwich and savored the taste. "This recipe is the best thing I learned in four years at UCLA. It has raisins in it."

"No shit—you went to UCLA?"

"Would you believe that I was a cheerleader for the basketball team?"

"Um. No."

"It is so easy to be stupid when you're young. Like doing things just because someone asks you."

"Amen, lady." We finished our dinners and sat back, fat and lazy, against the trees. Tania brought out a bottle of wine and two small glasses from her backpack. She poured and served up the booze. "So you do this every night," I said.

"When the weather permits," she said. "Being trapped inside makes me . . . ill-tempered." She did seem more relaxed—not controlled and deliberate like she normally was. Even when she was trying to be nice to you, she let you know who was boss. But not out here. Out here, she wasn't the boss, and she knew it. "We have time now. I've wanted to know about your ranch."

"Not much to say, really," I told her. "I just sort of hung around while my dad and his workers did all the hard stuff. I was the wild child who talked to the cows."

"It would be nice to be that girl with the cows. I do not like dealing to people. I would rather be out here. Do you return to your ranch often?"

"It's not in the family anymore," I said. "It just got too hard. So Dad packed up, sent me off to boarding school for senior year and started practicing corporate law. The American dream." Tania shook her head, finished her wine, and poured herself another. I sipped. Slowly. No repeats of grappa night. "I mean, I'd like to see it again. When I get really drunk, I get thoughts in my head about stealing a car and driving up to Wyoming to hang out with the cattle."

"Steal a car?"

I admitted to my criminal ways: "Only once, and only from bad people."

"Well, that's okay, then." I couldn't help but return Tania's smile. Then her expression became more sullen. "I could not imagine trading this for an office—in front of a computer all day, arguing on the phone about things that do not exist in reality."

"Wow. You've met my dad?"

"Your father . . . my brother."

"Your brother is Leo, right?" I thought back to the dapper-looking kid in a blue suit from the painting in the dining room.

"How did you—"

"His portrait is hanging in the villa."

"Ah, yes," she said. "When something is in the same place for so long, it fades from your sight. But my brother—yes. He always loved building things from spare parts, and when he was older, he went to work for a company in London to make machines. I do not remember now what they were. He had an office, two cabinets full of files, phones, calculators—it was his heaven."

"Your parents were okay with this?" I asked.

"They thought it was good for Leo to see the world, do many things. And when he was done, he would come back and take over the farm. My mother and father believed that they would be here for a long time." I already didn't like the direction of this conversation, but Tania seemed eager to keep talking, and I was willing to keep listening.

"Where is Leo now?" I asked, trying to sidestep the parent issue.

"He died," she said, almost matter-of-factly. "He and my parents were driving in Scotland on vacation. They had an accident, and . . . the other driver did not survive, either."

"Oh god. I'm really sorry."

"It happened long ago. Remembering is not painful. It is not . . . anything. What is done is done. Would you like more wine?" I looked down at my now-empty glass. I didn't think I was drinking that fast. I must have just been putting the glass to my lips automatically as I listened.

"No, thank you. I'm cool."

We spent a few more minutes sitting and listening to the breeze bristle the evergreens. Then we packed away the wine and glasses and stood up. I was a bit dizzy from the guzzling, and the rapid descent of night didn't help. Only the top edge of the Sun was visible on the horizon—what little horizon I could see beyond the treeline.

"Hey," I said, "Really. I'm sorry. I lost my mom, too, a couple years ago. It's funny—it was always her dream to visit Italy. I mean, she'd even play *Learn to Speak Italian!* language tapes in the car while she drove me to school. If the universe was fair, she'd be here, not me."

"May I ask how she died?"

It was a reasonable question. So I told her in the best way that I could: "I was really sad one night, and she came and held me until I fell asleep. The next morning, I woke up. She didn't."

"I see," she said, laying a hand on my shoulder. "Be sure to follow me closely. It is dark out here."

It was dark. Branches and thorny vines—seemingly made of pure darkness—snaked and spiraled around the stars before reaching down to snarl my pants. The moon and starlight were my only light sources, but the overhanging tree canopy blocked them out half the time. I was lost. And when you're lost, everything gets bigger, brighter, and stronger as your senses sharpen with the *fight-or-flight*. Every step on the forest's pine needle floor whipped up pungent evergreen.

Where was I going? I didn't know. I didn't dare stop. There were things in this forest that hunted at night—

things I didn't know the names for, that wouldn't recognize their own names if I said them in English. I pressed forward into a glade with a single tree in its center. At its far right edge was what looked like a pond, but when I got closer, I saw that it was little more than a large pool of rainwater that had collected in a low spot—a mirror made of obsidian. Two sets of footprints had been left in the mud—one noticeably smaller than the other.

"Baby," I heard a voice say.

I turned around. Next to the center tree . . . "Mom?" *Not fucking possible. Not fucking* . . . It *was* her. She wore that same pink dress the last night I had spent with her, that morning after her heart decided to stop working.

"It's been a while."

I ran over to her but stopped short. She looked exactly as I remembered her—the dimples, the tiny wrists, the way her wavy hair went crazy in the humidity. "Are you really here?"

"Lei è qui perché ho bisogno di aiuto." I turned around again to see the man who had been in my dreams every night I had spent at the farm. I finally knew his name: Domenico Tiburzi, the King of Lamone, the Robin Hood of the Maremma. "Tua madre—"

"Let me," said Mom. "Baby, it's okay. You're only dreaming." I backed away from the both of them. Part of me was screaming to wake up, to deny that this was happening. The other part wanted it to be real. "Listen. I want you to remember what I say. Can you do that?"

"I think so," I said. Then I watched as she made eye contact with Domenico Tiburzi. Then he started to talk:

Fate la vostra scelta al più presto.

"You make your choice soon," said Mom.

La terra sta morendo. Sei l'unica persona che può salvarlo.

"The land is dying. You are the only one who can save it."

Si deve seguire il raggio verde.

"You must follow the green ray."

Then Tiburzi looked straight at me. His eyes were the same color as the parts of the sky that didn't touch the stars—the absolute black of space: '*Sta bene avere paura.*

Mom hesitated before giving the translation: "It is okay to be afraid."

At that, Domenico Tiburzi took off his hat and bowed. He turned and walked back into the forest, leaving Mom and me alone.

"You're so big, baby," she said. "I don't even recognize you."

"Mom," I said, rushing forward. I had decided that I was going to hug her. No force in the entire universe was going to stop me. I was so close already. "Mom, I miss you so much. Please don't leave me again."

"Oh, baby. I wish . . ."

Closer. My legs felt like lead, but I pressed on.

"You're beautiful," she said.

One step away.

"I love you."

Orange. I opened my eyes. Sunlight streamed in past my bedroom door, cracked ajar. Over the door's edge curled Tania's fingers.

"Buongiorno, Miss Taggart," I heard from the other side. "There is food downstairs. Eat quickly. We have a long day ahead."

Four

t took me a while to get my balance back. That didn't stop Tania from putting me to work right away. She anticipated guests arriving around five o'clock (because she had told them to arrive at one to one thirty), but there was so much to be done that we were in a rush. My duties started outside, under the sun and a clear sky dotted with puffball clouds. Tania had me and Raffiano's girls as table committee: we set out tables and chairs, laid out tablecloths, and covered the hard seats with cushions.

"Come stai?" Daniella asked, smoothing out a tablecloth.

"Tired . . . er . . . stanca?" I really wanted to get some Italian under my belt before leaving, so I forced myself to speak it as much as I could.

"That's good!" She said. Cool. Of course, she could have just been buttering me up. She had that look on her face again. Girl had some questions.

"Spit it out, lady," I said.

"I want to . . . come si fa una bacia all'uno ragazzo?"

"Stupid American here," I said. Together, we set another table on its feet.

"Okay. Um . . . how do you . . . kiss a boy?"

Daniella didn't mess around. It's not like I didn't know the answer to the question on a purely technical level. I've kissed girls, I've kissed cows, and there was that one time with a lemur at the San Diego Zoo. And I've kissed a boy, too. But that wasn't what Daniella was really asking. She was asking this question: *How do you kiss boys so they know how you feel about them, but without embarrassing yourself?* And that I did not know. It sort of goes with the territory. I mean, you're jamming your face into somebody else's face. And all sorts of liquids flow in and out in ways that they probably weren't really designed to, and even though it doesn't make sense, it feels good.

Overcoming embarrassment is the easy part. It's the *feeling* part that's hard. Where is the line between *love* and *like*? Or even *like* and *meh*? How do we, through our tongues and lips and tooth avoidance, tell someone we could maybe, possibly, be in love?

So I just smiled. And nodded. And changed the subject to: "You have relatives coming today?"

"Si. Nonno e Nonna. I miei zii, i miei cugini."

"How many people is that, exactly?"

"At the last party, there were . . . twenty?"

"Twenty? Like two-oh?"

"No. Like two-oh-oh."

"Two hundred?" I said, feeling the air momentarily drain

away from my lungs. "Will there be two hundred people here today?"

Daniella put her finger to her mouth and thought about it. Then: "Si."

Afterward, we set up all the tables, Tania sent the girls to help Gemma and Gina cook while Raffiano and I followed Tania back into the villa. I assumed that we were on more chair duty, but that idea went bye-bye when we passed through the front room into the dining room where we ate awkward breakfasts every morning. The mix of garlic, fresh bread, and spicy tomato smells wafted in from the kitchen. At the foot of the stairs going up to the bedrooms, Tania leaned down, took hold of the upper lip of the bottom step, and pulled up, revealing a hidden passage.

"Sweet!" I said. Raffiano chuckled at my reaction. I thought it was cool, but maybe every Italian farmhouse had a kick-ass secret passageway. We continued to follow her along as she went down the staircase that she had just uncovered, down a dark hall lit up by Tania's flashlight. Raffiano hunched over and scrunched in his shoulders to fit himself in.

"What is this place?" I asked.

"Do you not have root cellars in America?"

"This is so much cooler than a root cellar."

"Maybe the soldiers who once lived here thought the same." Tania stopped when the hallway widened out into a small room. She shined the flashlight into a corner where two wooden crates were stacked on top of one another. "My grandfather hid Americans here for months while the *squadristi* swarmed these lands."

"Squa—what?"

"Blackshirts. Mussolini's pet fascists," she said. "Raffiano, porti il vino allo pianterreno. Mettilo nella cucina." Then she turned to me: "Raffiano will take one, and you will take one. Take it to the kitchen." I followed the beam of light over to the crates, marked with the word VINO.

"I can't imagine living in here." I picked up the heavy box and dragging it into the dining room. I resolved to go to the gym and work on these flaccid pieces of flesh and bone called my arms. "I'd even take the smelly haunted bedroom over it."

"Haunted?" said Tania.

"Um, 'cause of the ghosts."

She laughed. "Raffiano, ha paura degli spiriti."

"Anche qui abbiamo cavalli e mucche," he said back to her between labored grunts. "Ho piu paura degli animali." I recognized that lilt in his voice. I'd become familiar enough with it hanging around Paolo. Raffiano was totally making fun of me. Har-de-har-har. We got the boxes out of there and into the kitchen, where Gina ran around like a Roomba. One second, she was stirring a huge pot of marinara, and the next minute, she was beating chicken with a spiked hammer. Fiorentina and Vittoria, two of Daniella's younger sisters, mutely worked on a stack of onions and garlic, chopping them with big butcher knives no American mom would let near girls their age. Dumb move, because these little girls were buzzsaws, dicing and mincing like professional sous-chefs.

"Ah, Gina," said Raffiano. "Profumo." Raffiano laughed and joked with his daughters. "Non mi piace il sapore delle mani." They laughed, called him "Papa." I turned away to see Tania coming into the room behind me.

"So," I said, trying to change the subject for myself. "You think I'm crazy that I believe there are ghosts here?"

"Crazy?" she said. "If you are crazy, then we are all lunatics. Come with me. I will tell you a story." Tania and I walked together out through the courtyard and beyond.

My father told me a story his father—my grandfather—had told him of his own boyhood. One night before dinner, someone knocked on the villa door. On the other side was a scraggly-bearded old man who my grandfather did not recognize, but who his father— my great-grandfather—greeted with a glass of wine and a smile. This man dragged behind him a monstrous wild boar that should have taken three men to carry. "This beast is from your land," the man said. "I only ask a small portion. The rest is yours. Then I will leave." My great-grandfather would have none of it. He seated the man at the head of the table and introduced him as "nostro amico"—our friend—il signore Domenico Tiburzi. That night, he ate with our family, and afterward, he was given his choice of room. The one he chose would later become my bedroom, the same room that you are sleeping in.

"Bullshit," I said.

"Do you think I am lying to you?" Nothing in Tania's body language told me she was telling me anything but the truth. Her stride was as nonchalant as someone taking a stroll to the mailbox. "Why do you think I have interest in your dreams?"

"I didn't think it was because you thought I was possessed."

"Not possessed. You merely pique their interests."

"The ghosts' interests."

"You can call them ghosts or spirits or—"

"Dead people," I said. I felt my face flush with heat. "You could have maybe told me."

"It did not seem important."

"Not important? Tania, I saw my mom."

She furrowed her brow. Obviously, she hadn't expected to hear that little bit of info. "Perhaps it means that Tiburzi was trying to tell you something."

"Well, yeah!" I grabbed her arm. She looked at me all innocent-like. "What's going on?" From not far off, I heard the buzz of a chainsaw, and a second later, the sound of branches crashing to the ground.

"What you are describing—this is only normal life for us. Spirits, ghosts—whatever. All these things are parts of the world that we grow up with. I am neither surprised nor afraid. But you . . ." She paused, trying to mold her words diplomatically. "You are taught that all this is not possible. You learn that only crazy people believe. So when faced with the truth, it is easy—even preferable—to deny. I will tell you the truth: the dead speak. They exist all around us all the time. They see what we can see, feel what we can feel. They get bored. They get lonely. They like to play tricks. They speak in riddles. This spirit is one of those."

"But my mom . . ." I drew closer. "I mean . . . I sound insane, don't I?"

"What did she say to you?"

"She said she was there as a favor. To the old guy—Tiburzi, who was there, too. She was translating what he was saying—the land was dying, that I had to make some choice."

"It is just a dream, Miss Taggart."

"But I thought dreams—"

"Paolo!" Saved by the chainsaw. "Hey! Paolo! Si può scendere ora!" A few yards away and a few more yards up, Paolo was perched, chainsaw in hand, cigarette in mouth, spewing swears into the air just to make sure the other trees knew he was coming. Upon spotting us, he waved us away with his free hand, revving up the chainsaw again for another go, but either he couldn't hear her over the chainsaw, or he heard her and didn't care. "He is always like this," she said to me. "My uncle is not too fond of . . . people. But it is time for him to come down."

"So how do we get him out of the tree?"

"We are not doing anything. You are. I must cater to other matters before the guests arrive."

"Me? Really?"

"Yes," she said. I waited for the punchline. It never came. She turned to leave.

"Wait. You didn't answer my question."

She looked upward. "Perhaps you could throw a rock or sing an annoying song."

"I mean about my dream."

"It will have to wait," she said, starting back down the

61

path to the villa. I stood alone at the base of the tree. It went *waaaaaay* up. *Okay*, I thought, *if I stand here long enough, Paolo will get curious enough to come down and see what I'm up to.* This was not the case. Instead, he made a circle around his head with the chainsaw, sending not so small pieces of the tree raining down on my head. I jumped out of the way before a big branch hit me square in the face.

Plan A tanked. Start 'er up, Plan B:

"Hey!" I called up. "Remember me? The person you love to insult in Italian?" No answer. "Okay, so I'll, like sit down here by this tree," I said pointing to one comfortably away from falling debris. "I'm gonna chill out. Right here. Friends?" Aaaaand *nothing*.

I took a seat. In the dirt, I drew a tic-tac-toe grid with my finger. I'm not sure how long I was sitting there drawing up cat's eye after cat's eye, but at some point, I heard Paolo call out, "Dio mio!" snapping me back into the present. He stood over me, the chainsaw still growling as it hung from his belt. "Cosa stai facendo? C'è molto lavoro da fare!" Why did I get the impression that I was getting my ass handed to me? I stood and dusted myself off.

"Um, Tania told me to get you out of the tree."

"Perché?"

"Don't look at me," I said. "I guess she has a job for you."

Paolo grumbled and paced, but ultimately switched off the chainsaw, gathered his tools, and followed me back to the villa. Tania was overseeing a team of workers while Daniella and her sister, Ottavia, laid out white tablecloths onto each table. Tania waved when she saw I had captured my quarry while barking out instructions to some of the workers to set up twelve chairs per table. Paolo wasted no time and launched into a tidal wave of Italian directed straight at Tania. At first she brushed him off by stepping away, but he followed close, raising the pitch, volume, and velocity of his voice. Tania had to match his every move until she was forced to pull out the nuclear option.

"You will listen to me!" The switch to English had a palpable effect on Paolo, who stood there seething with no answer. Engaging her in the same language would just further entrap him in her web. He'd never out-argue her in a language in which she had the decided advantage, so he resorted to the old standby—stomping away angrily. He sat down at one of the tables and pulled out the last cigarette from its pack. A worker tried to straighten the chairs around where Paolo was sitting, but he only got a mouthful of cursing for his trouble.

"Miss Taggart," said Tania, composing herself. "Another job for you."

"As long as it doesn't have anything to do with chopping meat," I said.

"Watch my uncle. Make sure he is nice to the guests."

Meat chopping it is! We have Ryland-burgers on our prix-fixe menu!

"You want me to make sure he's nice?" I asked. "How am I supposed to do that?"

"I have no doubt that you will find a way."

"Thanks," I said. That was a change from normal—a boss actually thinks you can do shit. It didn't matter that she was wrong—it was still nice. "But seriously. I'm not sure anything will improve his mood."

"It is not easy to take orders from the little girl you used to balance on your knee," she said. "He is a proud man."

"What is the deal with that? Paolo was older than your dad—how come this isn't his farm?"

"If I tell you, you must promise to say nothing to Paolo about it." We both turned toward him at the same time. He sat at the table by himself, encircled but not approached by other farm workers, who had by now learned when to stay clear of him. He took a long drag from his cigarette. "My grandfather left the farm to my father and my uncle. Paolo sold his share to my father. He owns nothing now. Not even the apartment where he lives. That was my father's, too."

"Why would he sell?"

"I don't know," she said. Paolo ashed on the tablecloth. He didn't even bother to wipe it away. "My father told me that Paolo left for a short time after that. That is all I know."

No use delaying the painful task any longer. I took a deep breath and marched onward, taking a seat across the table from Paolo. I made sure to plaster the biggest shit-eating grin I could muster onto my face. That was when he got up and walked off.

Okay, so there were more than two hundred people at the farm that night. They started to trickle in around quarter to five, and at about six thirty, we were swarmed. Aunts, uncles, cousins, mothers, fathers, brothers, sisters—every worker employed at that farm had invited at least five relatives to eat and dance and play music. Vittorio, one of the men who took care of the horses, arranged for his cousin's five-piece gypsy swing band to show up and set up a makeshift stage in the center of the yard.

As for food—what didn't they serve? There were a full four tables reserved exclusively for the food spread. You had pasta of all colors, served with pesto or marinara or other things that I didn't know the names of. Roasted and cured meats (prosciutto rocks the house) sat on their own table. There was another table only for cheese and bread. Think of the biggest Thanksgiving you've ever been to. Then, square the amount of food and quadruple the amount of people. That'll get you close.

Daniella had the idea to drag me up and down the rows by the hand to introduce me to all her cousins. I reluctantly agreed, thinking that as long as I could keep one eye trained on Paolo, I was doing my job. After meeting her fourth cousin, Alessandro, a lean, olive-skinned youth with deep brown eyes and a swagger that said *you-want-my-body*, I started to notice a pattern.

"Now we will go see Claudio. He is my mother's cousin's—"

"Daniella!"

"Si?"

"I . . ." I'd thought that I was over this. Closet-stepping. Owning the gay. How many times in the last year had I just blurted it out—*I'm a lesbian*—without even caring who heard? Why was I having such a hard time right then? "I have to go." I looked around to spot Paolo in the crowd, but in that minute I wasn't paying attention, he managed to slip away. There was no indication of where he had gone. Dammit! I had one job, and I couldn't even do that right. "Tania asked me to stay with Paolo. I need to find him."

"But Benicio is the most handsome! You must meet him!"

"I can't." *I'm a lesbian*, I wanted to say, but didn't.

"Why Paolo? He is always so . . . scontroso, like when you are mad all the day, and you walk like this." She stomped around in a circle. "Scontroso."

"I'll be back, okay?" I took my leave to mount a search. The polka band was in full swing, and part of the yard was cleared out to make a dance floor. I narrowly dodged a bevy of men trying to snatch my arm and draw me into a dance. Everyone seemed to have this ease of movement, a kind of grace like they were moving through water. I, on the other hand, leaped from here to there, sticking my head into corners and behind trees, into nooks and between dancing partners. As I searched, I found myself farther from the music and father from the flood lights we had turned on when the sun had set. I found myself squeezing through the narrow spaces between the cars that the guests had parked in front of the barn.

A bright light suddenly lit up the space where I was. My eyes adjusted, and I recognized Paolo behind the wheel of the hatchback, its high beams streaming.

"Where are you going?" I yelled before jumping into the passenger seat.

"Non è interessante," he said. "Go away."

"Tania asked me to keep you company."

"Bah! I am not a child!"

"You're acting like it," I said. No more riddles, no more weirdo dreams or pregnant pauses. "C'mon, it's a party."

"I want to go home."

"This is your home," I said. "I know you grew up here. Tania told me so."

Paolo's gaze shifted from being a million miles away to being right in my face. He went from lost to angry to frantic to resigned in only a few seconds. At the end of it all, in the shadows cast by the reflection of the high beams on car bumpers, he did look all of ninety-plus.

"Tania talks too much," he said.

"But I'm right, right? Why did you leave it?"

"Pazzesca," he said, a small smile on his face. "Get out."

"I don't know what's going on with you, but I thought . . . like with the frame, and the lemonade . . . that was nice. I thought that maybe we could be, y'know, friends." I reached for the handle to open the door when Paolo grabbed my wrist. It hurt from how tight he had held it. We locked eyes. I swear words were right there at the edge of his lips, but they never came out. The way he looked at me—ilt was like I was some other person entirely. Then he let go and stared straight at the steering wheel.

"Mi dispiace. Your hand is hurt?"

"I'm fine," I said. "Look, are you coming with me, or are you leaving?"

He looked down at his hands. "I go."

"Fine." I opened the door and placed one foot on the ground outside.

"Tania will be upset," he said.

"Yeah." I rubbed my wrist. "Probably."

"You tell her, eh? 'Vado in biblioteca a leggere un libro.' You remember?"

"How am I supposed to—"

"Remember. Please. 'Vado in biblioteca a leggere un libro.' Good practice for Italiano."

"Whatever, okay?" I got out of the car and slammed the door shut. The car turned onto the road and soon became two pinpoints of light on the horizon.

The party was in full swing when I got back. People were either dancing or eating. One guy did both at the same time by taking a half-eaten loaf of bread as his dancing partner. Still shaken from the thing with Paolo, I wanted to lay low for a bit, sip some wine and slowly wind myself up into a party state of mind. Raffiano had other plans. He picked me up from my chair and launched me into the center of the dance area.

"Balla! Balla!" Now that the wine had been flowing freely for a while, the band's double bass player decided to throw his playing into the next gear. In a whirl of guitar, fiddle, and accordion, Raffiano and I danced—or more accurately, Raffiano danced while I hung onto his arm, went limp, and prayed to God/Allah/The Almighty Karmic Balance that I'd survive to the end of the song. I did, and when the music stopped, I found myself in Raffiano's arms, hugging him so tight. Happy. It was funny how fast the dancing turned my mood around. *Relax, Ryland,* and I did that, too, locking arms with people whose names I didn't know, whose names I wouldn't learn. All that mattered was that I was there. The last person I danced with before the band took a break was a short old man with slicked-backed gray hair and a prominent, dignified looking nose.

"Nonno!" said Daniella from across the way. "Quest'è la mia amica Americana."

"Americana?" The old man drew his face close to mine. "Ti piace l'Italia?"

"Sì!" I understood! That's progress.

"Non ascoliti le persone che ti dicono il contrario. Non vedono la magia." At that, he let go of me to embrace his four granddaughters who flocked around him like he was a movie star. That was my cue to get out of the way and get on with the hard stuff. At least I got a dance in before Tania chewed me out for letting Paolo go.

"Ciao, Ryland!" Raffiano called out.

"Ciao, Raffiano!" I called out, feeling all gooey and mushy inside. Either I was verklempt or Raffiano had crushed my spleen, and I was slowly bleeding to death. Either way, I had to find Tania and tell her about Paolo.

None of the lights were on inside the villa.

"Tania?" I went from room to room on the ground floor, but she wasn't in any of them. I went up the creaky stairs to the terrace, where she sat at a small table pushed into the corner. Out a half-circle shaped window, she watched the festivities outside. As soon as I stepped onto the second floor, her silhouette stood up, gaining color and texture as she stepped into a shaft of light coming from the outside.

"Hey," I said. It wasn't two steps later that I smelled a familiar rotten foot stink coming from a Tania's teacup. "Don't tell me you're actually drinking that stuff."

"I find its flavor to my liking," she said. "Apart from the strange aftertaste. What would you say that is?"

"Toe jam. And ass. Those are the major ingredients."

"You are enjoying yourself," she said. "How is my uncle?"

"About that . . ." I thought for a moment how I was going to explain what had happened, seeing that I wasn't really sure what did happen. Well, here it goes: "He sorta . . . well, he drove off, and—I don't know. He was really weird."

Sip. "Did he say where he was going?"

"Yes. He said . . . um . . . *Vado in biblioteca a leggere un libro*. He told me to tell you that."

"He went to the library to read a book?" said Tania.

"I tried to stop him."

Tania turned back to the window and sipped her tea.

"He will be here tomorrow," she said. "Please enjoy the rest of the night."

"So, are you coming out?"

"No. I have been doing this for many years. The workers know that I do not participate."

"Why?"

"It is not my place," she said. "It is theirs—their night to be happy, to forget the pains, to taste the foods they have worked the whole year to make. Tomorrow, they work. I will give them their tasks and expect them to succeed. It is my place to see that work on this farm is done correctly."

"I'm sure they wouldn't mind if you showed up."

She laughed. "You are correct. They would not mind, but

I would. You cannot be strong for others when you are so close to them. Too close, and you will fail them when they need you most. I learned this only after many years."

I had no rebuttal. "Well, I guess I'll be going, then."

"You asked me before about dreams." She put the teacup down on the table. "Tiburzi came to me once in a dream. Only once, when I was thirteen. I remember him sitting by the fireplace like in Nonno's story. I was not even in the room—more like a movie playing in my mind. He did not move, but I heard his voice, like rough hands: *Vivrai per vedere la morte di tutto ciò che si ami.*"

"What does that mean?"

"You will live to see the death of everything you love."

"Tania! Why didn't you say something?"

"I told you. We are all lunatics. Now, I must get ready for bed. The villa door will remain unlocked, so you may come and go as you please." She stepped away from the window. "Miss Taggart, do you think you will dream of him tonight?"

"I don't know."

"Buona notte, then," she said. "By the way, I rescheduled your flight for tomorrow in the afternoon. The plane flies out of Florence, so you must wake up early. You have quite the journey ahead."

Five

hit. I never listen. I woke up, but not early, draped on my bed with arms and head dangling off the side. All my clothes were on, including my shoes. I thought back on how I might have gotten into this position. All I could remember were vague, blurry images of me across the table from a big hairy man with the most righteous handlebar mustache. Between us was a bottle of wine that seemed to magically fill every time I looked at it. A drinking game? Why, yes. I wish I knew if I won or not.

"Miss Taggart," said Tania with a too-sweet voice that masked her annoyance, "Fifteen minutes."

I whipped out my best zombie impression.

"Uuuuuuugggggggghhhhhh."

"Fourteen," she said.

Fine. I sat up, the contents of my head swishing around. I hurt. A lot. But I pushed through because, well, I didn't have much of a choice. I crammed my stuff into my backpack, excluding my toothbrush, which I had to use because my mouth tasted like a family of muskrats had died in there.

Down below, Tania was sitting at the table and zipping up her boot. Raffiano sat next to her. He was wearing a suit.

"Special occasion?" I asked after coming downstairs.

"It is Sunday," said Tania. "Raffiano is going to church."

"You too?" I was commenting on how spiffy she looked with a white blouse and black pants. Simple and sexy. Tania pointed out a paper bag sitting on the table. I picked it up and looked inside. I could already smell what was inside. Food. Good food for the road, as long as I could guard it from jealous fellow travelers who had to settle for reluctantly purchased prepackaged snacks.

"I am driving you to the train station."

"What about Paolo?"

"Perhaps he has forgotten that you are leaving today." She slung a purse over her shoulder and proceeded toward the door. "We will stop by his apartment."

"I'd like that." And then, it hit me. I was saying goodbye to this place. Even though I hadn't even spent a week here, I felt that I knew it. I looked around at the rooms, took in the smells of toast coming from the kitchen. Then I set my eyes on Raffiano in his Sunday finest. Something told me that he wouldn't mind a hug, even though I was pretty scummy, so I went in. "Grazie per tutto, Raffiano."

"Prego," he said. "Siete sempre i benvenuti. Buon viaggio."

All three of us went out the door. Raffiano walked over to where Gemma and the girls stood waiting by the family station wagon. All of the girls were dressed to the nines in brightly-colored dresses. Upon seeing me come out, Daniella ran over.

"Goodbye," she said, and pressed a small piece of paper into my palm. "There is e-mail at school. You will send one to me?"

"Sure," I said. "I can already guess what it will be about." She confirmed as much with her dimples and ran back to her family. I took one more look around, at the far off trees, at the great horned cow in the pen, at the villa and the tables that were still set up from the previous night. I'd miss this place, all right. Tania and I watched the family pile into a car and drive away.

"Wait here," Tania said. "I will drive around." Two minutes later, she returned behind the wheel of a silver two-seat convertible with sunglasses on and a scarf trailing behind her like a 1940s movie icon.

"Holy starlets, Batman."

"It is ridiculous," she said. "But it was my father's car, so how could I get rid of it?"

It took Tania most of the ride to ask what she had wanted to ask. I considered her question while looking out at the spire that crowned Capalbio.

Did you dream last night?

"I don't remember." I said. I don't think I dreamed. "Besides, it doesn't really matter now. Ghosts? Really?"

"You still don't believe?"

"I don't know," I said, already imagining me touching down on the other side of the world.

"For what it is worth, Miss Taggart, you have made a difference. You made the sun appear."

"That's nice of you to say," I laughed, but she kept a straight face.

"It is true. For weeks, we had nothing but rain. You come, and it stops. You are the only thing that was different."

"If Herr Cutter heard that, he'd have a screaming fit about the principles of causality."

"Il professore is not here."

"Yeah, well . . . Thanks."

I felt like the king of Abu Dhabi rolling up in that pimp car. We drove down the twisty streets, causing passers-by to stop and stare until we were out of sight. At the train station, a tour group was just leaving the arrival platform, ready to shop and ridicule their tour guide when he was out of earshot. I felt a little jealous. They got to be surprised by the tastes and the smells, meet the people, smell the air and look at the stars. I'd done that, and I wanted a redo. Maybe I wouldn't fuck up as much.

Up through the old gate we drove, onto the cobbled streets of the ancient walled town. By the time we had reached Paolo's apartment building, my butt was sore from the bumpy ride.

We knocked and waited and knocked and waited some more at Paolo's door. No answer. Tania took out a ring of keys from her purse. After trying two or three keys, Tania plucked the right one from the crowd—an old-school skeleton key straight from One-Eyed Willie's private collection.

She inserted it into the lock and turned.

The night I came out to my parents was the night of junior prom. I hadn't planned to tell them, but a series of events made it happen. First: I didn't wear a prom dress. I had saved tips both as waitress and karaoke MC at Mr. Beaver's Western Round-Up (one of Wyoming's classier establishments, to be sure) enough to rent a tuxedo (I couldn't fit into any of their men's sizes, so I had to wear a boy's purple tux). Second: my date's name was Mya, and she had decided to wear a slinky pink one-piece deal straight out of a Sean Connery James Bond movie (y'know, the classy ones). Very nice. Very girly. Mya was under the impression that we were going as friends, which was my intention, too. Mostly. Okay, so I had a huge crush on her, but I wasn't planning on telling her and *definitely* wasn't thinking of laying the truth out on prom night. Third: I thought I was good enough to just make this thing happen. I figured that my parents would, for some reason, not be around to obsess over me. I forgot that parents live for that shit.

So Mya and I were upstairs in my bedroom getting ready, giggling about how stupid prom was. I slipped a corsage onto her wrist and fixed the headband in her curly black hair.

"So purple. Really?"

"I'm going for that insane-master-criminal-of-Gotham-City look," I said. "There." I stepped back and looked Mya up and down once she stood up. She was gorgeous. Mya was the captain of the volleyball team and the starting center on the basketball team. She took both to state that year and a year later went to Clemson on a full ride for—of all things—math. Yeah. She was a genius, too. Anyone would have loved to go on a date with her, and to prom—forget it. I had the hottest ticket in town, and I wasn't really sure why. I mean, I didn't hang around her friend circles, didn't know her except from sitting a seat ahead of her in Mr. Peterman's Geometry class. One minute I was joking that I'd show her a better time than any guy, and the next minute, we were scheming on ways we could avoid that harpy Dean Cundy at prom so she wouldn't kick us out for "insubordination."

"I'm not showing too much leg, am I?" How much was too much anyway? So the dress was a little short. The way I figured it was that if she had it, she might as well show it off, and she had the nicest legs this side of the Rockies.

"Coverage is good."

"Thanks. Really."

"You're welcome. I just fixed your headband is all."

"No," she said, laying her hand on my shoulder. She leaned down enough to look me in the eyes. "For all this. I hate prom. I mean, I don't hate it, but I hate everything around it. Like the asking and the gossip and the color coordinating and all that other bullshit."

You've been there. We all have. You're living and thinking at full throttle. Suddenly the world goes to Technicolor, and everything has real meaning. The Care Bear bedspread you never had the heart to get rid of because it makes your remember how your dad would bring you waffles and syrup in bed; the Queen CD that you hardly listen to anymore but keep around because you still think that Freddie Mercury was giving you life advice when he was saying "I want to break free"; the bottle of colored sand you keep on your nightstand because Daydre Phillips gave it to you in summer camp, and you thought she liked you; the rusty cowbell from around the neck of *Firestar*, the milk cow that died the year before, robbing you of both fresh dairy and a therapeutic ear. It's like the universe turned on a giant neon arrow pointing to your destiny. I didn't just want to kiss Mya at that moment. Every fucking thing in creation wanted me to do it. Fourth quarter. Three seconds on the clock. Two. One. Let it go.

Airball.

"Sure," I said, staring at my hands. "We're friends."

"C'mon," Mya said, taking my hand. "Let's show all those guys what they're missing."

It was a fun night overall. Mya wasn't really in any danger of being thrown out (being the school superstar helps in that regard), and all I had to do was make sure that my back always faced Dean Cundy when she was near (a boy cut helps in that regard). But I couldn't help feeling regret and burning jealousy every time a guy asked Mya to dance and she accepted. I knew it was crazy to think it, but all that ran through my head was that it could have, should have been me at the end of prom making out with Mya. Not Kirby Frink. Kirby Frink!

I dropped Mya off at home afterward, trying my best not to lose my cool on the trip to her place. After she got out and went inside, my lungs felt like they were melting into goo. I wanted to throw that shit up until I was an empty meat suit. I told myself that this was, most assuredly, the worst part of the night. I'd go home, go to sleep, and wake up refreshed.

Only when I got back, my mom and dad were arguing loud enough for me to hear from the outside. It was a bad one. I could tell. Things were pretty tough for the 'rents those days, with the ranch in the deep red. They got into fights—most of the time about money things, but eventually about little stuff like which brand of ketchup to buy, and whether it was more correct to spell it *catsup*. Stupid shit. As soon as I went inside and closed the door, both of them quieted down. Didn't take a super-genius to know the score: fucking bullshit: 1, Ryland Taggart: -45.

They entered the living room from the kitchen. Dad immediately went on the offensive: "Where have you been?"

"David, please," said Mom.

"No, I need to know," he said. "Who were you with?"

"My friends." I tried to move past him, but he stepped into my way.

"And that girl . . . Is she your . . . friend?"

"Ryland, go upstairs," ordered Mom. "Now."

"We're not done here!" Dad screamed.

"Our daughter is done here," she said. "Ryland, go upstairs now."

I did like Mom said, and Dad didn't stop me. For a whole hour, I sat on the floor with my head pressed up against my door, listening to them scream back and forth about who they thought I was and who they thought I should be. I cried, and I hated myself for being so fucking weak. In those moments, I hated myself for all that shit—why couldn't it have been easy? Why couldn't I just be who everyone wanted me to be . . . whatever that was? *God! So fucking stupid—about everything! What was I . . .*

I stopped crying when I noticed that it had gone quiet. Then: footsteps on the stairs, getting closer. Now at the top. In the hallway—one, two, three, four steps, and whoever's feet those were cast shadows that crept under the door.

Knock, knock. "Baby?" Her voice was hoarse and hollow.

"I'm fine," I said, trying hard to keep from sobbing.

"Can I come in?"

"I guess." I stood up, opened the door, and retreated under the covers, tux and all. Mom pushed the door open only a crack and slid inside, like she was sneaking into a tomb. She shut the door behind her and locked it again. Then she sat at the foot of my bed, but didn't come any closer. She looked down at me and attempted a smile. Her face was flushed like a bad sunburn.

"Your father and I . . ."

"You don't have to say anything. It's okay."

"No, it's not," she said. "It's not okay to be a jackass. Not to you. I told him as much."

"He hates me."

She closed her eyes, breathed out, before speaking again: "He was . . . I think he was unprepared to see you with . . . what was her name?"

"Mya," I said, inching closer to Mom. "But I mean, we aren't a thing, y'know?"

"You don't have to explain to me." She slid over and cradled me in her arms. Her hands shook and moved slow and labored as if suspended in water. But she held me close anyway, settled my head into the crook of her elbow. "Your dad just . . . it's not like we didn't know."

"You knew?"

"On some level," she said. "But I don't think he was ready to see it with his own eyes."

I hugged her and held her tight. For the rest of the night, she stayed in my room, and we talked. We talked, and when we ran out of things to talk about, I laid my head down on her lap, and she told me a story she would tell me when I was really little. It was about Winnie-the-Pooh having tea with his friend, Rabbit, only to find that he couldn't leave— he'd grown too fat with treacle and cakes and finger sandwiches to fit through the hole to Rabbit's burrow. So Rabbit called on Christopher Robin to help Winnie out of this pickle. Only, I never found out how Christopher Robin saved the day. That was always the part when I'd fall asleep.

And it was the same on that night.

"Paolo." Tania laid her hand on his head, his shoulder. He stayed still where he was seated—at his small table with his head and arms on a pillow of books. Pushed away from him were a plate covered with breadcrumbs and a small cup of cold espresso. "Paolo, svegliati."

But he didn't move. Tania continued to shake him— harder as the seconds went on—until she shook his reading glasses off his face. She felt for his pulse on his neck with her fingers. Tried again. Again. Again. For the first time, Tania looked truly scared. She stood up, stiff and straight, and walked over to the phone next to the sink. I rushed over to where Paolo was sitting and leaned in close.

No. I didn't want to believe . . . but then I saw how his chest lay still, how his eyes were open and dry. The skin of his face had the look of aged parchment paper—thin and brittle and cracked. Behind me, Tania was on the phone talking at warp speed: "Telefonimi il medico. Rapidamente." When she hung up the phone, she returned to Paolo's side, and together, we sat and waited for the doctor and the police to come. We didn't say anything to each other. I couldn't look at her or him or *anything*, so I kept my eyes locked on the one other thing that stood out in the room: the copy of *The Green Ray* laid out, pages down, pinned under Paolo's arm. The corner of the black and white photo peeked out from the pages.

Things moved fast. The doctor showed up after a few minutes. He referred to Paolo by name and moved around the place like he had been there before. I could only watch as he nonchalantly felt for Paolo's pulse, then unclipped his doctor bag and drew out a stethoscope.

"È morto," the doctor said after checking him. No dictionary necessary. He was dead.

"Ascolti di nuovo," said Tania. This caught the doctor off guard. He stood, locked in uncertainty. Tania wouldn't have it. She snatched the doctor's stethoscope away put it to her own ears. Reaching over Paolo's shoulder, she unbuttoned his shirt and stuck the stethoscope in.

"Tania." She stopped what she was doing. I wasn't sure who spoke until she and the doctor looked at me. My mouth went numb, suddenly. I couldn't say anything more. Another knock at the door, and a man in a police uniform stepped through. The doctor briefed him on the situation. As she listened to them talk, Tania deflated into one of the chairs at the table and pushed the stethoscope away from her. She didn't cry or get mad or any of the things you think of when a person discovers someone dead. She sat shell-shocked. I wanted to comfort her, but what could I say that couldn't, in some way, be the wrong thing? So I stayed silent, too. The officer and the doctor took the liberty of using Paolo's phone to call in people to take the body away. Tania and I continued to sit.

"Miss Taggart," Tania finally said. "I am sorry that your stay has ended this way."

"Tania, I can't leave. Not like this."

"You are kind, but you cannot help. This is only for family." She took out an envelope from her bag and pushed it into my hands. "Here is your train ticket to Florence. When you get to the airport, your ticket for the plane will be waiting for you at the Alitalia desk." I looked inside the envelope. Inside was a train ticket—along with two hundred Euros.

"Tania, I wasn't expecting to be paid."

"It was a surprise," she said, shifting around and then calling out instructions to the officer.

He nodded and continued to talk on the phone. "I've arranged for someone to take you to the train."

"I know where it is. I can probably walk there."

"No," she said. "You are my guest, and I will make sure you get there safely." We sat there for a few more minutes, stealing glances at Paolo like we were kids stealing sips of wine from our fathers' glasses. More people eventually came, including a young officer wearing the same dark blue and red uniform the other officer wore.

"Miss Taggart," said Tania. "This gentleman will take you now."

I got up to leave. How do you say goodbye in this situation?

"You do not have to say anything," she said to me. I followed the officer to the door when Tania called out. I turned around to see her holding the copy of *The Green Ray*. "I almost forgot. My uncle mentioned that he wanted you to have this. He did not say why." She handed me the book and smiled momentarily. "Buon viaggio, Miss Taggart."

I was restless on the train ride. A brief layover in Pisa did little more than allow me to stretch my legs. I couldn't stop thinking of how I had left Tania and Paolo. I hadn't done what I was supposed to do. But a deal's a deal, after all, and my deal involved me being on that train at that time as it screeched through the hilly Tuscan countryside. I tried to lose myself in the scenery, with the grape tresses on downward slopes next to tiny hillside villages. It was no use.

I could still feel his cold, dry skin on my fingertips.

Could still smell the espresso on his lips.

Still taste the cigarette smoke in his hair.

The worst thing was that I hardly knew the man. We maybe exchanged ten minutes worth of English. The rest of the time, he was making fun of me in front of my face or complaining about a job that someone didn't do quite right. It didn't make sense that I'd feel a sense of loss, but I did. Maybe it had something to do with this book.

The Green Ray, by Jules Verne. I tried reading it on the train, but couldn't bring myself to open it. Too early. In any case, I stared at the faded cover of the book while standing in Stazione Santa Maria Novella. It had an embossed illustration of people on the seashore all pointing toward a green-colored sunset. Why had he wanted me to take this?

The crowd disembarking from a newly arrived train pushed me along and out of my head. *Get with it, Ryland.* I still had to find the right platform for the train to the airport. I wandered, looking for a sign that would show me where I was supposed to go.

I was a wreck. Squeezing between comers and goers, trying to figure out the station map—I couldn't handle it right then. I didn't want to be there. After a few minutes of fruitless wandering, I sat down on a bench next to a mother, father, and their two teenage boys. From a little eavesdropping, I gleaned that they were a family from Newark at the tail end of their family vacation in the Cinque Terra. The boys whined to their parents about how their feet hurt and whether their hotel in Rome had a pool. *I just saw someone die this morning!* I wanted to scream. *There is nothing you should complain about!*

85

"Mi scusi?" a young, blonde guy said as he stepped up to the father of the family. He had a big backpack on and worn out boots. He was definitely a traveler. "Ah . . . parla franchese . . . français?" A Frenchman in Florence? He was more fucked than me right then.

"Je parle un peu français," I called out to him.

"Oh, merci beaucoup," he said, moseying up to me. "Où est le transport à l'aéroport?"

I laughed. "Je cherche la même chose." I held out my hand. "Ryland."

"I am Jonas. You are American?"

"The ten gallon hat and spurs were a dead giveaway?"

He raised his eyebrow and broke into a roguish smirk.

"Oui. Et ton accent."

"So where are you headed?"

"München."

"München . . . Munich?"

"Yes. And you?"

Did he mean to ask me where I was going in life? In about a day, I was going to wake up in Texas, in my dorm room, whose walls are only half-decorated because my old roommate Grace had gone home for the summer. I'd get up, brush my teeth, and probably have dangerously old pizza for breakfast. Then, maybe I'd call into work and see what shift I was on—if I was on the schedule at all. And I'd wonder. I'd wonder what the hell was going on at that farm and what the dreams were all about and whether or not I should be committed to a loony bin for even considering that any of that meant anything.

I looked down at the book in my hands and then opened

it. Naturally, it opened to where the pages had been bookmarked by the photograph, which fell out and drifted to the floor. Jonas knelt down, picked it up, and handed it back to me.

"Ah, c'est un photo de München," he said, seeing the note scrawled on the back. I took the photo and looked at it—the woman with the dark eyes and dark hair and the smile that hid a secret she was itching to tell. "We go together?"

I envisioned the framed picture of Domenico Tiburzi buried in my backpack, lying in wait like he did more than a century before, ready to strike when the stars were aligned and his prey was in sight.

You better be right about this.

"Oui," I said to Jonas. "On y va."

Part Two

Der Grüne Strahl der Sonne

Dear Daniella,

It's been a couple of days since we last saw each other. So you know about Paolo. I know that you thought of him as this grumpy guy (scontroso, right?). But I'm writing you to tell you that he wasn't just that. I don't know what he was, really.

It's not always easy to see who a person is. Like you. You're kick-ass, and someday, guys are going to fight over you. But right now, you need to just forget all that stuff I told you. Ride horses and play with your sisters and help your mom cook and hug your dad until he can't carry you anymore.

Right now, I'm in Munich, Germany. I just got in this morning after an overnight train ride. And boy, was it crazy.

So there's one more thing I have to tell you. It's kind of a biggie. You see, I wasn't exactly truthful to you about myself. I didn't lie, but I didn't tell you everything.

I'm a lesbian. Io sono lesbica. (I hope I got that right.) I hope that this doesn't change how you feel about me. I thought we became friends at the farm. I'd still like to be your friend.

Tuo amico,
Ryland

Six

ostly because we were both nursing epic hangovers, Isabella and I followed Jonas's lead. He told us that he'd been to Munich before, a couple of years ago, so he knew where a good, cheap hostel was. The last time he was in Munich, he and some friends stopped for a night on a road trip to Venice. Heh. *Road trip to Venice*. The sentence sounded absurd—a road trip to a city with no roads? But then I thought about how absurd it must be for Europeans to think about the crazy distances Americans cover in their cars. While waiting in line to check into the hostel, I stared at the map of Europe on the wall side by side with a map of the United States. The distance between Toulouse, France, where Jonas was from, to Venice was shorter than the distance between Yellowstone (!) National (!!) Park (!!!) and San Francisco—a drive that I'd done with little trouble. Relatively speaking.

"Welcome to Hunter's Hostel," said the lovely girl at the front desk.

"Guten Tag," said Isabella, in a booming Australian accent. She slapped the counter, snapping us to attention. "So I think we're checking in for three beds."

"Of course," desk girl said. "For how many nights?"

"Me? I got a flight tomorrow morning, so just the one," said Isabella. "How about you guys?"

"I leave, tomorrow, too," said Jonas after double checking his itinerary scrawled on the back of a tourist brochure for the Duomo back in Florence.

"And you?" the girl said to me.

"Um . . . I don't exactly know how long I'll stay." The girl's pen hovered over the schedule book where she recorded all the beds reserved for the night. Evidently, that wasn't a good enough answer. "Just put me down for tonight, I guess." It was just as well. I thought about how I had burned through the two-hundred Euros Tania gave me on two train tickets—one for me and one for Jonas. So how much money did I have left? Well, how much money could you make working part time at a cafe that caters to poor college students? Yeah. Bring on the pain.

You're probably wondering what the hell I'm all talking about—like *who the hell is Isabella?* Let me back up a bit, all the way back to Santa Maria Novella station in Florence.

92

"Oui," I said to Jonas. "On y va."

Once I finished speaking, it occurred to me that I had zero-point-zero percent chance in Hell of scoring a plane ticket for the same day. There went that non-plan. Still, I felt so sure of that crack decision. There was shit I still had to do here. The only things I needed to know were what to do, where to do it, why to do it, how to do it, and who to do it to. All Mom told me to do was to follow the green ray. I was determined to do that, in the best way I could—I was going to Munich, Germany, the place written on the back of the photo tucked inside of a book entitled *The Green Ray*. Best I got. Pause on the existential crisis. Jonas needed to get to his plane. Then I'd worry about my sorry ass.

I bounced from kiosk to counter, trying to decipher the mass of military times, incomprehensible train numbers, and ineffable Italian. Jonas labored to keep up. That backpack was impossibly huge. It had to outweigh him by twenty or thirty pounds. What the hell did he have in there? The neck of a guitar stuck out the pack's top, but the rest of the formless lumps? No clue.

We finally found a sign that read "Tram" alongside a picture of a bus overlain with a plane. As we worked our way through the line—inching painfully forward—we watched the time on Jonas's metal alarm clock—old-style, with bells and a hammer on top—that he kept in a pocket of his cargo pants. His plane was scheduled to leave at 3:30—I mean 15:30. He had a little over an hour to make the tram, ride to the airport, get through security, and board the plane. With any luck he'd have enough time to get an espresso and peruse one of Italy's fine gossip rags with bare boobies on the cover. That was the plan, anyway. Except right when we got up to the ticket window, the nicely coiffed man behind the glass beamed, cracked his knuckles, and hung a small sign in the window that had only one word written on it: *chiuso*. A quick flip through my dictionary revealed its meaning—*closed*.

"What?" I yelled. "It's like the middle of the afternoon! When do you open back up?"

"Sarò felice di aiutarvi, signorina. A diciassette ore."

"Diciassette ore," I mumbled to myself. I scanned through the whole dictionary until I got to the back appendix listing numbers and times. It took me a second to find it, but when I did: "Five o'clock? That's in three hours!"

"Vado a pranzare," the man said. "Lunch."

"We just need a ticket to the airport," I pleaded.

"Si," he said. "Dopo vado a pranzare. A diciassette ore." He got up and left. I turned around to face Jonas, who just looked confused by the whole mess.

"Trou de cul," I said, hoping the French term for asshole was all I needed to say. That ass-monkey behind the glass deserved a punch to the balls, but I couldn't lose my cool. We needed level heads to MacGuyver this sombitch. "Je suis désolée," I apologized to Jonas.

He looked disappointed, but not dejected, like I had assumed he'd be. Truth be told, I was more disappointed than he was. I mean, if he was having this much trouble with a ticket he already had in hand, how much harder would it be to grab one on the fly? It wasn't like either of us was made of money . . . wait. I had an envelope stuffed with a crapload of Euros. And I knew just what to waste it on.

"C'mon!" I said, pulling Jonas behind me. He asked me what I was doing, but I had no breath to answer. I dragged him and his humongous bag to the ticket counter where I hilariously tried to order up two train tickets to Munich in Spanish like I was ordering two enchiladas suizas, extra rice and beans, salsa on the side. The ticket agent looked at me like I was insane, and then asked what I wanted in English.

On the train, I quadruple checked the car against our tickets. Car seven. Sette. With the kind of day I was having, I wanted to be four-times sure that we were in the right place. Jonas and I squeezed through the narrow hallway alongside a wall of glass doors. A pair of huge men struggled to get past us and Jonas's backpack. One of them, a musclebound dude with wacky hair that made him look like a cross between the Incredible Hulk and Sideshow Bob, stopped mid-slide in front of me and did the most invasive check-out-ing I had ever seen. His eyes were like X-ray lasers hardwired to measure cup size and approximate ass diameter. "Buongiorno," he said, smiling.

"Andale, Fabrizio!" said the other, equally buff dude. He pulled his friend away from me, and together they crossed over into the next car. Nice name, I thought. I remembered that the object of Daniella's affections (and obsessions) was also named Fabrizio. Briefly, I imagined that tiny girl with that enormous man. Maybe she'd ride his shoulders, or they'd have a picnic close to the base of his beanstalk.

One of these couchettes was ours. Couchette seven. Sette. We followed the numbers until we found our new home—at least for the next ten hours. When we opened the cabin door, a redhead in cut off jean shorts and a tank top was lying across a whole seat. She had her nose deep into a stolen in-flight magazine (*Qantas the Australian Way*) with pen poised over a Sudoku puzzle. The entire contents of her suitcase had been draped all over the compartment. Apparently, she didn't have time or coin to properly dry her laundry before getting on the train.

"Hi," I began, but she cut me off with a wave of her finger. Jonas and I stood in the doorway as she filled in the last spaces in the puzzle.

"And still the undisputed Sudoku queen, Isabella Asher!" She threw the magazine against the opposite wall and raised her hands in victory. "So you're my new roomies, yeah?"

Seven

Everything hurt. I fell into the hostel bed. Never before had a cheapo pad on stiff springs felt so good. The night before had been hard on the beauty sleep. I shared the hostel room with Jonas and Isabella, because I shared the room with everyone at the hostel. There was only the one huge room, with bunk beds aligned into rows separated by lines of security lockers. It was like sleeping in the locker room at the Y. From not far enough away, a pack of Irish men caroused like only Irish men could carouse, even when stone cold sober.

Jonas set his pack onto the floor and crashed into the bunk across from mine. And by crash, I literally mean that his head collided with the bed at a perpendicular angle, pillow be damned. Unlike Isabella and me, he had been traveling non-stop for the past two days from Martinique en route to Toulouse, France. When I asked him why he'd hopped from spot to spot via boat to train to plane to hitchhiking instead of a simple direct flight, he countered with the world's best reason: his way was cheaper.

Five minutes later, he was snoring.

"Heya," said Isabella, hanging upside down from the bunk right above mine. Her fire-engine red hair hung down an additional foot past the top of her head. "Planning on going out later? You, me, and Frenchie can hit the clubs."

"You have got to be kidding. After last night?" God, I felt how Jonas looked. But even if the flesh was willing, I didn't have time to go bar-hopping. I was in Munich for a reason— even one as hazy as *I gotta find the girl in this picture*. It was my only lead, though, my only reason for existing right then.

"No wuckers," said Isabella.

"No . . . what?"

"No wucking furries, dearie," she said. "I'm a bit tuckered, too, to tell you the truth. How about this: I'm about to nap and then get a sausage. Then we can talk about going out."

I laid my head down on the pillow. Although I was exhausted, I couldn't get to sleep, no matter how hard I tried. So I lay there for a time, reading the graffiti scrawled on the bottom of the bunk above me. But that wasn't working. No rest for the wicked, as they say, and it was clear I'd been a bad enough girl to contract some vicious insomnia. So I got up and checked my e-mail, trying not to check Facebook and failing utterly. I didn't used to have this problem. Somehow, I'd avoided the thrall of God-Emperor Zuckerberg until I moved to Texas and signed up to maybe, sorta, kinda stalk this girl Alyssa in my freshman comp class. Two minutes after I clicked SUBMIT, I thought better of it, but TOO LATE! The Zuck had my deets, and people from my dank and dingy past started finding me.

Like these guys, offering such life-affirming messages as:

Lauren McGennaris

7 hrs

My stupid neighbors are have been playing The Best of the Police on Spotify all night. #SendingOutAnSOS

Bill Nusatz

3 hrs

How much brown gravy is TOO much brown gravy?

Same old bullshit. As I moved the mouse to log out, a message window popped up stating, "Lost contact with old friends? Reconnect with them!" Underneath were links to other people's pages, some who I didn't know, and some who I knew too well, like Shannon Gorski. Fuck. I clicked on the logout button four times.

That done, I started to pace with little choice in the matter. I'm a spaz when I'm stressed out and at the worst of times, I need to keep my hands and feet occupied. Now that

I was fully awake, I was in full on anxiety mode. It wasn't just Shan. It was Paolo's face, and then that woman's face—the one from the photo. Where was I supposed to begin? It wasn't like I could stroll down to city hall, whip the photo out, and expect some nice bilingual bureaucrat to escort me to her last known location. I didn't speak the language, didn't know the customs, didn't know a single soul in this town—wait. Shit! Herr Cutter!

I ran back to the room, where my companions showed no signs of waking up anytime soon, grabbed *The Green Ray*, and approached the front desk. The desk girl looked up from the horse she was doodling.

"How do you get to the university?" I asked.

I've always been amused by Rammstein. Till Lindemann's deep, gravelly voice sounds nasty and foreboding. But then you see the band in concert, and they're dressed in hot pink latex and marching out of a big rubber vagina. Funny, Rammstein. Funnier still was how Rammstein and naptime did not mix. Oh wait—not funny. I was not at all amused by "Du Riechst So Gut" pounding at me through the wall of the couchette. That would have been bad enough. But a second after the music started, someone began to physically pound the wall so hard that the beds in our tiny room were going to snap off the wall.

I slid open the couchette door and stepped out into the

hallway. Down at the other end of the car, I saw that beast of a man, Fabrizio, wearing only small, tight soccer bottoms to show off his pecs the size of porterhouses. We both walked toward the source of the noise.

"Hey," I said. "Can you believe this?"

"Eh . . . no English," he said. "Parla italiano?"

"Non parlo Italiano. Sorry."

Fabrizio shrugged, and in that gesture alone, he managed to flex muscles anatomists didn't know existed. Then he turned his attention to the couchette blasting the music. He pounded on the door, and immediately, the blinds blocking the window shot up, revealing a compartment full of smoke. When the door unlocked and opened, a plume of the stuff puffed out. There was no mistaking that sour smell—good ol' fashioned pot for a good ol' fashioned hot box. I counted at least five people, maybe six, huddled up in there. A skinny, blonde dude stuck out his head, and upon seeing Fabrizio up close, shirtless and snarling, the dude's eyes bugged out.

"There is a problem?"

"Non più musica," said Fabrizio. "O io ti ucciderò." Then he cracked his knuckles in the universal gesture for "potential ass-kicking."

I translated (more or less) "My friend is trying to say that if you don't shut off the music, he'll stick your head so far into your ass that you'll be peeing teeth."

"I promise no more music, okay?" He shut his laptop. Fabrizio wasn't convinced. Undeterred by, well, anything, he pushed his way into the couchette. Everyone else but me darted out of the compartment like frightened squirrels, despite being stoned out of their minds.

"Hai liquore?" said Fabrizio, mimicking drinking from a cup. "Vino?"

"Did someone say *vino*?" I turned around and saw Isabella holding two fat bottles of wine in her hands, one of which she handed to Fabrizio. "Hope you don't mind me inviting myself to the party." He broke out that devil smirk, and Isabella countered with her own. "Actually, I don't care if you mind."

With that, we popped the cherry on that party car, and soon even curmudgeonly old me was feeling pretty awesome. It was probably the pot—a special blend one of the German dudes (Gunther? Kaspar?) called "Geronimo Madman." Maybe it was the wine—one Euro specials from a Florence supermarket, courtesy of Isabella's forward thinking. Or perhaps it was because I was smitten by a smoking hot Finnish lass named Anna Elena. Yeah, that one. It's funny. You spend a whole semester trying your hardest to be hard—you don't talk to anyone except the row of UT basketball player mannequins leering at you in the bookstore (and that's when you notice that they're all repainted Michael Jordan statues). You don't smile. Ever. You don't accept any invitations to eat in the dining hall. All this to avoid interpersonal relationships of any kind. Once you have a little bit of that wacky weed, though, and that discipline goes out the window. Fuck, how long had it been since I'd touched anyone, since anyone had touched me?

What is the equation of a depressingly long time?

Answer: $y = mx + (I\ am\ so\ fucking\ horny)^2$. Next question.

I wasn't the only one feeling the good times. The entire

car came out for this makeshift party on rails. It turned out that most of the couchettes on this car were taken up by young Germans. They were all carnies—traveling workers who accompanied a German circus troupe called the *Circus Krone*. They weren't performers, mind you. They were the ones who drove tent pegs, sold tickets, and cleaned up after the animals. Then there was the contingent of rugby players, including Fabrizio and his equally beefy teammate, Javier, traveling from Rovigo to Munich to play an exhibition match against München RFC. Sprinkle in some random travelers—the luscious Anna Elena, Arash from Tehran, and Haifa from Tunisia—and we had ourselves a joint-rolling, liquor-swilling League of Fucking Nations.

Isabella, reclining in our couchette, was firmly seated in Fabrizio's arms. She played with his tight, springy curls and whispered sweet, incomprehensible-to-him nothings into his ear. Jonas sat on the hallway floor next to me, his guitar in hand, trying to get the strings in tune. Luckily for him (and all of us), Anna Elena was there to help out.

"I will fix it." Taking hold of the guitar, she moved her tiny fingers at light speed over the fret board and up to the guitar head. One by one, she turned the knobs, plucking the strings until they sounded correct to her ears. "You should be careful of this string," she said as she plucked the high E. "It will break soon."

"Are you in a band?" I asked.

"Yes. The name is *Kallo Hävittäjä*. I play lead guitar."

Hearing Finnish just sent me swooning. "What does the name mean?"

Anna Elena thought about it for a moment, her finger on

her lips before translating: "It means 'Skull Destroyer.'"

"¿Toca la guitarra?" Javier asked Jonas, mimicking a frenetic Eddie Van Halen-style jam session. This guy was every bit as physically imposing as his rugby teammate, Fabrizio, but you only had to sit with him for a little bit to get that he was different in most other ways. Instead of the playful, child-like goofiness that Fabrizio had, Javier sported an intense stare and seemed to be trying really, really hard not to smile.

"Oh. Ah . . . I can play, but not so good."

"Él no sabe tocar muy bien," I told Javier. He leaned back, rested his shoulders on the wall, and crossed his arms.

"No es importante," said Javier. "Toca la canción."

"Just play, Jonas," I told him. Suddenly, the spotlight had gone onto the one person among us who wanted it the least. Jonas blushed, but he didn't refuse or run away. Instead, he laid the guitar properly on his lap, wedging his leg into the curve of the guitar, and started to strum. At first, I didn't recognize the tune. But once he started playing, and definitely once he started singing, I knew—Bob Marley's "Redemption Song." An odd choice for the current vibe, but who the hell was I to judge on that score?

Eight

The desk girl at the hostel had traced out a route on one map, but the bus and tram lines were detailed on another map. Together, they'd get me to the university, but not without revealing me as a tourist of the lowest order. A pair of German teens rolled their eyes at me while I tried in vain to refold the maps into a more pocket-friendly size. I was pretty sure (read: hoping to high heaven) that this was the final bus that would take me to the university proper. With luck, an automated bus voice would buzz out my desired destination.

Luck. Yeah that and a Euro would have gotten me a couple of *Wasserbrötchen* from the corner bakery. I watched helplessly out the window as the streets passed by looking like any other streets in any other place save for the German on the street signs. Things got surreal. I started seeing avenues curl around themselves and meet back up with other boulevards that split into three or four lanes. And was I crazy, or did the bus pass over a bridge that had some guy surfing on the river raging below the stone walkways? *Get a grip, Ryland*, I told myself. *Stick to the plan.* The hot desk girl told me the street to get off. Since I had no hope of finding the street on a map, I resolved to listen to every incomprehensible word that came out of the bus driver's mouth until the syllables came together to form:

"Großhaderner Straße."

I got off the bus and stepped into what could have been an affluent suburb of any American city, so this was the Ludwig Maximilian University of Munich. Herr Cutter insisted on saying the entire name in the stories he told about how celebrated a hero he was in his home town and how, if only students at UT knew how esteemed he was in Europe, they wouldn't make such a mess of the salad station at the cafeteria near UT's Molecular Biology Building (because, of course, the entire student body knew that Herr Cutter loves his pear and mandarin salads).

Ten minutes after I arrived, I was lost. This place was less a navigable American campus and more sprawling city park—and I had no idea where I was going. The biology department was somewhere around here, but even if I could locate a sign, it'd probably be in German, putting me shit out of luck. After asking around, I was told that the best place to look for a botany professor would be at the *Biozentrum der LMU Biologie*, an imposingly huge half-concrete, half-glass structure that looked like the mall from *Dawn of the Dead*. At least there'd be a helipad on the roof in case I had to make a quick getaway.

How the hell was I supposed to find Herr Cutter in this place? It was like Disneyworld for nerds, but not in the fun way. No *Dance Dance Revolution* challenges, *Settlers of Catan* round robins, or Dario Argento movie marathons. The clipboard-toting profs shuffling around here were hardcore science-heads who, years ago, had fun surgically removed from their bodies. The sterile, white-washed hallways showed the same lack of joy. They turned at the same places and dead-ended in the same annoying ways every time. Classes didn't seem to be in session—it was summertime, after all—so the entire place was eerily quiet. Perfect for Herr Cutter. After covering the entire first floor, I took the stairs up to the next floor and did it again. And again to the third floor. And the fourth.

I paced the fourth floor much more slowly than the previous ones. I was starting to feel the tiredness from last night, like I was stuck in an Escher painting with stairs that infinitely led up or infinitely led down, but also infinitely went nowhere. That's when I smelled it—the athlete's foot smell that could come from no place other than Herr Cutter's teacup. I followed my nose around the halls until I came upon a door, left slightly ajar enough to let out that heinous bouquet.

Knock-knock. No answer. I strolled on in to find Herr Cutter hunched over a microscope, the few tufts of white hair on his head little more than a greasy, tangled nest perfect for a small family of pygmy marmosets to reside in.

"Herr Cutter, it's me," I said. "You left something behind at Tania's farm. Just saying." I meant that last part as a joke, but when Herr Cutter looked up, it was clear from the purplish bags under his eyes that he was living in a world where humor was a foreign concept.

"Did *she* send you?" he said upon seeing me.

"Oh, I'm great! Thanks for asking!"

"Answer the question, Taggart."

"I'm assuming you mean Tania."

"Yes. *That woman.* She does not stop with her calls."

"No," I said. I didn't dare edge in closer to him than I was. That way, if Herr Cutter lunged at me with a sudden pang for brains, I'd have a head start. "What is all this?"

By *all this*, I meant the books piled in stacks around the room. The one table without books on top had several microscopes lined up in a row and a small Bunsen burner heating a pot of Herr Cutter's bitters. Shoved into a corner of the room was a cot and blanket that looked like it had been used quite recently.

"You might as well be useful while you are here," Herr Cutter said, jotting down notes after looking into one of the microscopes. "I trust you know how to make slides?" He pulled a box of slides and slide covers, medicine droppers, and tweezers from a cabinet and instructed me to make four slides from four specimens that he had already prepped. I did as he said, trying my best to lay the perfect amount of greenish paste on each slide—too much, and the slide cover would slip off. Then I loaded them onto the microscopes, as he instructed, and stepped back to let Herr Cutter have his fill of Frankensteinery.

He looked into each microscope in turn, scrawling down his thoughts about each one into his notebook. After looking at the last slide, he set the end of his pen on the paper, but did not write. Instead, he took the notebook in his hands and threw it across the room. It hit the wall and flopped to the floor. *What the?* I looked back at Herr Cutter sinking his face into his hands and sighing loudly. I didn't know what else to do, so I walked over and picked the notebook up.

"Leave it where it is, Taggart," he said. "It does more good there." I didn't listen. Upon opening the notebook, I leafed through it. But I discerned little from the Herr Cutter's chicken scratch. Like his other notebooks, it was basically unreadable without a Herr Cutter brand decoder ring. "Why are you here?" He sounded totally spent.

"It's complicated," I said. Herr Cutter fetched the pot of boiling bitters from the Bunsen burner. He poured himself a mug and poured the rest into a beaker that he pushed toward me.

"We have time now, Taggart. You are in luck that I appreciate complicated stories."

So I told him one. He didn't seem to appreciate it at all and made sure that I knew it.

"What you did, Taggart, is incredibly stupid. How could you think you could ever mount a search for a person without a name, without any clue about her identity? You do not speak the language, nor do you know where to go to even start. I thought you were crazy before, Taggart, but to be senseless? Why did you not go home and away from this madness?"

Talk about having all my faults thrown into my face—this was not the first time I'd been accused of being irrational, hasty, and a general hazard to myself and society.

But I wasn't exactly keen on criticism, no matter how "constructive" someone thought it was. Frankly, it pissed me off. Who left me at Tania's farm? Where was Herr Cutter when Paolo was all alone dying? I wanted to get up and storm out, breaking as many slides and microscopes I could on my way out. But if I left that room, I'd have nothing to go on, and everything that Herr Cutter said about me would be true. So my butt stayed on that seat.

"I'm not asking you if you think any of this is a good idea," I said, careful to keep my voice steady. "I just want to know if you know where this photo was taken." I passed him the photo from Paolo's book.

"A woman and a house," he argued. "It could be anywhere in this city. How do you even know it was taken in Munich? This note on the back could mean anything."

"Please. There has to be something."

"Dreams of ghosts," Herr Cutter mumbled. "Ridiculous." He straightened his glasses and took one more look. I began grinding my teeth hoping he'd say something other than Taggart, you're a moron. He tilted the photo to one side and then the other. He licked his lips, furrowed his brow—these were good things in Cutter-land. Something had caught his eye, and the supercomputer in his skull was processing. *C'mon, Herr Cutter. Say you know where that is . . .*

"This is worthless, Taggart," he said, putting the photo down on the table.

I got right up into his face. "I know you saw something!" After giving me the look of death, Herr Cutter held the photo up for me to look at.

"Do you see this?" he said, pointing to a steeple point in

the background of the photo. "This is the top of the Rathaus in Marienplatz. You see, this is the backside of the pointed top." My eyes followed his fingertip tracing the outline of the point. "From this photo I would guess that this house here is no more than half a kilometer from the center of the city, on the backside of Marienplatz."

"Are you sure?"

"Like I am sure that you are not of sound mind? Yes."

I hugged him, even though I knew that hugs—and human contact in general—reminded him of his long-standing phobia of other ambulatory creatures.

"Taggart," he wheezed, "I cannot breathe." I let go of him and gathered my stuff up, ready to get back to downtown Munich before it got too dark. Meanwhile, Herr Cutter had opened his notebook back up and stared at the measurements he'd just recorded. He grew sullen.

"You need to get out of this place," I said.

"I'm busy."

"Have you even left this room since you got back? B.O. says that the answer is a firm no."

He put his finger up and looked like he was about to say something. Instead, he got up and opened a drawer at the other side of the room. He laid out a map on the floor—the same one that Tania had given us to plan our specimen collecting. I spotted the point—marked in black pen by Tania's own hand—where the villa was located and where she had drawn the boundary lines of her property. All the other marks on the map were numbers in red ink—the markings Herr Cutter and I made together.

"Those four slides that I had you prepare—go look at

them." I did. And . . . so what? What did he want me to see? Everything looked kosher to me. Cell walls intact, normal looking nucleus. Was I missing something?

"What's wrong with these?"

"Exactly. You remember this map, yes?" I nodded and he continued. "Each of these numbers represents the location of a sample." Then he pointed out a group of numbers toward the bottom of the map. "Those are samples that we took right by the beach. If you notice, they are just outside of the farm's old property line. Twenty-six, twenty-seven, twenty-eight, and twenty-nine." Then he moved his hand inward, deep into Tania's property. "Here is number fourteen—the same sample that is in the far microscope. Look at it."

Again, I followed orders and walked over to the microscope Herr Cutter was looking into when I barged into his lab. This slide was completely different from the others. The color was sickly brown, not bright green. Holes riddled the cell walls where the cytoplasm was leaking out. These cells were dying. Even a terrible student like me could tell.

"Radiation poisoning," said Herr Cutter, his voice suddenly hollow like I was listening to it from the other side of a tunnel. Radiation? "I am sure of it. I have seen cellular damage like this once before." Herr Cutter stood and gulped down the rest of his bitters, which, now cooled to room temperature, probably tasted like rotten pig asshole. "At Chernobyl. There is no question in my mind."

"You can't be serious."

"I did research in Kiev—Taras Shevchenko University. I walked in Pripyat, collected samples personally."

"Are you positive it's the same thing?"

He only stared back at me with an expressionless face.

"Then you have to tell her!" I yelled.

"More tests must be run to ascertain—"

"That's bullshit, and we both know it!" The vacuum of space between us at that moment was absolute. If a pin dropped, no one would have heard it. If a nuke went off, same thing. "Tania has to know. Now."

"And how do I explain this to her, Taggart?" he snapped. "*Hello, Miss Tania. Your family lands have been irreversibly poisoned, so I highly suggest you leave them and go as far away as possible. Forever.* When she asks why, I'll tell her that it is radiation of the most lethal kind, and when she asks how, what do I say? As far as I know there hasn't been a nuclear incident on her lands. How do I explain the discrepancies in the samples? Radiation spreads. It does not care about property lines. None of it makes sense!"

"I . . . but you . . ."

"I was brought there to find a solution, Taggart," he said, lowering his head and running his hand through his hair. "And . . . and I do not know if I can." He looked up at me. "How do you tell a person that everything she holds dear will die?"

Vivrai per vedere la morte di tutto ciò che si ami.

You will live to see the death of everything you love.

To be honest, it surprised me that Herr Cutter had such a problem with his findings. For all his insistence that science was settled, that causes and effects were clear, there he was admitting that it simply wasn't in this case. Guess he was human after all.

"You are right," said Herr Cutter. "I must tell her."

"I'm sorry," I said. "I shouldn't have been such a douche."

"Enough about this, Taggart," he said. "Perhaps I have spent too much time in here."

If I had to wait any longer for the bathroom to open up, I was going to ask either Javier or Fabrizio to rip the door off its hinges. I hate waiting for the toilet and especially hate waiting when I know the person (or more likely people) inside isn't even using it for its designated function. I won't mince words. I get pissed when people are having sex in the bathroom and I'm outside needing to pee. And not having sex. Anyone in my position would be a little miffed—not that I begrudge anyone getting lucky, but when nature calls, nature calls, and it does so for a reason—because piss doesn't belong *inside* the body. It belongs in a toilet, which was inconveniently located inside the same tiny room where people were doing the humpty.

"C'mon! Impending urination out here!" I banged on the door, and it had the same effect as the last four times that I shouted and pounded—which is to say, none whatsoever.

"Tu attends que la toilette?" said Jonas from behind me.

"Comment dire 'shitbag' en français?"

"Sac de merde."

Obviously. "Sac de merde!" I yelled at the door. A pointless move, I know. Jonas and I were probably the only

French speakers on that car. I turned back to Jonas in desperation. "Distract me. Tell me something."

"Quoi?"

"I don't know . . . I just need to be distracted so I don't think about waterfalls . . . and rain . . . and that one Chinese restaurant in Cheyenne with the statue of the little boy whizzing into a clamshell . . . fuck . . . like tell me about yourself."

"Okay. J'ai besoin de pratiquer l'anglais." Jonas cleared his throat. "I come back to Europe now after living on Martinique. Il est une île—er, it is an island, you know, and I spent one year there working with les pots."

"Pots? Were you a cook?"

"No, I make pots with clay. I worked with a man who owns a garden in Martinique. I make the pots for him, and he pays me and teaches me English." Ah—once he said that, his crazy accent totally made sense. He wasn't speaking English at all—he was speaking Rasta. It also explained why the only thing a clean-cut kid from Toulouse knew on guitar was a Marley song. "I liked Martinique. The sun is warm, and I like to sit on the beach. Sometimes we made a fire in the sand and cooked food. And the clay was good."

"But now you're back."

"Oui," he said. "I am back." I could hear how excited he was to return—as in *totally not*. "When you return to your home, it is sometimes hard, no? There are always people who want you to be something, but maybe you are not what they want. They are angry at you."

"C'est comme ça, quoi?" I said. Ain't it the truth. Another truth: I had to pee. I was about to embark on another assault on the bathroom door when the lock clicked. The door opened and out spilled two guys, both German carnies. They stumbled past us, leaving behind a gust of bad liquor breath. Whatevs. I leaped into the bathroom and did my thing.

When I came out, there was Anna Elena . . . making out with Jonas and tugging on his shirt like it was stubborn Christmas wrapping. I stood in the door for a really long time until they both stopped and looked at me—at which point, my mouth went on autopilot.

"I'll just be in here," I said. Then I closed the door back up and paced. In the dark. One step, two, then turn. *Okay*, I told myself. *In the future, when I look back at this, I'll blame the pot and the wine and laugh at how I'm feeling, but right now . . . I mean, goddammit, man!* I wasn't upset at either Jonas or Anna Elena. I was upset for two main reasons: 1) I was not drunk enough for my gay-dar to be this broken. Was I crazy, or was she totally leaning into me, looking into my eyes when she spoke, and doing the hair-flippy thing? *Yes, the hair-flippy thing!* And 2) it pissed me off to be mad. Because being mad makes me more mad. I like to think of myself as a cool cat, but really, it's a lie. Because when I get mad—like REALLY, REALLY mad—I feel things I wish I didn't. I see things in myself that I hate deep down inside.

I set my forehead on the door and counted. In French. *Un, deux, trois, quatre . . .* I told myself that this was karma cashing in its chips for all my past bullshit, that I deserved this. And, strangely enough, that made me feel better.

Knock-knock. "Ça va?" Jonas called out from the other side. I clicked open the door.

"Do you feel sick?" Anna Elena asked once I stepped out. "I have stomach medicine."

"I'm just gonna go lie down." I passed both of them up and continued down the hallway. "You guys should hang." I meant it. I mean, I felt like being a brat and saying *fuck off*, but thought it was better to distance myself from the action so I wouldn't do something that I'd regret later on. 'Cause I do that. A lot. Fate, though, was determined to give me that titty twister. As I approached the door to my couchette, I made out the form of Javier with his hands on his hips and his chest popping out of his shirt.

"Están dentro," he said curtly. I was about to ask who exactly was inside when I heard Isabella behind the couchette door making purring sounds. Followed by Fabrizio giggling. Oh. Okay. Well, at least *everyone* else on the train was getting some.

Nine

"You are impossible, Taggart. I hope you know that."

For the record, I did know that. And I knew that Herr Cutter had known that for some time. What Herr Cutter didn't seem to know was basic road etiquette. I told him that he didn't have to drive me anywhere and that I could search for the location in the photo by myself. But he insisted. And while it was very nice of him to do this, he put both our lives in danger every time he slammed on the brakes when a car zoomed by going in the opposite direction (as they usually did on, y'know, *the street*). Those, though, were brief respites in his otherwise maniacal quest to live inside the Kenny Loggins song, "Danger Zone."

"I hate driving," he muttered, the speedometer climbing toward heretofore unknown heights. "Taggart, let me see that picture again." I handed it to him with one hand while holding onto the roof handle with the other. He studied the photo carefully, as any good scientist would. Unfortunately, he did this while plowing through the middle of a four way intersection, narrowly missing two bikers, a truck towing a pair of large wooden horse statues, and a van full of blind children.

"Fuckity-fuck-fuck-fuck!" I yelled. "Dude, you have to watch the road! Like seriously!"

"I've seen this house before," he said. "I know it."

"And I've seen this movie before. In driver's ed. The ending sucks."

We sped down the curling side streets, Herr Cutter muttering all the way. Every turn felt like Space Mountain without the blessing of complete darkness. Suddenly, the car screeched to a stop and lurched forward. I would have gone through the windshield if not for the fine German-engineered seat belt keeping me secure. However, the book and photo were not so lucky. I lost my grip on both, sending them flying into the dashboard.

"We are here." Herr Cutter unbuckled himself and got out of the car. I waited for the little birdies to stop circling my head before grabbing the book and photo. Then I got out of the car and looked around, comparing my surroundings to the photo in my hand. And holy shit. Somehow, Herr Cutter had actually found the right place. I was standing across the road from the house in the photo. The door and window looked the same, down to the white, lacy curtains in the window. And indeed, the spire of the Rathaus poked the sky exactly like it did in the photograph.

"Are you satisfied, Taggart?" he called from across the

street. I didn't even wait to answer before making my move. "Wait! Where are you going?"

"Up these stairs," I said, climbing the house's front staircase. I knocked on the door. Herr Cutter looked suitably horrified. I backed off when I heard footsteps, locks unlatching, the seal of the door breaking with a *woosh* of air. On the other side stood an old woman with her white hair tied in a bun. She kept the door cracked just enough for her to get a good look at me.

"Wer sind Sie? Ich erwarte keine Gäste."

"Um . . . no sprechen Sie Deutsch . . . sorry?" I called over my shoulder: "Herr Cutter, I need some help here!" In response, he clomped his way to my side.

"Tut mir sehr leid, gnädige Frau," he said. "Mein Freund ist verrückt."

"What did you say to her?" I whispered to him.

"Only the truth, Taggart." I knew it—he had thrown me under a bus, probably said I was deranged (which is exactly what he said). He pulled me away from the door by the shoulder, and the woman began to close the door.

"No!" I whipped out the photo and held it up so that the woman could see it. She stopped moving right away. "You recognize this, don't you?" She opened the door wider.

"Dora?" she said. Dora? As in *D* for *Dora*. Oh my god, it felt good to connect name and face. "Wo hast du das Foto?"

I looked at Herr Cutter. "What did she say?"

"She wants to know where you got your photograph," Herr Cutter said.

"Italy," I said, praying that it would spark something. "Capalbio?"

"Nein," she said. "Aber kommen Sie herein," said the lady before disappearing back inside of her house, the door left open for us to follow.

"I guess we go inside?" I said.

"What are you getting at here, Taggart?" he said, scowling. "You barge into my lab, barge into this woman's home. I discern a pattern."

"Funny, right?"

"No. But I highly doubt that will stop you—"

I walked inside, leaving him out on the stoop. With a very audible groan, he followed, his toes touching my heels as we navigated through the tight wooden hallways of this woman's house. The hallway eventually opened up to a small sitting room with a sofa and coffee table. So we sat.

"I cannot believe you have placed us in this situation, Taggart," said Herr Cutter.

"Really? You can't believe it?"

"Fine. I can believe it," he said. "I cannot believe how I fall for it every time."

After a few minutes, the woman called out: "Hallo? Bist du da?" She walked into the room balancing a tarnished silver tray topped by an equally tarnished silver teapot, sugar bowl, and cup of cream. She poured and set cups of tea in front of us all fancy with tiny silver stirring spoons and molasses sweet biscuits on separate saucers. I felt bad that she had gone through all this trouble and I didn't even know her name to thank her.

"Frau . . ." began Herr Cutter.

"Müller. Rufen Sie mich an Lotte. Gefällt Ihnen Zucker in den Tee?"

"Nein," said Herr Cutter. Then Frau Müller looked at me. Not quite sure what the question was, I felt safest just parroting what Herr Cutter did. I said no, and at that, she sat down opposite us.

"Dora?" she said.

"Is that the person in the photo?"

Herr Cutter translated what I had asked.

Instead of answering the question outright, Frau Müller stood up and crossed the room over to a tall cabinet with a skeleton key stuck into the door's lock. She twisted the key, opened the door, and reached way inside to bring out a tattered cardboard box. Seating herself back at the table, she laid the box across her lap and lifted the lid off. Inside was a photo album, its leather cover cracked and flaking.

"Open," she said, handing me the album. Inside were photos in black and white, some in sepia. I recognized the younger Frau Müller in many of the pictures from her long cleft chin. Standing beside her in many of the photos was a woman that looked a lot like her, only a bit older.

"Your sister?" I said, pointing to the other woman.

"Ja. Meine Schwester Gerde."

I continued to look through the book with Herr Cutter's gaze just over my shoulder. As I flipped farther into the album, the sisters got older. Most of the photos showed them being carefree, running on the streets, chilling out in parks and having picnics by the water. Frau Müller and her sister were obviously close. Most of the pictures showed them holding hands. Then, abruptly, there was a change in the framing and lighting, when the sisters were seventeen or eighteen years old. Most of the photos from that time were taken indoors, without much light. Some of the images had faded so much that they were little more than brownish blurs. Gone, too, were the happy expressions on their faces, replaced by straight lips and weighed-down brows. Toward the end of this period—I guessed that the sisters were in their early twenties—a third girl regularly joined them in their photos.

D for *Dora*.

One of the first pictures of Dora in the album had Frau Müller's sister and Dora standing side by side in the central square of an unidentified town. They were dressed all in white and held identical black bags with the symbol of the Red Cross emblazoned on the side.

"This is how they met?" I asked.

"Ja. Sie waren beide Krankenschwestern."

"Traveling nurses, Taggart," said Herr Cutter. Each photo showed the two of them in different locales: inside a church converted into a hospital, on the banks of the Seine in Paris with the Eiffel Tower in the background, in Milan, tending to wounded men on one side of a freestanding wall amidst the piles of rubble. I scanned these pages trying to soak up all the details in each photo, but there were way too many to remember all of them. Then I flipped a page and saw a single photo staring back to me. A face that I didn't expect I'd ever see again. Paolo—younger and darkly handsome. He was arm in arm with Dora, her head angled upward in a way suggesting that she was lost in his face somewhere. He was lost in hers. Lovers.

"Him!" I exclaimed, holding the album up so that Frau Müller could see who I was pointing to.

"Doyouknowwhoheishaveyouevermethim?" She shook her head and looked at Herr Cutter for some clarity on what the hell I was babbling about.

"Kennen Sie diesen Mann?" said Herr Cutter, saving a few knife-edged glances for me.

"Nein."

I pressed on. On one page, I saw a copy of the photo that Paolo had given me along with *The Green Ray*. Frau Müller had more photos to complete the set. In them, Munich looked utterly ravaged. It wasn't the city I had experienced so far, a city that felt very old, never letting on that it had died and come back to life. Munich felt like a place that had been there for centuries, But that wasn't the truth. Post-war city planners must have painstakingly found each and every stray piece of stone, every shard of building that had been blown apart, and placed it all back together again.

Peeling back the last few leafs of the album, I started to worry. Almost all the way through and very few answers—in fact, many more questions. Like—if Paolo and Dora were in love, why didn't they get together? It's not like anywhere in Europe was very far from anywhere else in Europe. I mean, how far was it from Tuscany to . . . to . . .

"Frau, where was Dora from? What country?"

"Eh . . . Ich erinnere mich nicht. Ich denke . . . Dora . . . English. No German."

Okay, at least we were getting somewhere.

"Herr Cutter, could you ask her if she or her sister ever went to visit Dora any place else?"

Herr Cutter translated my question for her. In response, she called for me to hand her the book. She flipped forward a few pages to a photo of the pages at the very end. She scanned the page with her finger, and finding what she sought, pointed out a photo to me. Standing on a riverbank were Gerde and Dora—both looking in their mid-thirties—and another man who wasn't Paolo. Of particular interest in this picture were a few things: first and foremost, Dora looked very pregnant. Second, the tall, fair-haired man standing next to her frowned, as if someone taking his picture was a great crime. And third, the location where the picture was taken was notable in itself. Half-submerged in the river was a procession of huge statues frozen in mid-step.

"Do you know where this is?" I asked.

She took the photo out from under the plastic and flipped it over. One word was scrawled on the back in elegant pen: *Frankreich*.

France? Frau's answer only prompted more questions, like *who was that guy?* I pointed to the tall man and asked Frau Müller if she knew him, but she only shrugged.

She explained some more, and Herr Cutter translated: "That is Dora's husband."

"But . . ." I couldn't even speak. How could she have married someone else when Paolo loved her? And how could Paolo have just given up? I mean, why didn't he go after her? I wanted to grill Frau Müller with even more questions.

She laid her hands gently on the album, pulled it away from me, and rested it on her lap. Slowly, she turned the pages, looking lost in them. Every so often, she would pause and touch the corner of a photo of her and Gerde. To me, they looked the same—she and her sister posing, Gerde always on the left, either both sitting or both standing in various locales. But for her, the photos were merely gateways to another time and another place. The meanings of the photos stretched past the borders of their frames.

"I think it is time for us to go, Taggart," said Herr Cutter. He politely interrupted Frau Müller from her rumination, and they engaged in a short conversation in German. I was still processing what I'd learned about Paolo and his lady love . . . and then about her husband. How did this all fit together? I didn't see much of a choice—it was La France or bust for me, not that reducing my search to a whole country made it much easier to needle-hunt. At the end of their talk, Herr Cutter stood up and wished Frau Müller a "Guten Tag." As he and I turned to leave, she tapped me on the shoulder.

"For Dora." She extended three photos toward me. One of them was of the three girls standing in front of a fountain. I would guess somewhere in Munich. The next was of Dora and her hubby by the river. And the last was the one I had been so excited about—Dora and Paolo.

"Danke," I said.

Outside, Herr Cutter and I got back into the car. What just happened? And what did it mean for me? France was where I was being pulled to next. But where in France?

"I don't like that look on your face," said Herr Cutter.

"What look?"

"You are thinking. Bad things happen when you think."

"You know what I don't get, Herr Cutter?"

"Common sense, decency, propriety, respect for your elders. Shall I continue?"

"Ha ha—no. If I suck so hard, why did you pick me to come with you to Italy?"

"Why would you want to know such a silly thing?"

"Scientific inquiry."

"Very well," he said sternly. "I asked you because you make me laugh." Did not expect that one, mostly because I had never seen Herr Cutter laugh in my entire life, let alone smile, let alone imply any joy of any kind in anything. "I do it when you are not looking," he said.

"Well, I knew it," I said. "You're a softie. Wait till I tell everyone back home. I'm thinking a mass departmental e-mail. Hmm?" I placed my extended pinky on the corner of my mouth, Dr. Evil-style.

"You will NOT spread such lies about me!"

"Don't worry about it, Mr. Staypuft," I said. "I'll Bcc." He sat back into his seat, started the engine, and pulled the car out of its parking space—all the while holding his glare. "By the way, what was that last exchange you had with Frau Müller before we left?"

"She said that we could come visit her whenever we wanted. I promised I would, after finishing a few out-of-town tasks."

"Oh my god, you are the *sweetest old man!*"

"Taggart," he said.

"Yes?" I answered.

"I hate you." But he said it with a smile on his face.

127

"En Argentina, soy un abogado," said Javier. We sat in the hallway, keeping each other company until our friends finished having their fun. Our conversation revealed a lot of surprising details about him—namely that this huge rugby player was a trained lawyer back home. He'd make a pretty good prosecuting attorney, as he could carry out the death penalty with his bare hands. Also, he was twenty, maybe twenty-one years old? That either meant that he started school at age negative three, or he was a cyborg with a positronic brain. He certainly acted older than his teammate, Fabrizio. I guess that's what made them a good pair.

Javier told me about how he had traveled all the way to Italy to play rugby professionally, and that, yes, it was his dream, except for one thing.

"La gente de Rovigo . . . no es mi gente, mi familia."

What if someone gave you a chance to live out your truest wish, only you had to give up the things that you had already? Javier was homesick. It didn't matter that the rugby fans of Rovigo thought he was a god on the field. His mother, father, sisters, aunts, uncles—none of them were in the crowd. So that was his choice: stay and be a star, or go back home to duty and family as a lawyer. A tough decision to be sure. If it were me, I would have had an easier time parting with family. But it wasn't me.

Right then, the couchette door slid open. Fabrizio tiptoed out with a punk-ass sheepish look on his face. He knew what he did. He knew that we knew what he did. And Isabella, from how she was cooing inside the room, was *deeply* aware of what he had done.

"Hai finito?" said Javier, staring daggers into his friend. Fabrizio didn't care.

"Ho stanco. Dormirò," said Fabrizio. He helped Javier up, and together, they started down the hall, Javier behind Fabrizio to make sure that he no second thoughts about calling it a night.

"Buena suerte, Javier," I called down the hallway.

He turned his head, careful to keep his body blocking the rest of the passage, and said "Gracias."

"I see you've made a friend," said Isabella, who stood in the hallway. Her hair was tied up into a messy bun, and she was currently reapplying lipstick. Really. "Don't tell me that you've been out here all this time talking."

"Sure," I said. "What else would we be doing?"

She cleared her throat in an overly obvious way, as if to say *you know exactly what you could have been doing and don't be so thick because no one is buying it.*

"I'm not really into guys so much."

"Oh," she said, holding the syllable until her hormone-flooded brain was able to process exactly what I was saying. "That makes sense the way that Finn girl was all over you."

"You saw that?"

"Oh yeah. I just figured that you were being delicate. Y'know—with her up in your pink bits."

"Thank you!" I exclaimed.

"So where is she?"

"With Jonas. Somewhere."

Isabella scrunched up her face. "Didn't see that coming. Frenchie is cute. She could go both ways, you know."

"It doesn't matter," I said, staring out the window. It was

getting to that transition time between fuck-all late and holy-shit early, when the sky was an indeterminate dark blue. After making sure her makeup was applied neatly, Isabella joined me on the floor. "I take it you had a good time."

"Is it my glow?"

"Thin walls."

We sat and listened to the car roll along the tracks. "So when did you know you liked girls?" Isabella asked.

"For as long as I remember," I said. I think you always kinda know. It's not always obvious, but little things add up over time. And it was never a big deal. I wasn't angsty and shit—at least not at first. I mean, when you were a kid, did you go around saying, *Holy fuckballs, I am sooooooo straight! Like that guy is so hot! What am I going to do?!!!*

"For me it was simple," I continued. "I liked girls. Period. It wasn't until other people got worked up about it that it became a big deal."

"I never understood why people cared so much about who was screwing who," said Isabella, frowning over a chipped toenail. "We have enough to worry about with who's screwing us, right?"

"Wise fucking words, Bel," I said. Right then, in an act of epic timing, a doorway at the other end of the car slid open, and Jonas stepped backwards out of the compartment. Lights outside the windows flashed silhouettes on the wall—his mussed up hair, another face drawing toward his—before we heard the click of the door shutting in the darkness.

"The conquering hero cometh," said Isabella as he made

his way back toward us. Jonas shook his head and waved her away, preferring a straight-line trajectory into the couchette.

"Frenchie's got the right idea, mate," said Isabella. "I'm gonna lie down. You in?"

"In a few. You go ahead."

"You'll be okay?"

"Sure." And then she was gone, leaving me all by my lonesome. I wasn't sure why I didn't just crash right then. I felt like shit. I felt like the shit that shit shits out. But I wasn't tired enough to completely pass out. Or too tired. Or something. And it is in those kinds of quiet times that doubt starts to creep into everything. You analyze every single action that you've done recently and start to second guess your choices. What was my plan once I got into Munich? I had just come from an Italian farm—a haunted Italian farm—where a guy I knew a grand total of a week died, leaving me a mysterious book and an equally mysterious photograph of a woman that he may or may not have wanted me to do something with. Meanwhile, the ghost of my dead mother visited me in my dreams and translated a message in Italian from an equally dead highwayman whose heyday ended before the turn of the twentieth century. And what he said was that it was my job to save the farm, and that I was supposed to follow a "green ray"—a phrase that would repeat itself in the title of the book I was given.

I was insane. Completely *fucking nuts*. I mean, how was I supposed to find one specific person in a city of millions? I wasn't looking for a needle in a haystack—I was looking for one particular piece of hay in that haystack. And even if I could find it, what would I do then? How would I explain why I was looking for her when I didn't even know why? I could hear Dad's voice grow louder and louder in my head, see him looking down at me with his corporate frown: "What were you thinking, Ryland? I just don't understand how . . ." It was always that last unfinished statement that killed me—like he had grown so weary of my bullshit that he couldn't even finish his damn sentence.

I held *The Green Ray* in my hands. I opened it to a random page, not really looking for anything in particular. On that page was an illustration of a ship in a stormy sea. A huge whitecap was cresting just short of the bow. Beyond the wave, farther into the ocean, was a small single-person boat, barely visible. I couldn't make out the features of the stranded person, but it was clear from the distressed expressions of the crew on the larger ship that the small boat and its occupant were in serious trouble. The caption to the illustration read, "All eyes were fixed on this point." That's your *come to Jesus* moment right there—stuck in the middle of the ocean, alone and left for dead. You've either forgiven yourself for all the shitty things you'd done with your life, or you let your desperation fester into anger at the world for letting you drown or starve or whatever. Point is that there's no there one to say anything nice about you before you shuffle off to that all-you-can-eat Indian buffet in the sky.

That's when I saw it—out the window, past the rolling tree-packed hilltops, and just over the crown of mountains that bordered the Bavarian Black Forest. Just before the first shred of light broke the horizon line, a pinpoint in the murky, bruise-colored sky flashed bright green, as the rising sun brightened the sky to orange. I stopped breathing. Was I actually seeing what I thought I was seeing? Or had I strung myself out so much that I was hallucinating? Whichever the case, the flash lasted only a second, two at most.

I tried to deny what I'd seen, but I was too tired or too unwilling to let it go. So I spoke it out loud, gave it form, allowed it to sink in and take hold.

"Il raggio verde," I whispered. "The green ray."

My eyes shot open, and I fell off the couch onto the floor. When I tried to stand up, I found that the blanket had twisted itself around my legs, pulling me back down. One more time, and I managed to get up onto my knees. I was in a shockingly clean apartment, as if it wasn't lived in at all. Besides the couch I'd been sleeping on, the only notable things in it were a coffee table and a framed painting of a sailboat like you'd see hanging in Holiday Inn. This place had as much character as a pack of printer paper.

"Where am I?" The last thing I remember was riding along in Herr Cutter's car and listening to him drone on about how he, and not Dr. Hemmil, should get the biggest office in the department because, of course, Herr Cutter's work was the most pressing for the world at large. And right after that . . . nothing. This was all confirmed as soon as I detected the butt-cheese stink of Herr Cutter's bitters. A second later, he came through the far doorway carrying two mugs of the vile drek.

"You are not dead. That is better than the alternative."

"What happened?"

"You are a young woman of many talents, Taggart," he said, handing me a mug. I took it to be nice—to my erstwhile host, if not to my sense of smell. Herr Cutter sat next to me on the couch and took a long sip of his own mug. "I am most impressed with your ability to fall asleep in the midst of conversation. It is a rare gift."

"Very funny," I said. Then . . . wait. I looked over at the wall clock to see that it was 9:12, and then out the window to see the morning sun overhead. Shit! I was supposed to meet Isabella and Jonas the previous night after I was done seeing Herr Cutter. "I need to get my hostel."

"I would have taken you there yesterday, but there was no waking you up."

"Do you think you could give me a ride now?"

"Of course. After you finish your tea."

I looked at my mug—my gigantic, cavernous, bottomless mug. Well, bottom's up. After chugging the whole disgusting thing, I lowered the cup to reveal Herr Cutter's completely horrified expression.

"What? You look surprised."

"That tea was scalding hot."

"I'm used to putting hot things in my mouth."

"I will politely ask you not to elaborate." Okay, then. I wouldn't tell him that my mom used to grow habeñero peppers in her garden. Twenty minutes later, we pulled up in front of the hostel, where Herr Cutter parked the car, turned to me, and said:

"You are going to do something stupid, aren't you?"

"Probably."

"Ah," he said, swatting the air. "Exposure to you is killing my brain cells." I unbuckled my seat belt and got out. "Do you have everything?" He was referring to the bag of food that he hastily gathered from his cupboards, including a half-eaten jar of Marmite, a tin of a cheese called Milbenkäse, which, as I would find out much later (and, of course, after eating it) got its distinct flavor from an infestation of cheese mites, a pair of blood sausages that his brother, Helmut, had made, and a mysterious red and yellow colored can of something called surströmming. I had no idea what that was, but the fierce looking bulge in the can boded ill fortunes ahead.

"Yeah."

"Very well," he said. "You have my phone number. Call me if you are in dire need, yes?"

"And you will call Tania and tell her. Promise me."

"I should have thrown you out of class on the first day."

"True. Now is that a promise?"

He sighed loudly. "Yes."

"Thanks. It means a lot."

"I will see you in the fall, yes? You can stop by my office, too. We are colleagues."

"You got it. Bye, Herr Cutter."

"Goodbye, Taggart."

I leaned back from the car, watched it zoom away, then started toward the bright red awning of Hunter's Hostel.

Inside, the lobby was filled with travelers talking over complimentary breakfasts of tea and toast. I scanned the area for signs of Jonas or Isabella, but saw none. At the front desk, however, I spotted another familiar face, so I went up and said hi.

"Hello," said charming desk-girl. Her hair was drawn up into a ponytail, and I noticed the faintest trace of green eye shadow on her eyelids. "Do you know if my two friends have left yet?"

"Two friends?"

"An Australian redhead and a French guy."

She flipped through the guest log. "Yes. The girl checked out this morning. And the other . . . he has not left yet."

"He's still here?" I spun around again. This time my eyes stopped at a corner table where a blonde-haired boy was busy scribbling something, pausing every so often to take a long swig of coffee.

"Where did you go?" Jonas called out after spotting me.

"Long story," I said.

Part Three

Le Rayon Vert du Soleil

Ryland—

Je suis désolé. I am not so good with writing English. You did not return last night. I leave today in the morning for Toulouse. It is possible that I to pay you the money for the ticket. Send to me a letter to the address I write. I will send to you the money.

Merci beaucoup,

Jonas

Ten

o there we were, half an hour after meeting back up with each other at Hunter's Hostel, back on another overnight train, this time headed for Toulouse— Jonas's destination. At least this time, I only had to pay for my own ticket. Still, I was on pins and needles waiting for my debit card to clear at the ticket booth, and when it did, the knowledge that my plucky little bank account was now €78 poorer cut short any sense of relief. At least I still had Jonas by my side, giving me two advantages: 1) I'd know someone when I got off the train, and 2) according to Jonas, if I accompanied him home, I'd be able to recoup the money I spent on his ticket to Munich. Good enough for me.

Now that I finally had some quiet time, I took out *The Green Ray* with the intention of slogging through it. I opened up the book marveling at how detailed the woodcuts were on the pages. The one at the very end was my favorite—an image of people on a rock marveling at the green rays of the sun streaming from where the sky met the sea—all the people except a man and a woman in the foreground kissing and missing this amazing sight.

"What is this?" said Jonas tapping a photo sticking out of the book. It was one of the new ones from Frau Müller, the one showing Dora and her husband by the statue-lined river. "This is not the one from before."

"Yeah, I just got it," I said.

"C'est Le Jardin de Pierres."

I literally jumped out of my seat. "You're telling me you know where this is?"

"Not quite," he said. "But Henri knows."

"Henri?"

Jonas fidgeted just that little bit, enough for me to notice. "Mon père." More hemming and hawing. "When you talk to him, you can ask." I wanted to pry more into his business, but I'd had my share of parental crises to know not to poke that bruise too hard. So I changed subjects onto a lighter topic (for the time being):

"So what did you do last night?"

"Uh . . . *rien*," he said.

"You and Isabella didn't go out?"

"No."

Ooh. I knew that tone, that vocal inflection, that sudden look-away.

"You did not!" No answer. "Oh, shit. You did!"

"C'est rien!"

"*Nothing* is the opposite of what happened. Fess up!"

He threw his hands up in the air. "I am not at fault! She wants to . . . you know . . . all the time!"

"*I am not at fault*," I mocked. "*No* sounds the same in French as it does in English."

That was a long train ride. Fourteen and a half hours. I was only able to grab sleep small handfuls at a time—45-minute blocks pockmarked with half-hour long bouts of insomnia. And it was in those spots that I raced through a chapter or two of *The Green Ray* before nodding back off. So by the time the train pulled into Toulouse Matabiau station at 7:45 AM the next day, I'd endured the whole thing. Man, from somewhere far off, Paolo was probably having a great laugh—he'd tricked *la pazzesca* into wasting her time reading a book remarkable solely in its unremarkability.

So here it goes:

You have your privileged young lady, Miss Helena Campbell, who has come of age under the parentage of her two hapless uncles, Sam and Sib (short for Sebastian). So they do what Victorian Era parents do—they desperately try to pair her off with a man of high estate, which she is not keen on. Thus, her elaborate plan to delay her fate: before she agrees to get married, she demands to see something she calls "the green ray," a unique light phenomenon that occurs when the sun breaks the horizon. And to do that, she needs to travel to a place with an unobstructed view. Cue boat trip through the Scottish Isles, one horribly boring and uppity suitor, another much less boring, more swash-buckling, but still rather dull suitor, a badly timed trip into a cave during a thunderstorm, a daring rescue, and a kiss during which the two young lovers completely MISS seeing the green ray, and there you have it.

Not one of Mr. Verne's finest, I had to say. I also wanted to say this: now that I'd read the book, I wasn't sure what Tiburzi was talking about. What was I supposed to get out of this? That love conquers all, and that the green ray is actually neither here nor there? Or that I needed the adoration of a good man to make my life meaningful? Fuck both of those things. As far as I was concerned, the love train had not only departed my station, it jumped the tracks, transformed into a gargantuan robot, and burninated the countryside. So when Jonas jostled me awake, I was not in a good mood. Evidently he did not understand the ancient American technique of *I'm sleeping here, bitch!*

"Are we there yet?" I said, wearily.

"Oui." It was a very understated *oui*, one tinged with regret and ambivalence. We got up and stretched our legs. While we gathered our bags, Jonas seemed transfixed by something on the other side of the window. I looked out, too, but didn't see anything of interest. "Putain," he said. *Putain.* It's a classic French word. Its proper definition is "whore" or "bitch"—that sort of thing, but in usage, it had more in common with *fuck*. This tipped me off that something was very wrong. "See those girls?" he said pointing out the window.

Waiting on the platform, about a half train car up, were two girls. The shorter one was stocky—not fat, but strong, with broad shoulders. A normal girl. No insult or anything, but not really someone who would jump out at you in a crowd unless she was standing next to the other girl. I won't lie. This other girl was hot. Like way hot.

No other choice now. Jonas and I hopped off the train. Moment of truth. Come to me, Jesus.

"Jonas, qui est cette putain?" said the taller girl, as we approached. Wow. Still in the room.

"Angelique!" said Jonas, putting every ounce of fake cheer he could into his voice. Close up, Angelique was like an exquisite gem—every feature fine and sharpened, at once beautiful and deadly. I would have probably wanted to get to know her, y'know, if she wasn't pointing at me and giving me a liberal dose of nasty stink-eye face.

"Elle est ta femme?" She screamed this impossibly loud. The other girl pleaded with her to calm down, as did Jonas. Clearly, there was some sort of history here. Sexy history, I guessed, from her accusations that I was Jonas's new wife.

"Elle est mon amie," said Jonas.

"Hi!" I suddenly found myself between them. I extended my hand out in the international gesture of friendship, and had intended to say "Bonjour. Je m'appelle Ryland, et je suis des États-Unis." I got out one syllable before she clocked me a good one. Didn't even feel it when I hit the ground.

"That what you wanted, muthafucka?!" KoRanna Jackson was the hugest human being I had ever seen. And I was on the ground, my head flanked by "Massive K's" legs, each thicker than my entire body. "Say something else, c'mon!"

"I see London," I said, every word filled with pain. "I see France . . ."

"This is gonna be the worst year of your life, new girl," she screamed, spraying spit all over my face. And she didn't even know my name. I was simply *new girl*. Which was perfect. No, KoRanna, this was gonna be the best year of my life, because I wasn't going to fucking spend it at the illustrious (so say the promo brochures) St. Gertrude's All Girls Prep Academy in Los Angeles, California. And your fist was my ticket out of this Popsicle stand.

From the end of the hall, other girls ventured out of their rooms and watched the pit fight in the hallway. All good. I'd need witnesses, anyway. My focus returned to the beast hovering over me, her jowls tensed into a death stare, her hair a frizzy explosion of tight kinks.

I rolled away from KoRanna and got back up to my feet. Oh pain, welcome to my *Kobiyashi Maru*, my no-win scenario. My opponent looked shocked. All she could do was step back and wonder why the fuck I didn't stay on the ground like a sensible young woman. That was her first mistake. I'm Ryland Taggart, doer of stupid things. Not one sensible muscle, bone, or cartilaginous growth in this body.

"How 'bout you stop being a punk-ass bitch?" I said. That was all it took to spring her into action mode. She threw her M. Bison-style right haymaker at me, which I would have deftly dodged with my cat-like reflexes. If only I had cat-like reflexes. She connected again, slamming me against the door of the dorm room she and I shared. Oh yeah. KoRanna Jackson, "Massive K," and I were roommates in my senior year of high school.

And this was my first day.

Again I was on the floor. One more, I thought. I started to get up again. It was much harder this time around. For whatever reason, the theme song from *Baywatch* was stuck on loop in my brain, as was the playback of the Hoff's fuzzy man-boobs galumphing toward the water. The peanut gallery behind KoRanna had become a frenzy of hands over mouths, and Massive K herself looked legitimately scared. I knew what she was thinking: *She's not human. She's a piece of iron.* And like Rocky, all I had to do was weather the storm of K's *whatever-she-hits-she-destroys* punches and hope that the crowd starts chanting my name. So what if I conveniently overlooked the fact that she was kicked out of an all-girls street gang because she made the other members nervous. I wanted maximum carnage, so everyone—notably school officials and Daddy Dearest—would see just how horrible a mistake it was to bring me to St. Gertie's.

One more, I told myself again. *Just don't die, dude.*

I pushed myself away from the wall when a voice boomed from the back of the hallway.

"What the hell is going on here?" It was the principal, Carolyn Lewis, one of the hardest hardasses I had ever encountered. She strutted down the hallway in her Scooby-Doo PJs, her dreds mussed up and wild like a demon squid. "Everybody back to your rooms!" she screamed, clearing out the hallway, leaving me and K.

"KoRanna, go to your room. We're going to talk in a little while." K nodded and lumbered back into our dorm room. The principal then pointed at me. "You. To my office."

"Um, do you have a wheelchair?"

"Do I look like your nurse?" she said. "If you aren't right behind me, I'm going to make you mop this hallway tonight. With a Q-Tip."

Point taken. I dragged myself to her office, where she directed me to sit in one of her two luxurious leather chairs in front of her desk. We sat in the dark. The last time I was there (the morning of the same day), I sat in the left seat—the one I slithered into again—and my father was sitting in the right. Dad and P. Lewis were conspiring on how to make my life hell right in front of my face.

This time it was my face that was hell.

"What did you do?"

"I got the shit kicked out of me."

She leaned forward over her desk. "What did you do?"

"Nothing!"

"That's bullshit," she said. "And do you know how I know?" Then she waited for me to answer.

"Um . . . no?"

"Because it's 7:33 right now."

"I don't under—"

"*Dancing with the Stars* is still on."

"I still don't get—"

"Shawn Mendes still hasn't been eliminated."

Shit. She had me. Let me explain. So the first time I walked into the dorm room that KoRanna and I shared, I was a little shocked by her choice of décor. So, you know in movies with serial killers? Yeah, and then they show the bedrooms of said killers and you see that they've taped pictures of their victims on the walls and have shrines and shit, right? Well, from just stepping into that room, I concluded from the posters of Shawn Mendes in a slick Armani suit, the framed and autographed picture to "My Dearest KoKo," the jacket with a bedazzled portrait of Shawn's perfect face hanging from her bedpost, and her computer open to a YouTube playlist of Shawn's greatest hits that she either wanted to murder that pretty boy with a throat of gold or be the one on television dancing the Lambada with him. Naked.

"You must have done something to her to make her miss that show," P. Lewis said.

"Okay. Fine. So maybe I engaged in a little commentary that she sorta-kinda didn't appreciate."

"Such as . . ."

"Shawn Medes is a fucking no-talent hack he's probably lip synching dude's a cut-rate Justin Bieber." There. Got that out of the way. Just then my lip sort of burst into a fountain of blood. I covered my mouth with my hand and blurted something about some Kleenex in here.

"Use your shirt," she said. "You see, I know what's going on here. We've had girls like you. They all think that if they're big enough problems, they can go back to being spoiled brat princesses."

"I am not a spoiled princess." That kind of insult I will not tolerate.

"You'll have a chance to prove it."

"You're not kicking me out?"

"No."

"So what's my punishment?"

"Punish?" She laughed. It was a really, really evil laugh. "I'm not going to punish you. I'm giving you a scholarship. And I'm going to announce it tomorrow in the school bulletins that go out to parents. Everyone will know what a great asset you are to St. Gertrude's. A team player. Of course, with that scholarship comes certain requirements."

Now I was scared. I was clearly dealing with a seasoned veteran at punking people out.

"Your class schedule will be set up by me and other members of the school board," she said. "It will be very rigorous. Along with that you'll have extracurricular and community service requirements."

"So, I take it that I can't turn it down, right?"

"No. And every time you mess up, I'm going to give you another award and more responsibilities. And more people will look. Maybe if you screw up enough, I can even pull a few strings and get you up there in the running for Miss Teen California. Mess with me, *princess*, and I will shit on your life, put it between two pieces of Wonder Bread, and make you eat it. Comprenez-vous?"

I was shaking. Really. "What?"

"Your file says that you've taken five years of French."

"Oh . . . uh . . ."

"It means, 'Do you understand?'"

"Okay. Yeah. Sure."

She leaned back into her chair, into the shadows, and even though I couldn't see it, she was probably grinning ear to ear. "Now get the hell out of my office."

Eleven

aking up with a headache was a habit I needed to stop, second only to getting knocked out in the first place. Slowly, my world expanded from fuzzy blobs to less fuzzy blobs. I was in a car . . . and someone was dabbing my head with a wet towel. Eventually, my eyes returned to normal, and the sound of an argument in French rattled in my ears. A girl—not the one that decked me, but the other one—hovered over me, patting my head.

"You are okay?" she said.

I found it suddenly difficult to form words in French. "Je crois," I managed before switching to English: "Is Jonas . . ."

"I am here," said Jonas from the driver's side seat. I was in a car—more specifically an ancient Volkswagen Westfalia mini-bus with a fold-down bed and makeshift wooden table. Jonas was at the wheel, and Angelique the psycho-bitch was in the front passenger seat, leering at me and at Jonas in turn. Hovering over me, patting my eye with a damp cloth was . . .

"Comment appelles-tu?" I asked, using the familiar form because, hell, any lady doting on me like that I'd call a friend in a heartbeat.

"Madeleine. Jonas est mon frère." Yeah. Now that I looked at her, I could see the sibling resemblance. They had the same pretty blue eyes and the same strong jawlines. And when they smiled—as she was doing right then to put me at ease—they had dimples in the same places. "You are from the United States?" She leaned in closer, touching my face with hers. "You are the girlfriend of Jonas?"

I couldn't form words enough to answer.

"Press. We arrive at home soon," she said, placing my hand on the towel.

"Where is home?" I asked. She didn't say. Lightheaded as I was, I let the van rock me back and forth like a cradle. "Je m'appelle Ryland," I said. "Je pense . . ."

"Enchantée, Ryland Je Pense."

Eventually the van stopped rocking and turned uphill until Jonas set the parking break and turned off the engine. The people in front got out, and Madeleine, with me in the back, slid open the side door and yanked me up and out. My legs gave way under me, so she draped my arm over her neck and loaded my entire weight on her shoulder. I could feel through her shirt how solid and knotted her back was. She literally carried me out of the car and placed my feet on the ground, careful to keep a tight grip.

"Home," said Madeleine.

And what a home! Jonas and Co. lived in heaven, and somehow I had tricked my way past St. Peter to get through the pearly gates. From where I stood, green hills seemed to sprout from the ground and undulate off in all directions. Farther away, snow-capped mountains took up 360 degrees of the far horizon. Dotting this landscape were barns and small houses, and surrounding them, tilled earth. People in the distance were dots pulling slightly bigger, cow-shaped dots pens, or mounting old tractors that you could hear loud and clear even at this distance. The air smelled and tasted like real air. Like at the ranch in Wyoming. Like at Tania's farm. I started to think of Raffiano and his family. What were they supposed to do now? What did Herr Cutter's discovery mean for them?

"You are hungry?" Madeleine asked. As a matter of fact, I was starving. I'd even eat blood sausage and mite-cheese. She led me up the hill to a house that not only looked old, but felt worn and tired. The plaster on the outside had given way to exposed, gray wood and even grayer stones filling in the gaps between the beams.

"Um, bonjour?" I said, as Madeleine sat me down at a table and told me to be comfortable. Easier said. Two dudes seated there stared me down, looking a little curious and a lot confused. Madeleine did the introductions: Guy was the shorter guy with a characteristic big French nose (think Gérard Depardieu) and a perpetual smirk on his face like he knew not only all your secrets, but your mom's, too. Sitting next to him was Marcel: taller, dark-skinned, dreadlocks.

"So, you are Jonas's—" Guy blurted out.

"I am not his wife, not his girlfriend, have only known

him a couple of days." I hoped that was clear enough for him.

Guy laughed, apparently getting a rise out of my predicament. "Henri said that Jonas was bringing a girl home. When Angelique found out, she threw the phone against the wall. C'est le bordel, non?"

"Tais-toi!" Madeleine shouted.

"Quoi?" shouted Guy back in her face.

Madeleine buried her head in her hands, then looked up. "Sorry."

"Obviously, shit's fucked up. I can see that. Jonas wasn't exactly excited to come back."

"It is not like this here usually," said Marcel. He said it so matter-of-factly, like the *haute tension* of the past few minutes was no big deal. "I think you maybe came at a bad time."

"By the by, where is Jonas?"

"Listen," he said. "You will hear it."

A split second later, an argument erupted out of the silence. I recognized the voices. Jonas and Angelique. They weren't far away, probably on the other side of the wall. I could make out every word, so I knew they were arguing about me—whether I could stay here at this . . . whatever you would call it. Goddammit, I didn't mean for this to happen. Jonas really should have been straight with me. I understand crazy bitches. I am one. I could have at least prepared him for the onslaught.

He screamed at her, and she screamed back, obviously not caring who could hear. "Et moi?" said Angelique. "Et nous?" Ah. *Et nous?* Translation: *What about us?* It was all starting to make sense now, about why Jonas was so reluctant to come home, what had taken him all the way to Martinique. Her voice became quieter. "Ma robe était belle. Bleu et blanc."

Oh shit, Jonas. What did you do? I didn't like how she was talking about a dress, calling it "the dress"—you only call a dress "the dress" if you're talking about prom. Or your wedding. Add to that the combo of anger and sadness I heard in Angelique's voice, and I didn't have to guess very hard for the truth. These two were sweethearts, were supposed to be married. Only one of them decided that maybe it wasn't a good idea. So he booked it out of Dodge for the sunny sands of Martinique.

After a few seconds, I heard heavy footsteps on the gravel alongside the house. A moment later, Jonas burst through the front door, paused when he glanced inside the kitchen and saw me, Madeleine, and Marcel sitting there, and then stomped up the stairs. A door slammed. Then Angelique came into the house, breathing heavy, eyes swollen, jaw trembling. She stopped, just like Jonas had, right before she went upstairs. Her eyes were full of pure hate.

"Hey," I called out. She darted up the stairs out of sight.

"Un bordel. Oui," said Marcel. He sipped his coffee again. Madeleine offered me some baguette and cheese, but I'd lost my appetite. She nudged the bread on her plate a couple of times and decided that she wasn't hungry, either. She and Marcel helped me get the bags from the van and hauled them inside.

"Jonas told you none of this," she said. It wasn't a question. She knew her brother too well.

"It's cool," I said. "I should leave. I don't want to cause trouble. I just need to talk to Henri."

"No. You are a guest."

"Really. I don't want to interfere. If Jonas had just said something . . ."

"Jonas told me what you did. You stay." She hefted my backpack onto her shoulder and led me upstairs to a hallway so narrow we had to go single file. We followed it to a door at the end of the hall.

"Voila. Ta chambre, madamoiselle."

Calling the space at the end of the hall *un chambre* was being charitable. It was not a room. It was a closet. Of course. When you do stupid things, you tend to wind up exactly where you deserve. So I didn't flinch when Madeleine moved stacks of buckets and a mop or two to clear some space on the floor.

"Ah!" Pulling out a foam pad the size of a very, very small twin bed, she laid it out on the floor. "I will find . . . *un orellier*? How do you say this?"

"Pillow."

"D'accord. I will find a pillow and cover for you."

"Thanks," I said. "Say, where can I find Henri?"

"He went to Carcassonne," she told me. "He will return tonight."

Great, I thought. How many hours could I evade Angelique? I guess I was going to find out.

I was fucked. And not in the good way. Principal Lewis saw fit to load me up with seven full time classes—two more than most girls had to handle. As if that wasn't enough, I was assigned to after-school choir. *Glee* this was not. There was zero percent chance of a Lita Ford-themed episode in which I got to sing "Kiss Me Deadly" in tight black leather. Our hymn books didn't even have anything written after the 50s—the 1550s. After choir was World Club (in which students got together after school to "world" stuff, obviously), and after World Club was the worst—Academic Decathlon.

For those who are not so familiar with this ancient form of torture, Academic Decathlon is this thing invented by some teacher in the 60s because he felt that students weren't studying enough pointless shit in the classroom. Maybe the goal was to increase the student suicide rate. But what really happened was that students loved it. Finally, nerds of the world had their own competition by which they could lord their spoils over others! Unless, of course, you were like me—not sure whether *Magna Carta* was a document issued in 1215 which established natural rights of man, or if it was a new, mega-colossal experimental size of Starbucks coffee.

And then (and then!) . . . and then I had to go do my volunteering. This happened only twice a week, but straw on the camel's back and all. The first day I showed up to Grace House, the stink from my armpits was in direct violation of the Kyoto Protocols. I had woken up late that morning—too late for a shower. So I grabbed my books and ran to Discrete Math without looking back. Cue that up six more times and you had me *before* all the aforementioned clubs commenced. You can imagine a cantankerous me trudging onto the shuttle bus to take me to Grace House . . . whatever that was. There were three other girls waiting in the van in front of school, all ready to go, all nice and clean and tidy, and I think a little bit scared that I was more likely to demand gold coins from them when they crossed my bridge than help them do charitable work.

I took my seat without a word.

"We've been waiting for fifteen minutes," said the driver and Grace House volunteer coordinator, Mr. Leonard.

"Sucks to be you."

"Next time . . ." was all he said before jacking the gear out of park and rolling out. I didn't recognize any of the girls in the van. I had spent the week between my beatdown and right then minimizing my contact with other human beings. The two girls in the back seat—from their looks, no older than freshmen—looked completely mortified, like I had slit the throats of their pet hamsters and slurped up their blood. But the one next to me, this girl broke out in giggles.

Well, this would not do.

"Are you laughing at me?" I said, arching my back like I was about to pounce.

"I guess so." She giggled again. Ooh, she was the class-president-slash-valedictorian type. We all know them. Straight backed, shiny-haired, perfect-teethed, bronze-skinned, glittery-lipglossed, bowtie-headbanded, Nabokov-reading brown-nosers from quaint little suburbs where sweater-vest-wearing fathers cut their 10' x 10' lawns with riding mowers. This one was like the T-1000 of that line—a perfectly Stepforded young lady in a red plaid jumper that happened to color coordinate with the stream of vomit rising from my stomach.

"How 'bout you tell me your name so I can add you to my 'bad things gonna happen to you' list."

"Exactly how long is that list? I'd like to know how long I should wait for that bad thing so that I can put it in my planner. A date range is good enough." She reached into her handbag and pulled out a small red book. Then she cracked the book open to a fresh page, uncapped a fountain pen, and looked up at me. After jotting something down, she said, "You're really bad at this."

"At what?" I screamed, prompting Mr. Leonard to yell back, "Here we use inside voices! Think of this van like a library." Of course, except that it wasn't a building, there were no books, and I couldn't download pirated movies.

"Your whole bully act," she said. "It's okay. It's hard being new. At least you're getting noticed."

"I don't want to be noticed," I hissed. "And what the hell did you write?"

"That's really none of your business."

I wanted to say something like, *I'm gonna make it my business*, but I decided it wasn't worth it. I didn't want to talk to this bitch anyway.

"It's pretty special that you're volunteering with us," the girl continued. "St. Gertrude's only lets girls with 4.0s volunteer off school grounds. You have to prove that you can handle your schoolwork and outside activities."

"Special," I said. "You don't know me, so maybe you could shut the fuck up. Oh, and *please*."

"Poor dear," she said. "I've seen you. In choir. And World Club. And Academic Decathlon. I'm in all those, too. By the way, George Washington did not have wooden teeth, nor did he chase Moby Dick."

"Yeah? Well Caesar is still a salad dressing dude."

"You don't have to fake the tough girl routine. It's old. And you're not good at it."

"I don't even know your name," I said, "but I want you to die. I'd also like your children to die, their toys to break, your house to burn down, and the mice in the walls to eat the eyes out of your corpse's decomposing skull. But this world is unfair, and we don't often get what we ask for, so I'll settle for your head being crushed by a pneumatic press."

"That's a little better I suppose. Next time, maybe shake your fist more."

Aargh! Why was this happening? My cool had been lost a long time before, and we were approaching reactor meltdown. To stop critical mistake territory from being breached, I gave up. I slapped the seat and went limp. "Why are you even talking to me, huh?"

"I thought maybe you could use a friend," she said. "Last year was my first year. I know how it is."

"You know how it is, eh? Then riddle me this, _friend_—if you're in the same clubs that I'm in, how did you get to this van fifteen minutes before me?"

"Why didn't you use the secret passage?"

"Secret passage?!"

"Yeah," she said. "Secret passage. When we get back, I'll show you. I'm Shannon, by the way."

"Ryland. Enchantée."

"Ah! Tu parles français?"

By the time we arrived at Grace House, I had proven that I did not, in fact, speak French. But I had also somehow been tricked into letting Shannon tutor me. It wasn't until we all were walking through the front entrance that I started to wonder what kind of charitable organization Grace House was. I didn't have to wait long for the answer.

Mr. Leonard led us through hallways until we got to a large open room with fold out tables taking up the middle. Each seat around the tables was occupied by a person. A woman. Mr. Leonard was the only man in the room.

"On behalf of everyone at Grace House, I'd like to welcome our new volunteers." Mr. Leonard then had us introduce ourselves to the audience. When my turn came up, I rambled off something that resembled this: "Hi. My name is Ryland Taggart. I'm originally from Wyoming, but now I'm in L.A. Yeah. And I also don't know what you all do here, but whatever is cool because I'll be here to do . . . whatever. Um . . . I like walks on the beach—no just kidding 'cause I get sunburned real easily . . . "

"Let's welcome Ryland to Grace House," said Mr. Leonard, slow-clapping me into STFU. Once he was done with that, he kindly explained what Grace House was and what I was supposed to be doing there. "So, as a refresher—" He eyed me specifically. "Grace House is a non-profit for women who have fallen onto hard times, whether that be recent incarceration or domestic disputes. We provide temporary rooms, day care for kids, job placement services, and educational services. This, young ladies, is what you will help us with. But for today, I want you to go around, meet the women who are living here now, and get a feel for what we are trying to do here. Refreshments will be brought out shortly."

Principal Lewis had a sick sense of humor.

Twelve

ecause Jonas had gone AWOL, I ended up shadowing Madeleine as she went about the property doing her daily routine—which was insane when I learned how old she was.

"Dix-huit." She was eighteen years old, and barely that, making her the youngest person I had met that day. Marcel and Guy were both twenty, and Jonas and Angelique were both twenty-two. So it was kind of a surprise that while Henri was away, Madeleine was the one in charge of making sure the chickens were fed, the gardens were watered, and the place didn't burn down (more or less).

"Have you always lived here?"

"Oui," she said. "For Jonas and me, this is our home."

As we went along, passing by the chicken coop that everyone shared, and the vegetable garden that everyone shared, and the old stone well that everyone shared, I found out exactly what kind of home this was. In a word, Jonas and the others lived on a commune. So all things— including money—being pooled as they were, Jonas leaving was a great big *fuck* you to the whole group. No wonder him coming back was a big deal, in the positive and the negative.

Madeline led the way from the well, inspecting a line of piping that extended up out of the ground until it penetrated the wall of the house, where it led to a sink. With her handy-dandy monkey wrench, she tightened a few leaky joints while I held the pipe in place. We weren't a half-bad team. After that was done, she led the way to the other parts of the property that I hadn't seen yet.

If I had any doubts about what kind of work they did at this place, all of them were settled the moment I rounded the other side of the house. In front of me, on the downward slope of the hill, was nothing less than the end of a rainbow—one that was cool and smooth to the touch. Pottery of all sizes and shapes, from huge vases to tiny, delicate flasks, covered the ground. Each piece was glazed to shine a different color—not merely reds, blues, and greens, but subtle grades of fuchsia, aquamarine, emerald. No two pieces were the same shade. Many of the large pieces had designs of animals and landscapes on them. One huge jug was orange, but on a brown band that went all the way around were what looked like stencils or silhouettes of trees that I recognized instantly. *Pinus pinea.* Italian umbrella pine. As we passed it, I reached out and touched it, and for a second, I could hear the swaying of the leaves and branches in the wind, the soft stretching that maybe was more imagination than memory.

"Ça va?" asked Madeleine, breaking me from the spell.

"Wha—oh." I took my hand away. "I like this."

She touched the pot where my fingers had been. "Angelique made this design. Her father is from Florence. She loves those trees." So Angelique was Italian. We followed a footpath that wound through the field of pots toward a warehouse at the hill's base.

"What is that?"

"There? I do not know how to say this word. La usine de pots."

"A pottery factory."

"D'accord." As we got closer, I spied the cut out shapes of letters propped on the low slanting roof of the factory: O-T-E-R-I-E. It should have been *POTERIE*, but the first letter was missing. Through a huge sliding door, we stepped into the factory proper.

"Putain," I said. Yeah, so they made pottery at this place. Every single shape of pottery I saw outside and more were represented in stacks that rose ten or fifteen feet in the air. Some pieces made of thinner, more fragile material, sat in nests of straw and shredded newspapers.

"Soon we can open again," said Madeleine.

"Wait, wait. This place is closed?"

"Oui. We cannot open without Jonas."

"Why? Just because he's a good potter?"

"Because he is the *best* potter."

Madeleine blazed a trail through the high columns and between bizarre rust-coated machines clear through to the other side of the factory. I kept an eye on her feet as we walked. There seemed to be no method to where she stepped—no indication on why there instead of there or there. She probably wasn't even thinking about it. Nothing in this place looked like it had changed in years, maybe decades. As soon as we got near the other side, the temperature of the air went from the mild warmth of the ebbing day to stifling nuclear meltdown. At the very back of the factory was someone wearing a black-visored hazmat looking deal that looked like Marty McFly's get-up from *Back to the Future*.

"Qu'est-ce que c'est, ça?" I said, pointing at Darth Vader from Planet Vulcan.

"Marcel. Come!" We got as close as thirty feet before Madeleine stopped me. "Do not get too close. The kiln is very hot." By "kiln," she meant the silver refrigerator-looking oven thing that Marcel was standing next to. We both watched as he opened the door and extended a long pair of tongs into it to pluck out a red hot piece of pottery—this one a thin-necked vase. Without flinching, he plunged it into a coffee can full of wood shavings and used a small shovel to pile in more shavings until it was overflowing. The entire can burst into flames.

"You know about Raku?" Madeleine registered my muteness as a no, and went onto explaining. Raku is what Marcel was doing. It's a kind of pottery that involves the superheating of pots to a thousand degrees and then quickly cooling them off by smothering them with different materials. This kind of pottery is not for the timid or impatient. "Marcel does this pottery. Guy another kind. Angelique makes her glazes and designs."

"What about you?"

"I work with Henri. He teaches me to fix pipes and cars. Soon we can open the factory."

"That's exciting, right?"

"Oui." She didn't sound excited. In that moment, Madeleine was a thousand miles away, and it took the sound of a far off car horn to rouse her out of it. "Henri vient!" She sprinted out and back up the hill. I did my best to keep up, but you know what they say about either being a marathon runner or a sprinter. Yeah. They forgot to mention athletically inept people like me who'll be totally fucked when the zombie apocalypse happens. I crested the hill in time to see Madeleine hugging an older dude standing outside the house. I came over to introduce myself, but she beat me to the punch.

"Papa, c'est une amie de Jonas."

"Bonsoir, monsieur," I said as I shook his hand. "Je m'appelle Ryland."

"D'accord!" he said. "Vous êtes des États-Unis?"

"Oui. J'habite au Texas."

"Ah! J'aime beaucoup le *bar-be-que* de Texas!" We went into the house, where Henri sat down at the table and poured himself a glass of red wine. "Et Jonas?" he asked Madeleine.

I explained that he was tired from traveling and resting in his room. At least the part about him being in his room was the truth. Henri sat back, gulped wine, and reminisced about being young again. Then he told us to get Jonas and Angelique and bring them down. Ah, youth—tailor-made so older folks can order you to do painful things.

I accompanied Madeleine up the stairs to go fetch Jonas

and Angelique from their self-imposed exiles. Henri seemed to be in good spirits, almost too good, to the point that he was oblivious to the whole Jonas-Angelique saga. Of course, that wasn't possible . . . right? We stood in front of Jonas's door, which was still locked. Madeleine knocked and stepped back, waiting for the door to swing open.

"Henri is nice," I said, trying to fill the silence. What I really wanted to do was ask about his wife—Madeleine's and Jonas's mother. Neither of the siblings had mentioned her, or any older womanly person living with them. Were they like me? Did they lose their mom, too? "He's alone? I mean, Est-il marié?" She smiled like I had told her a joke. It was almost as if Henri was more friend than father. I must have looked troubled because Madeleine clarified: "My birth father is dead."

"I'm sorry."

"I don't know him. Only Henri. They were good, good friends, so when he died, Jonas and I came here."

"And your mother?"

"Oui. Same."

Jonas still hadn't answered the door. This time, I knocked.

"Jonas?" I knocked on the door again.

"Jonas!" said Madeleine. "C'est moi et Ryland."

The door clicked, then opened a sliver. Jonas scrutinized the scene before pulling the door and ushering us inside. He re-locked up tight after we came in.

"Tu es fou," said Madeleine.

"Dude. You can't stay in this room forever. Your dad's here."

166

"Henri?" Jonas sat down on his bed. "Putain."

"Yeah, and he wants to talk to you."

But he didn't move from his spot on the bed, where he cradled a book open to *Le Puits et le Pendule*—the French version of Edgar Allen Poe's short story, *The Pit and the Pendulum*. Not exactly the type of reading you want to do when you're going through an emotional crisis.

"Where is Angelique?" he asked.

"I don't know. In her room, I suppose. Henri wants to see her, too."

Jonas slammed the book shut. "I do not want to see her."

"That's gonna be hard. You kinda live in the same place." Yeah, and their rooms were across the hall from each other. He could avoid Angelique about as easily as he could avoid a fucking pot.

"I stay here."

"Go down," Madeleine commanded, her sternness catching me off guard. "I will find Angelique."

After she left, Jonas sprang up from the bed, opened his window wide, and stepped out.

"Uh, where are you going?"

"Down." Then he ducked the rest of his body out the window and onto a lower part of the roof which bowed under his weight. Shit. What else could I do but chase after him? Badly, I might add—he got a huge head start by jumping the fifteen or so feet down to the ground. I, being too chicken-shit, used divots in the outside walls to gingerly climb down. By the time my feet were on the ground, Jonas was out of sight.

The factory. There was nowhere else to go.

Before, with Madeleine and Marcel, the factory didn't seem so cavernous and foreboding. But alone, not knowing the lay of the land, the place took on this air of menace only heightened by the weirdly-shaped shadows cast by the pots. I followed the sounds of something dragging along the ground to find Jonas pulling bags of dry cement away from a door in the far back wall.

"Jonas!"

"Oui," he said, nonchalantly, as if this was normal operating procedure.

"Look. I'm going to ask you nicely to explain to me what the fuck." At first he ignored me, preoccupied with sifting through a heavy keychain for one key in particular. Once he found it—a thin silver number—he inserted it into the padlock that kept the door shut tight, then wiggled the lock out of the rusted-coated hasp. "Jonas!"

"Yes!" The word came out his mouth like a bullet. At once, he looked down at his feet and shook his head. "I am sorry. This is . . . je fais une connerie."

"You're right about that, Hoss. But running away ain't gonna fix it."

"Hoss?"

"Yeah. *Hoss*—a dude who rocks out with his cock out and hangs out with his wang out."

"Hangs out with . . . what?"

"Hoss means 'a person who's a bad muthafucka.' And trust me, you one bad mutha-fucking-fucka." I made a gesture of placing a ring on my finger. Jonas understood immediately. He lowered his head and mussed up his own hair. "I know about you and Angelique."

"Putain," he muttered.

"Yeah. Varying degrees of pissed with Jonas around here."

"She thinks I left because of another girl."

"You did leave her at the altar. Was there someone else?"

"No!" He punched the wall, then grimaced with regret. "There are some times you wake in the morning and there is too much everything. It comes so fast. All I wanted was to stop for a small time. Wedding and work and everything. Marcel told me his brother was opening a store in Martinique, so I go." He took a step back from me, as if preparing for the inevitable onslaught of *why* and *how did you think* questions. But I knew *why*. I knew *how did you think*. I had been on both sides of that shitstorm and was the last one who deserved to lecture.

"So why did you come back?" Okay. So I had one why question. "Sounds like a nice deal—pots and barbecues and ladies on the beach. Why come back now?" Instead of answering me, Jonas turned the doorknob, but paused before pulling the door open.

"Ready?"

"Ready for what?" I asked.

"There will be dust." And there was. A cloud of chalky awfulness stung my eyes and crunched in my teeth when he swung the door open. "Je l'ai dit."

"Thanks, Nostradamus," I said, spitting out gobs of gray slime between coughs. I patted myself down while Jonas went inside. He flipped the light switch to reveal a cramped cubby where one person could sit comfortably—if your idea of comfort was a hard wooden stool, surrounded by earthenware jugs, unpainted, unglazed teapots hanging

169

from bent nails hammered into the walls, and a lonely potter's wheel caked with dry clay.

"Bienvenue chez Jonas."

"Did you make these?" I pointed to the big jugs on the floor.

"Tout." He searched around his feet, and when he found his quarry, he hoisted it into the light: "You see this?" This jug was different from the others on the floor. This one had cracks spread across it like a spider web. It had been shattered and glued back together. "This is two-thousand years old—from the Gauls. I work with . . . like Indiana Jones?"

"Archaeologist," I said.

"Oui. I worked with them. I use this as a model to make new pots." He pointed to the other jugs on the floor, all the same shape as the one Jonas held in his hands. Jonas put the ancient jug down, then surveyed the workshop quietly. It was like a time capsule that captured the day, the hour, the minute he decided that he had had enough of home. "You make pots before?"

"Me? No. I've never thrown pottery."

"Throw?"

"I don't know. It's what we say in English."

"Here. I will show you how to throw the pots." Jonas took me by the shoulders and pressed me down onto the stool in front of the wheel. "You will make."

"You're not gonna, y'know, demonstrate first?"

"This is the best way to learn. The only way to learn," he said. After fetching a bucket of water and laying it by my feet, he slapped a liberal handful of clay onto the wheel from the pile next to it. Then he flipped the wheel's motor on. Gears moved for the first time in a year, at first making an awful grinding noise. After a minute, the spinning smoothed out. That was the signal to begin. Jonas, from behind, took my hands in his and dipped them in the water.

"I need to be close. D'accord?" He curled his sinewy body around to follow the contour of my back, aligning the joints in our arms so that when he bent his elbow, mine bent as well. "Tu dois assurer que l'argile est exactement dans le centre de la roue." Jonas used my palms—right hand first, then left—to press against the sides of the clay until the wet lump spun in the exact center of the wheel. "C'est bon. Maintenent . . ." He took my left hand and set it on top of the clay. "Appuies sur le dessus. Appuies doucement pour que l'argile se plie autour de tes doigts. Mais sois forte. Toujours fortement." With his fingers on top of mine, tensed so that I could feel all the muscles in his forearm go jagged, he pressed down onto the clay, and as he had said, it bent to his will almost too easily. A small, narrow tunnel gave way to a bowl-shaped opening as he guided my fingers to press from the inside out, widening the opening and making the sides of the clay thinner and more cup-like. "Nous mettons en place sur les côtés. Comme ça." Taking my left hand and creating a barrier on the outside of the proto-bowl, Jonas pressed my right hand into the inside and lifted up. The sides grew—equally from magic and physics. Almost finished, he tapped the fingers on my left hand like a pianist, creating ridges on the outside of the pot. "Voila." He took his hands off mine and switched off the motor.

The wheel slowed and eventually stopped. Where there

had just been a formless lump five minutes before, there was a flower vase. It's hard to explain how something could literally come from nothing. I wondered if Jonas knew what the pot would look like in his mind before he started. Did he keep to a mental blueprint as his fingers did the work? Or did he operate in barely organized chaos? Jonas tossed me a towel to wipe my hands.

"I know your problem," I said, tossing the towel back. "You're too dreamy for your own good."

"I do not understand."

"Of course you don't." I got up from the chair, but couldn't bear to look away from the vase. "It's really beautiful, Jonas. I can't get over it."

"It's a simple pot."

We closed up shop, turned off the lights, and shut the front door tight before journeying uphill.

"You didn't answer my question from before. Why come back now?"

"Henri sent me a letter. He wants to open the factory. I have to come back."

"How long has it been closed?"

"Twenty years. Many, many potters worked here once. It was the biggest factory in Europe."

"What happened?"

"Fighting. When his mother and father died, his brothers and sisters wanted to sell and move to the city. But Henri loved pots. So he paid money to buy the factory. But too much. He did not have enough money to keep the factory open. So it closed. It is always his dream to open it again."

At the top of the hill, we could see silhouettes in front of the house, black shadows cast by the indoor lights. Henri and Angelique, no doubt.

"Je déteste ça," Jonas said, keeping his eyes trained straight ahead.

"I'm sorry," I told him, motioning toward the fun times ahead. "This is probably going to hurt." I peeled off the trail, slicing through two terraces holding some terracotta statues of the Virgin Mary holding baby Jesus. I said a silent prayer as I watched Jonas join the shadows waiting for him.

Thirteen

s you could imagine, the first month of Principal Lewis's original recipe class schedule had left me little more than a greenish smear on the gym floor—the same gym floor that was being trotted on by soulless boarding school girls prancing in front of equally soulless boarding school boys at St. Gertie's annual Mazquerade Bash. Now, you may have some questions, which I will now preemptively answer: 1) I don't know why Masquerade suddenly contained a Z. At least the dance committee didn't call it *Mazquerade Bash X-Treme!!!!!!* And 2) Yes, I do know why St. Gertie's was basically holding a Halloween dance at the end of September. The answer is Samhain, as in they did not want to celebrate the high pagan feast day, on account of the school being a bastion of Catholic morality. Thus the solution: celebrate faux Halloween a month earlier and add a douche-baggy Z to the name.

As for me? I was not about to attend this little soirée. I was too busy witnessing the intrepid explorers of the Starship Enterprise, led by one James Tiberius Kirk, as they tried to wrest control of the Genesis torpedo away from 20th century genetic overlord, Khan Noonien Singh. It was just getting to the part where the brain slugs crawl into Chekhov's ear when someone knocked on my door.

"What's the password?" I yelled. Oh man, Khan does not play games.

"How about 'none of our doors lock'?" said Shannon, who showed herself in. Shuffling in with her was a small troupe of girls. They were Shannon's friends. Sometimes they'd pop in while Shannon was tutoring me to exchange the regular gossipy bullshit and, most strangely, drop off bottles of Coke for her. I mostly stuck to conjugation and stayed out of the chit-chat.

"Aren't you coming to the dance?" Shannon asked.

"And miss Spock's life-defining sacrifice?" I said. She blinked and waited. Was I not clear? "No. I am not going to the dance. I don't like dances. I don't like people. I don't have a costume." Then the peanut gallery chimed in:

"You could be, like, a sexy schoolgirl," said Montgomery Scott (dressed as a Minnie Mouse). Yes, this girl's parents named their daughter after the Enterprise's chief engineer, which was a win in my book.

"Or a sexy teacher if you had some glasses," suggested Carrie "Spider" Williamson, whose nickname came from the fact that she took up and won a dare to last an entire day only saying the word "spider." She was dressed as the Black Cat, Spiderman's bad girl sometimes ally/sometimes enemy.

Angela Wong, dressed as a ballerina, waved all those ideas aside. Of all the students I'd met at St. Gertie's, she was the one student I respected for being a hard-ass, even if I didn't like her all of the time. "A sexy serial killer," she said. "They look like everyone else. Except, y'know, sexy."

"All fantastic ideas," I told them. "I'm not going."

"Told you," Angela said to Shannon.

"We should show her, Angie."

Angela shook her head. "No."

Well, well. Things just got more interesting. "Show me what?"

"Angie, she's cool." Shannon again. While she and I got along at our tutoring sessions, it wasn't like we were friends. I mean, I kinda grew to like her company, but she had her group of girls, and I had "Bones" McCoy and Mr. Sulu. But now she and Angela were having a mini-argument over me and this secret thing they did/did not want to tell me. Truth? I wasn't really listening. I couldn't keep my eyes off Shannon's costume—a shredded sleeveless T, ratty jeans, oversized black leather jacket—a perfect Sid Vicious. Out of that schoolgirl outfit she looked completely different. No, she was completely different. It was kind of hot. No, really hot, really . . . wait. What the fuck? "Ryland won't tell. Right, Ry?"

"Um. Yeah. I mean no. I won't tell." I must have been convincing enough—or perhaps Shannon had been charming enough—because next thing I knew, she and I were sneaking through the halls away from the gym while the others headed toward the dance to call dibs on a table.

"Where are we going?" I said.

"Shh! C'mon." I followed Shannon through unlit hallways, totally trusting her sense of direction. Eventually, we got to a section of the building I recognized—the doorway to the secret passageway.

History lesson time: Sometime in the early to mid-1980s, a group of students at St. Gertie's—a proto girl gang who called themselves "The Pretties in Pink" (gag me with a spoon)—uncovered two things. One, a secret underground tunnel that linked up the east and west wings on the north side of campus. So, ordinarily, you'd have to wind your way around all the main halls of the school to get from the east entrance to the west entrance. Not so with the now-not-so-secret passage. They got an award that's still there in the trophy case in the main hallway for their "Determination and Ingenuity"—yeah, if determination and ingenuity was what you needed to spot a hidden door handle next to the fire extinguisher. After that, St. Gertie girls used the secret passage like any other school corridor. That's the spiel Shannon gave me when she showed it to me the first time. But this time, I got the rest of the story.

See, the school was none the wiser about the Pretties' other, much more important discovery. In this secret passage, unbeknownst to most, many of the bricks concealed little cubbies in the foundation. The same day that the Pretties originally uncovered the passage, they also uncovered what Shannon and company called THE STASH.

"Here." Shannon and I stood in the middle of the passage. No marks, no signals as to why we stopped in this particular pocket of shadow. And what does she do but take a bottle of Coke from her bag and place it into my hands.

"I'm not thirsty."

"You should have one sip."

Curiosity piqued, I unscrewed the top and bottoms up. "What did I just drink?"

"We don't know. There aren't any labels." Shannon knelt down and traced out a brick with her fingertips. Won't lie—I looked down her shirt. Holy mind-fuck, Batman. This kind of complication was not what I wanted. I was supposed to hate it here, get through this shit, and get out. That's what I wanted. Really.

Really?

"It gets stuck sometimes, but . . ." I heard cinder block grind on cinder block, and then: "Give me your phone." I handed it to Shannon, who told me to kneel down with her. And holy shit. Solomon's Mines of Booze. In that little hole, there were at least 20 smoked-glass bottles of different tinted liquid, none of them labeled. In front, was a folded piece of yellowed notebook paper that Shannon took out and handed to me. I unfolded it and read it by the dim cell phone LED:

Hey Girls!

If you're reading this, then you're having a pretty lucky day. Because you've just found THE STASH! Take good care of it like we have. Fill it back up if you run low. The future of St. Gertie's is at stake!

Rhonda, Edna, Chase, Vicky, Dana

"Angie found it last year, right before summer."

"You've been getting hammered all this time. Even in tutoring?"

"Especially tutoring. It's hard to keep my mind on . . ." She stopped. "I mean, it's pretty intense—French, I mean. Um, we should go. It's not good to hang around."

"Sure," I said. "Don't want anyone seeing us, right?"

"Right."

A hastily (and overly) spiked bottle of Mountain Dew later, we sat at a table in the gym, the thrumming heinousness of Chumbawumba liquefying my brain. I wasn't sure if I was drinking a whisky drink or a vodka drink, but it was a *something* drink, and holy fuck did I need it. Because this wasn't a dance. It was a re-enactment of *The Texas Chainsaw Massacre*, substitute the decrepit cannibal grandpa with sexy fill-in-the-blanks on one side of the gym and socially clueless MMO Masters dressed as *Dragonball Z* characters on the other.

And nary the twain shall meet.

So it's funny that single sex schools have dances at all, because, as I learned in Academic De-fucking-cathlon, balls and dances originated as events meant for high nobles to pick and choose their latest booty calls. Take away one of the sexes, and you take away the traditional point of the whole thing. But, ah! The schools had thought this one through. See, across town was another school with a similar predicament: St. Bartholomew's Academy for Young Gentlemen. One plus one equaling two and all . . .

"So . . ." How was I going to put this delicately? "Do these dances always make you want to swallow plutonium?"

Angela rolled her eyes, then downed another shot of the noxious cocktail Shan and I mixed. We each took turns, but even that stuff only helped to take the edge off. The dance still reeked of lameness. "Last year, Mr. Tanner was the DJ. Easy listening all night." Mr. Tanner was the school's physics and astronomy teacher—and also the blandest man alive. He could bore toasted Wonder Bread to death.

That's all I could take. I chugged down two gulps of the nasty juice, which made me want to die. Then I stood up. "Fine, I'll do it."

"What are you going to do?" asked Monte.

"What I do best." I'm a total sucker for those action movie walkaway lines.

"What do you do best?" Monte again.

"I'm going to save you all." Yes! What a fucking badass line!

"How are you going to do that?"

Dammit, Monte! Fine, if I had to do it, then I would. I whipped out the doozy, the crème de la crème of straight-to-the-gut, motherfucking epic lines:

"I have a plan."

"Oh?" said Monte. "What's your plan?" She looked up at me with her brown puppy dog eyes, but instead of petting and cuddling her, I wanted to set her up on a blind date with an industrial size woodchipper.

"Just wait here, okay?" Then, putting on a fake Austrian accent, I proclaimed, "I'll be back." I broke out in a full sprint away from the table. And even then, I caught the beginning of Monte calling out, "When will you be . . ."

Ignoring that, I set my sights dead ahead, directly across

the dance floor to the enemy camp. What I was doing there was simple: I was using the gift that my lesbian ancestors had passed down to me. As I looked around at all the guys, I could hear the pulse in my ears, feel myself being pulled along. And then there! Across the way, I saw him, dressed in an eye-piercing, silver-sequined, one-piece disco superstar suit. I wove around tables to meet him, and he did the same for me.

Our gay-dars had found each other.

We took each other's hands and stepped onto the dance floor.

"Hi," I said. "My name's Ryland."

"Rohit," he said. "What are you wearing?" Ah, yes. *My costume.* Seeing that I had exactly five minutes to conceive of and execute such a thing, I was left with few practical options. So, I pulled the white sheet off my bed, cut out eyeholes, and pinned up a pair a panties and my bra with its sad little A-cups. Voila—sexy *ghost*, only the sexiest fucking costume on the planet. I mean, how would you know I had anything on under there? The only drawback was that it was balls hot dancing under that thing. So not a minute into the song, I pulled off that shit and threw it to the side of the dance floor, where it landed in a sweaty pile.

"Eew," said Rohit. "But whatever. We have a lot of work to do." Of course we did. At every school there was someone like me: a little off, a little anxious, and a little too schemy for our own good. I was sure that if I looked hard enough, I'd find my counterpart at St. Bart's. Alone, we had no chance to shake things up. Together, we were a fucking neutron bomb.

"We need to stir up some shit."

"My thoughts exactly," he said. Rohit related his idea to me right then and there. It was obvious that he had thought about this for a while—ever since the junior mixer. As we danced, we hashed out a plan so nuts, so cockamamie that it *just might work*. We went over our roles one more time, making sure that we had every action coordinated. "Do you know all the names of the girls in your class?"

"More or less. I think."

"Let's make the call." I whipped out my cell and quickly texted Shannon:

I need your help. Run to my room and get my iPod and bring it back. Hurry!

Yes, I still had an iPod, because creaky-ass antiques were sometimes the best things for the job, and as a friend confided in me once, Spotify is secretly an alien conspiracy to beam "stupid rays" (her words, not mine) directly into our brains.

Out the corner of my eye, I saw Shannon take her phone from her pocket, check it, then dart out the gym door. The plan was a go. As the song ended, we took our leave back to our respective battle stations. I waited until Shannon got back to lay out what the girls had to do to make this work. iPod in hand, I scrolled to the right folder, and then the right song.

"All right, men."

"We're all girls here," said Spider.

"Metaphor," I said. "We're going to have to pull out the big guns." I held up my iPod. The girls looked at each other. "Okay fine. I know you guys know me about as well as that deranged guy who hangs out under the highway overpass eating paste, but what do you have to lose?"

Shannon gulped down the rest of the booze, and came up snarling. "What do we do?"

"When you hear your name called, come to the dance floor. That's it." After Shannon's little foray into face-melting awesomeness, the rest of the crew was on board. Getting that go ahead, I made my way up to the stage area. Across the way, Rohit was walking to meet me.

What the hell was I doing? I wasn't even supposed to be there. I should have been trying to memorize the starship Reliant's shield code in case I ever faced it in space combat. And what was that moment back in the tunnel between Shannon and me? That was a moment, right?

Gameface, Ryland. No time for angsty bullshit.

Rohit and I met in the middle of the stage, on either side of the table that Ms. Janowski was using as her base of operations as DJ. Beside the soundboard lay a stack of CDs that she planned to play during the course of the night. Aw, man. Creed? Matchbox 20?

"Can I help you two?" she asked, reaching for her Nickelback CD. We had come just in time.

"Ms. Janowski," I said, drawing closer to her ear. "I think I saw a pair of white mice scurrying around at the back of the gym." Ms. Janowski was St. Gertie's resident biology teacher, and her two best friends in the world were her pet mice, Ralph and Joseph Fiennes. "Should I call an exterminator?"

"No! I'll . . ." and then she ran off. The coast was now clear. I set up the iPod and flipped the MIC IN on the soundboard, and Rohit stepped to the mic stand at the center of the stage.

"Hello students of St. Gertrude and St. Bart's! It's time to announce the Mazquerade Bash Royal Court!" It is a singular feeling to have a hundred people look up at you at the same time with the same facial expression, that being "so you actually are the crazy guy underneath the highway overpass who eats paste!" And rightfully so, because there was no such thing as the "Mazquerade Bash Royal Court." Rohit delicately plucked a piece of paper from somewhere on his person. The paper was blank. As if that mattered. "Music please."

I hit PLAY and the familiar bass of "Another One Bites the Dust" (the karaoke version—courtesy of my days at Mr. Beaver's) blared out the speakers. "This year's Mazquerade Duke is Vladimir Fromgarten! Please step to the middle of the floor!" A nervous looking boy with pudgy cheeks and dressed like Maximus from *Gladiator* stepped into the center of the dance floor—prompted along by his cackling friends. I wasn't about to leave him there by his lonesome.

"And the Mazquerade Duchess is Carrie Williamson!" I announced. And to her credit, Spidey didn't hesitate at all. She got up and strolled right over to poor Vlad's side. We wasted no time with the next announcement—the baron and baroness—and then the third, and the fourth, and fifth, and so on. The point, you probably have guessed, was to give everyone a title, and thus give everyone an *obligation* to dance. As we winnowed down the as yet un-nobled, the names of girls I knew grew fewer and fewer, until I stopped Rohit just before announcing the "Grand Poobah and Poobah-ess."

"I'm spent." There were five remaining girls, and on the other side, six boys stood wondering what was going on. "I don't know any more names."

"Then start the music," he said.

"You're sure you know what you're doing?"

"As a heart attack."

At the same time I leapt back to the soundboard, Rohit announced, "Those who have not been awarded yet have a very special job. Please come up to the stage." On cue, the remaining girls and guys funneled up the steps to the center around Rohit. I started the next song and jumped back to center stage in time to hear his instructions: "Okay. You go with her, you with him, you and you over there. You all are part of the Royal Dance Troupe. All you have to do is dance. Dance when the music starts. Keep dancing until the end, and, most importantly, you have to always dance with the guy or girl closest to you. I may push you or pull you away, but always remember—find the nearest girl or guy, take their hands, and dance until the song is done. You got it?"

Everyone in the circle nodded except one barrel-chested, crew-cut-wearing kid who said, "What the hell is this, Patel?"

"You're in my world, now, Baumbrewster, so I suggest you listen or Lizzie Paraguay is going to see what a chump you are." Baumbrewster huffed and frowned, but ultimately backed down. That little altercation settled, everyone took positions around Rohit and I, who were paired dead center.

"You got my back?" he said.

"I'm your Hutch, Starsky." Then I launched into the intro of "Don't Stop Me Now."

That's right. Queen to the rescue. As soon as the vocals hit high gear, Rohit left the mic to concentrate on choreographing the people on stage. He pulled couples apart and pushed others together, all the while looking like he was part of the dancing—and it was legit, like it wasn't planned, y'know, ten minutes before. Then there was my job, which was injecting enough Freddie Mercury into this sonovabitch to make the gym explode. The dance floor below started to wind up slowly, getting faster as I sang louder. While I didn't have Freddie's stratospheric range, I made up for it with gumption and sheer volume.

I concentrated on two things up there: staying on key and spotting Shannon on the floor. My heart was pounding double time—from the excitement swirling all around me and the excitement that felt like a hot coal in the middle of my stomach. I mean, she was my French tutor. She came from an upper crust, genteel family with 2.5 kids, a mansion, and a boat. Two boats. I was supposed to beat her up and steal her lunch money.

And then I saw them. At the back of the gym was Ms. Janowski, carrying her mouse cage. Stepping through the doors with her was Principal Lewis. Oh shit. I wanted to run, but she'd seen me already (and would have suspected me even if she hadn't). All I could do was finish the song.

As soon as Freddie's keys faded out, and everyone in the gym clapped and cheered, I knew I was fucked. I tried to soak it all in because the glory would be short-lived. I heard the massive click and whir of the main gym lights, and I instinctively shut my eyes. My eyelids lit up that warm orange glow.

"Alright, everyone! We're done here!" the principal screamed. "St. Bart's students, get your stuff and line up at the bus! And you . . ." She was looking at me. I could feel it. If I kept my eyes shut, she couldn't turn me to stone. "You just had to do something, didn't you?" Was she talking to someone else? "Ryland Taggart! Are you deaf?" Well, fuck. I opened my eyes to see a mass exodus of students leaving the gym. Principal Lewis's death gaze beat down on me. "Both of you—to my office. Now!"

The chairs in front of Principal Lewis's desk were once again deceptively comfortable. I would have warned Rohit if it wasn't already too late. He sat back, his arms resting on the gigantic puffy armrests, looking completely relaxed. So when Principal Lewis sat at her desk, he was unprepared.

"What kind of shit was that?" The windows rattled. The floor shook. Fear flashed across Rohit's face.

"Ms. Lewis—"

"That's Principal Lewis! Am I clear . . ." She turned to me. "What's his name?"

"Rohit," I said, as quiet as Ralph Fiennes.

"Rohit! Do you understand me?"

"Yes, sir. I mean, ma'am."

"And you." Oh, that you was filled with the vilest, blackest hatred on Earth—blacker than the LaBrea Tar Pits, and nastier than raw sewage the morning after Mardi Gras. "I warned you about this."

"Technically, you didn't warn me about *this*." Rohit's eyes bugged out, as if I'd pinched a shit on a priest's head during Easter Sunday mass. C'mon. What the hell else could she do to me? "Maybe, in the future, we could, like make a list of things that you want to warn me about, because it's probably a really long list. Like, it could be a PowerPoint or an Excel spread—"

"Shut up! Just shut up!" P. Lewis set her forehead on her desk. "Rohit!"

"Yes!"

"I can't officially do anything to you, but I can recommend to Father Xavier that you be given two weeks mandatory detention."

"Yes, ma'am."

"Now get the hell out."

"Yes, ma'am."

Rohit made a hasty exit out the door, leaving me alone in Principal Lewis's clutches. She still rested her head on the desk, muttering something about meat hooks and a fire pit.

"Maybe you were right," she said. "Maybe I should have thrown your ass out on the first day." She lifted her head up. "I don't have much choice now. What's your father's phone number?" There it was. The prize my eyes had been on since the first day, and yet, I didn't want to go. I couldn't believe it and didn't want to say it because I couldn't answer why without seeing her face. Shannon's face.

"I want to stay."

"What?"

"I want—"

"I heard you the first time," she said. "I just said that for dramatic effect."

"Please, Principal Lewis. I don't want to go."

She sat back in her chair, then picked up her phone. "Look. What you did out there—you did it in front of teachers, in front of another school. Give me the number."

I stayed silent.

"Fine. If you won't tell me, I'll look it up." She hit the power button on her computer and it beeped to life. Routines and subroutines filled the monitor. Those meaningless numbers and letters would be my epitaph if I didn't say something.

"This isn't fair," I said, now dead serious. "You kept me here. You gave me the Titanic of all class schedules and then piled on the extracurriculars. And I could have dogged it, but I didn't. I'm still here."

"You're getting a C in Modern European History," she said above a symphony of mouse clicks.

"A C+. That doesn't count the extra credit paper."

More mouse clicks. Then: "206-334-8721."

That was Dad's office number. Principal Lewis picked up the phone and held it to her ear. I flopped back into my chair, not knowing what else I could do or say to plead my case. So I made one last desperate stab.

"Principal Lewis, how long has it been since you've sat through one of those dances?"

She put down the phone.

"Because, frankly, they suck," I said. "It's like someone decided to carbon copy a dance from 1993 and called it a day." I know, I know. It was a dangerous move—the debate equivalent of the Hail Mary pass. Did I have another choice? "Most students would rather shove pencils into their ears."

"That's enough," she said. "We're not in the party planning business."

"You don't even ask the girls what they want. Y'know, like poll or something? They work really hard all the time. They deserve something fun."

"Hmm." That was a good sign. "Maybe it's a good idea to conduct school-wide polls before social events."

"Yeah, something like that!"

"Good idea," she said. "That can be your job."

"Exsqueeze me?"

"You seem to know the pulse of what's going on out there, so why not you? The next dance is the Winter Formal in December, and it will be at St. Bartholomew's. So before that, I'd like a personally delivered report on what the St. Gertrude student body thinks about . . . everything."

I couldn't talk. The only thing that came out of my mouth was a stream of spit oozing out the side. I used my shirt to clean it up.

"Deliver it to me a week or so before the formal and make sure you make copies for all the teachers," she said. "Or you're expelled. That's fair, right? Feel free to use PowerPoint or maybe even an Excel spreadsheet."

I came out of the principal's office that night relatively unscathed. I wasn't going to be thrown out (yet), nor did I have to serve detention (yet), but why did I feel like a peg boy on a pirate ship? When I reached the door to my room, I stood there, my nerves fried by the night's highs and lows. I decided, once I could move, to bury my head in my pillow for a minimum of fifty-seven hundred years.

"Hey," I heard behind me. It was Shannon. She leaned

against the wall with her arms crossed and her lip curled up—a perfect Sid Vicious impression. "Did you really plan that?"

"Would it impress you if I said I did?"

She started walking toward me. "That was the best dance in the history of this school."

"Also the shortest. Principal Lewis was not pleased."

"It was totally worth it."

"You think so?"

"Yeah." She was so close. One more step, and she was pressing against me. My arm moved without me thinking, my fingers reaching beneath her jacket and tracing her spine upward. "I even saw Monte making out with some guy in the bathroom."

Her hot breath was on my neck.

"If that's what it takes to shut Monte up . . ."

We locked eyes.

"You can shut me up."

Fourteen

y feet felt frozen. That was my sole sensation, devoid of any other sight, sound, taste, or smell. A moment later, I heard water trickling through a small opening, a sound that grew louder and louder, until it became the roar of rapids. Then the unmistakable scents of freshly turned dirt and wet stone hit my nose, my tongue. Finally, the color switched on, and I was surrounded by the green of hanging tree branches, the gold of sunlight sneaking between the leaf edges. I was at the center of it all, floating in the middle of a frigid river.

In the distance, a single burning dot of orange flared up, and from that point, the rest of the scene lit up. Stones and moss and crags and the trunks of the trees where the low-lying branches found their roots. They all came into view, but they were not alone.

Someone was watching me from the riverbank.

"Buongiorno," he called out, not bothering to take the cigarette out of his mouth.

My breath left me. Paolo. "But you're . . . then I'm . . ." I flailed my arms out, groping for a handhold. At the same time, I arched my toes in the hopes of touching the river bottom. I only felt squishy ground threaded by sharp branches that threatened to dig into my heels and pin me to that spot.

"Pazza," he said. Paolo somehow laughed while inhaling on his cigarette, making it blaze red at the end. This place—I was inside Frau Müller's photo. What did Jonas call it? *Le Jardin de Pierres*. Next to Paolo were statues, the moss on their stony shoulders glowing a faint green. I spotted the tinge of unreality on everything. A dream. Was Mom there too? Behind the trees? Just past the bend in the river? That thought was enough to thaw my body out of its momentary stasis. I swam forward, toward the shore.

"This place," he said. "No good."

"Try being in the water!" I shouted between big breaths and breast strokes.

"Bah," he said. "I come here to tell you. You are too slow."

I had gotten close enough to the shore that the water came up to chest level once I placed my feet down. Total relief. I hadn't swum in more than ten years—my depressingly lonely day of water slides at WaterWorld hardly counted—and I was out of practice.

"Is that what you needed to tell me? To get my ass in gear?" I was already on edge. He had to have something else for me. Maybe some directions on where to go next? Or information about Dora? Dora! I wanted to say her name, but he cut me off before I could press my tongue to the roof of my mouth.

"Call Tania. You must speak to her."

"But Herr Cutter—"

"Bah! Not *il tedesco*—you. She needs you."

"Let me know what's going on."

"No."

"Why? Tell me what I'm supposed to do!"

"Call Tania. This is what must happen."

I wanted to scream, but it wouldn't have done any good. Was it possible that he was even more stubborn dead than alive? "I don't even know her number! How can I call her?" I yelled. "In fact, stay there. I'm coming!" I trudged toward Paolo, but the stony bottom gave way to a gulf of mud.

Paolo put his cigarette out against one of the statutes. "You are just like her," he said. "You never listen." As much as I tried to lift my legs out of the muck, it held me fast in place. I pulled with my arms, but I still couldn't get my legs to budge. "When you talk to Tania, eh—you tell her something. You say: *Lei non lo mancherà.*"

"I'm assuming you're not going to tell me what that means."

"She will not miss it."

Next thing I knew, I was on the edge of my bed pad . . . and then I wasn't. Not a big, you might think, but then you'd be wrong. See, after rolling off, my foot got caught on a ladder leaning against the wall. Said ladder then fell, hitting me square in the jaw. And because the universe was not done, the top of the ladder hit a shelf, on which sat a bucket . . . of sharp, heavy nails.

I walked down to breakfast trying on excuses for my cuts and bruises—something other than "the supply closet kicked my ass." Everyone was seated and eating when I got down to the kitchen. Jonas sat quiet and sullen at one end of the table, and Angelique sat at the other, holding her coffee mug, eyes transfixed on a point on the other side of the big front window. Henri was in the middle of telling a story about his friend, Theirry, in Carcasonne, and how his saxophone playing had whipped all the dogs in his neighborhood into a frenzy.

When Madeleine saw me, she rushed over with a hand towel to blot my full-body stigmata. I tried to tell her I was fine, but she wouldn't listen. She forced me to sit down, jammed a cup of hot tea into my hand, and cut me some bread.

"C'est bon. Je veux vous parler," said Henri, looking at me. He refilled his coffee cup, and took his sweet time buttering a piece of toast. All the while, my anxiety was building. Finally, the money, and none too soon. After a bite, a dip of his toast in his coffee, a bit more butter, another dip, he was ready to begin. Henri explained that while he admired and appreciated me helping Jonas, he couldn't just hand over a hundred Euros. That was a hella lot of scratch. My heart sank. I needed that moolah to continue my mad quest to . . . wherever I was supposed to go next. Nevermind eating or sleeping in the rain. And forget about a trip back to home. I'd have to steal a boat.

"Papa," Madeleine interrupted. She called him over and whispered something into his ear. After she was done telling him what she needed to tell him, she stood by, waiting for his answer.

"Madeleine . . ."

"Papa!"

He nodded, reluctantly. "Bonne idée."

"Merci, Papa." Then she kissed Henri on the cheek before he left to walk about the grounds. Breakfast broke up after that, with everyone but Madeleine and I leaving to prep for pottery-making. That's when she laid out the good news.

"Henri says that you can earn the money."

"That is awesome!" I hugged her.

"D'accord!" she squeaked. "You will work with me."

I let her go. "Aye, aye, Captain."

"Come. I will show you our new mission."

I changed into more work-worthy clothes before we went off into the fields. I figured that we had a task suited to my abysmal talent level, but nope. No simple clean up. No scrubbing pans. Madeleine led me down to the factory, where the potter's wheels were in full rev. We rounded the side of the building to where a curious little machine that kinda looked like R2-D2 was sitting all by its lonesome.

"Voila." She started to crank the ancient looking thing, which was, as it turned out, a cement mixer. It rumbled and tumbled and sprayed dried cement chips all over us. I kept mental notes as she explained exactly what "our new mission" was, which was to take the bags of dry cement, one bag at a time, pour the contents into the mixer, add water from a trickling faucet inside the warehouse, and churn, baby, churn. Post-mixing, we'd then transfer the whole mess to the most rickety looking wheelbarrow I had ever seen and then push said wheelbarrow through the warehouse to the far corner, where the old cement foundation had eroded away to rubble.

Easy peasy. Riiiiiiiiight.

I pulled water duty while Madeleine handled R2. She picked up the sack of cement like it was filled with corn flakes, slung it over her shoulder, slit it lengthwise with a box-cutter like she was gutting a fresh kill, and poured the gray powder in. That bag was twenty kilos!

Yeah! I know!

"Ça va bien?" she said, as she paused to tie a bandana around her hair.

"Oui," I said, still shocked at how easy she made it look. I poured the first bucket of water into the mixer while Madeleine turned the crank.

"It will become hotter today." I was already breaking a sweat, and it was going to get *hotter*? As it turns out, the south of France is a scorcher in the summertime, which is particularly annoying when you're in the sun cranking out cement. As soon as we filled up the wheelbarrow, Madeleine wheeled it inside.

"C'est simple," said Madeleine, raising her voice to be heard over the motors. She tipped the wheelbarrow over, and the cement oozed onto the floor, filling the cracks and the pits. With long ditchdigger shovels, we spread the cement as evenly as we could.

I lost count of how many times we repeated this process. All I know is, eventually, I looked like Rosie the Riveter, bandana and all, and Madeleine sported pigtails because her hair kept sticking to her forehead. It wasn't until we were nearly done filling up the corner with cement that I spotted Guy and Marcel standing across the way, enjoying a cigarette . . . and the view.

"Don't stop," said Guy. "Vous faites un bon travail." Marcel's only comment consisted of a puff of smoke that he let waft from his mouth.

"Trou de cul," Madeleine muttered, stamping down a lump in the cement with her shovel like she was braining a plastic rodent in a heated game of *Whac-a-Mole*.

"Ne fait pas le con," I said, which only seemed to encourage him. Sorry, but you don't heckle someone doing hard labor to make your life better. Shit, I was ready to throw down right then, but Madeleine held me back. Yeah, better to let some steam out lifting and cranking and wheeling and smoothing. Eventually, we finished mixing all the cement and spreading it into the cracks. The muscle part—the paid part—came next. In order to make the cement perfectly level with the floor, it had to be evened out by a large, flat thing. Shovels wouldn't cut it.

"How are we going to do this?"

"Comme ça." She went behind a stack of round plaster molds and came back hauling an iron beam. By herself. Like it was made of sugar and spice and everything nice.

"So why, exactly, do you need me?"

"Watch." I did as boss-lady said. I watched as she laid the beam on the floor at the edge of the wet cement. Then she took my hand and pulled it down so that I was squatting next to her. She quickly explained the plan: together we'd push and pull the beam, back and forth, and at the same time, we'd inch it toward the wall. This process would make the floor level, all right. Once it all dried, it would be a nice place to hold a memorial service in our honor—maybe even hang a plaque stating how we'd given our lives to even out the playing field.

On her mark, we started. Back and forth, up to the wall. Madeleine was doing most of the work. More and more, I tried to distract myself away from the pain in my arms and in my legs. So instead of smelling iron and sawdust, my nose focused on subtler scents, like sweat—Madeleine's sweat. A scent that was sweet and sour and perfect. Pheromones, man. And that wasn't all. Every time we pulled the girder, my bare arm would touch hers. Every time . . . I mean, her skin felt cool and smooth, her arm hard with muscle. Like I needed any more reminders that I'd been living the last six months like a misanthropic monk in Austin.

In short order, we had leveled the cement, shoveling the excess back into the wheelbarrow. And that was it. Lacking the strength to stand, much less celebrate, she and I sat against the wall and drank water from a pair of dainty teacups I spotted amongst the rest of the pottery.

"Nous sommes terminées?" I asked. *Please, please, please let us be done.*

"Mais oui." We clinked teacups and drank our hero's libation. "You did good."

"I hardly did anything."

"Ce n'est pas vrai." Oh, but it was true. How could Henri

even think of hiring other people to do it? Madeleine didn't need anyone to help her do this job, especially not my weak ass. She'd done me a favor, given me an excuse for her dad to pay me. I wouldn't forget that.

"Madeleine!" a certain whiny bitch-voice called out. Madeleine frowned and struggled to get up.

"I have to go," she said, frowning.

"It's cool," I reassured her. "That chick hates me anyway."

"Oh, oui," said Madeleine.

"I'll visit Jonas. Just go keep Miss Stink-Eye distracted."

Very, very reluctantly, Madeleine left. I got up and wandered about, finding Jonas in his cubby, churning out pieces. "You've been busy," I said, pointing to all the jugs, plates, and cups set on the shelves to dry.

"And you, too?"

"Yeah, but your sister did most of it. I just stood next to her and took credit." I paused to look around to make sure the coast was clear of angry ex-fiancées. "So, I don't know if this is too personal, but how did it go last night?"

"Henri said that we have to forgive. Opening the factory is more important."

"That's practical, I guess."

"But Angelique—"

"Jonas! Jonas!" Guy came running into Jonas's studio panting and holding his still-open flip phone. "Yeti joue ce soir au Bar Ô Crée Louche!" Before I could ask Guy to explain a little more, Jonas agreed for both of us that we'd go that night to a music show starring someone named "Yeti." Didn't know the abominable snowman did song requests.

A few things about this part of France. Apart from Toulouse, the landscape was made up mostly of hilly roads and isolated hamlets and farms. The bar we went to was not an exception to this rule. Situated right at the edge of the otherwise sleepy village of Engomer, France (population: 297), Bar Ô Crée Louche was a noisy, smoky, boisterous island in a calm sea. Second: this pottery thing was THE thing to do around there. When we walked into the bar, a swarm of people descended on our group. Marcel and Guy exchanged cheek kisses with other dudes, and even Angelique got into the act with a bunch of chatty girls who had huddled themselves into the corner booth. The lion's share of attention, though, was heaped upon Jonas, who entered the place like Aragorn marching into Gondor. Guys and girls alike swarmed him, hugged him, asked him how he was, inquired as to the texture of the clay in Martinique. All these people greeting him were potters, too.

Madeleine and I ended up standing next to the bar while Jonas and the rest of them melted into the crowd. Up on stage was a dude with a cowboy hat strumming an acoustic guitar (the opening act, I guessed) and singing "Highwayman" in a cool Johnny Cash baritone.

"You know this song?" I yelled at Madeleine.

She shook her head.

"Are you okay?"

"Oui. C'est rien," she said. But it wasn't nothing.

Something was bothering her. She was watching Jonas, Guy, and Marcel as they laughed with other bar patrons. Even Angelique looked happy in this element. But Madeleine . . . I knew that feeling. Knowing that you were not like the others around you. Not that they had anything against you, but they all knew that there was something different. She wasn't a potter like the rest of her friends, her own brother. She could never relate to the glaze and clay talk, the name dropping of obscure artists from far-flung Romanian provinces. I could relate. At UT, I hadn't said a complete sentence to anyone—save for Herr Cutter—the entire semester I'd been there. That's what I deserved for coming in a semester late, when cliques were already fully formed, complete with inside jokes. Too much like high school, and look what happened there. It was much easier for me to be the girl in the cafeteria who silently scowled as she ate her country fried steak.

"I wanted to tell you thank you."

"What?" Madeleine strained to hear over the music.

"Before, I mean. You didn't have to help me like that."

"You helped Jonas."

"Yeah, but . . ." It was like she wasn't in the same room with me. This wasn't the same girl who hauled girders to and fro like she was freebasing 'roids. It wasn't right.

"Stay here," I said to her.

"Qu'est-ce que tu fais?"

"Quelque chose de stupide." And with that, I stepped into and through the throng over to the young Johnny Cash who had just stepped off the stage.

"Mais oui!" I said to him, dishing up the "rock on!"

symbol with my hand (which doubled as the UT Longhorns symbol). "J'aime ta musique!"

"American?" he said.

"Oui!"

"What the hell are you doing here?"

"Hanging. So when is this Yeti person is coming on?"

"Twenty minutes, I think."

"Can I borrow your axe? I just need five minutes."

"Bien sûr! You will sing for us? What songs?"

"Song," I said, taking his guitar. "I only know one, and I don't think you've heard it." I climbed up onto the stage, under the lights, imagining that I was playing for an audience of one—that girl in the corner sipping her wine. She waved. That's all I needed.

"Uh . . . salut. Je m'appelle Ryland, et je suis des États-Unis. Cette chanson s'appelle 'Orange.' Je la joue pour Madeleine." I met her eyes one more time. "Mon amie." Then I made sure my back was straight as I pressed my fingertips into the strings, hoping that my uncalloused fingers could survive that one song, hoping that I remembered the chords, praying that I remembered the words. And go.

Eyes fall
Slowly to my feet
Time crawls
Trapped in heartbeat
And you could be here darling
For many lifetimes
As you could be here tonight

My hands
Reach where words can't go
And these demands
Lose weight half 'cross the world
For you could be here with me
For many lifetimes
As I could be here tonight

Teach me
Inside these walls of orange
To feel again
What had become foreign
And you could be here darling
For many lifetimes
As you could be here

When I finished, my fingertips were numb. My hands, arms, feet, lips, eyelids—no feeling. It had been almost a year since I'd heard that song played live, almost a year since Cas had played it for me. He'd never believe that I'd ever want to hear that song again, let alone play it for people I didn't know halfway across the world. But there it was—out there. The song wasn't his and mine anymore.

The crowd, which had been silent a second before, erupted into applause. I jumped off the stage and handed the guitar back to Johnny.

"Did you write that song?"

"No," I said. "Not really my thing. But thanks for the guitar!" I let the movement of the crowd carry me away from stage as I heard the voices curl around me:

Qui est là?

. . . des États-Unis?

Je pense que c'était une chanson de Coldplay.

Je pourrais jouer mieux que ça . . .

I waded through people back to Madeleine. She was all smiles. I love it when a plan comes together.

"T'etais extraordinaire!" she said, and she kissed me. On the lips. It lasted a second, but I could still feel it when she pulled away from my face. Just in time.

"You are a hoss!" shouted Jonas, coming through the crowd.

Joined by Marcel and Guy, we rearmed ourselves with drinks and secured a table butted up against the front window streaked with raindrops. My days as Tania's lucky charm were over. Even so, it felt good to not be in crisis mode for the first time in a while. So why did I want to be somewhere else? Anywhere—as long as Madeleine was with me? She had been holding my hand ever since I came off that stage and still held it under the table.

"Henri told me that you did good today," Jonas said.

"All this one," I said, pointing to Madeleine. She blushed and knocked my hand away. Ruining this precious moment was Angelique, who burst from the crowd, smacked her hand on the table, and screamed a single word: "Putain!"

I hung my head. Please not this now.

"You win," she spat—the first English I'd heard her speak. "Everyone is against me."

"For the last time, I'm not trying to steal your man or your friends!"

Not listening, or not caring—did it matter really?—Angelique stormed out of the bar. All of us at the table looked at each other. Slowly, our eyes settled on Jonas.

"She is like Stalin," said Jonas, face to palm. "I want to go away again."

"And when Henri calls?" I asked.

He looked up. "Why do you care? You will leave soon."

"I . . ." He couldn't know how much that hurt right then. I gathered myself and spoke. "Yeah, but . . ." I looked over at Madeleine, then turned back. "I'm still here. So I care."

"Go. I will find a ride home," said Marcel to Jonas, just as Yeti, the headlining act, took the stage. She wasn't abominable, let alone a snowman. Instead, she was a small-framed woman with an accordion strapped to her neck. Her first rousing song told about a man in Montpelier who broke her heart. So she slashed his tires but left a note on his windshield to apologize.

"Moi aussi," said Guy. "I will stay, too."

"Et toi?" Jonas asked me. Despite my gut telling me to run away, I nodded my head. Jonas, me, and Madeleine made our way out into the rain and over to where Angelique stood, wet and miserable, next to the car. We piled in and rode back to Henri's in silence. Madeleine held me the whole way back to Henri's. The tense atmosphere in the car was so thick and gooey that you couldn't cut it with a chainsaw, burn it with a flamethrower, or blow it to hell with a BFG 9000. Neither Angelique nor Jonas could bear to look at the other, and neither I nor Madeline dared to break that deadly silence. Maybe it was enough that we were there to share Jonas's pain. What else are friends for, right?

When we pulled up next to the house, Angelique bluntly ordered us out of the van.

"Jonas?" I said, my hand on the door handle.

"It is okay," he said. "It is time."

Madeleine and I jumped out and started walking toward the house. The rain was heavy, steady. Guy was right about something—that was a conversation that we didn't want, and really had no right, to hear. Still, I wished that he didn't have to be alone . . . or I wished that I didn't feel like I'd abandoned him. Then again, he made his choice one year ago, and this was the fallout.

Madeleine and I held hands on our way to the house's front door. I was immediately aware of how tight she was holding me and also aware that I was at the crossroads of two paths. I could keep going straight ahead, or I could interrupt the *should happen* with the *could happen* . . .

Fuck this overthinking bullshit.

I grabbed Madeleine's hand and pulled her alongside the house, out of range of the van, away from any windows, onto the downhill path to the factory. It was dark, so dark that I could hardly make Madeleine's face out save for when lightning lit up the sky.

"Embrasse-moi," I said. I reached up and touched where I last saw her face. It was there, in the same place. Her skin was smooth and cool.

Fifteen

on't lie. A small part of me was disappointed. Maybe that dangly thing on the frontal lobe of my brain. Or the hammer toe on my left foot. Whatever—the starry-eyed, ooey-gooey part of me was a nunchaku expert, hyped up on HGH, and getting some. For the next two months, Shannon and I would usually spend time outside of class and clubs in her room or mine making out. Sometimes we'd pass in the halls between classes and just smell the want off each other, and *BAM!* Duck around a corner or into a maintenance closet for a little action. Yes, badass Ryland wanted to hurl, but that hurl was made of rainbows and butterflies and smelled like honeysuckle and blackberries.

"I hate purple," I said reading over the ingredients on the hair dye bottle. We were in the bathroom K and I shared in our suite of mutual hatred. Actually, *hatred* is a strong word for what my roommate and I had. *Mutual ignorance* was more like it. She had her world of Shawn Mendes, boxes of Quaker Chewy granola bars, and schoolwork. I had my s'mores-flavored pop tarts, *Deep Space Nine* box sets, and pretending to work on French while I was actually French kissing my girlfriend.

"Shit, you know what's in this?" I said. "2,5-diaminotoluene? 4-aminophenol?"

"You forgot 5-amino-2-methylphenol," said Shan.

"I'm not going to ask you how you know that by heart."

"Good, because I'd have to kill you if you did." This girl. My life. Shan turned around and pulled off her T-shirt. "Could you . . ."

Why, yes I could. My fingers worked diligently to unclasp her bra, which went limp around her arms. Shan pulled it off and suddenly seemed to shrink as she pressed her arms to her chest. The skin on her back was smooth, without blemishes, like she'd been factory made with a seal of approval. As close as we had become in the last months, we'd never been this intimate. I mean, hands were free to move places they needed to go when we were together. Good places. The right places. But at least we had the clothing barrier to keep things semi-legit, like I wasn't really feeling like I was hovering off the ground all the time. If someone were to catch us right then . . .

Shan looked back with a pair of sultry eyes and mouthed, *Towel.* I complied without hesitation.

"Are you sure you wanna do this?" I said, wrapping a towel around her body. "I know girls who would kill to have your hair." With her long platinum hair, Shan was all set up to be "discovered" by a modeling agency in downtown Los Angeles. She'd proceed onto her whirlwind life of yachts and high teas, of movie shoots and strange men offering her flowers while she waited at crosswalks.

"They can have it. It's not me, anyway."

"It's your natural color, Shan. So in a way—"

She sat down on the side of the tub and swiveled her legs into it.

"No. Just do it."

I turned on the faucet, not because I had to, but because it seemed right to. That noise of the water tumbling into the tub and swishing around when Shan moved her feet. That's what this scene needed. Fuck, sometimes even I got swept away in the moment, trying to make it as perfect as possible. I knew perfection was impossible, but in these rare moments, I would think, there's that little sparkle past the bullshit. If only I could reach and touch it.

I followed the directions on the "Wild and Crazy!" hair dye box, and applied the goopy mess into Shan's hair. I'd done it to myself a bunch of times. In the last year, I'd gone from deep black to cherry red to a fine teal color. But eventually, I'd return to this mottled, off yellow mess that grew out the top of my head. Rinse and repeat, literally. It's different doing it to someone else, to touch someone's scalp, that new baby skin underneath the hair that had been sheltered from the elements.

"Comment ça va?"

"Alors, nous parlons en français? C'est très bon." She cleared her throat, like was going to give a speech. "Quel est votre nom?"

"No, I . . . I don't want to practice. I just didn't know what else to say."

"The queen of the harpies is speechless?"

"Queen of the harpies? Where'd you get that?"

"People have names for you," she said. "Not that it matters."

"What's your name, then? Let me see . . . She-Ra."

"No!"

"Okay, Princess Buttercup. *Mawwage is what bwings us togever today.*"

"Ry, stop. If you don't—"

"You're gonna what, Zelda? *Excuuuuuse me, princess.*" I turned her around and placed my forehead against hers, our lips less than a fingertip apart.

"Would you *please* shut the fuck up and kiss me?"

I complied without hesitation. The want was back, more ferocious than ever. It was the kind of want that made the tips of your eyelids tingle, that sapped your breath. The want that made you want to press and dig into the other person to see what was on the other side—if there was an "other side" that you could find your way to. I pushed, and she pushed. The towel dropped to the floor and stayed there. I leaned back to see her shirtless, unafraid in this tiny, enclosed universe. Her shoulders and neck were streaked with purple dye from my fingers. I wondered if I was looking at her like she was looking at me, with a singular longing, an *I need you now, please* look.

A moment later, the spell broke, and Shan reached down for the towel to cover herself up. Even though she had sounded so sure a moment earlier, she washed the dye out of her hair. It hadn't been in for long enough for the color to set in fully, but it did leave a soft lavender sheen on her hair.

"Second thoughts?"

"Not the right shade, after all," she said. I dried her shoulders and neck with the ends of the towel and leaned in to kiss her neck. She closed her eyes and shuddered. "What are you doing for Thanksgiving?"

That came out of nowhere. "Haven't really thought about it," I said. "I figured I'd just hang around here and split Lean Cuisines with Principal Lewis while we watch *A Charlie Brown Thanksgiving*."

"You're not going home?"

"What home? You mean to my dad's? I can OD on laxatives and watch *Cake Wars* right here for the same experience."

"Then come home with me."

Shannon lived in the house version of an Oreo with *holy fuck* instead of cream filling. I'm talking three stories of rustic perfection on the outside, and Swedish home-brewed-Ikea verve on the inside. Walking through the front door, I wished I'd worn a better T-shirt, one without the word "pussy" on it (even if it did pertain to a cartoon cat).

Shannon's mom had picked us up while her dad stayed home and cooked dinner. So when we rolled up, the eats were ready to be gluttonized.

"Your father is a lawyer, Ryland?" said Mrs. Gorski, spooning more stuffing onto my plate, as per the secret honor code of moms.

"Yeah. In Seattle."

"Is that where you're from?" This question came from Mr. Gorski, a lean, clean-shaven man with wire-rimmed glasses perched on his nose. He was totally not the person I envisioned when I thought of Shannon's dad. First off, he didn't wear a sweater vest. He had on a Phish T-shirt and brown corduroys. Nor did he speak like I expected—his conversation was free flowing and unintimidating. Charming. That's what he was.

"I grew up in Wyoming. My dad made the move this past summer."

"Ryland's a cowgirl," said Shannon, like she was showing me off.

The food was awesome, so I wolfed it down and welcomed second and third helpings. It was nice. What else could I say? It was a Hallmark Channel Thanksgiving, only with soy products instead of roasted meats. I hadn't had anything even resembling this since the Thanksgiving before Mom died.

When Mom was still alive, she and the wives of other ranchers in the area arranged a sort of community pot luck Thanksgiving. The plan was that each year, a different ranch would host a big 'ol dinner that everyone was invited to. A lot of ranchers had no children. Some weren't married, even, so this was the only way they'd spend the holiday in the traditional, big huge family way, even if the warm and fuzzy only lasted one day. My dad never attended—he always had some excuse, like he wasn't feeling well, or had to fix something. A few times, he said that he'd meet us later.

Later, as in never.

Back to the Gorskis: after dinner, Mr. Gorski and Shan's five-year-old brother Gabe settled in front of the TV to watch the L.A. Rams (Mr. Gorski: "They'll always be the St. Louis Rams to me.") take on the New Orleans Saints. Mrs. Gorski tackled the fairly substantial dirty dish pile.

"Would you girls like pumpkin pie and cocoa later?"

"Sure Mom," said Shannon. In the meantime, Shan gave me the nickel tour of her abode. Two fireplaces. Four bathrooms. Six bedrooms. *Holy shit.*

"What's this room?"

"A bedroom. Let's go to—"

"Your bedroom?" I asked. She smiled back, hoping to would dissuade me from pressing further. No dice.

"It's so embarrassing!"

"Hey, I bared my soul—and other things—to you. You owe me."

"The way I remember it—"

"Shut up. On y va."

Reluctantly, she opened the door. Jesus—Shannon's girlhood bedroom had been brought to us by the color pink. Plus, it was a veritable shrine to all things Shannon-related. Trophies, medals, certificates of merit. Shit you not, there wasn't enough shelf space to hold all her spoils of war. My eye stopped at a picture of a much younger Shannon on stage wearing a sparkly mini evening gown and sporting a silver tiara on her head.

"Honk my hooter, Little Miss Grand Teton."

"Where's chloroform when you need it?" She dragged me toward the huge picture windows that overlooked the woods around the house. "How about that view!" The Sun had already gone below the horizon, but its glow still lit up the mountains at the eastern side of the sky.

"Valiant attempts, your highness."

She punched my shoulder, then drew in close.

"Have you ever done it?" she asked, all fake nonchalant. I wondered how long she'd waited to ask me that question and why she'd picked now of all times to go through with it.

"You mean coitus?" She punched me again. "Fine! Fine! Yes. I have."

"What was she like? Or he . . . or . . ."

"Relax. No *hes.* Only *shes.*" Shannon fell quiet. "Her name was Faith. I know, appropriate, right? Anyway, she'd come into the place where I worked a lot, and we'd talk until closing time. After a while, I let slip that I was into girls, she invited me back to her place, and we—"

"Slept together."

"We met a few more times before she left town. Typical biker chick."

"Biker . . . like a bike messenger?"

"Biker as in motorcycle gang member. You should have seen my dad's face when I told him."

She looked totally shocked. "You told your dad about it?"

"We lived in a small town. It would have gotten back to him sooner or later."

"Wasn't it weird?"

"Weird like Loch Ness Monster weird?"

"Ry!"

"What?" I said, tiring of the twenty questions routine. "Let's leave it at this: that same day, he was on the phone with St. Gertie's, and a week later, I was getting my ass handed to me by Massive K. You know the rest."

Shan hugged me close and whispered, "I want to. With you. When we get back." Then she nibbled my ear before pulling back.

Our lips were a fingertip apart.

"I love you." We kissed. I don't know for how long. So I don't know how long Shannon's mother had been watching before she dropped the hot cocoa onto the floor. Shannon and I jumped up and apart when we heard the crash.

"Mom, let me help—"

"No!" she snapped. "Just stay there. I'm . . . okay." Neither Shannon nor I moved at all. Didn't make a sound until Mrs. Gorski left the room.

"Shan." She was quiet. She didn't move. Like her mom said. "Shan, talk to me."

"I don't want to talk."

I tried to take her hand, but she wriggled her fingers away from mine. "Shan, it had to happen sooner or later. Your parents are cool. They'll understand."

"You don't know them."

"It could never, ever be as bad as what happened to me."

"I need to be alone."

"Shan." She turned away from me. And it hurt. It really, really hurt. "Fine." I walked out and found a shadowed place at the top of the stairs where I sat, listening to the football game on TV.

Shannon and I didn't talk for the rest of the night. When we were called down for dessert, we went, but didn't speak. The worst thing was that her parents acted like nothing was wrong, including how their once talkative daughter had pulled out her emergency Helen Keller. At bedtime, Mrs. Gorski showed me to one of their guest rooms on the first floor, and that was that. I lay there vacillating between being pissed at Shannon and being pissed at her parents for not fucking coming out with it. Mostly, I was pissed at me. I should have known better. I should have asked if her parents knew about us. I mean, what was she doing bringing her lesbian girlfriend home for Thanksgiving? And what was I doing going along with the plan?

I should have known. I should have known better.

Gabe woke me that next morning by tugging my hair. Over (faux) Eggs Benedict (with soy ham), Shannon and I learned that our weekend would be cut short.

"Your Uncle Allen called late last night," her mother began. "Tyler's not doing so well." I initially thought that Tyler was uncle Allen's son, or best friend, or maybe even lover (on second thought, that was a really bad guess). But I learned through subsequent conversation that Tyler was Uncle Allen's decrepit, elderly pit bull.

"You know how close they are," Shannon's father chimed in. "We really ought to be there for him." What he had left out right then was that they'd decided late last night to be there *physically* for him. In Indianapolis. And their flight would leave early on Saturday. Of course, this was all bullshit.

"What about me?" said Shannon (conveniently forgetting someone).

"I can drive you back today," her mom said.

"Who'll take care of Gabe?" Her voice cracked, and her eyes got glassy.

"Babs said she could take him for a couple of days." Babs was the next door neighbor. They'd thought of everything. The chummy-sitcom breakfast couldn't mask the tension just under the surface of everything. Shannon managed to keep herself together, but barely. No thanks to me. I was ecstatic to leave early.

True to her word, Mrs. Gorski drove us back. All the way, we listened to NPR programs on the radio. It was a tentative peace. Anything was better than conversation. Around 2:30 in the afternoon, we arrived back at St. Gertie's. As Shannon and I gathered our stuff to leave the car, her mom softly spoke to Shan: "I'm going to pick up a gift for Tyler in the city. Why don't you come and help me?" She said this like it was a nothing proposition. Take it or leave it.

Shannon left it: "Get him a bone or something."

"It's more for uncle Allen, honey."

"I hardly know uncle Allen," said Shannon. "I've met him like twice."

Then her mother dropped all pretentions: "Shannon, why are you being so difficult?"

"What do you want, Mom?"

Clearly frustrated, Mrs. Gorski turned to me. "Ryland, would you please let me have a moment alone with my daughter?" Shannon's eyes begged me to stay. But I didn't.

"See ya later, Shan," I said, and left. First mistake of the day. It wouldn't be the last.

I sat on the floor of my room, my door slightly ajar, listening for movement in the hallways. An hour passed. Two. Eventually, I heard the click-clack of Shannon's footsteps. I jumped out in time to see Shan round the corner out of sight.

I found her at her door, struggling with the lock.

"Shan, we need to talk."

"About what?" She tried to close the door on me, but I stuck my foot in and pulled it back open.

"What is your deal?" I said. She threw her backpack on the floor and fell into her bed. I came in after her. "Can you just fucking talk to me? I've been there! Don't you think I know what you're feeling?" I sat down on the bed and reached to smooth out the tangles in her hair. She rolled away from me.

"No, you don't."

"Shan, why didn't you just tell her—"

"Mom was like, 'It'll pass. It's a phase.' Over and over. Like I wasn't even there." Everything got hot—like volcano levels—and I needed to break something—Shan's mom's face, for starters. "She said that if I didn't 'get better soon,' maybe I wouldn't be well enough to go to college."

"What does that mean?"

"Don't play stupid, Ryland." She was right. I was playing stupid. It was the same bullshit, different flavor. Instead of blasting away the gay like Dad, Shan's parents opted for some asphalt and a steamroller. Pave it right over and put up a tamale hut. No one would be ever the wiser.

"We can figure something out." I touched her hair and tried to smile even though I could feel a scream in my throat pushing upward. "Who needs them, right?"

"Me!" Shan pushed my hand away. "I need them! They're my family, not yours." My heart felt like it was going to explode—it was beating so fast. I bit down so hard that I felt like all my teeth would shatter.

"So is this it? You'll be what they want you to be, Little Miss Grand Teton?" My eyes burned. I dug my nails into my palms, hoping that the pain would override the sudden emptying sensation in the center of my chest, like a vacuum without an off switch.

"Fuck off."

That was it. I didn't—couldn't—say anything. I threw open the door and marched out. Past the soles of my shoes, I could feel the floor's cold, a cold that radiated outward from where I stepped, to the walls, to the ceiling. And still out more—into the bricks and between beams of wood, into the greened copper pipes that snaked around the steel girders that kept St. Gertie's straight up and strong. Cold crept inward, too, into my lungs where icy stilettos stung with each breath. Out. In. Out.

In: "I needed you," she said. I didn't turn around. "Why did you leave me with her? How could you just . . . you said you loved me—"

Out: "Don't you ever fucking say those words." And I walked away.

I'd be told much later on, and very much removed from this location, that I was too young to have regrets. Maybe that's true. But if it walks like a regret, and talks like a regret, what else could it be?

Sixteen

opened my eyes. At first, I only saw a pair of worn shoes, the soles attached with liberal applications of rubber cement. I followed the legs upward to Jonas's face. He stared, his mouth hanging open. Normally, I'd have taken offense. It's not polite to stare at a naked girl. Or two naked girls. Especially if one is your sister.

"Madeleine." I said, quietly, trying to nudge her awake. She stirred, cooed, but did not wake up.

Kicking in the door was Angelique, storming in to join the party. "Maintenant je sais!" she shrieked. "Tu et cette pute . . . mon dieu."

"It's not what you think," I blurted out, mostly because that's what you say when it is exactly what they're thinking.

The previous night, I kissed Madeleine in the dark, in the rain. We didn't stop. We couldn't stop. Managing to stumble into the house—we somehow made it up the stairs and wound up in the supply closet. Still locking lips, we stripped each other's clothes off, not caring about buttons or zippers or whatever dared get in our way. I had been starving, and I needed her to weave her arms in with mine, just taste her skin, slightly coppery from the rain, hear her breath rush into my ear when I kissed her neck, feel the muscles in her back go tense at my touch.

She made me giggle. I made her swear. Thank god for thunder.

Now, I had some 'splainin' to do.

Jonas and Angelique gave me and Madeleine some privacy as we got dressed for breakfast. I hated how quiet she was, how she didn't say anything. She was thinking all right. And so was I. I mean, I literally had just slept with the farmer's daughter.

As I walked alongside her down the hall toward the stairs, it occurred to me that I was shaking. My chest buzzed, and my arms and legs felt light enough to float. What was happening? I had to stop and say something before we went down.

"Hey," I said. "Last night . . ."

"Shh." The fingers of her left hand locked with the fingers on my right.

In the kitchen, Henri and Jonas hovered over a piece of paper, discussing something intently. I was too distracted to make out what they were talking about.

"Papa." Henri and Jonas looked up from the table. While Henri was none the wiser, Jonas went rigid. Did he know what was about to happen? I sure didn't.

"Papa," she said, after clearing her throat. "J'aime les

filles. J'aime Ryland. Elle me rend heureuse." No traipsing around the subject for her. It was just, "I like girls." Like a hammer to the forehead. Henri raised his eyebrows. He looked at Madeleine, then looked at me. Then Madeleine. Me again. Until finally he said:

"D'accord." Then he went back to talking with Jonas.

Wow. That was painfully, agonizingly drama-free. Madeleine sat me down, poured me coffee, and prepared some toast. That feeling I had upstairs—add a sinking, fist-in-your-gut sensation—only intensified. Maybe I had stomach cancer. Or maybe I had something much, much worse.

"We go after breakfast," announced Jonas.

"Go? Where?"

Henri passed me the paper that he had been going over with Jonas. It was a hand-drawn map of the area with the factory marked by a circled dot. At the end of a long twisty arrow, a big, fat X marked the spot: *Le Jardin de Pierres*.

The blink-and-you'll-miss-it mountainside village with the unfortunate name of "Alas" probably looked the same that day as it did five hundred years before. Take away the funny little French cars parked precariously on steep inclines, and you might as well be in the 1500s, leading your goat along the River Lez, backdropped by stonework homes and waterwheels.

We were back on the trail of Dora and Paolo. I could smell it, literally—the damp, the rot of soaked wood, and very, very faintly, the cigarette smoke. Now, we just had to find the garden. A simple task, yes, but complicated by Madeleine, whose presence made it hard to stay goal-oriented (unless my goal was pressing her up to a tree and making out), and also by Angelique, who had insisted on coming along on pain of whining like a spoiled bitch.

We wandered about the village, guided by Jonas's fingertip on Henri's map, hauling ourselves up almost vertical inclines that made me rethink skipping those free spinning classes at the UT fitness center. But past that was another gut feeling—despite the lack of people out and about, I could feel someone's gaze pressing down upon us. Just past the treeline, hiding behind curtained windows. Stores were shuttered closed. The roads were empty. No one fished in the river. But still—we weren't alone.

"D'accord!" Jonas hastened his pace, leading us ever higher. Ultimately, we found ourselves on top of a tall hill/pygmy mountain with Alas on the down slope behind us. In front of us lay a steep, muddy path that straight-shotted back down the other side. According to the map, *Le Jardin* was at the bottom. Jonas suggested we go down with partners, and it made sense that he'd pair with his sister, for obvious reasons.

"So," I said to Angelique, leaning on her arms to get past a fallen branch. "Still glad you came?"

Rien.

"Yeah," I said to myself. "Shut up, *Pazzesca*."

"You speak Italian?"

"No, I—wait, you speak Italian?"

"Oui. My father . . ."

"I know. From Florence. Madeleine told me."

She looked annoyed, but it passed. "You and Madeleine this morning . . ."

"Yeah." Oh shame. She hung her head like a puppy caught in the cookie jar (or something close enough). "I'm not here to steal him from you, Angelique."

"That is what he said last night, but I did not believe." We tiptoed across knotty tree roots that had been exposed by the rain. And then she lost it: "I do not understand him!" Jonas was by then already down the hill, out of earshot. "He goes and does not say anything. And then he returns? With you? And for the whole year, I think, 'when I see him again, I will hate him! I will spit in his face!'"

"You still love him."

"Putain," she said, tearing up.

"Angelique, it's okay," I said, tightening my grip on her. "Hold on. It's rough out here."

"Okay." She managed to hold on long enough for us to navigate the rest of the way down, through a vine-tangled stone archway, over to where we could once again see Jonas and Madeleine. I went first, warding away thorny brambles with my arms. What I thought was solid ground was anything but, and the leaves and branches gave way to what felt like ice-cold snowcap melt. Angelique tried to grab me, but it happened too quick. I belly-flopped right into the water. It took Angelique and Jonas to fish me out and drag me onto the shore.

After coughing up water, I wiped my eyes and reoriented

myself. This place—it didn't look exactly like it did in my dream. The edges on the statues were more worn, like they were slouching their shoulders. The river had swelled with the rains to completely submerge the smaller constructions. Despite those differences, we had come to the right place. This was *Le Jardin de Pierres d'Alas*, the same place in the photo—oh shit! The book had fallen into the water with me! I groped along the shore until I spotted photos floating face down in the water. No sign of *The Green Ray*. Jonas helped me collect the photos, but the book . . . it was gone.

"God-fucking-dammit!" I screamed. That book was a gift to me from Paolo—the only thing I had left of him. Diving down a couple of times, I came up empty. When I finally gave up hope of seeing it again, I sat on the riverbank, against the statue of a big head smoking a cigar. Madeleine pecked tiny kisses on my neck, and yes, that did help a little. But I still felt screwed by fate.

"I hope you know that you're kissing the stupidest stupid-ass on the planet." I clutched the remaining photos Jonas and I saved—the one of Dora and Paolo I got from Frau Müller and the photo of Dora Paolo had originally stuck in *The Green Ray*. One thought repeated in my head: *What do I do now?*

A scream yanked me out of my head. It was Angelique, leaping away from the brush and into the arms of a surprised Jonas. Behind her, a giant black mastiff stalked through the stones and plants. The beast was six or seven feet long and more than three feet tall.

"We go around to the van," said Jonas.

"I can't leave yet." I couldn't leave. This dog was the first sign that someone else was around—the collar around its neck gave that away. Maybe the owner knew Dora. Maybe the owner *was* Dora. "Good doggie." I started to approach the dog when Madeleine yanked me back.

"Tu es folle!" she yelled. She wasn't joking around.

"I'll be cool," I reassured her. "Good boy." I crept closer. "Good—"

"RRROWWRRR!" It jumped up and barked to high fucking hell, and haunched itself, ready to pounce, when someone on the path called out, "Qu'est-ce que c'est?" We waited while the footsteps got louder, and a man joined the side of his trusty attack dog.

Jackpot. I recognized him. He was the man Frau Müller pointed out as Dora's husband.

"Qu'est-ce qui faites à mon chien? Eh?"

"Um, I . . ." I said. "I mean, je vous connais. Vous connaissez une femme qui s'appelle Dora."

"Your French is terrible," he said. "Perhaps you did not understand my question."

"Mais, monsieur—"

"I don't know you. Leave here now."

"We go," Jonas said under his breath. He started to backpedal, and the others followed suit, but I stood my ground. The dog let out and held a low growl, so I made sure to move slowly and deliberately. I held out my hand, dangling Dora's photo from my fingertips. Puzzled, he reached out for it, but I snapped it back. The dog went crazy, but the man caught it by the collar before any throat rippage could occur.

"What do you want?" he said.

"Que parler," I said.

"Very well. If you want to talk, you will follow me."

"Valère Puisieux," he said, placing a small glass of red wine in front of each of us seated at the table. The inside of his house was remarkably small—made of corners butted up against corners that strangled the open space. Sitting in the kitchen, the largest room in the house, we were pressed against walls on all sides save for where Valère was standing, in front of an unlit fireplace with a large wooden crucifix on the wall above it. He refused to sit, opting to stand and cast a long shadow over the rest of us.

"That woman is not here," he said.

"Do you know where she is?"

"Yes." He didn't elaborate. Terse, one-syllable answers seemed to be his preferred way of communicating. "Why do you look for her?"

"I don't know why it matters—"

"A fair exchange, oui?" he said, his shadow oozing closer to me. "An answer for an answer."

"Fine," I said, adopting his adversarial tone. "A friend wanted me to find her."

"Who?"

"I get to ask a question now. Where is she?"

"She is dead." His words felt like anvils. I hadn't even met the lady, but I, all at once, felt an absence. Maybe I was channeling grief for Paolo and Frau Müller. "Now my next question. Who is the friend you speak of?" He spat out *friend* like a TB patient hocking up bloody phlegm.

"His name is Paolo."

Valère recoiled away from the table at the sound of Paolo's name. He ground his teeth in anticipation of my next question.

"Is she buried nearby?" I don't know why I asked. It didn't matter anymore. She was gone. Paolo was gone. And suddenly, there was no purpose to any of this. Why was I there? Paolo, Tiburzi . . . Mom. I followed the book, and what did it get me? Dead ends. Literally.

"Who are you? What do you want with me?"

"I wanted to know about Dora," I said.

"And you?" He eyed the others, Angelique specifically.

"We are her friends," she said. We exchanged a glance right before Valère pounded his hand on the table. The muscles in his forearms tensed up so tight that his veins looked like they were going to explode out his skin.

"You want to know, eh?" He took an ornately carved wooden box off the fireplace and slid it over to me. "Open it." My fingers slowly curled around its harsh corners, sunk into the spaces carved into its top. Inside were envelopes, all bound with a thick rubber band. Each was slit open, revealing a folded piece of onionskin paper. The bottom left corner of each envelope was charred and brittle.

"What are these?"

"A man can have two things that never lose value—his companion and his child. And that woman took both away from me." I lifted the envelopes out of the box, and the black turned to ash that dusted the bottom of the box. What he said didn't make sense. I mean, Dora was his wife (AKA "companion"), and she had been pregnant (AKA "child"). Was I missing something?

"I still need to know more."

"Leave me now," Valère said, winding his dog's leash around his hand. "Do not come here again."

We were all back at *Le Jardin*. Madeleine sat on the riverbank next to me, stroking my hair. Jonas and Angelique sat on the shoulders of a statue that looked like a man in a top hat half submerged in the shallow rapids lapping the tree roots just off shore. They were facing each other, talking. Neither looked away from the other. "Enfin." I felt the puff of Madeleine's breath on my ear. No doubt, talking was good. Much better than not talking, holding a grudge, letting things fester until they explode.

I had spread out Valère's letters on the ground. Each was authored by Dora MacCallum. Each was addressed to Paolo Rossi. Each was written from a different location in Europe, following Dora's travels as her nursing duties took her to Germany, France, England, parts of Hungary, Austria, Denmark, Poland, and elsewhere. Each letter started out with a story—like how she had fumbled over her French at the market in Orléans and unwittingly asked a shopkeeper the purchase price of his son, or how an Austrian soldier in

Warsaw had brought her home to meet his family after she saved his leg from amputation, or the one time she met Winston Churchill walking his miniature black poodle across the Serpentine Bridge in Kensington Garden. She regaled him with her adventures of her life as a Red Cross Nurse, but would always eventually come to the same point—she wished that he was there with her.

Then the last letter with an almost two year gap (from September 1947 to April 1949) between it and the previous:

P—

Though I have not written in years, this will be my last letter to you. I must stop writing not because I do not love to think of your face when you read my words—but because of it. So this is my goodbye to you.

I will be married this time next year. My husband and I will live in France, in his home. He is a good man. A doctor. He saved my life when I got very sick. I owe him everything, including my devotion. But, even now, as I write, I cannot help but shiver, even though it is summer, when I think about you sitting in the kitchen, with wine and bread, reading this letter. My hand shakes—can you tell in the stroke of my pen?

Do you remember my last letter, when I told you how I looked out from the window of my friend's cottage, saw the Alps, and thought that if only those mountains were not there, I could see you? Right

From where I was sitting, I'd be able to once again smell the salt from the sea, taste your mother's pasta, dance under those trees you make so beautiful.

You did read the book? Good. Close your eyes and think of it before you continue reading.

I look upon the sea in front of my mother's house. It is so cold and dark. Underneath my feet is sharp, black rock, endlessly lashed upon by the water. The cup of tea I had brought out here with me has gone cold. Can you see it? Can you see me?

—D

"Who is she?" Madeleine asked.

"Her name is—was—Dora. I don't know much beyond that. I thought finding out more about her would help me, but it hasn't." Truth. Now that I knew her last name and that she and Paolo had shared this transnational love, I was only one baby step farther along than when I had started this whole cockamamie thing. Actually, that wasn't true. What Valère said had stuck with me because it didn't seem to fit. He didn't seem to fit. I assumed he was the doctor Dora wrote about in that last letter—so how did Dora steal those things from him? She was those things, right? This, combined with the shit-ton of time and moolah it would take me to retrace all of Dora's steps, put me way behind where I wanted to be. We're talking out of healing potions, no continues, and no code for thirty lives.

233

I threw the letters back down to the ground and fell back into Madeleine.

She kissed my cheek, then picked up Dora's melancholy "Dear Paolo" letter and reread it for herself. "What is this book she writes of?" Book? She pointed out the line: *You did read the book? Good. Close your eyes and think of it before you continue reading.*

I shook my head. "It doesn't matter. The book's gone."

"Did you read it?"

"Yeah, but so what?"

"Here she writes about her home. It is possible that this book is about her home?"

The Green Ray was about a journey through the Scottish Isles. Could that be . . . *I look upon the sea in front of my mother's house* . . . could it have been that simple . . . *it is so cold and dark. The Green Ray* had come from Dora's library, and her note to him told him to return it there—and the *there* was hidden in plain sight. The book wasn't merely lovey-dovey bullshit—it was a guide for Paolo to find her.

Holy fuck. Next stop, Scotland. Right after a madly deserved kiss for Madeleine.

Seventeen

lavor of the week was *Karate Kid II*. I was settling into the movie and into a Butterfinger dipped into extra-crunchy peanut butter when someone knocked on my door. Over the previous three weeks since the Thanksgiving incident, the only person I saw outside of class or clubs was K, and she didn't have to knock.

"No one's home!" I shouted.

Knock again. "Ryland? It's Carrie." Carrie? Oh, Spider. I paused the movie and opened the door. All three of Shan's friends were there, looking like they'd just rung the wrong doorbell on Halloween night. 'Cause they had. "Can we come in? Please?"

"Did Shannon send you? Because I don't even want to hear it."

"Maybe you should listen," said Angie, pushing her way

in. "We're being serious here. Shit's gone down." *Gone* was the right word. So was *shit.* Between the three of them, they explained that Carrie had gone this morning to "fetch"—their code word for sneaking some booze out of THE STASH—only to find . . . nothing. The entire STASH was missing.

Monte came out with it: "We think Shannon did it. When we ask her about it, she acts weird."

"Like someone guilty," said Angie, narrowing her eyes.

"This has nothing to do with me," I said. "Shannon and I aren't really on speaking terms." That wasn't technically correct. In extracurriculars, we exchanged words, but only when necessary (passing along handouts or being a know-it-all at Academic fucking Decathlon). If she wanted it to be that way, that was fine by me.

"You need to talk to her," said Angie.

"That's funny, because *no.*"

"Ryland, please?" pleaded Monte. "She could get us into real trouble if she told." When she wasn't talking, she munched on her fingernails.

"Monte!" Angie shrieked. "I thought your mom gave you stuff so you won't bite your nails."

"She did," said Monte. *Bite-bite.*

"It's not working!"

"I know." *Bite-bite.* "I kinda like how it tastes, actually." *Bite-bite.*

"Well, it's really annoying!"

"Sorry." *Bite-bite.*

"Don't be sorry, be quiet!"

"I'm sorry!" *Bite.* "I mean . . . okay." She put her hands in

236

her pockets, solving that problem. But the bigger one—the fact that they were in my room—was still very much present.

"Look, Shannon's not going to fuck you over. You're her friends."

"Yeah, and what were you?" Angie said. "We're not stupid. Ever since you guys broke up, she's been AWOL."

"And this is my problem how?"

Angie blew up. "You knew about THE STASH and didn't tell anyone about it! That means you're an accessory."

"You've been watching the special features on your *Law and Order* DVD, haven't you?"

"Maybe it's about time I—"

"Can we all shut up?" shouted Spider. "Ryland, please. We'll owe you a favor if you help us."

"A favor, huh?" My rusty clockwork mind started to grind its gears. "Fine. Which one of you knows how to format spreadsheets?"

I searched school grounds all weekend, but Shannon managed to elude me. I wouldn't have a chance to see Shannon again until that Monday afternoon when she surprised me by appearing in Mr. Leonard's van en route to Grace House. The past three weeks, she'd been a no show. This week, she was there, in her customary seat, right up in the front seat behind the driver's side. The whole way to

Grace House, no one said a thing. It wasn't until we got there that I even tried.

"Hey."

Okay, so not much of a try. She ignored me. I sat in my customary seat, at a table across from Fabiana, the lady I had been assigned to help with her GED prep. When Mr. Leonard first told me that I'd be responsible for another person's educational future, I thought he was nuts. Ryland Taggart is neither greater than nor equal to a qualified tutor in *anything*. (Though, if someone needed help filling out a Paint-by-Numbers picture of Optimus Prime, I was your chick.)

"*x* times twelve divided by four equals . . ." I let my voice trail off. Fabiana chewed her lip, thinking about the answer. "You know this."

"Mmm . . . I think . . . eighteen."

"Fuck yeah!" She and I high-fived.

"Language!" Mr. Leonard scolded from across the way.

Whatever. It had been a rough couple of months for Fabiana. After getting kicked out of her boyfriend's home, and practically disowned by her own family, she and her one-year-old daughter, Tracy, found themselves at Grace House with no prospects for anything. She was barely seventeen—the same age as me, except that while I was busy emo-ing my youth away, the big city had chewed her up, spit her out, and stuck her on the underside of a desk to be forgotten. It took me two weeks to get her to read anything out of the training textbooks that Mr. Leonard shoveled onto us. That included her own name. But about three weeks ago, she slowly—really, really, slowly—started to respond. Turns out she could read perfectly well. In her spare time, she read boatloads of fantasy novels.

No, her bane was math, and her nemesis was that black-hearted harpy—Geometry.

"What is this formula?" I pointed on the page to the oft-maligned formula for a line on a coordinate plane: $y = mx+b$.

"Uh . . . I think it's the distance formula. Yeah."

"Try again," I said, just as I saw a flash of Shannon's back as she ducked into the ladies room. Over at the table where she had been sitting was her usual student, Corinna, looking pretty pissed.

"What's going on?" I asked her.

"That girl's got a problem."

"I don't get it."

Corinna squinted at me. "When she comes back you'll smell it."

Oh fuck. Fuck! That answered all my questions in one stroke. In the bathroom, I found Shannon bracing herself in front of the sink, rinsing her mouth out with water. In the unforgiving blue tint of the fluorescent lights, she looked like the wicked witch version of a girl I once had a thing with—her eyes were framed with dark circles that had sunken into her face. Her skin was clammy and pasty. And, yes, the smell—now I knew where THE STASH had gone. From her right pinky dangled her water bottle, which, I knew, had not one drop of H_2O in it.

"What the fuck, Shannon?"

In the mirror hanging over the sink, I saw her eyes dart toward me and then flit away.

"You are fucked up right now, and Corinna knows it." I

was perched on the front of my feet, as if getting ready and set for a race.

"Why do you care?" She tried to leave, but I blocked her path. "Get out of my way!"

"Not until you give me that bottle."

"Bitch." She pushed the bottle into my arms and used the leverage to squeeze out the door. I emptied the contents into the toilet, noting how epically lethal it smelled. I couldn't imagine drinking that shit. I came out of the bathroom and sat back down with Fabiana. Before returning to my lesson, I looked over to where Shannon and Corinna were sitting. There Shan was, diagramming sentences like she was fine, like she wasn't hanging on by fingernails.

"I'm gonna kill her," said Angie. "And then I'm gonna kill you." It was lunch, the next day. I was sitting outside with THE STASH crew, spilling the goods.

"What's your problem? I did what you asked."

"She admitted taking THE STASH—our STASH—and you don't do anything?"

"Did you want me to beat the shit out of her right there?"

"You could have told on her," said Angie.

"And then she would have told on us."

"And who would they believe? Us or drunkface?" Angie was right. I could have told and sold her out. Instead, I let her walk away while disposing of the evidence. "I'm going."

"Where?" said Monte.

"To Shannon's. To get our shit back and tell her what a cunt she is. Anymore questions, Monte?"

"Um. No."

"She's in class now," I said. "C'mon. We don't have to do it this way."

"Why all of a sudden, you're protecting her?" said Angie. She was right again. *What the hell, Ryland?* I had the most reason to want to screw with Shannon's standing at school. But I also had the most reason to want her to succeed. Maybe, somewhere deep down, I wanted her to get out of there and go to college and have the cajones to one day tell her mom off, tell her dad what a spineless shithead he is.

"Fine. I'll talk to her tonight."

"No, now," said Angie.

"Give me a chance. It's the stupid Academic Decathlon qualifiers. Her guard will be down."

"Are you sure that'll work?" asked Spider.

"It'll work," I said. "I promise."

It didn't work. I sat on the all-white couch in the all-white hallway in the hospital, wearing my stupid fucking blazer, stupid fucking leggings, and stupid fucking school-girl skirt. Old dudes, all dressed in big all-white napkins, steered their IV poles down the hallway.

Principal Lewis waited for the answer to her question.

"I don't know anything." The repetition of that answer—the same answer I'd been giving her for the last twenty minutes—rung hollow in my head for the first time. It wasn't that I was only *technically* telling the truth. It was that I understood how razor thin that technicality was.

"Then tell me again what happened," she said. "From the beginning."

I got dressed in my monkey outfit—oh, excuse me, my uniform—and was nearly late for the bus taking us to UCLA. And no, when I got on the bus, I didn't notice anything about Shannon. And no, I hadn't talked to her in a while—okay, so I talked to her yesterday, but not for a long time, and it was in a bathroom . . . but anyway, where was I? Oh yeah. We got off, we were shown to the staging area behind the studio set, and I sat there dotting my Ts and crossing my lower-cased Js when I heard a ruckus across the room. I look over, and Mrs. Volino is holding Shannon by the shoulders, propping her up, 'cause Shan was convulsing and throwing up and screaming. Someone called the ambulance, and apparently, you. I was about to get on the bus taking the other kids home when Mrs. Volino calls me over and tells me that I was to come with her. And I was like, "Why?" and she was all shaking and red and pissed, and said, "Principal Lewis wants to talk to you." And she was right, because here you are talking to me, though I'm not sure what—

"That's enough. And close your legs. You're wearing a skirt." P. Lewis was livid. *Livid* is a nice word, though, when you're referring to a psychotic, cannibalistic, demon-possessed bride of Satan. She continued the slow-motion relay race between interrogating me and conferring with Mrs. Volino standing at the doorway to Shannon's room. I watched P. Lewis grill Mrs. Volino as harshly as she did me. I think P. Lewis was mounting her case against me, using Mrs. Volino as the primary witness. I mean, we were both there when Shannon broke down. We both heard what Shannon was screaming, even though I denied it: *Why did you do this to me? Ryland, why?* We both saw the silver flask drop out of her bag. It was empty, but smelled like moonshine. My sins of omission were gonna see the light.

And then things got worse. The swinging doors at the end of the hall burst open. Shannon's parents rushed through to meet P. Lewis and Mrs. Volino. They, understandably, looked mega-stressed—veins bulging out their foreheads, red blotches spread all over their cheeks. They'd been fighting. I could tell. I can always tell. P. Lewis kept them from entering Shan's room until she could upload the skinny to them. I watched without being able to hear the conversation. I didn't really need to hear.

After more exchanges, Shannon's mom looked down the hallway. At me. I tried to hide my face, but it was too late. Following her lead, everyone looked at me. I froze and hoped that I wouldn't be called over. I didn't want to talk. Not to them. What the hell would I say, anyway? It was a silent tête-à-tête (à-tête-à-tête-à-tête) between me and the four of them. And for three out of the four, it was whatevs. I knew that P. Lewis and Mrs. Volino hated my guts. And it was a reasonable assumption that Mrs. Gorski shared their feeling. But Mr. Gorski—the way he looked at me, the way he held his head, stood on his legs, leaned into his hip . . . for a nanosecond, I was no longer in that room. I was somewhere else, somewhere that didn't even exist anymore.

I got up and went to the water fountain. The cold jet danced on my lips, but I didn't drink.

All of them were gone when I looked down the hallway again. Returning to my seat, I sunk my head into my hands. I didn't want to be there. Maybe if I wished hard enough . . .

"Let's go." It was P. Lewis.

"Can I see Shannon?"

"No."

I didn't put up a fight. As we passed Shan's room, I heard her talking inside, but could only see the backs of her mom and dad and Mrs. Volino. What was she saying? Did she rat us all out? Was I being taken to the gallows?

"Move faster," commanded P. Lewis. I followed her to her car, and soon, we were on the expressway headed away from the hospital. After a minute, I figured out that we were also headed away from St. Gertie's. The downtown L.A. skyline was moving away from us.

"Where are we going?"

"Shut up and put on your seatbelt. You're paying the ticket if I get one." After ten minutes, we peeled off the highway and pulled into the drive-thru of In-And-Out-Burger. "What do you want?" It was not a motherly, please-tell-me-what-you'd-like-sweetie-pie kind of tone.

"I'm not a fan of burgers. I grew up on a cattle ranch."

"If the next thing out of your mouth is not one, two, or three, I'm throwing you out of this car."

Okay, then: "Two." After picking up our orders, we parked in the parking lot and got moving on our dinners. Turns out the number two was your traditional cheeseburger, fries, and drink combo. P. Lewis's preferred dinner—or her preferred method of suicide—was an In-And-Out specialty called "The Animal 4x4," a quadruple meat and cheese extravaganza slathered in orange special sauce. That fucking thing was so heinous that it didn't even appear on the menu.

"Aw, shit, In-And-Out," she exclaimed. "You can do no wrong!"

"Um, thanks for dinner, Principal Lewis."

"I only bought it for you so you could shut up. So eat."

We ate. That was a lot of burger, enough to buy at least half-an-hour silent eating time. It didn't last nearly as long, as P. Lewis surprised me.

"You fucked this one up, didn't you?"

"Look," I said. "I told you everything I know."

"Mrs. Volino told me Shannon was screaming your name," she said.

"I . . ." But there was no defense. "You don't know the circumstances—"

"Oh, you think I don't know, eh? I know plenty. You and Shannon. Don't take a rocket scientist, and I sure as hell ain't one of those. Let me tell you a little secret. Teachers have no lives. They grade papers, they eat microwave dinners, and they go to sleep. The shit that happens in these hallways is all we have. So student dramas—yeah, we talk about it all."

"That's depressing. And horrifying. Like that burger."

245

"Shut up about my baby."

"Hold on. So you know. Did Shannon say anything at the hospital?"

"She talked, and not only about you two. All the beans spilled out—how she'd smuggled in alcohol, how it was all in her closet, if we bothered to look. *If we bothered to look*—you know how that makes me look in front of her parents?"

Didn't need three guesses: "Pretty bad."

"Fired—that's what." You'd think that maybe my first reaction to the downfall of my arch-nemesis would be joy. But it wasn't. She didn't deserve it. She ran a good school, and despite all my directed efforts to fuck it up, she kept it a good school. Until now, when a tiny little insignificant (read: titanic) omission had led to this: the last supper. I could have said something. I should have.

"You ever hear that French poem, 'Ballade des dames du temps jadis'?" she asked.

"No."

"Did you sleep through French?"

"I'll have you know that *j'ai étudié beaucoup pendant cette année.*"

"Not bad," she said, nodding. My first piece of approval from her! A little too late, but I'll take it. "There's a line that I love—*Mais où sont les neiges d'antan?* It means, 'But where are the snows of yesteryear?' I think about it a lot here because it hardly ever snows. Maybe I'll move somewhere it snows. Like Chicago. See the kids."

"You have children?"

"No, I have baby goats," she snarked. "Yes, I have kids. They're with my ex." Ex? I glanced down to the wedding

246

band on her left hand. I must have been really obvious. "What the hell are you looking at?" she said.

"Oh, it's just that some people were wondering if you were married, or divorced, or—"

"Or maybe it's none of your business."

"Or that."

"You know what? I know Shannon was lying to me."

"Principal Lewis—"

"You wouldn't know who she's covering for, would you?"

"I . . ." The right answer was poised on the tip of my tongue, ready to thrust itself into realspace. That itsy-bitsy syllable that wasn't about justice, or fairness, or anything else from the opening credits of *Quantum Leap*. With it, I'd doom Angie and Monte and Spider. And bury P. Lewis even deeper than she was in now. Those were excuses, though. The truth is that I'd gotten pretty good at putting myself through the grinder, but when it came down to really taking a stand, I stood as strong as tinsel in a hurricane. So that word? Yeah. I roped it back in, but not out of a sense of duty to others. That'd at least be medal-worthy. No. I was scared shitless of what would happen to me. One point for selfishness. It was easy enough to audible that sombitch and save my worthless ass: ". . . don't."

That night, I walked down the hallway to my room. The phone in my pocket vibrated for like the thousandth time. I

247

knew that it was one of Angie, Monte, or Spider—probably all of them huddled around one phone upset that I wasn't picking up. But I didn't feel like talking. I won't lie—it really bothered me what Principal Lewis had told me about Shannon. She had taken the fall for us. Big time.

I didn't get it.

I didn't understand.

I didn't know that I was crying until I had reached my door, but once I did, the waterworks went into overdrive. I just felt so fucking confused and angry and betrayed all over again. Except this time, I didn't know who was responsible. I couldn't blame anyone. So I blamed me. I crawled under the covers and held the pillow against my chest, pulling against the seams until the pillowcase started to split. But I felt nothing. It was like my body was possessed, but my mind had gone numb.

Until K showed up. She stepped inside the room just as I had thrown a gym shoe, hitting the wall inches to the left of her head. We stopped for a second. Had a high noon staredown. I didn't know what was going to happen next, but I was completely alright with K knocking me into next century. I wanted it.

But she didn't do it. She offered me a tissue. And that's when I felt everything finally wash over me. Not only was I crying, but I was wailing, sniffling and all that. I felt the lamest I had ever felt in my entire life—*you're being a fucking whiny soap opera diva.* But I couldn't stop myself. I took K's whole pack of tissues, and she turned to leave.

"K!" I spat out between sobs. "Thanks."

"S'cool," she said, and shut the door.

Eighteen

fter our trip to Alas, we returned to Henri's, where he'd prepared a sumptuous duck soup. Not only was this the closest thing I had tasted to the food on Tania's farm, but after one bowl, I had to cut myself off. Too rich for my thin American blood. I should have seen the hidden motive behind such a grand meal.

"Ryland," Henri began over dinner. It unfolded quickly. The short of it was this: Henri didn't have the money to cover Jonas's ticket. Every other sentence out of his mouth was *Je suis trés, trés, trés désolé*. Henri explained that now that he was embarking on opening the factory, there was very little cash to spare. One hundred euros was too much to scrounge up and give away.

"Mais, je suis heureux que vous êtes venu," he made sure to tell me. "Pour Jonas et Angelique. Et ma petite Madeleine."

I thanked him for that. It was a small solace to not be seen as a nuisance, but not quite enough solace to overlook the bigger, less fuzzily happy reality. I was stuck. Nevermind getting back to the suckhole that was my real life—I needed the cash infusion to get to my next destination. All through dinner, I tried to hide my disappointment. Finally, after the millionth time Henri apologized, he asked what I was going to do. I told him that I'd have to figure out a way to get to Scotland, which prompted the strangest response. Henri told Jonas to give him his cell phone, then dialed a number.

"Sylvia! Une faveur, s'il te plait."

So, remember those sisters and brothers who sold their shares of the pottery factory to Henri? Well, turns out that he did many of them a favor by taking the family legacy out of their hands. Sylvia was one of the most excited to depart southern France and migrate to the wide, picturesque boulevards of *Gay Paree!* where she promptly got a big girl job at a cheap, no-frills airline outfit. After twenty years at the same company, she rose to Vice President and got all the perks that come with the position—which included free tickets to anywhere she wanted at any time.

And lucky me. She was so excited to hear her brother's voice for the first time in years that she agreed to leave a plane ticket in my name at the ticket counter in Aéroport Toulouse-Blagnac. I totally thought Henri was shitting me. It was hard for me to buy the sequence of events that would wind up with me holding a comp ride to exactly where I needed to go. Despite everything that had gone on. Despite fucking ghosts chasing me in my sleep. But that's how it happened.

250

The next day, I woke up, and Jonas was ready to take me to the airport. I just had to pack up my shit and we were off. My flight was early—eleven AM—leaving me little time to settle things with Madeleine. I was never good at saying goodbye. I preferred to make Batman-style, smoke-screened exits. I couldn't do that here. Madeleine deserved more than that, and, frankly, I deserved more. Up until then, hook-ups—long and short term—were filled with mostly anxiety. It helped that my tendency to fuck up relationships made the goodbyes quick, albeit painful. But Madeleine was different, and not only because she and I had so little time together. No. It felt different because maybe I was different.

We took a walk that morning amid the pottery on the hillside. Every five minutes or so, we'd pause from the conversation and make out, then return to talking.

"So it's really happening," I said. "The factory is going to open."

"We will be very busy here, but I am scared a little."

"Could you use some help from a totally helpless, inexperienced, untalented American who'll drink all your wine and offend the locals?"

"And who is this?"

We stopped walking. It was about time for the next break.

After we resumed: "What do you think you will find in L'Écosse?" she asked.

"I want to find Dora's family," I said. "She has to get me closer to figuring out Paolo." Oh shit. Just then I remembered what Paolo had told me. I had to call Tania. I totally forgot. What's more, I had to call Herr Cutter to get her number. I wasn't exactly enthused at the prospect of phoning up Herr Cutter, interrupting his meticulously assembled schedule. Well, whatever. It had to be done.

"Madeleine, I'm going to come back," I declared.

"I will keep the bed in your closet ready."

"Alors! C'est comme ça entre nous!"

"Only kidding."

We parted ways, and I headed back to the house with her cell phone in hand. She went down to the factory. It was a big day—the test run for the big kiln that hadn't run since Henri closed the place. Inside the house, I tossed the shit out of my bag until I found the Salt Lick Bar-B-Que napkin with Herr Cutter's number. Then I rang him up. He picked up after half a ring.

"Cutter," answered a dry voice on the other end.

"Herr Cutter, it's Ryland Taggart."

"You are still alive. Surprising. What do you want? I am having my morning egg."

"Scrambled? Poached?"

"Weich gekochtes Ei—surely you did not call me to ask my breakfast preferences."

"Of course I did." He didn't laugh. "Ooookay. I really called because I need Tania's number."

He sighed. "Has she contacted you?"

"No. Why?"

"I am set to return to the farm tomorrow. I am running the tests again."

"But you were so sure," I said. "The radiation?"

"I still am, but I . . . I believe you have been a bad influence on me."

"Anything for a friend."

"Plus 39, 342-745-8759. That is her mobile." I wrote the new number next to the old on my trusty napkin. "Do not tell her that we spoke. She asked me not to bother you. I suspect she already knows what I know—you are afflicted with a chronic and highly contagious brain wasting disease. From this conversation alone, I find that I cannot recall my favorite quotes from Charlemagne."

"*Let my armies be the rocks and the trees and the birds in the sky*, right?"

"I am hanging up now." Wrong side of the bed, Herr Cutter? Did he have a right side? No matter. I got right to dialing Tania's number and waited until the voice-mail picked up. I hung up and dialed again. I hate voice-mail for multiple reasons, but mostly because the people I know never listened to them. On the fourth call, someone finally picked up with a weary, "Pronto?"

"Tania? It's Ryland Taggart."

"Miss Taggart? Why . . . is this a French phone number you are calling me from?"

"Um, yeah?"

"I am sorry if I sound . . ." she began. "I did not expect to hear from you. Why are you not in America?"

"About that." I thought for a moment how I was going to sum up everything that had happened in the days between my leaving the farm and right then. I decided, ultimately, to scrap that plan and just try to shoot the shit. "I decided to extend my vacation."

"I see. You are enjoying yourself."

"Well, not quite. I mean, I'm having fun . . . mostly."

"There is something you are not telling me." Shit! Why did she have to be so perceptive? Fine. Chase, consider yourself cut to.

"I saw him," I blurted out. "In my dreams."

"Tiburzi?"

"No." I had to muster up a fair amount of courage to make it through the next couple of minutes—courage to be okay with sounding crazy, and courage to admit that I hadn't exactly been truthful to Tania. "Listen—I need to tell you some stuff. It's going to sound insane." Here it goes. "I should have told you that morning we were talking about my dreams. That guy—Domenico Tiburzi—he said that the land was dying."

"This you did tell me. And it is true—Il professore informed me of his findings. It has been hard these past days, for all of us here."

"But that's the thing—I didn't tell you that Tiburzi said I was the only person who could save it."

"Miss Taggart, I told you that sometimes spirits try to fool with people—"

"That's not what's happening!" I had started to pace up and down the upstairs hallway, scuffing across the floorboards. "I've been to Munich and then to France tracking down this lady . . . In the book you gave me was this photo. . . Did you know anything about Dora? She's this lady Paolo was in love with . . . I've seen the green ray, and that's the name of the damn book that you gave me!"

"I cannot follow. How does this concern Paolo?"

"*Lei non lo mancherà,*" I said.

"Pardon?"

"*Lei non lo mancherà.* I don't know what it means, but Paolo told me to say it to you—in my dream. But he wouldn't say what it means 'cause he's so stubborn!"

"It means 'She will not miss it,'" said Tania. "You remember my grandmother's vase? My uncle found me crying, sitting on the floor trying to piece it together like it was a puzzle. He gathered up the remains and threw them away. *Lei non lo mancherà.* He told me that she would not miss her vase because she was dead already."

"What is all this? What's happening, Tania?"

Long pause. Then: "I do not know, Miss Taggart."

Deep breath. "Everything that's happened with the farm and Paolo and right now—it's all connected somehow in this crazy way. I can't prove it. I don't really know how."

"I do not think there is a how, Miss Taggart," said Tania. "The more important question is what will you do now?"

"Follow the green ray, I guess. Not much choice."

"You always have a choice," she said.

I closed the door on the storage closet, the one thing at Henri's that I was glad to leave, and walked downstairs. The kitchen had been through post-breakfast cleanup. The coffee pot was off the stove and hung on a hook over the sink. The butter and bread had been packed away.

Marcel sat by himself at the table, his customary cigarette dangling from his lips. In front of him were the pieces of pottery I'd seen him firing the day before. He was using a brush to scrub the outer surface of each little pot.

"Bonjour," he greeted me without even looking my way. The cup in Marcel's hand was small—the size of my fist. Post-scrub, he held it out for me to take. It felt hard to the touch, and cold, like stone. Not completely smooth. The surface undulated, felt slick on my fingertips. The colors, though, were striking—a band of jet black, then of brick red, then a gray that shone copper in the light.

"Do you plan out the colors?"

"It is not possible to predict," he said, refusing the cup when I tried to give it back. "It is always a surprise how they look. Like a baby, no? You take it."

"I can't take this."

"C'est bon. There will be more tomorrow."

Outside, Jonas loaded my bag into the back of the van. Through the windows, still stained with rain-grime from the downpour the other night, I tried to take all of it in because I didn't want to forget what it was like to be here, in the mountains again, only on the other side of the world. As the car eased off the property, I thought I saw Madeleine—it was far away, so I couldn't be sure it was her—standing amidst the tallest pieces of pottery like they were trees in a thick, glazed forest. As the car moved, so did she, disappearing and reappearing from around the backs of the jugs and swan-necked vases. I placed my hand on the window to wave one last goodbye, and that's when the figure stopped, watched us until she faded from sight, until I faded from her sight.

Mais où sont les bisous d'antan?

"Ceci est votre nom?" the ticket agent asked, holding up the plane ticket for me to see.

I once more stood next to Jonas and across from a ticket agent, but this time, I was the wayward traveler, and Jonas played the role of good Samaritan.

"Oui." I handed over my ID, and after a short comparison, the ticket was in my hands. I felt such a rush of relief. *Départ: Toulouse et L'arrivée: Édimbourg (Écosse).* The clock indicated that I had an hour till boarding time. That left about twenty minutes to enjoy one last cup of coffee with Jonas at L'Horizon Cafe, a surprisingly pleasant vantage point to watch planes take off.

I was leaving Jonas, leaving France, leaving the European continent for things unknown.

Leaving Madeleine.

"I was thinking that it is possible we will not meet again." Jonas sucked his cup of coffee dry and gingerly placed it back on the saucer. With his finger, he traced the cup's lip, maybe imagining the mechanical hands that stamped it out, fired it up, packed it in, and shipped it here.

"I'll be back. I promise."

"It is one thing to promise, but another to do," he said.

"I don't think your sister feels the same way."

He laughed, then pointed up at the clock. "Drink, or you will miss your plane."

Promise me something.

I spent Christmas break at St. Gertie's with the girls whose parents were atheists and one who I think was a practicing Satanist. I pulled away socially from everything and everyone, even more than I had before. It wasn't anyone's fault. It's just that Angie, Monte, and Spider were never my friends. Just girls who were there because their friend had become someone special in my life. When she left, so did they. I didn't blame them.

I never saw Shannon again. The teachers stopped calling out her name for attendance, and her name gradually stopped being said altogether. Principal Lewis, as well, disappeared for a month after Christmas break ended. Apart from the stunned look she gave me when I handed in the report for the Winter Formal, we didn't have any communication after our burger rendezvous. Then one day, I opened my door to go to class in the morning, and there she was, tapping her foot and holding a thick manila folder under her arm.

"I swear to God I didn't do anything," I declared.

"Come with me."

"I'm going to be late for class."

"Then I'll just give you the detention ahead of time."

Well, shit. I went with Principal Lewis not knowing where she was taking me. At least at first. Right as P. Lewis and I passed up the last classroom in the hall, I figured out where we were going, and my brain lit up with ways to weasel out of my sudden and probably unavoidable death. We were headed for the secret passage. P. Lewis opened up the hidden door and bade me to go in before her.

"I want you to see something," she said. My fears were on target. P. Lewis stopped me in the precise spot that Shan had stopped me all those months before—where THE STASH used to be.

"On my desk this morning was a note from one of our maintenance men." She presented me with a piece of paper—a note written to P. Lewis with a little map to the location we were at. "He and his crew were cleaning here last night and noticed one of these bricks sticking out from the wall. Turns out there's a little cubby hole here perfect for stashing things away. It was empty when he opened it up. What do you think of all this?"

"Um . . . crazy?"

"Yeah. Crazy."

"What am I doing here?"

"I just wanted your opinion."

"I think that Dexy's Midnight Runners was way underrated."

"I'm gonna miss you," she said. "Wait, I think I was actually talking about the corns on my feet."

"Miss me?" I turned to face her. "Are you leaving?"

"I already left. Turned in my resignation yesterday."

I held up the note she gave me. "What am I supposed to do with this?"

"It's paper," she said. "You write on it, or maybe make it into an airplane."

259

"What? I don't get it."

"You always ruin my jokes," she said. "Look, it doesn't matter. I don't know what this thing is, or if you had anything to do with it. I really brought you here so you could promise me something."

"Promise you what?"

"You have to promise first."

"That's not how this usually works, Principal Lewis."

"First of all, I'm not your principal, and second, that's how I work, so promise. C'mon." Reluctantly, I promised and hoped that I hadn't just committed a valuable body part to a grotesque and sinister experiment P. Lewis was conducting in her basement. "Don't burn down this school. It's a good place. And double promise that you'll keep working your ass off. I took a look at your grades the other day. Not too shabby." I thought I saw a glimmer in her eyes, a twinkle maybe. Maybe she and I didn't disagree on that many things. Maybe, in some way, we understood each other all too well.

"Thanks," I said. Were we sharing a moment? Because I think we were honest-to-fucking-God sharing a moment. "I know you could have sent me home all this time, but you didn't. I really appreciate that."

"Part of my job. It *was*, anyway."

"Maybe it's . . . maybe I remind you of you as a girl?"

P. Lewis scowled and leaned to meet me at eye level.

"You take that back," she said.

Part Four

The Green Ray of the Sun

Buongiorno Ryland!

Nonno has a new computer so I write to you. Mama and me and my sisters stay now in Nomadelfia. That is the place Mama and Papa grew up. On the day before Tania told Papa that we must leave. He says the farm is sick and we to go.

How do you make it clean when you kiss boys? It is always so wet. I tell this to Fabrizio, but he does not listen. He drols. Is that the word?

You are practicing Italiano, si? Read this: Non è importante quello che sei. Siamo amici. Write back to me! Better to phone! +39075432719

Daniella

Hey Shan,

It's been a while. I know. I just wanted to drop you a line. Facebook seems to think it's a good idea, anyway. RT

Nineteen

ontrary to what he might believe, I did listen in Herr Cutter's class. One thing always stuck out, and that's how evolution works. See, scientists—including his royal grumpiness—still tend to think that things changed slowly over millions of years. Look how that saber-toothed tiger got less sabertoothy and became a Survivor song, or how amoebas became fish, elephants, or gorillas. But that's not how it really happens. Change doesn't happen over millennia.

It happens in moments. That fish one day decides that legs might be a good idea. The ice age ends, and mammoths figure that fur coats are totally last epoch. Gorillas trade in bananas for skinny jeans, cellphones, and double bacon cheeseburger meals. A second before, it's all one way, and the second after, it is something totally else. And it's all about your choice—*vostra scelta*—in That. One. Moment.

The Green Ray of the Sun

A plate and glass—two glasses, a cup of hot tea—begin to slide across the tilting rattan surface.

On the plane ride to Edinburgh, I raced through my memories of *The Green Ray*, trying to recall important plot points. It may have been more helpful if I remembered some names of places. Then again, in the days just before the book plunged into the river, I was a little distracted.

Strangely, I didn't freak out. Not that I wasn't concerned, but my existential self-flagellation was absent. My outlook had changed. I'd accepted bewilderment as the new normal.

When I got off the plane, I took a piss and went to the ATM. The big fat £ symbol on the ATM screen flipped me the bird, even before I put my card in. I was in the land of the pound, which meant that everything cost roughly *twice* what it would have cost at home. After taking out £50, I took note that I officially had £65.23 left to my name. Not enough to get back home for sure. The line had been crossed. There was no turning back. Two men enter, one man leave.

Bah. What else was new?

I indulged in a banana from the airport Relay shop (£.50), rode the Lothian bus into downtown Edinburgh (£1.20), and wandered around until I found a hostel—nothing less than an old church converted into a makeshift inn (a refreshingly inexpensive £7.00). After scratching my internet technology itch for an hour, I found myself with time. Only, I had grown so used to rushing here and running from there that my body had to transition from always being on edge to being okay with the calm. Needing to get my head on

264

straight, I lay aside any aspirations on furthering my Dora quest for the moment to concentrate on beer.

Yes, beer. The friendly desk clerk from Cameroon marked the joint where tourists went to wet their whistle. Only, when I arrived there, I was a little disappointed. Okay, more than a little—I hadn't been that disappointed since the time I was seven years old and the *A-Team on Ice* show got cancelled because half the cast had contracted the clap.

I was standing in front of T.G.I. *fucking* Friday's.

At the bar, a busty beer wench waited for me to order up a drink-and-perhaps-food. A part of me wanted to order the *Nawlins Cajun Spiced Bourbon Street Turkey Club Quesadilla*, but a cheap ass beer was more in my price range. Relaxing there was a welcome blip of levity. Notice I used the word *blip* because my respite didn't last very long.

In a deluxe booth at the other side of the room, a rowdy bunch of athletic, rugby-looking dudes were aggressively screaming the lyrics to *Purple Rain*, clearly annoying the larger T.G.I. Friday's population: powersuit-wearing, post-workday warriors slinging back their happy hours, families with their children in highchairs, disheveled travelers like me enjoying their bargain basement ales. One of the bigger guys called over the waitress and ordered yet another round for the table. And in that split second, I did the thing. The bad, worse, worst thing.

I made eye contact.

"How about her?" one of the dudes with a green and white soccer tee said. He meant me. "She's pretty enough." Now there's a compliment to get you on base. Even though I looked away and feigned interest in a stack of napkins on the bar, two guys from that table walked over to me. They were twins—both tall, lanky, scruffy guys with the same narrow chins and the same spiky haircuts.

"Oy!" said the one on the left.

"Hullo," greeted the one on the right.

Me: "Gentlemen."

Left: "Why don't you join us?"

Right: "Yeah! We'll make room at the table."

Me: "Um, no."

Right: Well, if you don't want to sit with us, maybe you'd like to help us."

Left: "Yeah."

Me: "I don't think so."

Left: "C'mon, then! You haven't even heard what we're proposing."

Right: "We need your help."

Me: "With what?"

Right: "Excellent!"

Me: "I haven't agreed to anything, yet."

Left: "C'mon. It'll be fun."

Right: "Our brother over there is getting married, see? His wife-to-be is beautiful, dazzling, the whole fooking lot. We just want him to enjoy his last day as a free man."

Left: "We want you to kiss him."

Right: "I hear he's a good kisser."

Me: "I'm not exactly feeling my sexy back right now."

Understatement. I looked like a sack of shit. I felt like a sack of shit. I probably smelled like a sack of shit, and how come these dudes weren't getting the high sack-of-shittiness quotient in this situation?

Right: *Looking around the bar for a potential new target.* "Well, thanks for your time anyway."

Left: *Pointing down the bar to a woman in a sequined dress.* "What about her, Sebastian?"

Right: "We had a chance with this one, Samuel. No chance with that one."

I did a double take. Samuel and Sebastian. Sam and Sib. This was too weird. Correction—this was *exactly* weird for this week's edition of Ryland Taggart. I called to them before they were out of earshot: "I changed my mind."

"Fook yeah!" yelled Samuel. They led me across the room to the carousing at their table.

"Eowin!" shouted Sebastian. "You have a lovely girl waiting for you!"

"Ach, gonnae no dae that!"

"How?" Samuel said. "What kind of brothers would we be if we let you live happily ever after?"

"Just gonnae no—hey!" Sam and Sebastian plunged their hands into the mini-mob and extracted their brother from his social cocoon. He hung from their outstretched arms curled tightly around a tree branch. He was the opposite of his brothers—squat and stocky, his head clean shaven. Their friends around the table started chanting "Eowin! Eowin! Eowin!"

"May we present you our dear brother, Eowin," said Samuel proudly. The twins dropped their brother—arms tucked in, eyes shut tight—down on the ground in front of me. Slowly, he opened up until we were eye to eye with each other.

Motherfucker.

267

"I'll be buggered," said Eowin. "Ryland?"

"Hi Clancy," I answered. "Are we making out or what?"

Out the window next to the office's front desk was a breathtaking forty-fourth story view of Mt. Rainier and the Space Needle. Claudia, the secretary manning the front desk did what secretaries did best—type stuff, talk on the phone, and look pretty. This one was especially pretty. While I sat in the waiting area, I caught a glance or sixteen at her full, heart-shaped ass. Very nice.

Too bad I had to hate her guts.

"They done yet?" I asked for the ninth time. I'd been waiting an hour.

She glanced over to the double doors that had been shut since I'd arrived. I'm sure Claudia enjoyed my presence as much as I enjoyed waiting, which is to say *negativo*.

"Not much longer," she said for the ninth time. "I like your hair. Is that a special style?"

"Purple. You know, like Picasso had his blue period. This is my purple period." Insert joke about menstruation, grape soda. "How much longer?"

Claudia could only smile and shrug.

"That long, huh? I'll set my alarm," I replied, twisting the invisible knob on my invisible watch. I leaned back against the wall, swiped on my crappy-ass phone, and hooked onto the hilariously un-passworded wifi to watch the same video

I'd been binging on that whole morning. "Living the Geek Dream!" it was titled. It showed a packed convention hall, lights a-blazing, with the main action happening on a stage at the front. A trio of people sat up there in front of a set of video screens. Each furiously jammed their fingers on joysticks to control pixelated characters shooting at each other. Even though I knew what was going to happen at the end, I still gripped my phone as if this was the first time I'd seen the video. It reminded me that once upon a time— roughly twenty-four hours before, as a matter of fact—I'd (finally) done something worth being proud of, even though it had landed me in the shittiest of shit situations.

The double doors swung open, and out walked three shitheads. Okay, so maybe I should be more specific. The shithead on the right with the bolo tie and cowboy hat was probably some oil tycoon getting the skinny on how to skirt environmental regulations. The shithead on the left was a sharp-looking black lady holding a bunch of manila folders and sporting really nice runner's calves and a form-fitting, blue dress. The shithead in the middle was the king—the shittiest shithead of them all. David Taggart. My dad.

"Mr. Chisholm, once again, thank you for paying us this visit!" Dad was so good at sucking up. He took the cowboy dude's hands in his like he was the pope. "Our continued good relationship means so much to this firm."

"Thanks, Dave. And thank you, Deanna." He took the lady's hand and kissed it. After Doc Holiday made his exit, I called Dad over to let him know I'd arrived. I was surprised when the lady lawyer approached me and started talking.

"Are you Ryland?"

"Yeah?"

"Hi, I'm—"

"Deanna. I know. I have ears."

"I think your father wasn't expecting you this early." Dad made no effort to join our little dialogue. Had he hired extra people around the office so he wouldn't have to talk to me? That's pretty . . . typical.

"You don't have to make excuses. He forgot."

"I didn't forget," he said, still not looking at me. I hadn't physically seen him in almost a year, not since he dropped me off at St. Gertie's. He looked different. More svelt. Buzz-cut. And it wasn't until I dressed him down fully that I noticed the blonde tuft of hair underneath his bottom lip. A fucking soul patch. My dad. My life.

"I'm so glad that you decided to visit," Deanna said. Hmm. Looked like the whole truth and nothing but was on a need to know basis. And the help didn't need to know. Fine with me. If daddy-kins wanted the real nature of my "visit" to stay vague, I had no problem with that. "Are you hungry? I don't know if you've eaten, but I'm sure David would love if you joined us for lunch." David. Dad. It was jarring to hear this lady call Dad by his first name like he was a newborn puppy. And for sure, he didn't look at all like he'd love it if I joined them for lunch.

"The reservations were for two people," said Dad. He checked his watch, polished its face with the cuff of his shirt. "And I think Ryland's pretty beat from the trip." Reservations? Like who makes reservations for lunch on a workday? Oh. Lawyers. Understood.

"I'm sure we can squeeze one more in."

270

"It's Canlis, Deanna," said Dad. "I made these reservations a month ago."

Wait, wait, wait. I sat there while the tide of comprehension lapped at my ankles before drowning me in a sudden tsunami of obvious. Dad. Deanna. I looked at each one in turn, and stopped on her face. I totally got it. Everything made sense: the first name basis, the being nice to me, the private lunch.

This was the woman who was fucking my dad.

"I'm actually not really hungry," I said, my mouth dry and gritty like sandpaper. "I'll just go to Dad's and lie down."

"Let's let Ryland rest," he began, pressing a pair of house keys into my palm. "And we'll see her later, okay?" He turned to me. "Okay?"

"Yeah."

"Get the address from Claudia. We gotta go, Deanna."

"It was so nice to meet you, Ryland," Deanna said before she and Dad boarded the elevator.

I waited five minutes before getting on the elevator myself. I wanted to avoid any awkward lobby run-ins with Dad and his new little woman. That being done, I followed Claudia's directions to Dad's swank pad, where I had half a mind to call up the Swedish authorities and report the illegal Ikea factory outlet Dad ran from his living room. Everything in his condo was white-colored and business-efficient, from the kitchen table that folded into the wall, to the toilet with three seashell-shaped buttons on the side that controlled the built-in bidet. The couch cushions were still robust and bursting, not yet downtrodden by the parade of asses that oppresses couches worldwide.

271

Yet, despite the dominance of Swedish-made décor, Dad had taken pains to embellish the place with an Asian flair—as long as by "Asian" you mean, "decorations stolen from the set of a *Godzilla* movie." A tea set was laid out on the counter by the sink, and a kimono hung framed on the wall opposite a small bar filled with unlabeled, probably expensive liquors made by enslaved children crushing spiny fruits with their bare hands.

The bedroom was decked out with similar Japanese shit—at least it looked like Japanese writing on everything: a set of metal bottles with various foul smelling powders inside, a print of a Japanese scroll featuring a seascape, and a katana. Yes, Dad owned a samurai sword. (Mid-life crisis much?) And while I would not have been surprised to find a pair of nunchucks in his kitchen cupboards, I was a little peeved that he had no food around. I hadn't eaten anything besides the $4.00 fruit roll-up I bought at the airport, and it had been a few hours already. So when the refrigerator's only contents were a pack of honey mustard from a Wendy's six-pack chicken nuggets and half a container of gorgonzola crumbles, I groped for other possibilities, chief among them the number for Via Tribunali pizza magneted to a whiteboard on the fridge door.

I had just picked up the phone when someone knocked on my door. On the other side was a pizza delivery boy. That's some service.

"Hi," said the pizza boy in a sexy baritone. Dude was seriously stacked, a full 6'2" broad-shouldered linebacker type holding an extra-large pizza with one hand.

"I think you have the wrong place," I said. "But I'll buy

that pizza off you if you're willing to tell the real owner you got mugged by the Ninja Turtles."

"The pizza's for you. My mom was worried that you hadn't eaten anything."

"Your mom? Who—oh." His mom. Deanna. Which meant that this was a charity house call. Well, far be it from me to leave the Trojan Horse outside the gates. I showed him in, making sure to liberate the goods from his possession. I oppressed the couch, folded back the top of the pizza box, and went to town. Mmm. Pepperoni. My favorite. "I'm Ryland, by the way," I said, spitting up a piece of crust which landed on the sand mandala on the coffee table. I used the mini-rake to cover it up.

"Casimir."

"Pizza," I said. "Have some."

"No thanks. I work at a pizza place. I'd rather eat anything else."

"Suit yourself," I said, partaking of my third piece. "So Deanna sent you to spy on me?"

"Nice to meet you, too."

"Sorry," I said. "Where are my manners? Can I offer you a drink? A refreshing glass of honey mustard?"

"I'll get it." He popped up and went into the kitchen. A second later, he came back with two cups of water. So. He was a gentleman. That was nice. "Mom said you just got in today."

"Yup. Thanks for the pizza, by the way."

"Y'know, David never really talks about you." I choked on a piece of pepperoni. "I didn't even know he had . . . has a daughter."

273

"Yeah. Surprise." I said.

"Usually parents talk about their kids."

"Jesus, okay! Apparently, there are exceptions! You're endangering the pizza truce."

"Sorry," Casimir said. "I'm not very good at talking to girls."

"Then pretend I'm not a girl."

"That's kind of hard."

"I'm a lesbian—does that help?"

"Not really."

"*Not really?*"

This was not going well, and it was mostly my fault. I'd been on edge since I woke up that morning in a jail cell next to a charming man named "Tabitha," who, the night before, had educated me on the dangers of bacteriological infection from supermarket carts. In depth. Like with Latin scientific names. Cas didn't deserve bitchy Ryland, so I apologized: "Look, I've just had a rough day, okay?"

"Care to talk about it?"

"No."

"Why not?"

"Because." I smiled to let him know that this line of questioning would go nowhere. "How about you tell me about yourself, instead?" He didn't have a problem giving up the goods because there wasn't much to hide (unlike myself). Cas had graduated high school that past May, like me. Since then he'd been working at Marco Trafficano's Pizzeria and playing in a band.

"What instrument do you play?"

He shook his head. "Nothing."

"You're in a band, but you don't play an instrument. So what are you—a go-go dancer?"

"I write music," he said. "If I need to learn an instrument, I learn it. But I can't really claim to specialize in any one, which kinda sucks. If I was any good, I'd be able to get into the U.S. Army band."

"The Army? Why the hell are you doing that?"

"My dad." Oh, that old, familiar tune. "He's a major at Fort Bragg."

"So your mom . . . and my dad . . ."

"My parents are divorced. Four years now."

A key jiggled into the lock in the front door. A second later, the deadbolt slid open, and in walked Dad and Deanna, both beaming and holding hands. I had a sixth sense about Dad, and it went something like this: if he was happy, there was something out there that you should be sad about.

"Hey guys!" he said.

"Hey David," said Cas.

"Ryland," said Deanna, "did Cas bring you food?"

"A whole pizza."

"Guys!" Dad called out once again. It was irritating, like he was talking to a bunch of his friends. I was not his friend, and I had a name. He gave it to me. Not that his soul patch and thousand-dollar suit didn't make me want to piss all over the couch and sand mandala and samurai sword. "Deanna and I have some news." He raised her hand to show off the sizable rock on her finger. It hadn't been there when I had last seen her in his office.

No fucking way. I was about to stand up and open my

mouth—not knowing exactly what would come out of it—when Cas stepped in front of me and pushed me back onto the couch.

"Congratulations," said Cas. "I . . . we're so happy."

Ooh, I wanted to kick the shit out of all of them.

"It's a really great day, you guys," said Dad. "I'm glad that we could share it with you. Now, if you excuse us, I'm going to walk Deanna home." I tried to get a word in, but Cas used his ass to play human shield. It wasn't until Dad and Deanna had left that he turned around to face me.

"Before you say anything—"

"ANYTHING!" I screamed.

"I deserve that," he said, wiping spit off his cheek. "I didn't want you to do something you'd regret."

"You don't know me! You don't know how I feel!"

"Okay, then. Tell me."

When I next opened my mouth, I made a noise like the last breath of a dying cat. He had put me right on the spot. How did I feel? Mad, for one, and hurt, for another. But I couldn't place exactly what I was mad or hurt about. The emotions just swam through me. I could feel it even in my hair and fingernails—it was that intense. "Doesn't . . . aren't you mad that your mother is getting married to another man?"

"Truth? I'm happy for her. She's dated enough scumbags."

"How is my dad NOT a scumbag?"

"He seems like a good guy."

"You don't know what he did!"

"What did he do?" One thing became very clear to me.

Cas didn't mess around when he set his mind on something. And with my snark temporarily disarmed, I embodied title as queen of the harpies:

"Thanks for the pizza," I said. "Now get out."

For hours after Cas left, I sat on the carpet in front of the door. I felt drained, so much so that I'd continue to sit and be in the way when Dad came back from his walk. But he didn't come back that night. So I spent my first night in Seattle on the floor, processing Dad being married again, a new wife, a new son. An entirely new life with me as the only vestige of his past.

Twenty

un fact—Clancy wasn't a first name. His full name was Eowin Aldous Clancy, aka *Whitest Name Ever*.

The last time I'd seen him—a whole year before—he'd been operating the only bike taxi outfit in San Francisco. Insane, I know, but he did corner the market. By luck or fate or something even more mysterious, we were together again—this time on his home turf where he had a secure hold an altogether different market. Apparently around these parts, Clancy had quite the reputation as a cosmetologist and haberdasher. In normal-people talk, that meant that he was a hairdresser who also knew how to apply makeup and fix up your hat. Hey, at least that beat out what his bros did for a living, which was help run the family business, Clancy Paper Corp., with their father.

"So," started Sebastian, "how do you know Eowin?"

"I want to know where she's fitting all that liquid!" said Samuel. "I had thirty quid before she showed up!"

"I'll buy you a pint if you shut the fook up."

"You got it," agreed Samuel. To me: "How do you know our little brother?"

"I met Clancy—er, Eowin—last year. In the States."

"San Francisco," said Eowin leaning back into his seat. "I miss that bay, the cool mornings and perfect afternoons, the string bikinis."

"Your brother helped me out with his bike taxi when my car broke down."

"Free of charge, may I add," Eowin said. "Sorry the polls lifted ya."

"Um . . . yeah." I raised my glass of beer and toasted: "For all the times we've fucked up!" Everyone in the bachelor party clinked glasses. "Speaking of fuck-ups, Clancy—"

"Which one?" the brothers said simultaneously.

"I mean you," I said, pointing to Eowin. "Tell me about this lady love. She's gotta be better than the chick who kept hitting you in the face, right?"

Samuel spit up his Belhaven and burst out laughing. Sebastian was a little more discreet, hiding his giggles behind his hand. Eowin turned beet red.

"What? What did I say?"

Samuel, after cleaning himself up with a napkin: "Eowin's marrying that same girl tomorrow. Her name's Elspeth."

"Right," said Sebastian. "Mean right hook, our future sister-in-law."

"You two are bloomin' idiots," said Eowin. "Aye, it started off bad with me and Elspeth, but once I came back . . ."

279

"Came back—tell her the truth, Eowin!" shouted Samuel.

"Okay," Eowin began. "Maybe you know this, Ryland. In the U.S., they do this really funny thing when you get pulled over for running a red light at three o'clock in the fooking night. They take you down to the police station and they ask you for your ID, and you say that you don't have one. Then they type your name into their bloody computers and talk about you in front of your face and put you in jail. And after a bit—this is the funniest part—you get a plane ticket back to where you came from."

"You got deported."

"Such an ugly word. Say, what're you doing here? Vacationing? The others aren't with you, are they?"

The others. Jesus, from late last summer up until I'd gotten to Tania's farm, not a day would go by that I didn't think about Double-J—LeRoy Jupiter Jenkins—and the rest of the crew for at least a few minutes. Those crazy days felt like a lifetime ago—or more like twelve lifetimes with all the shit I'd been though on this trip. And as much as I wanted to believe that we'd keep in touch, time and distance did their thing. Communication became sparse save for the occasional inclusion on a group text, and my life got shit-fucked enough so that watching funny YouTube videos wasn't enough to counteract the daily fucking slog. I moved on with my life. So did LeRoy. Same with Austin and Saff and Clancy. Until now.

I shook my head. "I'm here solo," I said. "In fact, you'd have me committed if I told you why I was here."

"We'll make sure that the paddy wagon was pink on the inside," said Sebastian.

"I hate pink."

"You in some trouble?" Samuel asked. "If you're a friend of Eowin's, you're part of the family."

Cutting across the plate are two strips of bacon pointing at twelve

o'clock and three. Coffee spills onto the plate and sinks into the

waffle, soaking through the bottom and welling around the sides.

What. The. Fuck. The Clancy brothers had failed to mention two things before we left the hostel, where a gang of Estonian boys helped me gather my things to check out: 1) the Clancys lived in a castle, despite their protests. *Turrets? Check. Square-shaped cut-out doo-hickeys along the roof? Check. A moat? Check, even though Eowin insisted that it was simply a "natural contour" of the land.* And 2) an Asian nation had declared war on their drawing room, and had sent its elite, prepubescent girl ninja squad to make sure the highlanders were cut off at the knees.

"Chinese," Eowin clarified. "They're Chinese. Ninjas are Japanese." "They" referred to the throng of people chatting, eating, drinking, sewing, dressing up, dressing down, dressing sideways in white satin-y bridesmaid dresses. "They" were his peeps—or at least would be once his marriage was legit. Twenty-four hours before, I was in the middle of nowhere with the quiet French countryside, a beautiful girl on my arm, and all the pots I could piss in. Now, I was in *Mulan* meets *The Princess Diaries*.

"There he is!" A tall Asian—I mean Chinese—girl with a Scots accent ran over, jumped on Eowin, and laid kisses on his bald head. "How are you, love?"

"Hi Elspeth," Clancy's brothers said together.

"And who is this?"

A shrill voice rang out above the din: "Are those ruffians back yet?" A stout woman emerged from the crowd to greet us at the door. "Aye, here you are you good-for-nothings."

"Hi ma," said the Clancy bros.

"And you, young lady—have you come to find out what mother could birth such barbarians?"

"Uh . . . well . . ." I stammered. "Your generous sons insisted that I could spend the night."

"Is that right?"

Eowin for the save: "Ma, Ryland and I go back. Remember when I was in America—"

"Oh yes, Eowin. If I could only forget."

"We couldn't let her stay at a hostel," said Sebastian. "Scots hospitality, after all."

"You're lucky you're my favorite, Sebastian. Why don't you show your friend some 'hospitality' and get her something to eat. Your father insisted that I let Elspeth's mother take over my kitchen." Samuel took my stuff up and hit the sack early while Sebastian showed me around. Eowin had the hardest job—mingling with members of his extended-family-to-be, who insisted on his opinion on which bridesmaid looked prettier, which looked fatter, that sort of thing. *Abandon all hope, all ye who enter . . .*

Upon entering the kitchen, Sebastian and I found it to be the polar opposite of the boisterous girlie-fest we had encountered in the living room. The mood was quiet, almost somber. A bunch of men stood with drinks or with bowls of soup ladled out of a kettle on the stove.

"You think China is any better? The banks fecked up the Irish economy, the whole U.K. And forget about America." Led by Sebastian, I stuck to the far side of the room, drawn toward the food on the stove that smelled delicious. It had been almost an entire day without meaningful food. Sebastian ladled up a bowlful of noodle soup and handing it to me. "Perhaps it is just as well, then. If money is what gives meaning to your life . . . boy." Sebastian snapped to attention like an electric current had jolted him straight. The man who was speaking waved us over, and we did as he commanded. "You'd, perhaps, like to make introductions."

"This is Ryland, da. Eowin's friend from the states."

"Ryland Taggart, sir."

"I wasn't aware there were guests from the U.S."

"She's not exactly here for the wedding. Just a visit."

"That won't do," he said. "I'm David Clancy. Eowin's father."

"Pleased to meet you, sir."

"Your name—Taggart—it's Irish. From Ulster, in the north. It means 'son of a priest.' Is your father a priest?"

"Far from it, sir. He's a lawyer."

"Ach. 'Tis the same. Am I right?" The guys in the room all burst out laughing at his joke perfectly on cue. "Well, Miss Taggart, I wish to rectify a grievous offense and formally invite you to my son's wedding. I trust that since you're here already, you will accept."

"I . . . of course. Thanks."

"Good," he said. "Now, where were we? Ah yes." Mr. Clancy refilled his glass with whisky and shot the whole thing back, licking his lips afterward. Mr. Clancy (sir) returned to regaling men huddled about him while we slurped up our soup.

"Sorry about that," Sebastian apologized. "When my da gets pissed, he's a tosser. When we were kids, he'd whip the shite out of us for any reason. Eowin, being as small as he is, was the most afraid. Da, I think, smelled that, because he gave Eowin holy fooking hell. Those were bloody beatings."

"He seemed okay."

"Yeah, well he's got an audience," he said. "But let's not think about that."

After finishing the soup, food baby set in, and I was ready for bed. Before heading off to one of the many guest bedrooms, Sebastian pointed out that "Samuel and I are down the hall, last room on the left. If you need anything during the night, just knock."

"Thanks," I said. "Actually, there is something . . ." How to say what I wanted to say without sounding like a psycho? Best, I thought right then, to leave the ghost stuff out. "You think you could help me find a specific person who lives in Scotland?"

"That's simple. Catch me tomorrow morning before we leave."

Not a priest, but Dad did attend mass, along with Deanna, every Sunday. Cas told me this on a Sunday morning, standing inside World's First Starbucks, guarding our narrow piece of counter space like it was the Alamo. Cas showed his impeccable sense of timing in waiting a week (about how long it took to see what a *sac de merde* I had been) before inviting me out for a peace offering cuppa. But why World's First Starbucks? This place was more packed than constipation. And why? It's Starbucks! Large was still stupidly called a "venti," and the biscotti was still hard enough to crack a few crowns.

At least I had unlimited refills, courtesy of Cas.

I shook my empty cup in front of his face, swishing the last little remnant of coffee at the bottom. With a playful sneer, he snatched the cup from me and got in line behind a tour bus worth of vacationing French tourists commenting on the décor.

"The French guys sure seem to like this place," Cas said, upon returning.

"Not really," I said. "They're criticizing everything. 'Look at zis! So disappointing! Ze one in Paree is better, no?'"

"You understand them?"

"Comme ci, comme ça."

"That's how you're passing the time? Studying foreign languages?"

"Yeah," I told him. But not really. My second day in Seattle, Dad and I had the dreaded sit down (I refused to sit down, opting instead to pace) about the reason I had come to town. Not even bothering to look straight at me, Dad let it out that UT had contacted him and was *this close* to throwing me out of school (an accomplishment, since I wasn't technically going there yet). Only after more wheeling-and-dealing did Dad get UT to merely delay matriculation. In other words, they were putting me on ice for a semester so that I'd have time to think about what I did. I almost expected Dad to (gleefully) produce an official UT dunce cap and tell me to sit in the corner until Christmas break was over.

Me: *I didn't even do anything.*

Dad: *Wait, wait—what? Maybe I need to remind you. Let's see . . . you stole a car . . . from Yellowstone National Park. Then you took it across three state lines. That makes it a federal crime, Ryland. You're lucky I got them to drop charges. You understand what that means?*

Me: *I'd be a long shot for that CIA internship?*

Dad: *If they pressed charges, I couldn't help you.*

Me: *You're a lawyer.*

Dad: *A corporate lawyer. Not Perry Mason.*

Me: *Perry Mason's a lawyer? That Ozzy song finally makes sense!*

Dad: *Be grateful you can make jokes.*

Look, I know I should have been grateful, because yes, he was right. Thanks to a letter writing campaign by former St. Gertie's principal, Carolyn Lewis, I'd been working as a "conservation intern" (read: souvenir shop cashier) at Yellowstone for a fat blob of a manager named Eugene. He taught me to conserve, all right—conserve outward signs of loathing, conserve my disappointment that visitors to Yellowstone would willingly buy literal jars of dirt for $12.99.

Then one day, opportunity showed up with a need for emergency wheels. What was a little vehicular "borrowing" between me and ye olde U.S. government, anyway? I figured snagging a van that wasn't being used for an extended joyride to San Francisco made me and the National Park Service even-steven.

Nope. It didn't matter that I helped break the Internet for a moment or two, gaining immortality in meme Valhalla next to Doge and 10-hour video loops of a baby dancing to "Gangnam Style." The worst part was my punishment. No, not the 500 hours of community service, a revoked driver's license for one whole year, and a lifetime ban from America's most cherished national park. That was all shit I could deal with. What I really hated was how Dad smeared my face in the fact that he—David Taggart, Esquire—had once again saved the fucking day.

Fuck-a-doodle-do.

"Is something wrong with the coffee?" asked Cas. "You're just staring at it."

"I'm fine," I said. "Just, y'know, contemplating the next drink I'm gonna make you buy."

"How about we make a deal. If you help me out with something today, I'll buy you as much coffee as you want—after payday."

I liked the cut of his jib. "One more refill."

"How about you skip the refill and we get some apple chips in the market. Then you're mine."

"You really know how to treat a girl," I said. "Maybe afterward we split a Capri Sun?"

He didn't dignify my snark with an answer. Instead, he led the way across the street and straight into the throngs at Pike Place Market, past and around vendors hauling their makeshift shops on squeaky-wheeled carts to set up on tables that they'd been assigned that morning. I admit that at first, the crowds put me off venturing into the wilds of the market. But I couldn't resist investigating the hawkers hollering to *try our new ghost pepper/raspberry blend!* from the pepper jelly nook or inviting me to *sample our cream cheese vatrushka!* at the Russian pastry shop.

With every blink, Cas melted into the crowds and emerged several steps ahead of where he had been—quite a feat for a dude his size. My pigeon legs could only take me so fast, and the fact that I stopped every other second to process the latest change in smell from fresh berries to tulips to tanned leather to smoked salmon.

It wasn't until we stopped at the front entrance of the market on Pike Street and 1st Ave. that I noticed the floor.

"What are all these names?" I said, pointing to the tiles under our feet. Each tile had imprinted upon it a unique name. Most times, they were normal people's names. *Gertrude Stedmond. Alex Derringer. Artie Yonkers.* Other times, they were really strange.

"Back in the '80s, the city raised money to fix the market floors by letting the public buy a personalized tile."

I pointed to the one right under my heel. "This one just has a number 3 on it."

He shrugged but paid no more attention to it. We stepped over to a kiosk, where Cas bought a small bag of shriveled looking apple chips for the road. Nearby, a couple of kids were riding a big metal pig statue like it was a horse. Their mom, camera in hand, begged them to stand still and smile. I liked this place. Seattle seemed to fit me okay. It was funky and weird and unapologetic about it.

Now to work. Strung along by the sweets, I blindly

followed Cas as he led me up Pike and half a block over to a storage facility.

"Hey," I said, as we stepped through the front entrance and onto a badly-lit walkway between rows of blue-doored storage units. "I know I agreed to help you, but you need to understand that I'm an unrepentant weakling. I can bench press a gallon of milk if I'm really angry."

"Relax. I don't need you to lift anything." He walked, with me on his heels, until he reached compartment number BV948. After sifting through his key ring and unlocking the door, Cas revealed an almost empty space save for a drum kit, a few amps, and shelves with two guitars, a bass, revealed an almost empty space save for a drum kit, a few amps, and shelves with two guitars, a bass, and a keyboard. "Welcome to the practice space of Faze Shadow."

"Faze Shadow?" I said. "The bad guy ninja from G.I. Joe?"

"That's Storm Shadow, and ha ha. You're so funny." Cas slid an acoustic guitar off the shelf and started to tune it by ear. He blazed a lick, and okay—I was genuinely impressed.

"Try not to touch anything, because the other guys in the band'll freak if they knew I had you here."

"C'mon. Don't tell me you haven't taken a girl here to—ahem—polish the horn section."

"Um, no."

"What kind of rock star are you?"

"I'm not a rock star," he said. "Anyway, I need your French. I've been trying to write this song."

"What's her name?" Cas gave me this quizzical look, but I didn't buy it for a second. "What is her name? No straight guy writes a song IN FRENCH unless a girl is involved."

"How do you know I'm straight? Like you're an expert."

"One—I'm more of an expert than you are. And two—you are straighter than the Prime fucking Meridian."

"I think the Prime Meridian is actually curved," said Cas.

I cast a leery eye at him. "It's just like you to use geography for nefarious purposes. Both Rand and MacNally would be disappointed."

"Fine," he said. "Her name is Caroline."

"Ooh. Caroline. Caaa-rooo-liiiiine. Caaaaaaaaaaah—"

"Could you stop?"

I threw my hands up in surrender. "Okay, okay. What's the name of your song?"

"Um . . . Caroline."

"Wait, wait—you're naming the song after her?" I picked up a pair of drumsticks and hit the snare drum—*ba-dum-bum*—and then the cymbal—*ching!* "Dude, I think you're a cool guy. So as a member of the vaginatory population of the world, I have to tell you—that's a shitty idea. You'll totally come off as desperate."

"It's not like that!" He was legitimately losing his cool.

"Fine," I said, backing off. "I'm sorry. Just let me hear the song, and I'll see what I can do."

Vous êtes joli
Vous êtes belle
Vous êtes fantastique
Vous êtes magnifique
J'aimerais être avec toi?

Oh Caroline

J'etais aux parc
Tu etais aux parc
J'etais heureux
Nous nous étions réunis
Aimerais-tu être avec moi?

Oh Caroline

Tu as dîné
J'ai dîné
J'vaise ton attention
Vous avez mon coeur
Aimerais-tu danser avec moi?

Oh Caroline

J'taime Caroline
J'taime Caroline

"What do you think?"

"Um . . ." I said, way too obviously for me to just wave off. "It's cute."

"It's stupid." He turned away from me to fiddle with the head of the guitar.

"No!" If it wasn't obvious from the name of the song, it certainly was from the lyrics. This Caroline lady had his balls in a vice grip. "Okay, your French is pretty good. Mostly."

"Mostly?"

"A little bit of confusion between the formal and informal. Not a huge deal . . ."

"But?"

"But . . . there's the one line—*J'vaise ton attention.*"

"I want to say, *I had your attention.*"

"Yeah, but it kinda sounds like I *fuck* your attention."

"Oh man." I caught his guitar as he melted down to the ground. "I suck. I suck! Tell me how much I suck!"

I instantly shifted to healer mode, laying on hands and all. "You don't suck. Just stay off Google Translate, okay? That's a pro-tip." That didn't do much to cheer him up. "I wasn't lying before—the song's cute. Besides, she probably won't even understand it."

"She's from Belgium." *Caroline de la Belgique.* That changed things. "It's all a stupid idea."

Shit, I thought. *I gotta do something now. Just because I'm blessed with the love life from hell doesn't mean that everyone's has to suck.*

"Hey," I said. "If you're after this lady love, you're gonna need some help. C'mon."

What kind of help? one may ask if such help is offered to him. Ah, but not tall, dark, and *naïve* Cas. So after closing up the Faze Shadow (*Coooobraaaaaaa!*) practice space, I made a phone call that wound up with us at a practice space at the Cornish College of the Arts in downtown Seattle.

"Um, I'm not sure how this'll help," Cas whined. But I— firmly in drill sergeant mode—wouldn't have any of it.

"Daniel-San didn't know that the only thing standing between him and a karate championship was sanding a fucking floor, painting a fucking fence, and waxing a fucking car. So just keep your finger on your nose and your toes pointed down." Okay, so maybe the bacon double chee was rubbing Cas's face in it, but whatevs. All that coffee made me hungry. It was real hard work sitting on a padded folding chair—coaching his ass—but hey, it could have been worse. And then it got worse:

"When I snap my fingers," instructed Rohit, "you're going to switch legs. I don't want you to waver at all. Do you understand?"

"Uh, yes?"

"Was I not clear? DO YOU UNDERSTAND?!"

"Yes!"

"Good. Now just wait for me to snap." Rohit turned to me. "That stuff will kill you."

"Don't talk about my sandwich."

So, back to Facebook for a second. Though I think that ultimately Facebook will become the Book of Revelations Mark of the Beast, it did come in handy for certain things—like timely updates letting you know where some of your favorite people are. Facebook and Cas had become my only real lifelines to the outside world. But then who did I find out was also in Seattle? Rohit, as a choreography student at Cornish. Damn skippy. I figured if anyone could help out Cas with his not-being-a-stylish-man issues, it would be Ro.

"I'm not sure what you want me to do, Ryland," he whispered to me, "It's like teaching Bigfoot the Nutcracker."

"He doesn't need to be Michael fucking Flatley. He just needs—"

"A makeover?"

"Fuck no," I said, squelching Rohit's happiness. "He just needs some confidence. And, maybe, a few pointers—like one or two, tops—on how to dress." Ro's eyes lit up.

"First thing's first—what do you know about the girl?"

"Her name's Caroline, and she's Belgian."

"As in *from Belgium?*"

"Hey! Excuse me!" Cas called out. "I can't feel my legs! Is that supposed to happen?" Ro mouthed "oops!" and snapped his fingers. Cas tried to pull a Baryshnikov— switching pivot legs with a little hop—but instead landed flat on his ass with a sickening *ka-thunk*. He rolled around on the gym floor, his groans growing louder as pins and needles gripped his legs.

"Close enough," said Ro, quietly gathering his things to leave the scene.

Twenty-one

"Mazzesca."

I saw nothing, even though it felt like my eyes were open. I did, however, smell something: gunpowder, wet dirt on the soles of old boots that had seen more days than I had. Abruptly, the scent was overtaken by the over-whelming perfume of pine. It was so strong that I could feel it travel up my nose like a flame burning its way to the center of my forehead. Then, a spark of light—a match struck on a flat surface, and around the flame, the light grew wider to illuminate a matchstick, held by a hand, an arm, connected to a shirted chest. The flame traveled upward, where it stopped to light up the end of a cigarette, and behind a puff of smoke, I made out the contours of Paolo's face. Only then did I see his other hand, holding what looked like a rock under my nose. But it wasn't a rock, judging from the smell.

It was a pinecone—the kind that grew on Tania's farm.

"Like a stone, eh? Ma è una pigna."

"Wha? Where?"

"Sta 'zitto, Pazzesca," he said with his finger to his lips. "Others are sleeping. Come." I started to ask him where we were, but it occurred to me that it was a pointless question. Paolo held out the match, and its light faintly outlined a door just a few feet away from us. He beckoned me to follow, and looked back at me just as he laid his fingertips on the doorknob. "I come to say goodbye."

"Wait—where are you going? I'm so close," I said, tugging on his free arm. "I've almost found Dora. You can't just leave me! I'm doing this for you!"

"No, pazzesca. I do this for you."

"I'm not letting you leave!" And I meant it. I pulled on his arm, digging into the floor with my feet for added leverage. But he didn't move, didn't even look like he was trying to resist. He was like stone—as I pulled and tugged, my own arms grew weaker. I finally gave up. "So that's it? Like you drag me all this way, and fuck Ryland? Next stop, sweet hereafter?"

And, as if he hadn't heard me at all: "I give you a gift."

"I'm not going to pay the five Euros I owe you if you leave. So there!"

"Keep it. Now come." I stood as he drew open the door. On the other side was the open air, the salty smell of the sea. The sky was a similar Technicolor blue that I had seen in my first dream at the farm, except that as it got closer to the horizon line—where it met the water—it got whiter and whiter until it was painful to look at. The land met the ocean abruptly, as green pasture turned to gray-colored slates of rock lapped by whitecaps. Paolo motioned me to go ahead, so I stepped through the doorway. As soon as I did, I heard from behind me: "Ciao. E gratzie," followed by a door shutting. I swung around to find nothing there, only a structure that resembled a cottage far in the distance.

Before I could take another step, I heard a hard sole tap on a rock behind me.

"Now you're fucking with me!" I yelled.

"Hi, baby." I instantly drew in a breath and held it. Slowly, I turned around, and there was Mom, in her pink dress. She held it against her legs so to keep the wind from puffing it out. "You sure have made a lot of good friends." There was no way that I was squandering this opportunity like I did the last time. I didn't open my mouth or even think—I just sprinted to where she was and hugged her tight. It didn't matter if this was a dream. She felt real. She was real. Her hands squeezed my back, and I knew that in this place, we were actually together.

She laughed. "You don't have to hold on so tight."

"Yes, I do," I said.

"We have a little bit of time," said Mom, lightly pushing me away. "Let's walk. There." She pointed to that house far off along the coastline. "I'm supposed to show you something. I'll explain what I can, but for now, c'mon." I walked alongside Mom, my head exploding with all the things I have wanted to say to her about the last couple of years. They came on so fast and so strong that my brain and my mouth were short circuiting. "I've wanted this for so long. You don't even know."

297

"I do know," I told her.

"Keep your eyes on that house." She pointed into the distance at a small structure.

"Where are we?"

"You are in Edinburgh, at your friend's house. Asleep."

"And you?"

"Not asleep."

"Mom, let me stay with you. Please, I want to." And yes, I knew what that meant. At that moment, I didn't care.

"Baby, that's not how it's supposed to happen."

"How do you know? And why haven't any of you told me what is supposed to happen?"

She took me by the shoulders. "Because *your choices* are what matter. Not mine or anyone else's. We had ours already. The dead aren't allowed to interfere with the living."

"Not allowed?" I said. "Then what have you and Paolo and Domenico Tiburzi been doing all along?"

"Simple, baby," she said. "We've been breaking the rules. At least as much as we could."

It didn't dawn on me until right then that there may have been other forces in play besides just the ghosts I was seeing. *Rules . . . supposed to . . .* it all seemed totally insane, but that was par for the course, I suppose. And then I thought about what could happen to them because they were breaking rules. I was experienced in that department, after all. "You won't get in trouble, will you?"

She stopped and laughed out loud. Very loud. "I don't know. I don't care. What are they going to do—kill me?"

"That's not funny." But she kept laughing.

"Whatever happens," she said, holding herself up by my shoulder, "it was worth it. Just to see you, it was worth it. But it's almost time now."

We walked farther. I didn't want to talk—I just wanted to be there. I guess Mom felt the same because she didn't say anything until she stopped me suddenly.

"Okay, now we're close enough. Stand right here." She took me by the shoulders, pushed me onto a rocky outcropping. The sea spray hit my face. Then she turned me so I was facing the house square on. "Don't take your eyes off that house."

"What am I looking for?"

"Just a little bit now."

"Mom, I—" But as I moved to look at her, she squared my shoulders back up to the house. "You remember before how you said that it was okay to be afraid? Well, I am. I'm really, really scared." As much as I wanted to turn around, I kept my eyes trained on that house, just like Mom said. "Something's going on all around me, and every time I think I have a handle on it . . . I mean, I don't even know how I'm supposed to get home."

"You do know." She was right. I knew exactly what I had to do, even though I wanted with all my heart for her to tell me something else.

"But it's not only that," I said. Just then, a light in the house's lone window turned on. Through the sheer curtain, I could see shadows moving around, but couldn't make out what they were. Time was running short. "I met someone, Mom." A large shadow passed right by the window, in the direction of the front door. "And the thought of never seeing her again after this ends . . ." The door opened, and out stepped a woman with dark hair in a blue and white dress. We were still too far for me to make out her face. Who was it? Was she what Mom was supposed to show me?

Mom wrapped her arms around my shoulders and nestled her head next to mine.

"Shh, baby," she whispered, her wet cheek pressed on my neck. "Remember—there is no end."

Morning. I leaned my head on the staircase banister, listening to the marriage-prep commotion of Clans Clancy and Kwan, but was preoccupied with something totally else, something—someone—a million miles away, if such a measure even applied. I wouldn't see Paolo or Mom again. That last dream—that was goodbye. I'm glad I got that second chance to see them, but I also felt profoundly empty from the experience. It was like they'd taken some of me with them to wherever they were going.

"Shite!" The shout roused me from my stupor. I looked up, and Elspeth was barreling toward me at full speed. There was no dodging this charging rhino. "I need your help!"

"Oka-aaaaaaay!" She yanked me to my feet and into the room where we spent last night. It's not every day that you get to wake up next to a hotty-McHottenstein like Elspeth, but I can truthfully say that I did—if only because there were no other available beds or rooms for her to shack up in, on account of her entire family sleeping under one roof.

"Just give me a minute." She took her hair down and sat on the bed right next to me. "This is all mad. Mad, mad, mad." She looked over to her cell phone sitting on the nightstand. "We leave for Oban in . . . an hour! Ryland, right? Sorry I'm in the cream puff right now. I can't decide what dress to take for the reception tonight. You choose." She took a pair of dresses out from an armoire—one frilly and pink (blech) with an alarmingly short skirt, and the other a sleek, steel blue deal that included a kind of collar fastened with buttons.

"Aren't you wearing a wedding dress?"

"No way am I wearing that thing when we eat. It weighs twenty kilos! Woman to woman—which one would you wear? Pink or blue?"

"Blue, I guess," I said. "I like that collar thingy, but really, I'm not a dress person."

"Hmm. Let's see." And then she took her pants off.

"Whoa, lady," I said. "Not sure we're at that stage in our relationship."

"It isn't as if you're leaving anything to the imagination." *Tou* and *ché.* Left with very little clean clothing left (most of it was spattered with clay or cement), I'd resorted to sleeping in a long T-shirt and panties. I grabbed pillows to cover myself up. "It's too late," she said. "I've seen everything. Just tell me if this dress looks good." And oops, her top came off. The only thing I have to say about that is, goddamn, Clancy was a lucky man. A lucky, lucky—

"How's that?" She did a runway purse-your-lips-and-twirl

shtick like a model. That's because she was a model. Tried and true, signed to a fat contract with L'Oréal, which explained all the makeup bottles in a stylish carrying case. She strategically thrust her hips into the light, studied her own ass in the tall mirror hanging on the armoire door. "You don't think my ass looks big?"

"Feel lucky you have an ass. I use mine to draw straight lines."

"What dress are you wearing?" A very good question with a very easy answer: none. It's not like I planned to attend a wedding, or anything. "Don't tell me you don't have one."

So I didn't. Point gotten across.

"Wear the qípáo," she said. "I'll go with the pink." She slunk out of the dress and tossed it over. The fabric was cool and smooth to the touch and featured a flower design that crossed over the left shoulder and hugged a plunging neckline. I could not wear a dress like this. I didn't meet the minimum level of hotness. "Don't even think of arguing with me," said Elspeth conveniently right before I was going to start arguing with her. "I'm the bride, and no girl at my wedding will look less than spectacular. Next you'll tell me you don't have a date."

Again, I was quiet.

"Ryland!"

"Elspeth!"

"What kind of girl are you?"

"Lady, if I only knew the answer to that question."

Knock-knock. "Love?" Eowin knocked again. "You in there?" Elspeth got back into her sleep attire and opened the door a crack.

"We're having some girl time."

"Oh!" he said when he caught sight of me. "Well, two birds, then. There's breakfast downstairs."

"Five minutes?" said Elspeth.

"I'll come back. Oh, yeah—Ryland, Sebastian was looking for you."

Elspeth closed the door. "So nervous!"

"You're going to be fine," I told her. "I'm impressed. Like really. You don't have to be this nice."

"Bollocks. Of course I do. You're Eowin's friend. He doesn't place his trust in bad people. Now take that dress and get out of here so I can seduce my future husband." Done and done. I grabbed a quick change of clothes—my last—and left. On my way to the bathroom for a shower and a change, I ran into Eowin, who was leaning over the railing. He watched as his relatives and people who were going to be his relatives skittered about, getting ready for magic time.

"Morning, guvnah," I said.

"It's mad, you know. All this. Fooking marriage!"

"Your conquest awaits, Casanova."

It took him a second to get what I was talking about. Then: "Shite!" He bolted toward the bedroom door and disappeared behind it. I heard a giggle, and that was my signal to vamoose. My to-do list awaited: shower down, put on some pants, and find Sebastian all before we had to leave—whenever that was supposed to be. I figured that as long as folks were buzzing about the house fretting over what they were gonna wear, I was still in the clear. Twenty minutes, a squirt of soap (how I had forgotten ye!), a bit of toothpaste (and ye, too!), and I was two thirds done with my itinerary. All that was left was tracking down Sebastian and zeroing in on one Dora McCallum—or at least her next of kin.

With trepidation, I wandered into the first floor frenzy and navigated my way to the kitchen, where a crowd of people massed around the middle table reaching for sweet rolls and toast and pots of coffee to smash into their mouths. I ducked and weaved closer to the center, as I was hungry as well. I reached out and had my pinky finger on a croissant when a loud-mouthed Chinese lady swiped it. I let it go. I wasn't about to launch into a diatribe about how dibs rules worked in the Western World.

"Everyone, everyone!" shouted Sebastian—or was it Samuel?—standing at the center of the hub bub. "There's more food coming! Everyone will have some! Please, everyone!"

"Sebastian!" I called out once, twice.

"Sebastian's out buying every fooking scone in Edinburgh!" Samuel replied. "He better hurry!"

"Whose idea was the whole Brady Bunch on steroids, anyway?"

"Me mum," he said, holding his head with both hands as if coping with shellshock. *"We don't even know her mummy and daddy! We should invite them to stay with us before the wedding! Invite all of them!* Da didn't even fight it. Anyway, wha's going on?"

"Nothing," I said—my usual automatic response. "I mean, not nothing. Sebastian was going to help me with stuff this morning. I need to find a Scottish person."

"I'm a Scottish person."

"I mean a specific one."

"Like find where someone lives?"

"Exactly. Except she's dead."

"Hmm. That rules out Facebook. Maybe . . . let's go to—" The cell phone in his pocket started to vibrate. "Oh, hold on. Hello? Sebastian! What do you mean 'The albatross flies at midnight?' Did you get scones or what? By the back door? Okay, I'm coming." He turned to me. "Tell you what. Meet me in the study. I have to open the door for Sebastian."

"Sure thing." Samuel pointed out where exactly the study was ("that way, then right, then left, and it's the first door on the left—the one with the lion's head"). It took me a bit, but I managed to find the study, hidden away from the hungry mob the kitchen clamoring for second breakfast.

On the other side of the lion-headed door was a dimly-lit room lined with floor-to-ceiling bookshelves. It smelled musty, like the part of the library that's usually hidden away, where all the rare books are kept. I sat down in the leather-covered a Boss Hogg swivel chair in front of a computer. I fired that sombitch up. First stop: Facebook. My fingers got it on with the keyboard. And . . . no messages. No nothing. But lookee on my news feed. The evil gerbils in my brain got cracking on a particularly fiendish plan. Was she online? *Type-type-type.* Yes. Was she willing? *Type-type-type.* Yes! Was this gonna happen? *Type-type-type.*

Um, hell yes.

From behind me, I heard the door open. I swiveled the chair around in triumph.

"Samuel," I called out. "I think I've scored a date to the

prom, er wedding." Only, it wasn't Samuel. Or Sebastian. It was their father.

"Miss Taggart?"

My legs moved of their own accord and stood the rest of me up, straight as an arrow. "Hi, sir. Samuel said I could use the computer."

"I'm sure he did, Miss Taggart. Continue. I am only here for a book. I detest these insufferable ceremonies." Mr. Clancy stepped over to one of the dusty shelves and scanned the spines until his finger stopped at one in particular. "Do you know who you are riding with?"

"No, sir."

"Let me know if you don't find someone."

"Thank you, sir."

"As you were, then." I watched Mr. Clancy—because it was difficult to not watch him—stride toward the other end of the room, his tattered tome in hand, and pull open the door. There was Samuel, his arm raised in mid-knock. "Boy."

"Da."

"I trust things are under control."

"Yeah. Sebastian is back, and everyone seems better."

"Good." And then Samuel stepped aside to let his dad through. Once Mr. Clancy was out of his sight, Samuel let loose with what he really thought:

"Jesus fooking Christ."

"Good news," I started, trying to lighten up the situation. "I got a date for the wedding." Samuel's face brightened up instantly. "She said she could be in Oban by tonight."

Oban—where the wedding was taking place. Elspeth

mentioned it earlier, and I vaguely remember hearing about it when I was out getting pished with the boys. Why did it dig at me, as if I should have known about it before? Fortunately, the information superhighway was at my fingertips. I wikied "Oban" up and found my answer toward the bottom of its entry: Oban figures prominently in the Jules Verne novel, *The Green Ray*. That's right! Yet another creepy link to the now lost book. I clicked the link to *The Green Ray*'s own entry and found the plot summary. Oban—the second to last stop of Helena Campbell's journey, and one of the places where her view of the green ray was thwarted.

"Tell me about this dead person," said Samuel, who was all business. He brought up the website for *The Scotsman*, one of Scotland's more prominent newspapers. "What's the last name?"

"MacCallum. Dora MacCallum."

"It's a pretty common name. I played footie with Duncan MacCallum. Any relation?"

"I have no idea."

"An obit will be in one of the papers." Made sense. There were many obituaries in papers like *The Scotsman*, *The Daily Record*, *The Telegraph*, *The Times*, *The Daily Star*, *The Guardian*. But none for Dora MacCallum. After half an hour, Samuel threw his hands up. "I don't know if we're going to find her."

"Hey, it's okay. I appreciate you trying."

"No way. There must be . . . wait." He took his phone out of his pocket and hit one of the speed dial options. "We might'nae be able to find about where she died. But where she was born . . ." The phone on the other end picked up: "Aye, Michael! Yeah. It's the wedding day. Ach, it's all mad. Yeah. Me too. I was calling to ask you a favor. You have access to birth databases at the Herald, yeah? Could you look up someone? . . . Yeah. . . . Dora MacCallum. . . . Aye, in Scotland. . . . Yeah, it's on the way. Ryland!"

"Whoa, yeah!"

"Your date. Can she be at the Weedge around thirteen hundred hours?"

"The what?"

"Glasgow at one o'clock. Central Station."

"I'll check." I switched browser windows back to Facebook. *Type-type-type.* Aaaaand yes. "No problem."

"It'll work, Michael. I'll see you soon. I love you, too." Click. "I have a friend. He works for a newspaper in Glasgow. He'll help us."

"A friend."

"Boy. Friend."

"Does he know?" I asked. We both knew I was talking about his father.

"No one knows," said Samuel. "Maybe Sebastian, but he hasn't said anything. Eowin and mum have been too busy. And da? Pfft. You don't tell a man like him that his son is a nancy-boy." *Nancy-boy. Queer. Gay.* It all starts so benign. Then: *Flaming, Fairy, Faggot.* All these fucking names. Take back one—*dyke*, for instance—and three more pop up in its place to beat the shit out of you.

Milk and orange juice clash in mid-air, mixing into a pink sludge, and landing on the floor with a splash.

308

"Not that I have any right to give advice—especially on this—but I've seen it handled different ways. You don't want to come out the way I did. Believe me." I paused, thought about Madeleine, and couldn't help but smile.

"What is it?" asked Samuel.

"I have a . . . my 'friend.' I like how she did it. She marched straight up to her dad and said 'I like girls.' Just like that." I snapped my fingers.

"I don't think it'll be that easy for me."

"I never said it would be."

I lied to Samuel. My wedding date did not say "no problem" to a hasty arrival in Glasgow. She said, "No wuckers." No matter. Both of us rode in Sebastian's car with Eowin and Elspeth en route to Oban. "We need to take a small detour," Samuel explained to his brother.

So come thirteen, we were parked on Hope St. outside of the Weedge's Central Train Station. While everyone else waited in the car, Samuel and I got out to make our respective rendezvouses. Now, where was that crazy redhead? I thought it too uncanny that I logged onto Facebook to see Isabella's freshly minted status: *Now I know why the Beatles left this place. LIVERPOOL SUCKS! HELP GET ME OUT!* So a little bit of the F-Chat, badda bing, and she's here, dragging her little suitcase behind her.

"Arvo, dearie!" We hugged, and then (of course) her

attention was drawn to the fine Scots lad I had brought with me. "And who might this be?"

"Samuel, this is Isabella."

"Samuel," she said, raising her hand so he could kiss it. "I'm so glad you got me out of there. It was like a nightmare. There's nothing to do in Liverpool!"

"I like Liverpool," said Samuel, still on the lookout. "It has good pubs."

"You should show me around, then," said Isabella.

"Oh . . . uh, well . . ." Samuel said.

I laughed. "This one's spoken for, Bel. But I have one just like him in the car."

"Samuel!" A slender man with black curls called out from down the block.

"Stay here," Samuel instructed before running to the guy—Michael, I presumed.

"You are crawling with boys," commented Isabella. "I think that's why we get along."

"Hey, thanks for coming."

"No sweat. Who's dark and curly over there?"

"Michael. Samuel's boyfriend."

"The best ones are always taken," she joked. Man, it was so nice to see her again. It felt like forever since we'd been in that hostel in Munich, even though it had only been a few days. I wanted to ask her about what she had done in that time, where she had gone. But she beat me to the punch. "You talk to Frenchie after we all left Munich?"

"Actually, I went home with him."

"Took you to meet mum?"

"Actually, his father, and the way I hear things, he should

have been taking you." Isabella had this amazing ability to not blush at anything. Was it because she didn't care? Or did she have the embarrassment receptors in her brain surgically removed? Probably both. "There was maaaajor drama back in France." I gave Isabella the Cliff-Notes version of what happened at Henri's farm, the (stupid) love triangle with Jonas and Angelique and me, and finally about meeting Madeleine.

"You and his sister?"

"Yeah."

"You're glowing. You know that?"

After a laying a discreet peck on Michael's cheek, Samuel came dashing back to where Isabella and I were waiting. He held the papers up.

"He found her!" At that, I jumped and hugged Samuel, then look past him to see Michael standing far off, watching. I waved to him and screamed: "Thank you so much!" We made our way back to the car to find Sebastian closing up the front hood and slamming it shut. He wiped his greasy hands on his pants and offered his hand to Isabella.

"Charmed. I'm Sebastian."

Isabella took the offering. "You weren't kidding," she whispered to me.

"Figured the bobbies wouldn't do me if I was making like I had engine trouble," Sebastian said. Samuel raised his hand to start speaking, but his brother cut him off. "I know, Samuel. You don't need to say a thing. Me and Eowin will always love you, mate. So how 'bout we get out of this sodding town!"

Twenty-two

o. Community service. The quiet of the Seattle Children's Hospital ICU made time move slower. There weren't any real tasks to do, no one to talk to, no busywork of any kind to distract me from thinking how I'd been trapped in a stasis. But—as all good Catholics are taught—purgatory is preferable to hell, aka my dad's condo. Both of us used any excuse possible—and eventually didn't bother with excuses—to avoid being in the same place together. Dad, for his part, made more of an effort to stay at Deanna's. I asked for more community service, which more or less entailed me sitting on a chair in a hallway in front of the head nurse's desk. That's it. Yeah, I know. After a few days of this, I begged to be given something to do besides sit. So the ruddy, corpulent head nurse, Nurse Beefman, gave me the official title of "medicine technician." I got to follow her around while she visited each room with the kids' allotted pills. My job was to take the paper cup of medicine from her hand and then place it in the patient's hand. Little victories, right?

One day, after rounds, I decided to hover around Beefman's desk instead of my usual herculean undertaking of . . . sitting in a chair.

"What do you want?"

"Nurse Beefman, I think—"

"It's pronounced Bef-man."

"But . . . your nametag says 'Beefman.'"

"Why are you bothering me?"

"Nevermind." What I had wanted to talk about was maybe how emulating the asylum scenes from *12 Monkeys* wasn't so conducive to kids' mental health. But what did I know? I was just some random delinquent doing her time, taking her punishment from society. And between Beefman and Dad and the rotating mystery meat specials in the hospital cafeteria, I was starting to believe it.

So call me surprised when I was walking to the bus stop on the way back to the Temple of Doom (Dad's pad), and Cas texted me:

> *Faze Shadow is playing a Battle of the Bands tonight. It's on your way home, and I know you don't want to go home. Show's at 8, but we're setting up now before grabbing dinner. Wanna come? 2101 22nd Ave S. Call when you're near.*

The last thing I wanted to do was go to a concert with local (read: bad) bands. I started to text Cas as much, but as

I did, I thought about my alternatives: alone, in bed, with a bag of stale Doritos and Netflix. Again.

So I erased my old message and replied with:

> *Woot! SYS dood*

At the other end of an interesting bus ride in which I promised my first-born child to a Puerto Rican dude with a Mohawk, I stepped off the bus in front of a bomb shelter looking building that turned out to be a bowling alley.

Cas sat at the snack bar, staring at a nacho round dabbed with flaming hot cheese product. He seemed conflicted about whether or not to eat it. So I walked over, plucked it from his fingers, and popped it in my mouth.

"Finders keepers," I said, spitting chip crumbs all over his sweater vest. And, um, sweater vest? "Dude. Buddy Holly is dead, and he wants his style to rest in peace, too."

"Rohit thinks it looks good. He picked it out."

"Blargh. Where are the other guys from the band?"

"Out back smoking."

"Why aren't you out there?"

"I don't smoke."

"Tattoo?"

"No."

"Drinking problem?"

"I like cranberry juice."

"Foot fetish? Any fetish?"

"Why are you asking me all this?"

"Just saying, Mr. Rogers. That's all." Before he could rebut, the other members of his band walked in and sat at the bar next to us. In stark contrast to how Cas was dressed, they had random T-shirts and jeans on, with the only oddity being that one guy had a scarf around his neck.

"Hey, hey," said Anton, the blonde-haired, droopy eyed drummer. "This your girlfriend, Cas?"

"No way man," said Nate, the buzz-cut bassist in a semi-ironic Quiet Riot tee, after ordering a root beer float. "You know who he's really after."

"Hello," said scarf dude, whose manners fazed me (Ha! Get it? Faze Shadow!). He set his deep green eyes right on me, shook my hand, and told me that his name was Shawn. "And you are?"

"Ryland," I said. "I'm a friend of Cas's. And let me guess. You're the lead singer." It didn't take much to guess that the band's horn dog was the lead singer—like all the other bands in the universe. Cas by that time had lost his appetite, and I was conveniently there to scavenge his leftovers. The rest of Faze Shadow gobbled up barely heated hot dogs and microwaved crinkle-cut fries.

"Thanks for coming," said Cas. He slurped up the last of his Coke, then continued to catch the spare Coke droplets from between the ice cubes. I snatched the straw away and threw it onto the floor.

"Nervous much?" I said.

"Yeah. Some of my friends are coming down."

"Friends, as in a certain friendly Belgian mademoiselle?"

"Maybe." Maybe means maybe except when the person turns away, lowers his chin, and mutters it under his breath. That kind of maybe really means, *I fucking hate you that you've guessed exactly what I was trying NOT to say right on the dot. Thank you for destroying my only sliver of self-worth, you horrible, despicable person.*

"So this is your chance," I said.

"Yeah," Anton taunted. "Just like all the other times it was his chance."

Cas tried to stay all business. "What number are we?"

"Second," said Shawn. "Right behind No Exit."

"I hate those guys." Nate tossed aside the rest of his fries. With the end of a straw, I slid them over to me. Ass-tasting or not, they had the distinct smell of free, the best flavor in the world. "Didn't they win the last Battle of the Bands?"

"Nah," said Cas. "The one before. Betting on Angels won the last one."

"They're the chick band, right?" said Shawn. "Oh yeah."

"Their guitarist is awesome." Cas didn't kid about that sort of thing. We occupied those choice seats as more and more people filed in to bowl, or to watch the show, or to do both. Three other bands showed up: No Exit, your stereotypical nu-metal angst rockers; Betting on Angels, the chick glam rock band (think Vixxen—scarves, strawberry-scented lip gloss, and Aqua-Net Extra Super Hold); and Natural 20, a band I could only describe as Nerd-core acapella, complete with a Tina Fey lookalike as the lead.

First up, No Exit, and, oh man, I wish there was an exit. I mean, was there a way you could make Korn covers sound good? No? You mean *No Exit*. Next up, Faze Shadow. Cas was the first on stage to do a quick sound check. He played a few random things on his guitar—a piece of which I recognized as the song he wrote for Caroline . . . which reminded me. I looked around the bowling alley for someone who fit my mind's depiction of Caroline, a coquettish diva being fanned by her personal troupe of eunuchs like the resident Khaleesi. Cas continued to strum away at his guitar, showcasing off pretty pieces of songs— and it occurred to me that I had no idea what kind of music Faze Shadow played. If this little dose was any hint, I had reason to be excited. That was soon quashed when the rest of the band got on stage, and Shawn said into the mic, "Okay, no more pussy shit. We're gonna rock and kick some ass!"

And then . . . they didn't rock. Or kick ass. Because Faze Shadow was a fucking Screamo band. And yes, I stayed through every second of that repetitive, whiny, one-and-a-half-chord bullshit. Shawn tore up his vocal cords like a howler monkey, but the crowd wasn't buying it.

"This is shit," said the lead of Natural 20, who had sidled up to me with a bottle of Coke pressed to her boobs. "I wanna slap that singer."

I turned to her. "Not before me you don't."

"Who are you here to see?"

"These guys. The guitarist is a friend."

"He's cute. I like the sweater vest."

"That makes one of us," I told her. "You should talk to him after the show."

"That a tip?"

"Yeah. It is." I let her drift away from me back toward where the rest of her band mates stood. At the end of Faze Shadow's set (every band got three songs to win over the judges—whoever and wherever they were), Cas and Co. hopped off the makeshift stage and plowed into the crowd.

"I don't see her," said Cas when he got close. "I was hoping that she'd see us play."

"Other fish, Cas. Big sea. The lead singer from Natural 20 asked about you."

"What are you saying?"

"I'm saying that the lead singer in Natural—"

"I heard you, but . . . I don't know." Then: "I'm going to go to the bathroom." And he went off. Fucking boys always fucking up their own shit. And, with perfect timing:

"It's not even a contest!" Shawn screamed into my face. "There's no use even sticking around."

"Great. Leave."

"How 'bout you come with me. Help me celebrate."

"No." I tried to walk away, but he got in my way.

"C'mon," he said. "Cas doesn't need to know."

"Fuck off." Again, I tried to slip by him, and again he managed to get to my spot before I could, this time sliding close enough for me to smell the noxious frat boy cologne off of him—ah, the fine piquant of unprosecuted sexual assault.

"What's your problem?"

"My problem," I started, snatching a plate of nachos from the girl next to me, "is that I'm really clumsy." And then I smashed the plate—flaming hot cheese product and all—down the front of Shawn's pants. He screeched and ran away from the crowd to a decidedly female laugh track. After collecting high-fives, I decided this place had worn out my welcome. I texted Cas that I was taking the bus home.

About ten minutes went by, and no bus. But then Cas drove up and called out: "Get in!" Inside, Cas looked real serious. Pissed, even. I guessed it was because Caroline was a no-show.

"No Caroline, I take it?"

"Fuck Shawn!" he shouted, either not hearing or ignoring my question. "He's always fucking up, and I have to deal with it!" He slammed the steering wheel. "Are you okay? Did he touch you?"

"I—no. He didn't lay a finger on me."

"Because if he did—"

"Cas, relax. Nothing happened."

"Something happened—I quit the band."

Wow. I didn't expect that. It kinda touched me, y'know. I had to think back to when someone braved the storm and stood up for me. It was hard. I had to go all the way back to Junior year of high school, prom night. "You didn't have to do that."

"It was overdue. I'm tired of playing with assholes."

"Well, not to be all Yoko, but the universe just gave you a second chance. Imagine if Caroline had seen you up with that shit crew."

"It wasn't shit."

"Fine," I said. "But it wasn't you."

"No, you're right."

"So?"

"So . . . what?"

"So get out there and play! You don't need a band. Just you, your guitar, and your voice."

"I've never been on stage by myself."

"You were up on stage by yourself tonight. You and three dudes pretending to play instruments."

He hedged, contorted his face in every way, but I wasn't going to have it. I was right on this one. After a minute of my icy glare, he relented: "Okay. I'll do it, but only if you help me. I have some harmony parts that I'd love to use, but I need someone else to sing with."

"Deftly played, mon capitaine," I said. "I think we have a deal."

With the Faze Shadow storage space unavailable, Cas and I took a different approach to practice—by making the rest of Seattle our rehearsal space. The only instruments we needed were Cas's guitar, an egg shaker, and our voices. Soon, we settled in Fremont—a neighborhood known to its own residents as "The Center of the Universe"—as our regular stomping grounds. The ratio of cheers to angry stares tipped strangely in our favor—no surprise to Fremont's more statuesque inhabitants, which included Lenin (Vladimir Ilyich Ulyanov), a dog with a human face, and a lumbering troll who must have lost quite the sum of money investing in Volkswagen stock. The non-sculpture denizens of Fremont were just as strange: a mix of old-guard hippies and new-guard hipsters, both of whom seemed perfectly willing to subject themselves to a couple of punk kids busking on the corners. One day we were playing next to comrade Lenin when a pair of old dudes (think ZZ Top with less leather and more fleas) walked up and started jamming with us. One cut it up on his harmonica, and the other played the spoons.

"Hey man, dig the tunes! You wouldn't be interested in playing a gig, would you?"

And that's how we scored a phatty-phat set, two weeks from that day, at Cronie's, a Chicago-style pizza joint run by Duke, a former temporary axeman for obscure metal outfit S.A. Slayer (the San Antonio band, not to be confused with L.A. Slayer, which is the band you've probably heard) and Dutchie, the self-professed "fastest shovel in the northern provinces." He never explained what he was digging up, nor did he elaborate on which northern provinces his legendary speed had lorded over.

We had a venue. Now we needed to make me a musician.

That next Wednesday (Beefman sent me home early . . . again) we were at Cronie's, which had kinda become my second home. I was eating the Duke special—roast pork, bamboo shoots, and fresh garlic—and Cas was doing his customary pizza fast.

"Does he not like fun?" asked Duke.

I told the truth: "Hates it like the plague."

Dutchie chimed in: "Hey Cas, play that one about having a new mission. What's it called?"

"Mission."

"Yeah, man. Excellent name."

Cas sat up straight and got his guitar set. He looked at me for the go ahead. We had been practicing this one for a few days, with me as harmony most of the way, then switching to melody. I slurped up a piece of bamboo, and Cas started the reggae-style riff:

Dreams are between
What we can believe, but not conceive
It is possible to be free,
But impossible as a nation.

We have a new mission
We've got to find a way
All we can know of our position
Is our position will always change
Is our position will always change.

I had to ask: "So, heard from Caroline lately?"

"She sent me a text apologizing for not coming."

"Did you invite her to our show?"

"No, I—"

"Invite her to the show, stupid! This is your chance!" After practicing for a couple hours more, we left Fremont to catch some dinner. We didn't stay at Cronie's because there was no way Cas was going to eat any variation of pizza whatsoever. So, barring any other bright ideas, we crossed over the Aurora Bridge, through *gentil* Queen Anne and its gaudy mansions, all the way south back to the downtown area. He suggested that we walk back to his place, where he'd whip up some sort of leftover icebox creation for dinner. As "luck" would have it, (lucky like a stomach pump) Deanna and Cas lived in the high-rise condo building across the street and two blocks away from Dad's condo. The small distance between his office, his place, and Deanna's meant that Dad could strategically plan to stop home for changes of clothes and any other things he needed when I wasn't there. Don't think that I didn't appreciate the "kind" gesture, because I did. It came out roses at the end for both of us. Until right then.

Cas inserted his key into his front door, only to find it already unlocked. From inside, we heard the unmistakable clink of silverware on dishes. Small talk over glasses of wine. While Cas ventured in, I stood outside the door, around the corner and out of sight and eavesdropped.

Deanna: "Hi honey! We set a place for you."

Cas: "Hi Mom. I thought you were working late tonight."

Deanna: "The county dropped the case."

Dad: "We're celebrating! You like chicken Vesuvio?"

I had heard enough. I had walked back to the elevator and tapped the down button when Cas called out after me. Why did these things never come when you needed them?

"You should come in."

"Not hungry," I said.

Cas walked over and blocked the elevator. "Ryland, please. I really want you to stay."

"Get out of my way."

When the elevator doors opened, he stepped in my way.

"It won't be weird. I promise."

"No! No, Cas . . . I mean . . ." I didn't care that Dad or Deanna had heard my tantrum out in the hall. All I wanted was to get out of there. "Look, I'll see you later, okay?" Thirty seconds of quiet, of stillness as we waged our silent war of wills until Cas stepped aside.

I don't care where it is.

In the blur between when I got off that elevator in Cas's building to when I got on another elevator going up, all that stuck in my head were the sounds of eating, the ease that I heard from Dad's and Deanna's voices. And then somewhere in there was Rohit telling me an address, me hopping a cab and using the last of my cash on the fare, the sounds of loud dance music as I walked—more like floated—down a dark hallway to 4F.

After I knocked a couple of times, a girl with a septum piercing and angel wing chest tattoos opened the door.

"Is Rohit here?"

"I don't have a clue who that is. Wanna come in?"

It took some searching, but I did eventually find Rohit talking with a bunch of dancer guys. He introduced me to his conversation partners, who had names that managed to slip through my brain without leaving a trace. I stood there, listening to their back and forth, unable to penetrate the world of whatever they were talking about. Out here, with the stale tortilla chips and store-brand salsa, it was a wall of sound that blended in with the pulsing beats of the *oonce-oonce* music. Rohit only addressed me directly after they had all decided to refill their cups with booze.

"You haven't said one thing in twenty minutes. I didn't think it was possible."

"Maybe I'm tired," I mumbled between chomps.

"Pee-shaw. Come with me." He led me to another part of the apartment, thankfully farther away from the annoying stereo. "I hope she didn't leave."

"Where are you taking me?"

"Looking for a friend."

"The last thing I need now is a friend."

Rohit led me to a bedroom, where a bunch of people were lounging on the floor, all over the desk, on the carpet. And wouldn't you know it—the girl lead singer from Natural 20 was there. Other than her hair being pulled back into a ponytail, she looked exactly the same.

"Ryland Taggart, this is Julia Styles. She's a design student at Cornish."

"We meet again," she said, raising her beer bottle.

"Julia Stiles? You looked a lot different in *Save the Last Dance*. Blonder. And taller."

"It's Styles with a *y*," she clarified. "But sometimes, I mistakenly get e-mails from her friends. And boyfriends."

"You know each other?" Rohit said.

I made it clear: "We don't, but we shared a moment wanting to kick the same guy's ass."

"Which you ended up doing very nicely," Julia added.

"Okay!" Rohit announced, trés loud and trés, trés obvious. "I'm going to leave you two to . . ." He stopped before saying it, but both Julia and I knew exactly what filled that gap. "I'll be in the other room, okay? Okay!" He flitted away, back toward his man gang, leaving me and Julia to salvage this ineptly assembled conversation.

Thankfully, she was on the ball.

"So I'm assuming you're . . ."

"Yup," I said.

"And Rohit introduced us because . . ."

"I think so."

"I mean, that's why I talked to you back at the concert."

Julia took an ill-timed swig of her beer. Most of it ended up on her shirt. Five minutes later, we were sprawled on the bed making out. Ten minutes later, I shut the bathroom door, and pushed in the lock, and I KNOW THAT I'M GUILTY OF DOING SOMETHING I SUPPOSEDLY HATE! But she was hot, and I was . . . I don't know. I knocked all the toiletries off the sink. She lifted herself up and sat on the edge of the sink, both of us kissing furiously, fingertips pressing into shoulder blades, her stomach rigid, tense, and pressed against me. In a movie, there would be repartee, a pithy comment about her brand of underwear or hilarious pun with the word, "toilet." But not here. There were only animal grunts, shallow breaths that caused little highs from the lack of oxygen.

I pressed into her, licking and nibbling her collarbone, then followed it down, down between her breasts. With my hands I reached under her shirt and undid her bra, feeling where the clasp had left indentations in her skin. That's when I pulled her down, onto the floor, and rolled over so that I was on top of her. I touched the tip of my tongue to the skin around her belly button, and she moaned softly. At the same time, my fingers traced her legs up into her skirt, hooked onto her panties, and then . . .

There are those times when you suddenly see yourself in the third person. You get an image in your head, as if watching yourself on a security camera, and you're totally horrified that the reality doesn't fit with the fantasy you've created. Not horrified. *Horrified* isn't the word. It's something between surprise and disbelief—almost like some small part of you has started to doubt your very existence. Everything is gimmickry, only exists until some guy just behind the lens yells cut, and you dust yourself off, laughing about how you'd never do that in real life. There I was, on the floor, on top of this girl I hardly knew, looking at her, feeling her heart pulse, tasting her skin—play-acting like I felt anything at all for her. But I didn't.

I didn't, and I wished I did.

"What is it?" said Julia. I pushed myself away from her. "Is something wrong?"

"No, I . . . I'm sorry. This isn't . . ." Instead of completing the sentence, I got up and left, making sure to close the door behind me to give Julia time to fix herself up. It literally was the *most* I could do with my head pounding in rhythm with the pumping bass. Did I just do that? Left a girl humiliated on the floor of some strange guy's bathroom? Shame wasn't what I was suddenly feeling.

Worthless. I felt entirely worthless. I managed to find the door back out into the hallway. This time, I wasn't floating. My legs lagged behind me like ten-ton weights. It wasn't until I was at a gas station five blocks away, waiting for the ATM to spit out my dwindling savings so I could take a cab back, that I got a call from Rohit. But I didn't answer. Not the first time, not the fifth time, not the ninth. And when I got back to Dad's, I deleted all his texts and voice mails before I went to sleep.

I lifted my head up. Looked straight at the nurse's station, where Nurse Beefman sat. According to the clock, there were two more hours till I could leave.

It had been six days since I had last seen Cas, Rohit, or pretty much anyone besides Nurse Beefman and the constantly rotating children populating the ward. Oh, I'd gotten calls, but I didn't have the heart to pick up. After a while, they stopped leaving voice-mails, and their texts trailed off. Day four marked the end of Rohit's communiqués, but Cas's never stopped.

"What do you think of your time here so far?"

Did Nurse Beefman just ask me a question? Ill prepared for this eventuality, I stumbled over my words until I blurted out: "S'cool." At that, she returned to writing on one of her endless supply of forms. And then, another question:

"If you were a kind of bird, what would you be?"

"What?" I said, and then she wrote another thing down. "Are you recording my answers?"

"No," she said, eyeing me strangely. "That bother you?"

"Well, yeah," I said, before realizing that she'd asked yet another question! Right then, my phone rang. The display indicated that it was Cas calling. Just as I silenced the ringer, I heard him yell from down the hall:

"I've been trying to reach you!" Oldest trick in the book.

"Are you here visiting someone?" said Nurse Beefman.

"Her." He pointed at me. Beefman nodded, then noted something else down on that same form. "There's one week left till the show, and I have a couple more songs to go over. Are you free now?"

"I'm working. And you don't have your guitar."

328

"Please take her with you," said Beefman, finally throwing her pen down. "I've been trying to make her leave for an hour."

"No," I told Cas. "I'm fine. Me and Beefman. BFFs."

"Bef-man!"

"C'mon," said Cas. "I'm trying this new thing: being spontaneous."

"Wow, did you read that in *Cosmo* between 'How to tame your man' and 'Achieving the Big O'?"

"Actually, yeah."

"Okay, I'm seriously not going anywhere with you."

"Oh yes you are," interrupted Nurse Beefman. "You've used up all your hours this week, and if you don't leave, you're fired."

"Tell me again why we're here?"

"Because you haven't been here before."

"I also haven't been to a toxic waste dump."

"Just say the word," said Cas. "I think I have a couple hazmat suits lying around." Damn! One more indication that we were meant to be related: Cas was getting harder to *pwn*. How else was he able to coax me to, of all places, the Space Needle?

Leaning my head forward until it touched the glass wall of the elevator, I looked downward, watching the elevator leave the platform and spring upward like a rocket ship.

"You're going to get sick," Cas warned.

"Oh, I'm counting on it. Hope you brought your mop."

In less than a minute, we were up at the top. The doors opened with a swish, and it was time to get off. I lifted my head off the glass, and right away, my legs swung one way while the entire world swung another way. But no sir was I going to give Cas the victory lap. I resorted to my genetic predisposition for grace—meaning that I fell on my ass and immediately made thinly veiled threats against his family if he said even one snarky syllable.

"Told you so," he said with a smile. I hate those three words. After helping me up, we stepped past the elevator door and onto the outdoor deck. Man, we were high. Seattle was just the right size—and we were at just the right height—that I could peer at cars and even whole buildings through two fingertips.

I could see my house from there. I crushed its head.

"This is amazing," said Cas.

"You sound like you haven't been up here a zillion times."

"I haven't. Ever, actually."

"No joke?"

"Swear to God," he said. "You always figure that it'll be here later, but later never comes. The closest I came was five months ago."

"Oh yeah? Did 'David' wanna come up here? Father-son bonding?" I didn't even try to contain the bite in my voice.

"No," he said, suddenly icy. "My girlfriend—my ex-girlfriend—Jacinda." Extra emphasis on *ex*.

"Wow. It already sounds painful."

"She wanted to come up here to have that movie ending

kiss scene. Y'know, the one where two people in love stand under a clear night sky." He laughed. "Those are usually the movies with shit scripts. *Oh, you're the one, baby. You're my superstar.* Then the kiss, fade to black."

"Right before they remember that they hate each other."

"You've seen this one?"

"No comment."

"It just . . . I wasn't the guy for her. She wanted me to get in with the popular crowd, go out for sports, do all that social pecking order shit that came so easy to her. Actually, David set me straight."

"And I was just starting to like you."

"He's not what you think," said Cas. "He told me that I didn't have to be anyone for anybody. If Jacinda didn't like who I was, then fuck her."

"That's the pot calling the kettle . . . uh, uniquely suited for stews and casseroles." Our roles had suddenly reversed. My face was red hot. I gritted my teeth. Hearing Cas talk about Dad made my nausea return. I mean, what business did he have dispensing life lessons when he was emperor fuck-up supreme? I spat a loogie down onto Seattle proper.

"I know that you and your dad—"

"Don't," I said. "I mean, I appreciate what you're trying to do, but you don't know what the hell you're talking about."

"My dad's no hero, either," he said, staring into the bay. "I love him, but he's an asshole most of the time."

"Can we cool it on the dad talk?" Cas didn't argue the point. We both leaned over the railing, casting our gaze outward to nowhere in particular. "So you and Jacinda—you never made it up here?"

"No. I stopped her in front of the door and told her it was over," he said. "Three whole years."

"Three years? Shit, you were married. I haven't had a relationship last three months. We last three weeks, and it's cat shopping *and* U-Haul time."

"Cat . . . U-Haul . . . What?"

"It's a lesbo thing."

Cas's cell phone started playing a few measures of Van den Budenmeyer's 2nd Concerto in F (his most underrated, according to Cas), and he pulled it out to check the new text. "It's Rohit asking if I'd found you yet. I don't know what happened with you and him, but he's worried about you."

"Did he say that before or after he called me a 'herpes-infected cunt rag'?"

"After," he said. "Look, we need you back. I can't do this show without you. I miss you—I mean . . . I've had such a great time playing music and hanging out and just being okay with being me, even if you don't like sweater vests. I don't have a lot of time left before boot camp, and I think I'd rather have you around than not. That's the reason for the Space Needle and me talking like a fool and you making funny faces like I'd been talking about dog turds this entire time. I wanted to find a place where you couldn't get away so easily. Rohit suggested here."

"Wait, you haven't been talking about dog turds?" Cas crossed his arms and frowned. "Okay, okay! So could we just have a do-over then? Dinner tonight, my place. No pizza. I promise."

I looked up *mandala* on Wikipedia:

> *In various spiritual traditions, mandalas are used as spiritual teaching tools. They are thought to aid in creating sacred spaces fit for mediation and prayer. Thus, the symbolic nature of mandalas are meant to focus the consciousness to align the unconscious in order to achieve personal "one-ness" with the ultimate unity of the cosmos.*

I wondered why Dad had one on his coffee table. Oneness with the ultimate unity was the opposite of what he'd be in for. Maybe he thought it was an ant farm. I etched out designs using the rake hoping one of them would unlock eternal wisdom. The repetitive action quickly became less transcendent and more tedious. After a while, I was playing tic-tac-toe with myself, and when I tired of the endless cat's eyes, I ended up trying to smooth out the sand's surface with the rake's wooden handle, blanking out the canvas, trying to get it pristinely flat and even.

Cas was late.

On the kitchen counter sat a box of spaghetti and a jar of pasta sauce. I figured that once he got there, we could whip it up fast and vege. All relaxed, like. That was before I started getting the munchies. And not the light, "I could eat" munchies. I'm talking piranha munchies. I knew I had it really bad when I traced out the shape of a chicken leg in

Dad's little sand garden. The knock at the door came just in time.

"I'm going to attach the spaghetti corollary to the Pizza Treaty," I said, unlocking the door. "You make me wait, we do the feats of strength." But it wasn't Cas at the door. Nor Dad. It was Deanna, dripping wet. I hadn't noticed, being immersed in universal oneness and all, that it had started raining. A second after I opened the door, I smelled it. Oh, heavenly deep fried things! With one sniff, I IDed chicken fingers, and with another, something slathered in teriyaki sauce.

"Cas had to work late," she said. "Some soccer league party or something. He said that you'd be hungry, so I got you some food." In two large plastic bags were cartons of every single kind of pub food that you could imagine: steak quesadillas, fish and chips, mini-burgers, sweet potato fries. I swooned. I'm not kidding. I wanted to bear the firstborn child of the chicken satay with peanut sauce. "I just got one of everything."

"Thanks . . . I, um . . . do you want some water?" *Good one, Taggart. Offer the drenched lady the one thing she has plenty of.* "Make yourself at home," I said, which was stupid. That place was more of a home to her than it was to me.

"I'm okay." I let her in and she sat on the couch.

"I'll go get a place—I mean some plates—if you're hungry."

"I ate," she said. And then she said, "Ryland, it's okay," probably noticing how I was doing the pee pee dance—a common reaction my body has to stress. I nodded and ran to the can, where I did my deed and where I found myself looking into the mirror. *C'mon, man. Chill the fuck out. So she's probably spying for Dad. So she's totally doing this out of pity. Make like you've been there. Eat the waffle fries. You love waffle fries.*

"I do love waffle fries," I said out loud. To the girl in the mirror. Right. Wash and rinse.

I sat down on the couch and loaded my plate with everything I could fit on it.

"Thanks again," I told her. "I'm starving."

"Your father doesn't keep much food around," she said. "But anyway, I wanted to come here to apologize for last week. We should have invited you to dinner, but we didn't know you were there. By the time we heard your voice—"

"Don't worry about it," I said.

"Well, see, I do worry about it, because I don't want us to start out on the wrong foot." She resettled in her seat. It's that thing that psychologists or school counselors do when they have to lay the heavy on you. "I know that things have been difficult between you and your father for some time." I listened, chewing slowly on a bar-be-que spare rib. "When I ask him about you, he changes the subject. In fact, you're the only thing he won't ever talk about. I want to know why."

How do I answer the most loaded question of all time? Like this: "I dunno," and shrug.

"I bet you have no idea how alike you are," she said, shaking her head. Then she changed the subject: "Cas told us that you're helping him put on a show. David and I will try to make it, but he's . . . there's a lot of work we need to do." *We.* She and Dad. Did he really have any intention of going to the show? I didn't believe it. Mutual ignorance had been the foundation of our relationship for the last two years, and it had been working splendidly, thank you very much. "I'm glad you're encouraging Cas to do more music. God knows his father hates it."

"Do you still talk to him?" I asked. "Your ex-husband?"

"Only when I need to."

"He must be glad Cas is going into the Army."

"Ecstatic." As in *she totally disagreed.* "But it's Cas's choice." Oh, fuck. Why did I like Dad's fiancée? Like really like her. Respect her, even. That wasn't supposed to happen. I was supposed to plan evil practical jokes involving buckets of pig intestines to make her break off the engagement. But she was so . . . so nice. And eloquent. And a good mom. And somehow knew that the fastest path to my heart was down the yellow brick road—yellow being the delicious color of fryer fat.

"I'm glad that Cas and I had a chance to meet," I said.

"He adores you, you know."

"I think he's pretty swell, too."

"You don't understand," she said. "He's in love with you."

I froze, the tortilla chip between my fingers suspended mid-way to my mouth. Because that was totally *im-fucking-possible.* Cas was not in love with me. Deanna had to be mistaken.

"That's not true," I said. "He knows—waitaminute. Do you know? About me?"

"Yes. Your father told me that much."

"So you know that Cas can't possibly . . . I mean, he's in love with Caroline."

"If there's a girl named Caroline, he never talks about her," said Deanna. "It's you. Only you, all the time. Ryland this, Ryland that. A mom knows when her son is in love." Mind successfully blown. How could I argue with her? *I miss you*, he had said, qualifying it right after. But he still said it. And *being spontaneous*? Reading *Cosmo? Cosmo!* Clarifying that Jacinda was his *ex*? Oh God, I am so dense. Cas was sweet and kind and really, really stupid. Of course he was in love with me.

Fuck.

Twenty-three

"The hotel isn't in Oban itself," said Eowin, who had taken the driving duties from Sebastian. "But we're going to pass through the city." I was taken aback by yet another beautiful, old place that seemed built for picture postcard perfection. Stonework buildings sprang up from the ground like they had always been there, and tree-lined hills filled in the gaps. A series of steeples dominated the sky above the town, as did a coliseum on the top of the hill overlooking the bay. As we drove through, teens played what looked to be field hockey on the broad side of one of the hills.

"Shinty!" Eowin exclaimed. "I remember begging mum to let me play, but she said it was too dangerous."

"So she let you play rugby instead," laughed Sebastian.

"You?" asked Elspeth. "Rugby?"

"Is that so hard to believe?"

"Not at all. I'm sure you kept those water bottles nice and topped off. Hydration is important."

"Ooh, I like her," Isabella noted.

"Laugh now, love," said Eowin. "Or should I say, *Mrs. Waterboy.*"

The repartee continued, but it gradually faded, replaced by the hum of the engine and the tires on the road. We were driving on a stretch called the Corran Esplanade, which placed us on the other side of a metal railing from Oban Harbor itself. The water was dark. It looked cold, as the Scottish lochs are always said to be. But the harbor wasn't on a lake; past the nearby islands that made up the Hebrides archipelago, the harbor opened into the Atlantic Ocean.

And in between was the piece of paper Samuel's boyfriend had given to us:

MacCallum, Dora Blair
DOB: 24/7/1925
Place of Birth: Glasgow
DOD: 15/2/2005
Buried: St. Oran's Cemetery, Iona Abbey, Iona

The *where* had been staring me in the face since I took my leave of Tania's farm—Iona, the tiny Scottish Isle where Helena Campbell and company found themselves at the end of *The Green Ray*. It was daring me to take that leap beyond logic and accept the *what is supposed to happen*. I had been wrong with what I said before. The book wasn't only a guide for Paolo, it was a literal map—one that would never change boundary lines or fade in the sun or become outdated—a calling card, a connecting point before cell phones and e-mail, when lines of communication across Europe had been ravaged to the point of non-existence. Even drowned, hundreds of miles away, it was still working to take its reader back home.

Once away from Oban's city limits, we drove ten minutes north to the hotel. This wasn't some shabby roadside econo-motel that charged by the half-hour. This was a gated, sprawling estate. While maybe the Clancys and Elspeth didn't think this was a thing, Isabella and I—used to bed pads and sleeping next to Yuri, the mad Russian beet farmer with the amazing talent to fart Mozart concertos—were silent because we feared, like a birthday wish, that these sweet digs would disappear if we made a peep.

Samuel and Sebastian already knew which room was theirs, but they accompanied us to the front desk to see where we could be squeezed in. To our surprise, the desk clerk looked under my name and handed me a key to "Room 6, second floor." It wasn't until we closed the door and put our bags down that Isabella and I finally spoke.

"This is incredible!" I yelled.

"I call shower!" said Isabella, running to the bathroom.

After freshening up and getting dressed, we all piled back into cars and made our way to the wedding ceremony. So, okay, I was wrong about one thing before. The Clancys didn't live in a castle—at least compared to the real castle he and Elspeth were getting married in. The best way to describe Barcaldine Castle—a "small" one, where castles are concerned—is to imagine it with Rapunzel's hair streaming down its side.

Isabella and I sat next to each other in the audience, with the groom's side of the family, in the castle's grand hall. It wasn't quite the ballroom with chandeliers and marble steps that you usually see in Disney movies, but it was, in a word, *grand*, in a deluxe hunting lodge kind of sense. All along the wood-decked walls were trophies of ancient kills—buck antlers and boar heads—along with paintings depicting the process of killing such animals. And at the far end of the room, where the stately-looking Father Patrick Keegan waited for the bride and groom, was a massive stone fireplace, big enough to roast small-to-medium sized game.

The perfect place to get hitched.

More than once, I caught Sebastian angling to look down Isabella's shirt. Not that I could blame him. I mean, BAM! There were her girlies, braced by the lacy push-up bra she made sure was visible. When the bagpipe music began playing the wedding march, everyone in the audience stood up as Eowin—in a proper Scottish kilt—slowly marched down the aisle, his mother's arm tucked under his. He looked a little deer-in-the-headlights (maybe this wasn't the perfect place to get married) at the amount of people there to see his big day. He kept his eyes trained straight ahead and let his proud mum do the eye-to-eye hellos and the tiny waves to greet long lost relatives.

"Shouldn't one of you be the best man?" I asked Samuel.

"Eowin didn't want to choose between me and Sebastian," he said. "So he didn't." Props to the bride and groom for not being wedding-zillas. After reaching the front of the room, Mrs. Clancy left her son's side, and he turned to face the audience. This did not change when the bride, in

341

a brilliant red wedding dress with massive train, walked the aisle arm-in-arm with her very small father. The wedding photogs did their duty.

Eowin and Elspeth looked at each other. *Snap! Snap!* And then they laughed.

There. Mom's *split second*. Electrical impulses.

Twenty-four

Over the last few practices before the concert, I weighed my options.

Plan A: Run away. Over the phone, I begged Nurse Beefman to give me max hours. She refused. In fact, she informed me that she was so *pleased* with my service (evidently that chair really needed to be sat on), she was giving me a week off. The Beefman game plan was firmly based on P. Lewis's technique of screwing over Ryland Taggart by being inopportunely "nice."

Of course, the effect of this was obvious: more practice time with Cas. Armed with what Deanna had told me, every interaction I had with him had a different edge to it. No longer were those back pats expressions of encouragement, and when he said, "I really like how you harmonized with my voice," was he actually talking about what I sang or some other stretched metaphor? I made a promise to

Deanna before she left Dad's condo that day that I'd figure out a good way to tell him that this shit will not stand (my words, not hers). But how, without hurting his feelings? Without humiliating him?

Thus, *Plan B: You're fucked.* I resolved to just bear it for that week. After all, it was only a week, and then the show, and then only another week until he left for boot camp. I could take it till then. In that final week before the concert, I planted my Caroline bombs strategically: You think *Caroline* would like this song? I wonder what *Caroline* would think of that. Is there some way this could be more *Caroline*?

"Can we focus here?" said Cas.

"Yeah. Sorry."

"Let's start from the top."

Take me home,
Back to the unknown.
I don't wanna be
Traveling.

Oh this winter is
Not what I remember
But oh to kiss her might
Even the scorn

But I don't know how to answer you
In your fairy-tale kind of world

Jesus, even the song lyrics were warping themselves to fit my paranoia. Cas had been short with me all day, which was to be expected on the eve of the show. After practicing for two hours that afternoon, he was still not satisfied with how we sounded. I thought we were great. I thought we'd be great that night—if I didn't strangle him first.

"Maybe I should restring the guitar. It feels tight."

"You said that fifteen minutes ago," I reminded him. "And then you restrung the guitar." I smiled at him to put him at ease—and about a second later, I thought about how that was a really bad idea. I mean, it worked, but I was going to hell for it. We finished practicing and then helped Dutchie arrange the tables and chairs to make room for our setup. Duke was working in the kitchen double time to fix up pies for the anticipated audience. I wasn't sure how many people would show, though Rohit, in a pointed phone conversation, had informed me of his own attendance:

Ring

Me: *Hello?*

Ro: *Miss Ryland Taggart. You answered the phone.*

Me: *Yeah. Old dog, new trick.*

Ro: *So I'm calling to tell you that I'm coming to your show. Cas was nice enough to invite me.*

Me: *And me! I told him to call you, so really—*

Ro: *A likely story, mademoiselle. But, since we're such good friends, I'm going to forgive you . . . as long as you do something for me.*

Me: *Name it.*

Ro: *It'll be a surprise.*

Me: *I HATE surprises.*

Ro: *I know.*

Click

That's how I knew that this was going to be *so much fun.*

Turns out that we were in store for a packed house. Cas basically invited his entire high school graduating class, so that was some of the crowd. The big surprise was that Duke and Dutchie had called up some of their associates from parts unknown. The result of this was a crazy mix of old hairy ex-rockers and day laborers next to college freshmen with flipped up collars and wallet chains. I tried my best to be all business-like, getting the two vocal amps and mic stands set up, while Cas more or less held court. And he did it well. Oh, he'd whisper to me between songs how out of his element he was, but you wouldn't have been able to tell.

"Good evening," he said to start the set. "Thank you everyone for coming out. I'm Cas, and this is Ryland, and we are . . ." He turned to me. "What's our name?"

"I knew we forgot something."

"Go ahead and call yourself 'Slayer'!" yelled Duke. "Everyone else does it."

"Okay," said Cas. "We're Slayer."

That night, R.C. Slayer slayed. We started with a fast-paced tune called "Travelin' On":

I don't believe
There is another
Life waiting for us to discover
And I don't believe
From under our thumb
We find salvation
I believe I don't know
I believe I can't see

All that surrounds my body
I believe in action
I believe in here
I believe motion
Is the opposition to fear

And then we progressed to the grunge-esque "Temples":

I see the change
Clearly before me
I see the stage
All so disturbing
I'll raze this house and
Not before I'm done you'll feel this

And it all will crumble
And it all will remain

With each song, the crowd grew more into it, putting aside quiet conversations to concentrate on the music. I felt like I was part of the audience, too, just with a better seat than anyone else. Cas was a rock star, no matter how much he protested, and he proved it on that night. Way in the back, next to the front door, were Cas's old band mates (sans the douchebag singer) from Faze Shadow. Even they were into it.

Cas and I had the audience's undivided attention until the very last note of the very last song. We were a hit. No. Cas was a hit. As soon as he said "good night," I leaned over and said into his ear: "Every girl in this place wants to make out with you. Right now." I swear he blushed at that. I was close enough to tell. But did he look out into the audience to peruse his selection of lovely ladies? No. He just stared at me. There it was—that look that I had been dreading, and the moment that I didn't want to come.

The crowd came to my rescue, as the people at the front came forward between Cas and I to give him their congratulations. I used the distraction to leave the scene, ask Dutchie for a Coke, and blend into the background. Unfortunately, that's where Rohit was waiting to strike.

"Hello!" he exclaimed, latching onto my arm and showing no interest in letting go. "Just the lady I was looking for. Great show, by the way."

"Okay, so I can tell you're upset."

"Upset? I'm not upset." He was upset. Saying the actual word seemed to make him more upset. "Oh, are you talking about the not picking up the phone and the not calling back and the treating her friends like shit? I'm sooooo over that. Water, bridge, flowing like a gentle stream. I just need you to come with me." He pulled me to the front door, intent on taking me outside. When he did, I think even he was surprised by what we saw: the single most beautiful person (man or woman) either of us had ever seen. Ever. Her hair was gold-colored. Her skin, also gold-colored. Her dress: I remember more gold. In fact, everything about her seemed unreal, from her Botticelli angel face to her Michelangelo-sculpted curves, to the breeze that blew through her hair at just the right angle. And was that pixie dust?

"Je présume que vous êtes Caroline," I said, followed in my mind by *humina, humina, humina.*

"This is where Casimir's concert is?" she said in heavy accent. "I hope I did not miss it."

"You did, but Cas is still inside," I told her. "I'm sure he'd play something if you asked." And with that, she ventured into the crowd, which parted ways for her to walk up to the stage. Goddammit, man. If Cas wasn't going to ask her out, I would. Because why shouldn't I? The answer to that question was walking up to Cronie's when Rohit and I stepped onto the sidewalk. The instant Julia saw me with Rohit, she tried to cross the street. Rohit ran over, took hold of her wrist with his free hand, and pulled her toward me. She and I faced each other, neither person wanting to look the other in the eye. No, we were both focused on Rohit, stoking our mutual and growing desire to beat the shit out of him.

"You tricked me," said Julia.

"That's true," Rohit said, freely admitting his guilt.

"You tricked me, too," I added.

"Again, correct. And you know why? Because sometimes you have to rip the band-aid off. Oh, it starts quietly, but then come the shitty text messages and the catty calls at 2 AM and . . . you get my point." He faced Julia: "So you are going to listen." Then me: "And you are going to do what you should have done that night."

I raised my eyebrow.

"I don't mean THAT!" he said. "I mean apologize!"

Rohit let go of us and stepped back to give us room. He was right. This is what I should have done. "I'm so sorry, Julia. If I wasn't so messed up right now, it would have turned out different. You don't have to accept my apology, but I'm giving it freely and honestly. I made a mistake and wish you hadn't been dragged into it. For that, I apologize."

I searched for any sign of acceptance, but she kept it all shut behind a blank stare.

"Fine," Julia forced past her lips. "I accept. Just stay away from me. Both of you." She walked past Rohit and me, and we watched as she disappeared around the next corner.

"She'll be okay," Rohit assured me, even though he didn't sound so sure. "What's important is that you were sorry. You are sorry, right?"

"You are so not helping the situation."

"Ryland!" It was Cas, sticking his head out the door. "Could you pop the trunk? I have the gear." He tossed me the keys. Rohit loaned Cas a hand with the amps and stands and paid an ample amount of compliments Cas's way.

"We rocked the house, man," I said to Cas. "I think I'm gonna head out of here. Rohit owes me a cab ride anyway, so don't worry about me." I didn't hear a peep out of Rohit for that one. "Listen," I said, tossing Cas's keys back to him. "I'll be right next to the phone if you need some advice. I am here for you, guy. Especially on going down. I got diagrams."

"You're doing that thing again where I don't know what you're talking about," he said. "I'll give you a ride, and you can explain along the way."

"What about Caroline?"

"What *about* Caroline?"

Fuck me. I was on edge the moment I shut the car door. Cas, on the other hand, was giddy about the concert, how good it felt to play his songs—finally his songs!—for people. And then the look.

"Thanks," he said.

"Don't worry about it. It was my end of the Pizza Truce."

"I mean for everything. For not staying mad at me. For convincing me to leave Faze Shadow. For helping me arrange these songs. For making these last weeks the most fun I can remember having. Is that everything?"

"Just about," I muttered. Happy thoughts. For me, the mantra wasn't working. It had something to do with the phrase *last weeks*. Moreso the word *last*. Though I had known it the whole time, it was easy to forget that Cas was really leaving, that he'd be gone for who knows how long, and who knows where? Off in some Middle East country where he didn't know anyone. And I'd be off in some other foreign land (one called Texas) where I didn't know anyone. It made me sad because while having to face Dad and all the change was hard, Cas made it better. He didn't unconfuse my confusion, but he made it easier to take. But knowing that I wouldn't have him there in a week . . . I already felt alone. In that car. On that night. Stopped on the bridge. Wait, what?

"C'mon," said Cas, getting out of the car. He had pulled us over to the far side of the Aurora Bridge. As I got out to confront him, he pulled his guitar out of the back seat.

"Cas, what are you doing?"

"Putting the strap on the guitar."

"Why?"

"Because I want to play it."

"Here?"

"Yes, because it has my favorite view in the city." I looked down at the waters of Lake Union, at the marina. Its outlines of light topped the swirling black water—a miniature floating city in a tempest. "I want to play a song."

351

"No you don't—"

"Yes, I do. Humor me." And like that, he played the first chord of "Orange." A lot of songs addressed a *you*. You *know, girl . . . How do I live without* you *. . .* You *are my sunshine . . .* In most of these songs, you hear the line and imagine the singer in front a crowd, tossing out the *you* to no one in particular. In this case, however, the song's *you* hadn't been tossed out like a penny to a beggar. It was directed intentionally to its audience of one.

To me. Just me.

"Stop," I said.

He didn't hear me.

"Cas, stop!" This time he did.

"I wasn't done."

"We are done here." I went over to get back into the car.

"What's wrong?"

What *wasn't* wrong? I had tried everything to escape this moment, and yet here it was, and nothing I said would make it all like it was before. He had to push it. He had to take it here, and not listen to me, and *what the fuck, man?*

"What the fuck did you think was going to happen?"

"What? I . . . I just wanted to play you the song."

"That is not a song you *just play* for someone, Cas. I know how you feel about me."

No answer.

"How did you think this was gonna work?"

"I didn't expect you to—"

"No, you didn't!" I yelled. "You didn't think, and you didn't care! I can't ever feel the way you feel. You knew that from the very beginning, and you didn't care!"

Now he raised his voice: "Didn't care? Like I can control how I feel? You are the most overbearing, rude, irrational, difficult . . . incredible, beautiful person I have ever met. Without you, there'd be no show, no songs, nothing. I'd still be in someone else's band playing someone else's music, pretending that it's okay to feel smothered all the time."

"So, I'm like some manic pixie teaching you how to live your fucking life?" I flashed to Julia walking away, her figure getting smaller and dimmer until she turned the corner and was gone. "Here's a tip. You got out of this—you and me—lucky. Truth is, I ruin everything. Truth is, everything I touch turns to shit."

"That's not true, and you know it. Everyone knows it. Except for you. Even David—"

"Fuck you! What do you know?"

"I know that I love you."

Oh God. He said it. It wasn't real before, like really real, but now I felt that ache in my chest, like an open, gaping cavity had been carved out by those words. And a raging fire—at one time a lone flame—exploded into the empty space. I turned on my heels and started walking south along the bridge, hoping, in my mad hazy mind, that he wouldn't come after me. But of course he did.

"Ryland, please don't go."

I couldn't stop myself. I turned back around: "Those words—those fucking words! You know what happens to people who say them? They all leave. They all go away and never come back. Ever! And you're going to do it too."

"But I'm . . . it's not forever."

"Leave. Me. The. Fuck. Alone."

When he turned his back to leave, my heart broke. I felt the beats go slower and wind down, get weaker until I could barely feel them. But I was still there, on that bridge, alone just like I had asked, overlooking the lights illuminating unoccupied boat cabins and empty boardwalks. I should have gone straight back to the apartment right then, caught a bus or even hitch-hiked back downtown so that I could dive headlong into sleep and put this shitty day behind me. But I couldn't check out that easily. The hot-cold cycle of rage fueled my legs like a perpetual motion machine that would char me from the inside out.

I needed to burn off the excess heat.

I needed to walk this shit off.

An hour and a half later, I found myself back at Pike Place Market just as a light drizzle was starting to come down. In contrast to its lively daytime, the market at night was a dark, empty shell. Apart from a couple of twenty-something punks in leather jackets and tattered jeans sharing a cigarette between them, there were no people by the market stalls, no one to stop me from wandering right in. No one to ask me why I couldn't stop my lip from shaking or why my fingernails had dug so hard into my palms that they bled. No one to ask if I was okay. No one.

Well, almost no one. I pulled out my phone and tapped back to the string of texts I hadn't touched in weeks—the one shared between me and Double-J. At the beginning of the summer, I was just a fan, one of dozens of people who'd catch his YouTube livestreams where he'd down the worst kinds of food (think one very small step above actual dogshit) for minimal value entertainment.

Then we got to talking.

Then he showed up at my door.

And then we went on the most batshit adventure I'd ever been a part of.

I started to type out a text to him, my fingers moving faster as the seconds passed, my feelings seeping out from underneath my nails onto the electronic screen. Then I stopped. What the fuck was I doing? Seriously? Like, what the hell would I actually be asking from him?

Too much, probably. Way too much, certainly. All throughout our back and forth, Double-J and I had our set roles. He was the misunderstood underdog needing guidance, and I was the all-seeing, all-knowing mama bear leading her lost cub through a shitty, shitty world. I was the one who was supposed to know how to do things, how to be, but in reality, I didn't know shit about anything.

I couldn't endure him knowing that. I powered down my phone and stuck it in my back pocket.

So I really did have no one—just the names stamped onto the tiles on the floor of Pike Place, embossed phantoms to keep me company. Reading by the light from the street lamps shining through the entrance ways, I whispered each name aloud right before placing my foot on the tile. *Linda Kaswell. Victor Masden.* Who were these people? Why leave a mark like this that would exist after you were gone? *Henriette Berg. Kevin Mack.* Step by step, I treaded on the names, quietly asking them why it mattered to stay. *Steve Xavier. Harlan Tobias. Nanette Williamson.* Who the fuck cared? Hardly anyone even looked down while they rushed back and forth before work or on their lunch breaks. What was the point?

There were names, but no faces. No people. No pasts or presents. No futures. All dead ends.

Frank Millstone.

Tracey Frominger.

Elliot Drake.

Heaven's Gate.

I stopped at that last one. *Heaven's Gate 6-8-85.* Unlike the others, I knew the fate of this name. In 1997, the 39 members of the Heaven's Gate cult thought comet Hale-Bopp was the cosmic signal heralding aliens who would take them to paradise. To prepare for their ascent, members drank cocktails of pills chased down with vodka-pineapples, laid down, and awaited their just rewards.

When their deed hit the news, TV screens were flooded with images of feet hanging off beds and still images of the members' austere wardrobe—simple black shirts, sweat pants, and never-worn Nikes. TV personalities grappled with the question that always followed events like this: *Why did they do what they did? What was the point?* Right then, with my toe touching the tile with the Heaven's Gate name stamped upon it, a slightly different question came to mind:

Did they know what they were destined for when they bought this tile on 6-8-85?

I think they did. As with most get out of jail schemes, the

Heaven's Gate master plan had a catch: to get past Saint Pete, they had to let go of every attachment they had to the planet. First, this meant parting company with their families and identities. Ultimately, it meant separating themselves from their own bodies. The members had to have known from the very moment they joined that they were destined for their end. Maybe that's what made them join in the first place—the intoxication of letting go, of separation. Of leaving everything behind.

I didn't have to imagine the overwhelming urge to leave. There was comfort, as delusional as it was, in the hope that on the other side of the shit lay something so much better than what you had. But when you were knee deep in the shit with the level rising and no handhold to pull yourself up, delusion was all you had. So yeah. *It's time for me to leave*, I told myself. Not that I was gonna shed my knock-off Keds, shave my head, and pop a few dozen pills in an epic sayonara to this mortal coil. But I couldn't bear to be there—to be me—anymore.

When I arrived at Dad's, I had my plan in mind. Fuck community service. Fuck Nurse Beefman, fuck Dad, and fuck Cas. I was going to take the last cash I had, walk over to the Greyhound station, and get a one way ticket somewhere. Wherever. Anywhere. Maybe back to Faith.

I held open the apartment door in case I needed to make a run for it. I could have sworn that I heard someone rummaging through drawers in Dad's room. I peered around the corner and jumped back when Dad stepped out with a bunch of shirts in one hand, a duffel bag in the other.

He had stopped in just to grab a few shirts for work the

next week. I froze as soon as I knew he was there. So did he. Then I let the front door close behind me.

"Where have you been?" His voice was dry and stern.

"Like you care," I said. I decided that I'd hole up in my room, wait for him to finish, and then prep for my own exit. Dad stopped me short of my goal.

"Did something happen?" What was this? Like he even gave a shit if I ended up floating face down in Elliot Bay.

"Just finish your deal. I'm going to bed."

"Is Cas with you?"

"No, okay?" We stared each other down, kept our gazes locked as I walked into the bedroom. Once in total darkness, I slid headfirst into the covers, plowing my face into the pillow so that Dad wouldn't hear the noise bubbling out my mouth and nose and eyes. My entire face burned—I hadn't quelled the fire completely. The walking hadn't been enough.

It became harder to stop the tears, harder to keep my tongue from stuttering. I melted into the bed. My entire body suddenly became heavy, making it feel like I was sinking into it—which was exactly what I wanted. I wanted to sink so far that no one would be able to find me. And far enough that I'd never find my way out. No such luck. I heard two feet step into the bedroom.

"Go away!" I screamed.

"I'm really tired of this bullshit, Ryland," Dad said.

"You know how much I love bullshit."

"I didn't have to bring you back here."

"You shouldn't have. You'd be happier."

He flicked on the light. My eyes burned. I sat up, and

when I could see again, I noticed that he had stepped closer. His face was pulled taut, clenched against bone. All the muscles in his body seemed to be holding each other at bay. Holding back. It's how I felt, how I must have looked to him, too.

I was here. Again. I always came back here. Again.

"Do you hate me?" he said.

"Just go, okay? I don't want to—"

"We can't do this anymore! I have a new life!"

"The old one was so horrible you had to get rid of it?"

"Your mother died, Ryland!"

"Like you care! You never cared! But now you have your nice little wife and the straight fucking son you always wanted!"

"That is not fair!"

"I hate you," I said, my voice low. Like water from a broken faucet, the flow didn't stop: "I hate you. I *hate* you. It's your fault that Mom died." And like that, the fire inside was gone, replaced by the sudden intake of air. It was like I could breathe again, but that I couldn't take enough oxygen in to save myself from drowning. And like before, as I knelt above Julia on the bathroom floor, I was pulled out of me and into the third person. I saw myself on the bed. Dad was standing just inside the door. But we weren't in Seattle. We were back on the ranch. I was 16 years old, dressed in a purple suit and jacket. Mom's cold skin . . . her eyes sealed shut . . . her heart permanently broken . . . her pink skirt darkened by my drool. And like paging through a flipbook one frame at a time, I watched the breakfast tray in Dad's hands fall when his fingers lost all strength. The glasses and the dishes and the silverware all shifted to one side, and the orange juice and milk collided into a single wave of liquid that washed onto the bed and floor. Then the crash of porcelain and waffles and bacon at Dad's feet, bits and pieces mixing together. We looked at each other. Our faces felt the same.

Again.

"I . . ." He didn't finish the sentence. He hardly started it. He just took his bag and left and didn't come back. I don't know where he stayed, but I guessed that his full move-in with Deanna and Cas was final after that. I don't know why I didn't skip town right then, too. I guess with him gone, the thing I had been trying to shed was gone. So I kept going to the hospital to fulfill my service, despite Nurse Beefman's protests. Every afternoon when I'd come back to the apartment, I expected Dad to be there, ready for our final showdown. I dreaded it, and yet I anticipated him being there every time I opened that door. I bit my lip, held my breath, and braced for impact—an impact that never came.

On the seventh day, I knew he wasn't coming back. I noticed that the bathroom door was closed when I'd left it ajar that morning before leaving. Dad's room had been swept clean of all his stuff. That's when I noticed that other things from the kitchen and living room were gone. The toaster was missing, a dusty imprint of its shape left on the counter. Even the sand mandala was gone.

The operation had been quick and decisive. No note left, no voice mail. He left nothing that he valued at his place, and in the process, emptied it of any semblance of a habitable space. No clothes. No decorations. No names.

That's when I knew that it was finally time for me to go, but I didn't know where. So after I packed up my shit that night, I schlepped myself to the closest place I thought would still take a shithead like me.

I never even had to pretend to give an explanation to Duke or Dutchie. They let me crash in the spare room above their pizza place for the rest of the summer. When I wasn't doing my community service hours, I was earning my keep (and enough scratch for the occasional hang with Rohit) by learning the pizza trade. Duke showed me the right way to spin a pie crust from a glob of dough, and Dutchie sat around, taught me all the Spanish he learned while being a roadie for Menudo.

The only communication I got from Dad before I left for UT was a plane ticket to Austin mailed to me in December. I had no idea how he found me (probably through the hospital), but I came back one day to see Duke holding an envelope with my name on it. Along with the ticket, Dad had a note typed up nice and official on his company letterhead. All it said was:

JANUARY 3
3:00 PM
CENTRAL TERMINAL , CONCOURSE B, GATE 6

Save for that, he had done what I had asked. He left me alone.

As for Cas, I didn't talk to him before he left. The next time I heard from him was a letter I pulled out of my dorm mailbox one day in the spring. In the envelope was an unlabeled CD and this handwritten note:

Ryland,

I hope that I got the address right. I had a hard time finding you and didn't think that asking Mom or David would be the best idea. Sorry it took me this long to get brave enough to record the songs. Double sorry because the quality sucks. But they're all there. Even the one you never let me finish.

I hope you're still not mad at me. I was mad at you for a long time. I debated with myself whether or not to tell you how I felt. And I thought for sure that I was doing the right thing. But when I did tell you, and it all fell apart, I guess I couldn't handle being so amazingly wrong. I didn't know what to say. You wouldn't listen. So I didn't even try. I walked away.

I'm not mad anymore. Now, I just miss talking to you. It's easier to bust down doors and yell than it is to write this kind of letter. Maybe I can visit Austin sometime. We can work on a new truce.

If you'd like to call or e-mail, the contacts are the same. I'd love to hear from you if you have time.

Cas

P.S. My buddies are right behind me, teasing me for "writing my girlfriend." I said that I was writing to my sister. I hope that's cool.

P.P.S. See. I'm still here.

For the rest of the semester, I listened to that CD on repeat, ripped the mp3s off and put them on my iPod so I'd have them wherever I went. I'd walk around campus with them blaring in my ears and sing my parts over his. I was hooked. I even tried to learn how to play a few using my roommate's guitar when she'd go on all-night benders/hook-ups with her frat boy boyfriend. I learned exactly one song.

Despite me having the recordings, there was a part of me that felt uneasy listening, as if eavesdropping on someone else's life. What made me feel better was imagining him sitting next to me, guitar in hand, trying to get his fingering right. That was all I had of him, though—a wisp of an image in my head—because I never called. I never sent an e-mail. I never got brave enough.

Twenty-Five

From the branch of a birch tree high above my head, a leaf drifted downward, and against all laws of probability, it landed in my cup of electric raspberry punch. My reflection rippled away from the red-colored surface.

"I wouldn't touch that if I were you," said Sebastian, startling me. "My great-cousin Martin makes it for all the family weddings. It also doubles as petrol. You look beautiful, by the way."

"The dress hardly fits."

"Me da says that bad excuses are worse than none." He smiled. "Take the bloody compliment."

"I'll take it on behalf of Elspeth's dress." He seemed to be content with that.

"Something the matter?"

"A little preoccupied, but it's nothing."

"Have you danced?" He motioned toward the section of pier where people were getting their groove on.

"No. For the safety of the children, it's for the best."

Sebastian took the cup from my hand, plucked out the leaf, and downed the whole thing.

"You said that stuff was dangerous!"

"Natural Clancy immunity."

The Clancys spared no expense to shut down the Oban Marina, hire out every local fiddler and bagpipe player, and put on the rowdiest outdoor dance party this side of Aberdeen. It didn't seem to bother anyone that there were many, many more people at the reception than at the ceremony. There was plenty of space on the grass, on the piers gridding the boatyard, and on the yacht where all the food was laid out. Isabella and Samuel, who had been bounding about, twirled off the dance floor when the band took a pause for a booze refill.

"Bloody hell! I need a break," said Samuel. He pointed the finger at Isabella as the culprit.

"So none of you blokes is gonna dance the next one?" She glared at all of us before pulling me into the throng. How could I say no? Once the bow hit fiddle strings and the pipes started to hum, we melted in with the rest of the dancers. The resistance in my joints gave way to Isabella. "Flailing" is the best word to describe what she was doing, along with "epic," and "infectious." She was a tangle of red hair, elbows, and smile, and it was really, really hard not to follow her lead. Slowly, her buzz-saw style multiplied through the crowd, infecting everyone it came into contact with—and I was at ground zero, not caring who I was or what I had done. This was how Isabella did *everything* from dancing to tying her shoes.

"You having fun yet?" she yelled.

When the song was done, I leaned on my knees, gasping for breath, just like Samuel had. All I saw were shoes—all kinds of heels and flats, loafers and wing-tips . . . and one pair that didn't belong—hand-tanned leather boots, cracked and caked with mud from endless days of trailblazing. The iron nails holding the soles in place exposed themselves with each step to look like a dying man's ribcage. When I stood up, I spotted a brown speckled hat that bobbed slightly above the heads of other partygoers.

Isabella pulled me up and away. "You're not tuckered after one song!"

"I gotta go do something. I'll be back. I promise."

"Hey," she said. "This is exactly what I want to be doing at this point in the history of me. I just wanted you to know that. Hurry back."

Argh! Elspeth's heels—her "grandmummy pair"—slowed me down in the chase. I caught glimpses of the man's threadbare coat, his salt and pepper beard. People crossed my path, and I was scared he'd disappear. He seemed to leap farther away every time my eyes left him.

It had to be Tiburzi. If so, was I in a dream? No time to wonder. I gave chase down to where a boat was docked to carry the party onto the water. By the time I had reached the pier, he was all the way at the other end, where he stepped onto the boat and out of my sight. Fuck it. I threw off my shoes and ran the rest of the way barefoot.

On the boat, I saw no trace of Tiburzi among the partiers

partaking of the buffet table. I butted my head into convos about family gossip, interrupted proto-romantic small talk between cousins of cousins. Fuck. He was gone.

Over by the stairs to the lower deck was Eowin, his once prim tux now missing a jacket and cummerbund, his shirt untucked and his bowtie slung around his neck. Also quite sauced, I must add.

"Hey, Ryland!" he called out.

"Clancy!"

"AHHHHHHHH!" we screamed together, then fell into each other's arms. "I am so fooking happy right now." He shook me by the shoulders. "What's better than love, eh? I used to hate weddings. But it's fooking great, I tell ya. Are you in love with someone? Someone you'd marry?"

"I'm not drunk enough to answer that question."

"Well, it'll happen. And when it does, then you hold on and don't let go, even when she punches you in the face. That's what I learned."

"You talking 'bout me, love?" Elspeth came up from the lower deck, a little wobbly as well.

"Just saying how much I adore you."

"Sod off, Mr. Clancy."

"Ach, your voice is so sweet, Mrs. Clancy." And then they kissed. I stepped away and made like I was deliberating between the stuffed mushrooms and the unidentified roasted meat. Then I crossed over and out to the other side of the deck, finding a rare empty spot along the rail looking over the Marina.

Well, shit. Where else could Tiburzi have gone? The lower deck was the only place I hadn't looked yet, so that was my next destination. The breeze caught my hair, and I let it tickle my forehead. A breath. A moment. I closed my eyes and thought of absolutely nothing, and it was a relief. Just then, I caught a whiff of cigarette smoke blown just over my shoulder.

Goosebumps. Maybe this *was* all a dream, and I'd wake up in some fucking depressing dorm room. Or worse, back in Seattle right after I fucked everything and everyone up.

I turned around, hoping and dreading at the same time, only to find Mr. Clancy—the elder Mr. Clancy—standing on the threshold of the deck.

"Did I startle you, Miss Taggart?"

"I thought you were someone else."

"You have an eye for choice spots. May I join you?"

So I wasn't dreaming, which meant I was probably just crazy. Not much of a surprise. I nodded to Mr. Clancy and stepped aside so he could lean on the handrail to watch the clouds spread apart and merge together.

"Quite the view," he said. "It is more beautiful than everywhere I have been save one: Caratra, on the other side of the Firth of Lorn and the Irish Sea. In Donegal, where I was born. It is like what you see here, but there is nothing visible between you and the sunrise—nothing between you and what counts for things."

"It sounds like a place I'd like to see."

"I could tell you more about it tonight if you wish." His expression seemed to crack into something other than his usual cold authority. "That is, if you desire such company." Was he asking me . . . yes. Yes he was.

"Wow, um . . ."

"Don't feel obliged to accept. It was an invitation. Nothing more."

"I can't," I said. "For a number of reasons."

"One is enough, Miss Taggart."

"I don't know if this is too personal, but aren't you married?"

He chuckled. "If you must know, Mrs. Clancy and I have an arrangement. It has served us well for some years." I must have looked puzzled because he proceeded to elaborate, in his own peculiar way: "See those there." He pointed directly ahead to the island of Kerrera and its dense forests close to shore.

"You mean trees?"

"Yes. To make money, we take those amazing things and reduce them to a wet mush." He mimicked holding two fistfuls of this mush in his hands. "And then we spread it, dry it, and roll it until we get paper that others can make into something like this." From his inside coat pocket, he pulled the small paperback I saw him take earlier from his library. "On these pages, we print words of vast and incalculable wisdom from our greatest thinkers and artists." He handed me the book. I read the author's name out loud.

"Henry Howard."

"The Earl of Surrey—briefly, before he was beheaded by Henry VIII. Are you familiar?"

"Brit Lit wasn't my best subject."

He took the book back, opened to a dog-eared page, and started to read: "*The happy life be these, I find:— / The richesse left, not got with pain; / The fruitful ground, the quiet mind; / The equal friend; no grudge, no strife / No charge of rule, nor governance; / Without disease, the healthful life; / The household of continuance; / The mean diet, no delicate fare;"* As he read the poem, his voice slowed, and his eyes strayed from the page upward to Karrera. But he kept speaking the words. *"True wisdom joined with simpleness; / The night discharged of all care . . ."* Then he looked at me: "What do you think of all this?"

"Well," I started, feeling not unlike a student looking for gym and finding AP Comparative Literature, "A happy life is a peaceful one, right? You have all the things you want, and then you can relax. It's sort of like Florida, but without the geriatric VD."

"What it is, is bollocks," he said. *"The Means to Attain a Happy Life,* indeed. His grace, Henry Howard, had his head up his arse. Tell me, has your life been tranquil, Miss Taggart?"

Let me count the ways. "Well, if you *must know*—this week, I've seen a friend die, learned a whole farm has been poisoned with radiation, been plagued by crazy dreams, and am currently stranded thousands of miles away from home without any way to return."

"Let's say I gave you the chance to undo it all—everything that has placed you through and into those circumstances—would you do it?"

"No," I said, almost like I was actually sure about it. Shit, I think I was. "If I hadn't gone through all that, there'd be things I would have missed out on. Wonderful things. So no, I wouldn't undo it, no matter what my regrets would be later."

"Heh," he laughed. "You're too young to have regrets."

"Try me." Serious face.

"Something tells me, Miss Taggart, that I shouldn't doubt you. Let me tell you about an old man's regrets. The worst part is not feeling them. It is forgetting them—knowing that once you bore that regret, and it pained you to think of it. But with time, the fog of age wipes away those pains, takes away the hurt—the feeling—until it becomes one more curio to dwell upon. Like vague shapes in dull glass. The faces of past loves that fade because you are too tired to hold on. And you wonder if it isn't you, in your *tranquility*, who is fading away."

"I don't want my pain taken away," I said staring into the sea. "I need my pain."

"Said more eloquently than I."

I smirked. "Not me. Captain Kirk in *Star Trek V*." Who'da thunk?

He puffed on his cigarette and blew out a plume of smoke. "You ask about me and Mrs. Clancy. All that matters is that we made that decision together. To judge us—to judge me—by some arbitrary measure is a waste of time. I am happy to live my life, to make my own mistakes—for I make many—and to one day atone, when I know how."

"When do you know how?"

"I'll send you a message when I find out." He smiled and tucked the book of poems into his jacket. "So where does your path go from here? Are you now looking for ways back to America?"

"Not yet. I still have one place left to visit. Would you happen to know how to get to Iona?"

"Iona! You will need a boat."

"Shit." I looked around, patted the guardrail a couple of times. "From the looks of these things, they cost a pretty penny—er, shilling. I mean, maybe there's a ferry, but I don't know anything about it."

"What about this boat? It seems seaworthy."

"This one? I'd need to sell my kidney for the down payment."

"Down payment? Simply ask the owner for permission."

"Well, if you see him around . . . it's your boat, isn't it." Vintage Ryland Taggart, circa the last two weeks.

"I will leave the keys with the concierge at the hotel. The only thing I ask is that you give them to Eowin and Elspeth afterward. I hope they enjoy their wedding present." We stood together on the deck for a while. I respected Mr. Clancy, even though on paper it'd be easy to be disgusted by an old married guy who propositions a random teenage girl. But that wasn't who he was—not entirely, at least. He was a person looking for something, even though he wasn't sure what it was. I could relate, at least on that level. Besides, if there was anyone fit to judge him, it sure as fuck wasn't me.

After a while, we heard a ruckus behind us, and climbing onto the deck were all three Clancy brothers, the new Clancy wife, and Isabella.

"So this is where you've been!" Isabella said. "We've been looking all over, girlie."

"Da," said Eowin as he approached his father, "Is everything to your liking?"

"Yes, boy . . . Eowin." He turned to Elspeth. "More importantly, do you approve?"

"Yes, sir," said Elspeth. "It is the wedding of my dreams."

"Ach, don't be so uptight around me." He drew closer to Eowin. "A bit of advice. There are five words that will help your marriage considerably, and those are: *you are right, my dear*."

Elspeth looked elated. "You better listen to your father, Eowin."

"Enough with this touchy-feely rubbish!" said Sebastian. "We have more dancing to do!" All of us started to file out behind Sebastian, leaving Mr. Clancy to his quiet contemplation. As one of the last in line, I noticed that Samuel was staying behind as well.

"You coming?"

He shook his head. "I think I need to stay here for a bit. With da."

"Are you sure?" I placed my hand on his, resting on the deck rail.

"Yeah. I'll be okay."

Two things in the hotel room that night: A) I formally proposed marriage to the concept of jeans and T-shirt, because I could not imagine living a happy life without them, and B) at approximately 11:45 PM, I declared Isabella officially NOT sharing my bed. To which I could only have these reactions: *good for her*, and *no shit, Sherlock*.

I held Paolo's photo in my hands. "I'm so close," I said out loud. I knew that Paolo had said that I'd never see him again. But I also knew that he DIDN'T say that he wouldn't ever be here, close, maybe right next to me on the bed.

Knock-knock. "Ryland are you inside?" Samuel. Or Sebastian—wait, probably not Sebastian. I had a hunch he was otherwise occupied.

"It's not locked!"

Coming in was Samuel, each hand brandishing a bottle of wine.

"Let me guess—you were kicked out of your room."

"Almost. The door was closed, and there were . . . noises."

I patted the bed, inviting Samuel to carve a spot out for himself. He plopped himself down and whipped a Swiss Army knife from his pocket. In magician style, he got to uncorking the bottles.

"I forgot the glasses," he noted.

"Glasses are for nancy-boys." I winked at him. "Tonight, we are kissing the bottle."

"Who do we have to keep up appearances to, anyway?"

"Speaking of," I said, "are we celebrating something?"

"How about a toast?" We clinked bottles. "To my boyfriend. His name is Michael. I love him. And I don't care who sodding knows, because fook all!"

"What made you do it? I mean why now to come out?"

"You," he said. "You and your friend. I couldn't stop thinking about how she just announced to her father the truth, and then I thought, *Why the hell should I wait?* So when I saw da there, I decided to do it. I was pissin' in my kilt, I was, but I did it anyway."

"What did he say?"

"At first, nothing. Then he said that Ma would be upset,

and to let him handle telling her. He said he was—get this—glad that I came to him. It's mad, right? And then here's the strangest part. He tells me that he's going to go visit with Elspeth's family. But before he goes, he gives me this." After digging for a moment in multiple pockets, Samuel produced a familiar beat-up paperback. I already knew the title, the author. "I've never read this guy before. Henry Howard . . . wasn't he a Royal?"

"The Earl of Surrey—briefly, before he was beheaded by Henry VIII."

For the rest of the night, Samuel and I traded our war stories. Mine were about the horror show that was my own coming out, about the time when I maybe thought I kinda could have something with someone named Shannon, but how it ended badly, about kind boys who get crazy ideas in their heads and the punk-ass girls who break their hearts. And then about love.

Yeah, at the end it was about love.

Twenty-six

The next morning, they had ganged up against me.

"Absolutely not," said Sebastian. "No way."

Eowin was the next to speak: "He's right. You can't."

Okay, then Samuel: "I don't understand why you'd even consider it."

Elspeth? "I can't believe I'm agreeing with ALL the Clancy men."

And Isabella: "Why are we debating? We outnumber her."

And that was that. Despite my insistence that I had to complete my quest alone, these people—my friends—had decided that they were coming along with me to Iona. And really, who was I to argue? (Because I'd lose, on account of the outnumbering thing.) I thought I was being sneaky, getting up early, packing up quietly while Samuel snoozed away on the bed. I was almost sure that I had escaped. Then I opened up the door to find Isabella and Sebastian on the other side.

After a few phone calls by them and futile protestations by me, we were all standing in the hotel courtyard, packing gear into Sebastian's car to take to the marina, where we'd make use of the Clancys' boat—"The Shackleton," named after Sir Ernest Shackleton, the Irish explorer whose tenacity and leadership saved a doomed South Pole expedition.

A turn of the key I got from the concierge, paired with the rumble of the boat engine, meant that we were off into the clear Scottish waters and into the legendary mist that had tumbled down from the mountains. Elspeth insisted on taking the wheel, citing her participation in something called the *Three Peaks*, which must have been pretty prestigious because no one bothered her after that. The Clancys spread out over the deck, with Eowin up front with his new wife, and one twin each on the port and starboard sides. Isabella and I chilled in the back, watching the piers of the Marina and the rest of Oban shrink into the distance.

A part of me still felt uncomfortable taking people along with me to Iona. Tiburzi's tiny little phrase—*vostra scelta*—had branded itself into my head. I had made my choice. I made it the first time I chose to brush off Paolo's insults, then when I forced Herr Cutter to call Tania, when I kissed Madeleine. And following the green ray to the end, even though I didn't know what would happen—I chose that, too. But I had a hard time understanding why all these people had made their choices the way they did. Samuel had every reason to want to be in Glasgow at that very moment, Eowin and Elspeth should have been en route to their honeymoon, and Sebastian and Isabella could get to know each other on a walking tour of charming Oban.

Instead, they were there with me.

"What's on Iona, anyway?" asked Isabella.

"Truth? I got no clue."

She slid a pair of sunglasses on. "I like it better that way. Lots of people don't like surprises, but I do. On the train to Munich, for instance."

"What are you talking about?"

"Right before I feel asleep, the sun was coming up. I looked out the window, and just for a moment, I saw this green—"

"You saw that, too?"

"Of course," she said. "I was supposed to see it."

It's like what my uncle told me. Back in Oz, my Uncle Lawrence—more a family friend, but we call him uncle—is Karadjari, and when I was little, he'd come over for Christmas and tell me stories. My mum and dad hated these stories. They're both astrophysicists—not exactly the most fun people to be around, especially when you're keen on taking an indefinite gap before uni. Anyway my favorite story was about these guys Uncle Lawrence called the Bagadjimbiri Brothers. They were the great ancestors of man who created the world by bumbling around, calling things names, and making naughty bits for the otherwise boring things called human beings (I am pretty happy for that one).

So one year, Uncle Lawrence tells me that he's got a special Christmas present for our entire family, and he drives us to "Uluru"—what you all call "Ayers Rock." Uncle Lawrence stopped the car, but he didn't say anything. We waited for fifteen minutes before mum started complaining. Then we all heard the thunder. Five minutes later, it started raining right on the rock. You know how dry it is in Australia? Rain like that doesn't happen very often. We got out of the car and watched as the rain poured off the rock in purple waterfalls.

Then Uncle Lawrence leaned down and whispered only to me: "Remember that we are all descended from the Bag Brothers. We make things true by believing that they are true. We make things happen because we need them to happen."

"And I still believe that," Isabella said. "I needed that night to happen. People tell you that traveling gets lonely, but all you read about is how fun it is. And it is fun. And it is lonely. Maybe the green ray was a sign that we'd meet again? Or maybe we're just *both* crazy."

"It's hard to imagine you needing anything," I said.

"I would have thought the same of you," she said back. "What does it matter now, anyway? We're here now, together, right? Who the hell cares how the universe works? Point is that it works."

She was right. It was the same thing that Tania was trying to tell me with the rain and the sun. Really, what makes things happen when they do? What determines the timing of the universe? Maybe it was gravitational fields bouncing off each other, stardust streaming from supernovas into black holes. That's the stuff Isabella's parents could handle. But two brothers having fun, laughing the world into existence? I liked that better. It made more sense to me.

"You are the real deal, Bel."

"I know. I'm pretty awesome."

The beaches of Iona's largest town, Baile Mor (literally "big town" in Manx), would have been nicer if I had 1) some nachos and a margarita, 2) an experienced lotion girl, and, most importantly, 3) ANY SUN WHATSOEVER. Scotland's legendary fog had come in hardcore, making necessary the map and compass we bought from Baile Mor's tourist office/grocery store/bike rental/boat repair/bait shop.

Samuel and Sebastian combined their rusty boy scout knowledge to guide us up a mountain path and through glades and ruins until we came upon a single structure ripped from another time and place: The Abbey of Iona. No trace of the modern construction down in Baile Mor. This place was ancient. You could feel it in the stones that made up the walls, breathe it in air that tasted like grass and seawater.

"We going in?" said Eowin.

"That's why we're here," said Samuel, taking my arm. He

led us through, inside to the abbey's main chapel. First thing, it was notably colder than it was outside, which, by this point, was not a surprise. Places with history all seemed to all share that unshakable chill in common. We all spread out into the long, stone room. It wasn't like any other church I had ever been to. It wasn't fancy—conventionally fancy, anyway. There were no elaborate paintings of the crucifixion or statues of Mary or the Holy Spirit. There was only the one huge window at the far end, and the walls themselves were made of roughly cut stones piled on top of each other, almost as if a church-shaped rock had stood here since the dawn of time, waiting for a stonecutter with a major case of masochism to go to town with chisel and hammer.

Luckily for us, a tour group had gathered at the front. We hung around toward the back of the crowd as the leader started his spiel: "Reverend George MacLeod, who led the restoration of the abbey in 1938, called Iona one of the 'thin places' of the world, where the barrier between the material and spiritual realms 'had the likeness of tissue paper.'"

"I haven't been too comfortable in churches," Samuel whispered to me. "At least not recently." No more explanation needed. I learned plenty at St. Gertie's about how God loved us all . . . unless you did one of these ten things over here, and also some of these other less egregious, but still serious things, and, oh, how about these totally stupid, arbitrary, yet still sinful, things like eating a bagel within one hour of taking holy communion (not lying, that's really a sin). And yet, I remember how much my mom loved church. She wasn't even Catholic. She just loved the ritual—the stand up, sit down, kneel thing. I think it was meditation for her. And let's not mention the free donuts and Tang after mass. She loved it, so a part of me would always love it, even if it hated me.

"I got your back," I told Samuel. "Let them try to throw us out."

The tour leader took us to the next room—a courtyard type area, where, in the middle, the ceiling gave way to the sky. In the center of a patch of grass sat a bronze sculpture shaped like an inverted heart with Mary, the mother of Jesus, at its center. All around the grass, like the bars of a cage, were dual sets of columns. On a clear day, I imagined the sun shining in and the blue sky casting the background between the columns. It reminded me of my first dream at Tania's farm, the dream of dancing. She was totally right about Tiburzi being a trickster of the highest order.

"Now we're going out to the cemetery of St. Oran's," the tour guide announced.

Eowin gave me a knowing look. We were here, about to find the person at the center of this all. We filed out the back door into a small, fenced-off plot. I was off, my legs possessed, my eyes scanning the markers. Most of the gravestones had lost any trace of writing. But Dora died in 2005, so the words on her grave would still be sharp. But after a full twenty minutes of looking, none of us found her grave.

"But . . ." I took the paper Michael had given Samuel out of my pocket and unfolded it. "It says here that she was buried at St. Oran's. Michael's info couldn't have been wrong, could it?"

"That's straight from the government," said Samuel.

"Maybe we missed it or the marker's small or what," said Eowin. "Let's look again." So we did. Halfway through my second run, my legs lost all strength. Every blanked out headstone began to look like all the others. Had I seen that one before? Was Dora lost in the grass or covered by dirt? Was this what was supposed to happen? Me getting this far and failing? Was this Tiburzi's ultimate trick? Let's see how far we can push *la ragazza stupida—la pazzesca*—before she cracks? That's fucking bullshit! I sat my ass on the ground and sank my head into my lap.

Nothing made sense. I wished someone would come and tell me where to go next, what to do. Closing my eyes, I tried to concentrate on the images of Paolo and Mom and Tiburzi, hoping that I'd catch a hint from one of them on the wind. In my lap, my fingers curled around the photographs of Paolo and Dora. Dora. I was looking for *her*. Was she there now? Dora?

"Dora?" Her name slipped quietly out of my mouth. "I know you're here. I know you can hear me. I'm here. Paolo sent me all this way. But what do I do now? Please help me. I can't do this all alone."

I felt arms come around my shoulders, a chin lightly touch my neck, warm breath on my ear: "You're not alone, dearie." Standing over me was Samuel, and next to him Sebastian, Eowin, and Elspeth. Isabella was kneeling, her arms around me. I placed my hand on hers.

"How long have you guys been standing there?"

"About two minutes," said Eowin, which elicited a punch to the shoulder from Elspeth.

"What my lovely husband meant to say was, 'Standing? Where? We have no idea what you're talking about, and we didn't see a thing.'"

Sebastian laid out the status report: still no info on Dora's grave. Elspeth was able to stop the tour guide and ask a few questions. The guide said that we should talk to members of the abbey community and that they'd be inside the Abbey's refectory (whatever that was). We all went back inside, asked around, and eventually found the refectory, which turned out to be the cafeteria. Several groups of people sat at the picnic tables in the room, eating and discussing. After inquiring about a person in charge, we were directed to a young ginger-haired lady named Katie, who sat at a table, her only company being the schedules and itineraries she was studying. After a whole minute of our group staring at her, she looked up.

"May I help you?"

"We're looking for this lady," I said, placing Dora's photo on the table. "Dora MacCallum?"

Katie picked up the photograph. She stared at it hard and for a while. Then she looked up at us. "Aye. I knew her well enough to spread her ashes." Bingo. All of us sat down around that table, eager to hear what Katie had to say. "Who are you all? You do know that Dora's dead, right?"

I did the talking. "A friend asked me to find her." I laid out all the other photos of Dora I had gotten from Frau Müller, then laid the letters out in a stack. "Actually more than one friend. I came here because she's buried here. Only, now you tell me that she wasn't buried at all."

"You know Dora." Katie smiled, but it wasn't a happy

smile. It was the smile of momentary remembrance—of a time now gone.

"Actually, we don't," I told her.

"Here's what you need to know, then. There is only one person in the world that could ever stop Dora MacCallum from getting what she wanted, and His name is God. I remember when she was sick in her last days. She came and told me personally that she wanted to be 'burned to ashes and travel eternally on the winds.' Those were her exact words. She threatened to haunt me all my days if I let anyone do otherwise."

"How did you know her?"

"She volunteered here as a cook for many, many years. Her father was actually one of the first to come here with George MacLeod to rebuild the abbey, so she had a long history with this place." I turned the photo of Dora and Paolo around so that I could look at it right side up. Then I fanned out the letters, touching each of them in turn with my fingertips while recalling the places she had told him about.

"Dora had a child," I said.

"Aye, a daughter. Marguerite."

I got really excited. "Is she on Iona?"

"Why wouldn't she be?"

"Please, you have to tell me where she lives!"

"I don't know about that," said Katie. "I don't know who you are. We're a pretty close community here. We protect one another, just like we do to anyone who comes here for spiritual guidance. I can't give out that kind of information when I don't know what you want."

"But we have all these," Samuel said, meaning the photos and letters.

"They're just things. I don't know how you got them or what you mean to do with them."

I picked up the photo of Dora and Paolo. "Please, look at this picture. This is Dora, right. And this guy—he was my friend, and seventy or so years ago, he and Dora were in love. A little over a week ago, he died, and before he did, he gave me a book . . . which I lost . . . but which also led me here. Right to this spot. To you."

She considered my words. "You're a pilgrim, then?"

"Yeah, I guess so."

"Then it's my job to give you guidance."

What do you know? Even after her death, what Dora wanted, Dora got.

Katie marked an X on my map. Before we set out on yet another trek across Iona, I gave my friends one last chance to bow out.

No takers, no problems, no regrets, no wuckers.

We followed the map back down the hill into Baile Mor, and from there walked west along Iona's southern shore. Much of the land we passed through was open common for the island's sheep raising industry. Indeed, we passed several flocks of sheep hanging out, getting where the getting was good. Soon, the road petered out into a trail, into a footpath, and then into nothing. Fiercely steep black crags streaked with green dropped right into the sea.

"How does anyone live out here?" asked Eowin. "It's so far away from all the other people."

"I think that might be the point, little brother," said Sebastian.

"I don't know if I like it. I'd miss folks." He hugged Elspeth.

"But you'd make the sheepdogs so pretty!" said Samuel.

"Is that it, then?" said Isabella, pointing to a spot along the horizon. Major déjà vu. To the right of us was a ridge of rocks forming a wall, as if someone had broken the island into two pieces and raised one side before fusing them back together. And to the left were the black rocks, slick with spray. And then there was what Isabella was pointing at: a single, small house. Marguerite MacCallum's house.

X marked the spot.

"Yeah," I said. It took us ten minutes more to close the distance. It took me another minute to get brave enough to knock on the door. And then one more for the door to open.

"Yes?" said the woman at the door, but I was too much in shock to say anything remotely intelligible. Because it was Tania who stood on the other side. Not literally, but this woman—Marguerite MacCallum—could have been Tania's twin, the main difference being the crow's feet at the edges of her mouth and her brow clutching down on the dark bags under her eyes.

"Is there something that you all want?" she said, eyeing us all with suspicion.

"Marguerite MacCallum?"

387

"Boyd. My husband's been dead for three years, but I still have his name."

"I, um . . ." C'mon, Taggart, say something! But I couldn't. So I held out the photos I had of Dora and Paolo together and hoped that they'd say everything that wasn't coming out of my mouth. Marguerite took them and stared at them so hard I thought they'd catch fire.

When she finally looked up, she asked, "Who are you?"

I gulped. Now or never. "My name is Ryland Taggart. I think we should talk."

Sometimes being a friend is about guessing and keeping still—not wanting to know everything, but only desiring to know just that much, understanding when you should back your friend up or let that friend go. Being okay. That's what I think that means. Just being okay with you being you, and whatever else being what it needs to be.

I ventured into Marguerite's house alone, and this time, none of my friends insisted that they come along. Not that they didn't want to. Isabella asked me six times if I was sure, and I answered back "yes" six times. This was my trek, and I had to travel it. Marguerite led me through the rooms of her house until we came to a small room at the other end of the cottage. She pulled out an old photo album from an ebony trunk in the corner. Then we sat at the kitchen table, a pot of lukewarm tea between us.

"Who is this man?" she asked, pointing to the photo of Dora and Paolo together.

"His name was Paolo Rossi." She flipped through the album, and every time she came to a new page, she double-checked the photo. Marguerite stopped her finger in the middle of the book and let out a sound like someone had punctured her lung, deflating her whole body. "I knew it."

There he was. Paolo—on Iona—arm in arm with Dora.

"He was here," I said, dumbfounded. "Paolo came here." *Of course he did*, I thought. How else would Valère have had the letters Dora sent to Paolo? He must have brought them to Iona from Italy, and later on, Dora took them with her to France. So he hadn't simply pined for her on the other side of Europe. He must have come to Iona when he sold his share of the farm to Tania's father—in September 1949, according to the flowing script written in the border of one photo. Did he try to convince Dora that she should marry him instead of the French doctor? If so, why didn't he stay? He'd given up everything to be with her. "What happened?"

"My mother happened." Marguerite's lip quivered. She arched her fingers on the tabletop. "She could say anything and have you believe it, do anything and have you love her." Her fingers curled into a tight fist. "But she would never let you close. I would not be surprised if she told him to leave."

Did Paolo tell Dora he loved her, only to have her turn him away? Something told me that was less my own fiction and more the truth than I cared to admit.

"Where is Paolo now?" asked Marguerite.

"He died. About a week ago."

Tears streaked down her cheek. "Do you know what it is

like to find out more from a stranger than your own mother?" I didn't. But I did know what it was like to feel closer to someone I'd only known a day than a parent who shared my name, who was responsible for my entire existence. "I hate her," said Marguerite. "I hate her for what she took away from me."

"I . . ." I was unprepared for this. I had been so sure at this point that everything would just turn out. I had been so positive that I was doing the right thing, that everything would just generally be okay. But this was real, not a dream. Not a storybook or a movie that fades out to credits. Dora wasn't just a set of pictures and a collection of stories. She was once a real person, too. With a real daughter.

"Every time I would ask about my father, she would tell me that he was terrible and that we should be glad he sent us away." That could only be Valère. No wonder he was angry when we stumbled into his life and even angrier when we spoke Paolo's name. Valère was a doctor. He would have noticed his new bride already many months pregnant. Imagine him finding those letters and piecing together the truth. I could only pity him. At the same time, Dora's personality was rounding into form—as someone I couldn't like, but also someone a little too familiar for comfort. "I would find her here, sometimes in the wee hours, staring at these pages, at this man. I've always known who he was."

"These are his," I said, pressing the letters into her hands.

"They are *hers*. Please take them when you leave."

I figured that was my cue to go. I gathered up my stuff and left Marguerite hunched over her album, holding up the photos I had given her, carefully tracing their travel-dulled edges with her finger like they were slices of time that let her reach backward to touch her father for real. Questions raced through my head as I walked back through Marguerite's house. Did Dora regret her choice to stay with a man she respected, but did not love? Could she really love anyone? And what did it mean for me, for Paolo and the farm and everything else? Here, at the end of it all?

And then I remembered what Mom told me. No end.

"Wait," I called back to Marguerite. I asked to use her phone, and she led me into her bedroom, where the phone lay on the nightstand. She waited close by while I made that call—one only I could make, one I was *supposed* to make.

"Tania?" I said when the other end picked up.

"Miss Taggart? Where—"

"Scotland," I said. "I have someone you should talk to."

Pins and needles for the next ten minutes as Marguerite and Tania talked. To give them privacy, I walked back into the far room where Marguerite had left her photo album open on top of the trunk. Paolo. He was so young and handsome in those pictures, and maybe for a moment, I knew that person—the person he once was. Before disappointment. Before his heart was crushed. I liked to think that we were friends while he was still alive. Then again, we were friends enough after he was dead. He gave me the greatest gift anyone had ever given me.

"Ryland?" Marguerite called out. "Tania would like to speak with you." Back in the bedroom, I raised the phone to my ear. Marguerite excused herself, probably returning the favor I did her.

"Hello?"

"I think I finally understand what il professore says about you," Tania said.

"And what's that?"

"You will drive him to an early grave."

"Herr Cutter's got no business talking about driving anything. Helpful health hint—don't let him anywhere near a steering wheel." Tania laughed. She laughed hard and long. It was a beautiful sound, even through the static on the phone.

"I apologize," she said, quieting down. "I have had a . . . a dramatic day. Professor Cutter is here."

"I know," I said. "He told me everything."

"Then you know? You know the sickness has disappeared?"

"What?" I dropped the phone on the floor and picked it up right away, hoping it still worked. "Tania? Are you serious?"

"I do not joke about my farm," she said. "He has not been able to find a trace of what he had seen before. Perhaps he was mistaken the first time."

"No, he wasn't," I said. "I saw those samples."

"Then there must be some other explanation."

"Lunatic to lunatic—I really don't care how or why."

"That is exactly how I feel."

Tania and I said our goodbyes. I hung up the phone. My arms and legs felt jolted by electricity. I wanted to cry my eyes out, and at the same time, jump and punch the air in excitement. I was so happy that the farm was safe and healthy—for whatever reason—and I was glad that I could make the unlikely connection between Tania and her cousin, Marguerite, happen. But mostly I felt happy that on the other side of the front door were my friends—people who I always wanted in my life, who I cared about.

Loved, even. *That fucking word.*

I went out into the kitchen to say goodbye to Marguerite. She was pulling food out of cupboards and laying them on the counter.

"I hope you don't have to go yet," she said. "I haven't been to the market today, but I do keep some supply in case my grandchildren visit. I could fix supper for you and your friends. And maybe, if it's okay, you could tell me more about Paolo."

Didn't need to think about it.

Epilogue

he universe started with *hello*. Presumably, it will end with *goodbye*—that is, until you remember that there is no end.

Hello!

Marguerite prepared a stew from beef scraps, barley, leftover veggies from her pantry, and a small amount of dark beer she kept for special occasions. Nothing fancy, especially compared to Henri's duck or Gina's lasagna, or the catering at Eowin and Elspeth's wedding. But it was good. It was enough.

Over dinner, we all talked, traded stories around the table. Marguerite told us about life on Iona, about how, despite fantastic stories her mother told her of far off lands and exotic, mysterious locations, she never once thought of living anywhere else. Next, Elspeth and Eowin relayed the story behind how they had first met—Elspeth as a frantic runway model with a hair emergency, and Eowin as a new salon trainee with the unenviable task of saving the day. He did, and she asked how she could ever repay him. He said he'd accept a date. Then it was my turn to spin a tale.

"So it was pouring," I began. "Yet my stupid botany professor insisted on lecturing me on complexities of time and space in the middle of the rain . . ."

Buongiorno!

So far, so good with Tania's farm. It's been a couple months, but still no sign of radiation. This didn't mean the farm was in the clear. Because of the delay, the workers toiled double-time to overcome the heavy rains and the lost know-how from Paolo's absence. I think it turned out okay, though, because I got an e-mail from Daniella:

Ryland!

We are at the farm again! Yay! Your friend from Germania is here too. He is always scontroso.

I do not like Fabrizio anymore. That is because Giacomo is nicer and does not spit so much when I kiss him. He gives me flowers and tells me I am pretty.

I miss you. When do you come back?

Daniella

As for Tania herself, the last time I spoke to her (about a week ago), she sounded good. Happier. She also told me that she was close to coaxing Marguerite off of Iona to visit the farm.

"We talk often," Tania said. "It is only a matter of time."

Bonjour, mademoiselle.

Madeleine convinced Henri that the factory needed a website to let the world know that it was open again, which was true. A nice side benefit was that having a website required a new computer, allowing me and Madeleine to video chat. We talk once a week, usually on Thursdays at 10:00 PM for me (7:00 AM for her). I tell her all about the boring goings-on in my life, and she charms me by just being her. Fuck, I think I just made myself throw up in my mouth. I've talked to Jonas over Skype as well. He and Angelique are still working on being friends. There have been flare ups, especially after Jonas started seeing other girls. He says that everything's going to be fine. Madeleine's not so sure. God, I miss them both—all of them, even Angelique. I'm gunning to return next summer, but maybe I can swing something during Christmas break.

G'day!

Isabella is still traveling, and has no intention of stopping anytime soon. Currently, her Facebook status reads:

> **Isabella Asher**
>
> 4 hrs
> I've got a fever and the only prescription is more lutefisk. In related news, Norwegian boys are almost as hot as Scottish boys.

396

Hoi bhoy!

Eowin and Elspeth posted the pictures of their honeymoon to Rome and thereabouts. An interesting observation (and potential smash hit drinking game) is seeing how many of the photos include groups of men standing and staring at Elspeth as she poses in front of the Vittorio Emanuele II monument, the Coliseum, the Vatican, and the Trevi Fountain. It's hilarious, as are Eowin's comments on the pictures: "And here's another gang of young Roman men trying to look up Elspeth's skirt. The one in the purple pants is named Leonello. We share a mutual love of my wife's hair." On a suggestion from yours truly, they took a scenic road trip to Capalbio, and to a certain farm, where they were received with open arms. I got an e-mail with a picture attached of Elspeth, Eowin, Tania, and Raffiano standing in front of the horse stable. As soon as I get back to school, I'm going to hang it on my wall next to my autographed picture of Leonard Nimoy and the poster from the limited edition of *Forever Throne*.

"Hello, Armin and Associates. How may I help you?"

"Hi, I'd like to speak to . . ." I said quietly into the phone, not wanting my voice to be heard on the other end. I felt that now-familiar feeling of my mouth drying out, my throat clenching, and my mind filling with things OTHER than what I needed to focus on, which was saying my father's name.

"You right?" asked Isabella, sitting on the sidewalk next to me in front of Auley's Pub in Oban.

"I'm good." Liar.

It was nighttime. Inside the bar, the Clancys were

relaxing after a day of trekking Iona's steep hills and after a filling dinner at Marguerite's. Outside, Isabella lent me her cell phone and her moral support. There was one more thing I had to do, and I needed all the help I could get.

"Hello?" the secretary's voice repeated. "Do you want to speak with someone?"

"Deanna?" I blurted out.

"I'll connect you with Miss Avery right away." Oh shit. What was I gonna say? Maybe something like, *I'm kinda in Scotland right now. How are the Mariners doing?* I wanted to snap the phone shut and run far, far away. *No. I'm not doing that anymore. That's not me.*

"Good afternoon, Deanna Avery speaking."

"Deanna?"

"Who is this?"

"It's Ryland. I don't know if you remember . . ."

"Of course I do." Shit. I hate phones. I couldn't tell if she was pissed or merely confused over me calling after all this time. "I'll connect you with your father."

"No! I . . . I can't talk to him. I mean I have to, but . . ."

"You're not making any sense," she said, calm and cool. "Are you in trouble?"

"I'm in Scotland."

"That's not a town in Texas, is it."

"They play bagpipes," I said. "The dudes wear skirts."

"That'll be a hard one for your father to swallow."

"I know." My hand was shaking. My lip was shaking. The whole universe was shaking.

"I can talk to him if you want," Deanna said. "He's just next door."

"No, I have to do this. It's just . . . I don't know . . . I've never known how to talk to him. Mom always—oh, I'm sorry. I shouldn't have—"

"It's okay, baby. We all have moms." I started crying. Not hysterical weeping, or in heart-rending rending sobs. The tears had to come, and they did. Instead of feeling painful, they felt good. Isabella squeezed my hand.

"Deanna, why are you so nice to me? I mean, after everything?"

"Why shouldn't I be? Even after everything?" And there it was. The perfect answer to a perfectly stupid question. But Deanna didn't judge me for it. She hadn't ever judged me. "I'll tell you what. Let me call up your dad on three way. If things get too tough for you, say so, okay?"

The three tone transfer rang in my ear, and a second later, I heard: "David Taggart speaking."

Breathe, lady. Breathe. "Dad?"

"Ryland," he said in a one-word declarative sentence.

"I'm . . . there's no other way I can say this, so here it goes. I'm sorta stuck in Europe, and I don't have any way home."

Loud sigh on the other end. "Are you serious, Ryland? Dammit, why—"

"You can be as mad at me as you want," I said. "I just need your help. I'm so sorry for what I said last year. I don't mean it now, for what it's worth. I want to go home."

"How are you even—"

"Please," I said. I had to hold my arm with the opposite hand to keep from dropping the phone. "Please help me."

Dead silence. A long silence. I'd have to buy Isabella

another SIM card. I slipped her a ten pound note, but the dwindling minutes on Isabella's phone were a small distraction from my real fear—I was about to get what was coming to me. Two years of bad karma cruising toward me like a tidal wave of negative mojo. I deserved it. All of it. Maybe not from Deanna directly, but Dad? Yeah. I saw it in him that that day. In my room. With Mom. *Don't do it. Don't leave like she did. Don't leave me alone.* But I did. I took that hate and ran with it, woke up with it every day fresh and new to define myself.

And now? Nothing left to say but *bring it on, pops.* Couldn't say I wouldn't wilt and die from it, but maybe it's what was supposed to happen. My fate, no longer in my hands.

"What is the biggest city closest to you?" said Dad.

"What?" I said. "Uh . . . Glasgow, I think."

"Scotland?"

"Yeah, but—"

"Alright." I heard typing on the other end. "Can you stay on the phone? It might take a while to buy the ticket."

"Okay," I said, handing my entire wallet over to Isabella.

When I got back to the States, Dad, Deanna, and I had a long sit-down. I won't lie—it was hard. There were a lot of tears, some all-out crying, but I think we all came out better on the other side. Not that everything is hunky-dory. I still have a $2000 plane ticket debt to work off, so it's all work and no play when I get back to Austin. Fortunately, I have a new job as Herr Cutter's lab assistant. I know—I'm not sure what he's smoking either, but the per-hour on it is pretty nice, as long as I can cover the costs of all the test tubes I'm going to break. It's still awkward between Dad and me. A lot of shit happened between Mom's death and this summer, and I pretty much had to tell Dad all of it. "No secrets," he said, to which I remarked, "Fine. Then no secret engagements." He turned red. Deanna howled with laughter. She's awesome. I'm excited to have her as a stepmother. Last night, before leaving again, I had dinner with her while Dad finished up a case at the office. We didn't talk about the upcoming school year or even my gonzo travel stories. No, she sat down across from me at Dad's kitchen table and asked, "What was your mom like?"

So I did.

Hey.

I'm still not able to drive on account of that suspended license thing. So when I had to get my ass, and a bunch of my shit, from Seattle to Austin, I had a little problem. Cas to the rescue. Cas always to the rescue. He explicitly asked for time off to drive me back to school. I told him that he was wasting his leave, and he told me to shut my trap: "How I use my leave is my choice."

So now we're on the road, me in the passenger seat, and he taking captain duties. That means I have the important task of maintaining a lively vehicular environment.

"I've come to a conclusion," I say. "I think I want to sue Funyuns."

"You want to sue a bag of chips?"

"Not one bag. The whole Funyuns corporation. On the back, it promises me fun—hell, *fun* is built into the name! But Funyuns are not fun. They're actually kind of disgusting. And while I'm at it, I want to sue candy bars in general, because 'fun size' is false advertising, too. It's half the size of 'snack size' and therefore *less* fun."

"You did not just spend vast amounts of brainpower on that, did you?"

"You'll see. I'll e-mail your mom, and she'll be like, 'you are a genius,' and I'll be like, 'that will be one million dollars.'"

"I dare you."

"Your momma taught you better than to mess with *this* lord of badassery. Now where's your phone?"

On cue, his front pants pocket starts to ring. He takes it out, shoots me an evil smile, and answers it. I taught him that whole "being evil" trick, and when he gets off the phone, I'm gonna sue him for copyright infringement.

"Hello? Mom? Wait, wait. I'll put you on speaker." Cas sets his phone down on the dashboard and hits speakerphone.

"Hi, Deanna."

"Hi, Ryland. How's the trip?"

"Smooth sailing," I say. "It's funny that you called, because I just got this idea—"

"Mom," says Cas, "we're both good, except that Ryland is DRIVING ME CRAZY!"

"It's only been . . . how long?"

Cas doesn't even have to look at his watch. Asshole. "Thirteen hours, twenty-five minutes, fourteen seconds. Now fifteen."

Deanna laughs. Even through her hand covering up the receiver, we can still hear her laugh. "Cas, a package came for you here, from someone named Samantha?"

Well, well, well. Who is Samantha?

"She's a friend from the Army, Mom. That's all."

"Right. Ryland, your father wants to talk to you." Oh, Jeez. I sit straight up on instinct. Like I said before, it's a work in progress.

"Hi, you guys." I still wince when he uses "you guys" but at least I know that he actually includes me in it. "How's the road out there?" I look at Cas to see if he wants to answer that question, but throws it back my way.

"Um, it's going well, Dad."

"I want you to call when you stop for the night."

"We will," Cas says.

"And no seedy roadside motels, okay. You have your mom's card, Cas."

"Yeah," I say. "La Quinta or bust."

"Don't forget to call."

"We won't," Cas and I say together.

"Talk to you later."

Hello.

While five-dollar bags of Cheetos and fifteen-dollar *no-fun* size bottles of soda, courtesy of the hotel mini bar (and Deanna's card), lay in our immediate future, Cas and I have more pressing business to attend to. We pull into the parking lot after a forever of the hills and the trees and the streams and the majesty of nature that is Yellowstone National Park. And yes, I understand that the phrase "lifetime ban" should be self-explanatory. But hey—doer of stupid things, right? We ease into the parking lot next to the world's most trustworthy geyser, pick a spot, and park.

Cas looks nervous. "So why are we here again?"

403

"I promised to meet a friend."

"But why here? Someone's going to recognize you."

"That's what the disguise is for!" And by disguise, I mean a dress. A fashionable, pink (shudder) dress with a wide-brimmed hat, matching purse, and Audrey Hepburn sunglasses. "No one will suspect that it's me." *Yes,* they'll think, *at least Ryland Taggart has a soul. That girl in the hat clearly feasts upon the brains of newborns, and puppies, and newborn puppies.* "Ten minutes, tops. I promise." Then I added: "Keep the engine running, just in case."

"You owe me." We raise our hands for a fist bump and touch knucks.

"Thanks for driving, Cas."

"I'd drive around the world just to see you in a dress. Two words: *Insta* and *gram.*"

"You wouldn't dare."

"Already done."

"You fucker!" I'm not worried. Lemons, meet lemonade: "So . . . Samantha. Is she your *superior* or your *subordinate*?" I stick my finger in my mouth suggestively.

"She's just a friend, and please don't ever do that again."

"I've heard that before. I bet Samantha's an acronym for your harem of naked, bazooka-toting nymphets: *S* for Stephanie, *A* for Ariel, *M* for Mary, *A* for Aileen . . ."

"I need to stop making it so easy."

"I love you," I tell him. I really do, whatever the words mean to me now. That's the thing—meanings change. So understanding the words when you say them, or when you hear them said—it's all alchemy, all smoke and mirrors, dreams and memories and regrets blended together so you don't know what you have, even after it punches you in the face. I've come to the conclusion that ain't nobody gonna know where any shit's gonna lead. All you can do is believe.

Believe and buckle up.

Hello. I'm okay. I love you.

"Get that stupid look off your face," I tell him.

"You first," he says back.

The End

Background and Acknowledgements

irst and foremost, this book would never have gotten off the ground without the generosity and hospitality of Samantha Lotti, owner of Tenuta San Carlo, a farm located near the town of Grossetto in Tuscany. My thanks to her extends to the Montorsi family, who treated me like a family member for the time I spent at the farm, and to Andrea—expert farmhand who is more awesomer than Chuck Norris. No collocation of words can accurately describe the haunting beauty of this place, so I suggest that if you're willing, you should go ahead and take a trip over there (http://www.tenutasancarlo.com/).

This book is dedicated to those people, places, and events that fell into my life in the winter/spring of 2009 as well as the ensuing production of the first versions of this novel. Some events in these pages are based on real-life occurrences. Like in my previous book, *Lords of Badassery*, I certainly took liberties with history to make the storyline smoother. In *Green Ray*, the largest deviation I've made from our history is in the description of the Jardin de Pierres

D'Alas, an amazing feat of environmental art created by Robert Mathey in the sleepy village of Alas in Southern France. The book locates the creation much earlier in time than the 1970s and 1980s when Mr. Mathey constructed his incredible riverside rock garden. It's a small change, but an important one to make the history that Ryland uncovers about her quest just a little more colorful (and an opportunity to wax poetic about one of my favorite locations in the entire world). Nonetheless, many of the locales based on real places have been portrayed as I remembered them during my own travels.

To say that those places and events—and the people I met through them—were life-changing would be to sell them short. I would not be the person I am without that time in my life and without those experiences. There aren't any characters that are strictly based on one person—they are more composites melded with pieces of viscera yanked from my brain to fill in the details. My only hope is that I— in little ways—do justice to just how much I love and respect those friends who shared the road with me, whether for a long time or a short time. There are too many to name them all here, but I'll try (in no particular order): Anna Nikunen, Elina Lahtiharju, Elizabeth Jaxon, Amandine Besse, Jon McDonald, Camille Aragon, Yolanda Aspland, Valerie Van Kerkhove, the kind elderly couple on our train to Frankfurt who taught us EVERYTHING we know about German (that being, *was is das?*), Victoria Martí, Leslie Demaso, Philippe Van Den Bossche, Sam Wilson, Octavia Monelli, Helene Maigne, Pierre Goula, the gas station attendant in Brussels who taught us how to say "very far away" in French (*très loin*) along with the English-speaking student at the same gas station who helped us not be so lost, Charlotte Fanny, Makiko Okubo, David and Jaime Golitko, Ric Manteigas and his main man, PJ, Karen Van Craenenbroeck, Wim Proost, Renata Escarpelli, Daniela Marugo, Matt Szymanowski, Douglas Deleu, Beverly Dobson, Madeleine Thörn, Greg Maxey, Janet Kownacki, Roberto Aguilar, Sara Aguilar, Pieter Van De Peer, Chris "Coz" Costello, Hannah Freeth, Barbara Lafaye, Ali Fischer, Rocío Morales García, Reuben Payne, Christian Rouget, Tiffany Calcagno, Miray Caylar, Sabrina Grimilde Merola, Janne (AKA she who needs no other name), Yanna Berthouloux, Tim Van Aelst, Stéphanie Arenou, Jonas Van Baelen, Marcus Greenslade, Imane Bacardee (Our Heroine), Haifa Haudry, Alan Vuchichevich, Ruth Martin, Keith Warnack, Slim Rand, the late and great Bar Ô Crée Louche, Francesca Robinson, Veronica McHale (I miss you dearly), Thomas Courcelle, Aya Okamoto, Robert "Rob Fucking G" Gremmer, the kind hostel desk attendant in Madrid who let us make out with our French girlfriends way past curfew on our last night in Europe, 2009, Derek Martinez, Allan Desquins, Zhun Mao (the first forester in Chinese history, at least according to him), Jesse Lewis, Celeste Ragone, Emily Matthews, Andrew Twiss, Dirce Rainho (the universe is less beautiful without you, my friend), Leopoldo Pellino, Julien Bertrand, Gilbert Serres, Said from Friend's Hostel in Paris, Juan Aráoz, Marcello De Gasperi, Ary Gonzalez, David Gunter, Maria Hetman, and Lucas Medeiros (Brazilian brother from another mother).

I also want to take this opportunity to thank my classmates, teachers, and friends in New York City who helped me through and after The New School MFA program (again, in no particular order): Nicole Audrey Spector, Emily Fitz-Randolph, John Weingarten, Sara Ross Witt, Stacey Schick, Lee Matthew Goldberg, Dani Grammerstorf French, Angela Veronica Wong, Amalia Ellison, David Levithan, Marco Rafalà, Amanda Miller, Sharon Preiss, Lucas Klauss, Jeffrey Renard Allen, Connor Coyne, Camellia May Phillips, Scott Larner, Stacey Malo, Morgan Matson, Randi Jørgensen, Meredith Franco Meyers, Pete Meyers, Jason Everman, Vladimir Kowal, and Ed Harris (not that Ed Harris). I must also recognize the lovely staff at NYC's City Bakery for their irresistible pretzel croissants. Though you are gone, my most favorite bastion of baked goods, the memories will last forever.

Special shout out to Carolyn Crawford. When I told her I was thinking of basing a character on her for this book, she immediately stated, "You better. I belong in a fucking book." So there you are.

This manuscript benefited greatly from input and insight from very astute readers and editors: Camellia May Phillips, Daydre Phillips, Marco Rafalá, Amanda Miller, Christine De Luca, Wes Alexander, Anne Cunningham, Kristin Fitzsimmons, Brian Quinn, Mercedes Landazuri, Christine De Luca (again, squared), Maria Butauski, and Samantha Lotti. I'd also like to extend a very special thanks to agent Stephen Barbara, a true and magnanimous gentleman who took the time to pen a crucial critique of the manuscript in its middle stages. It was a tremendous help.

The dazzling Risa Rodil is responsible for the covers to *Lords of Badassery* and *The Green Ray of the Sun*. She is a world-class talent, the best in the YA cover biz—whether traditional or indie—and I consider myself so fortunate to have her art adorn the cover of my books. It is a double treat to feature the work of a Filipina artist on my books as well.

Finally, but not leastly (ugh . . . I was an English major), there are no words to encompass my appreciation for Wes Alexander—friend, band mate, and travel companion. This story—our story—would not have happened without Wes's constant cheerleading, his relentlessly upbeat attitude, his insistence on going to 12 (why stop at 11?), and his penchant for getting us into all sorts of mayhem. I'm so proud of what we've created together. As we were coming home from our European odyssey, our heads cloudy from processing all the craziness we'd been through, we wrote down promises that we'd made to ourselves to ensure that the spirit of the journey would never be lost. Through this project—the words and the songs—they never will be.

Remember—there is no end.

About the Author

einhardt Suarez is a Chicago-born, Minneapolis-based writer, editor, and raconteur. He has an MFA in fiction writing from The New School in New York City. Among other things, he enjoys a good slice of deep dish (Lou Malnati's is manna from on high), a night of quality karaoke, and eking out thoroughly undeserved victories at Friday night *Magic: The Gathering* events. He lives with his wife, Kristin, their daughter, Morrigan, and their feline overlord, Karl.